ALL
THROUGH
THE
NIGHT

Also by Connie Brockway

ALL THROUGH THE NIGHT

CONNIE BROCKWAY

First published by Dell Publishing, a division of Bantam Doubleday Dell Publishing Group, Inc., in 1997.

This edition published by Montlake Romance in 2013, Seattle

www.apub.com

ISBN-13: 9781477849019
ISBN-10: 1477849017

Cover design by Mumtaz Mustafa
Illustrated by Dana Ashton France

Library of Congress Control Number: 2013911345

Printed in the United States of America

With gratitude and affection to Marjorie ~~B—— the~~ "best" of editors, who always ~~mo———ted~~ me to be "better"

Prologue

The landlady shuffled into the long narrow room ahead of Colonel Henry "Jack" Seward and headed right for the curtained window overlooking the square.

"You don't know how many times over I could 'ave rented the use of this 'ere room," she said, eyeing Seward's tall, punishingly straight figure. "'ad a baron's man come round just last hour offerin' me twice over what you paid. But I'm an honest woman."

And a shrewd one, Jack thought as he inclined his head in gracious recognition of the landlady's honesty. She knew quite well not to cozen the likes of Whitehall's Hound. He counted out a short, thick stack of coins and handed it to her. She snatched them from his outstretched palm and stuffed them deep into the pockets of her worn skirt before yanking back the dingy piece of threadbare velvet hanging over the window.

With a glance outside and a mutter she turned and waddled over to the single chair in the room, a straight-backed wooden one sitting against a water-stained wall. With a grunt she lifted it. Jack immediately came forward and took it from her. "Allow me. Did you want this taken somewhere?"

She gaped at him. Doubtless no one had ever extended the woman a simple courtesy. "Ah." She snapped her mouth shut and open and blinked. "Ah. Aye. To the window. So you can sits durin' the show." Jack strove to keep his repugnance from his face while he set the chair in front of the window. The woman craned her neck to look out and down the road leading to the square. A shout arose from the mass of humanity crowding the streets below. "There he comes now," she said with unmistakable satisfaction. "I'm off then."

Jack didn't hear her. He was looking outside.

The crowd pressed eagerly in around the cart carrying John Cashman into a cordoned-off area in front of the gunsmith's shop, the same one he was alleged to have robbed in order to arm himself in a revolt against His Majesty's government. Men, women, and children, mostly poor people, had come to see "the gallant tar" hanged for treason.

Few, Jack knew, thought young Cashman deserved his sentence, and the injustice of it frightened them. Some hoped for royal clemency.

And who was more worthy of mercy than Cashman? Jack asked himself sardonically. His greatest crime had been trying to collect his arrears payment and prize money from the Admiralty. The crowd contained hundreds just like him. Men who'd fought for their country only to return home to discover they had no jobs, no pensions, and no futures.

Jack's gaze remained mild, but the hand pulling off his black leather gloves trembled just the tiniest bit. He took his seat, his posture as straight as a papist's at mass. Yes, Cashman had broken into this gunsmith's shop during the Spa Fields riots, but liquor and his own discouragement had been the reason for his presence there, not treason.

Premeditated? John Cashman, Jack knew, had received severe head wounds thrice in the line of duty. He was not even reckoned by most to be competent enough to handle his own affairs.

No wonder his fate frightened the crowd. Hell, it enraged them.

"I always fought for my king and country, and this is my end!" Cashman shouted once more as he stepped down from the cart and gazed resolutely at the scaffolding before him. Thousands shouted back in a frenzied chorus of support.

They'd been gathering since five o'clock that morning, and now they spread as far as the eye could see: choking streets and alleys, crowding windows with angry faces, thick as bees in an over-crowded hive, clinging to balconies, hanging over rooftops.

Without hesitation, Cashman mounted the steps to the gibbet, his courage firing the masses. At the top, a clergyman hurried to his side, laying a comforting hand on his arm. Cashman shook it off, his eyes blazing. "I want no mercy but from God!"

The executioner led him forward. When he moved to place a hood over the condemned man's head, Cashman jerked away and said, "I want to see till the last."

The executioner and clergyman left the scaffold together and took their positions beside the tripboard beneath Cashman's feet.

"I could not get my own, and that has brought me here!" Cashman shouted. "I have done nothing against my king and country but fought for them!"

He was still shouting when his words were cut off, strangled in his throat. Jack's hand jerked involuntarily to his own throat. He ground his teeth, pain and anger mixing together as he forced himself to watch the man below swing crazily, his tied limbs spasming.

The crowd went utterly silent. The silence lasted while he was cut down, while the clergyman finally placed the hood over his contorted features, while they hefted his body into a plank coffin. It lasted as they set the coffin in a cart and drove away.

Jack stood up and drew on his black leather gloves. He felt cold, as if a bitter wind buffeted him, yet not a breeze stirred the skeletal branches of the trees outside. He checked the buttons at his wrist and adjusted his coat, his expression carved in concentration, his movements economical, deliberate.

Below him, a single utterance rose from the stunned crowd. It gathered pitch and momentum, growing louder with each added voice until it reached a horrendous din.

"Murder! Murder!"

Colonel Seward finally ceased adjusting his gloves and looked out over the crowd to see the cart disappear from view.

"Indeed," he murmured soberly, "indeed."

Chapter One

London
December 1817

Never assume you are safe. Never drop your guard. The thief's father, a cracksman the likes of which London had never known before or since, had drilled that lesson home above all others.

Ears straining to detect any sound above the murmur of a night breeze stirring the bed curtains, the thief known as Wrexhall's Wraith lifted an ormolu clock from the mantel. Too heavy. A delicate porcelain figurine nearby tempted but was too fragile to survive the leaps across rooftops that night work entailed.

Another of the old man's imperatives whispered just behind the thief's conscious thoughts: *Five minutes in, five minutes out.* This was taking too long.

Long, sensitive fingers lightly roved along the gilt frames of the pictures on the walls, searching for hidden caches, finding none.

With a small utterance of annoyance, the Wraith roamed deeper into the Marchioness of Cotton's suite. Her fabled jewel collection had to be some-bloody-where.

At the far wall the thief pushed aside the unease that came from being so far from the window and bent over an ornate dressing table. A music box, pretty but no more than a dab. A pearl-inlaid snuffbox. Bah! Nothing worth the £5,000 promised. Only a gem would suffice to pay *that* debt.

The thief moved more quickly now, thrusting hands along the contours of various furnishings, tipping a mirror, opening drawers, and then . . . there. Innocuous, noteworthy only for its relative stodginess among its opulent companions, a thick, marble-slabbed washstand.

White teeth flashed beneath the band of black silk masking the Wraith's face. So obvious. Father's most elementary wisdom: *Hide in plain sight.*

The thief dipped to one knee and felt along the undercarriage of the washstand, immediately finding a small metal tab and slipping it back. A drawer dropped beneath the marble top. The smile broadened. Now just a quick plunge of the hand into the secret drawer and . . . It was empty.

"No joy there, I'm afraid," a calm voice said.

The Wraith bolted upright and spun, looking frantically about for the author of those words.

There, in the lightest shadows, in the center of the room, his dun-colored coat blending with the gold settee, he sat on with telltale perfect posture.

Hide in plain sight.

No fashionable scent signaled his existence. No quiver of readiness shivered through the air, telegraphing his presence. Colonel John Henry Seward. Whitehall's Hound.

Every fiber in the thief's body coiled in preparation to take flight as Seward's lean figure slowly rose, blocking any access to the window. The thief was fast but no one was that fast. London's underworld regarded Seward as their most formidable opponent. Still, there might be no other way, and if—

"I wouldn't, son." There was nothing but gentleness in Seward's soft advice, a hint of raspiness in his tone, as if his throat had been injured at one time.

"Coo, what would ye have me do?" the thief said. "Stand here docilelike while you tie the bow 'round me neck? Not bloody likely." Only a slight tremble ruined the thief's cocky certainty.

"You should have thought of that before you embarked on this career. Give over, lad." Incongruously, a touch of pity laced Seward's voice.

Pity? Nothing of the kind from Jack Seward. That "pity" was only a spot of wishful thinking best eradicated now. There'd be no pity from Jack Seward. Best keep one's wits clear, alert for an opportunity to escape.

"There's nowhere to run," Jack said as if reading the thief's mind. "My men are in the outer hall and I"—he shrugged apologetically, lifting his hands—"well, I am here."

"So you are," the Wraith murmured.

Abruptly Seward tilted his seal-sleek head. Even in the dark, one could discern the intensity with which he suddenly listened.

Damn. The thief had only one trump card to play—surprise— and that was a long shot. Jack Seward looked as if he'd given up being surprised a long, long time ago. Yet there was no other option. If unmasked . . . Well, there was only one possible end for a thief: the Tyburn Tree.

"Right-o, *Cap,*" the thief said, using Seward's former rank and swaggering forth with hard-feigned bravado. "You got me fair and square. But why, I'm wonderin', ain't you screamin' to your lads for help?"

"Very good. Very astute, lad," Seward said approvingly. "But not so fast, if you please. I'd like to see your hands, above your shoulders and straight from your body. Anyone as good with a pick-lock as you are is bound to be just as good with a sticker."

"Right, mate. But I don't carry no knife. Bloodlettin' ain't what you'd call a gentlemanly trade, and I—within me means a' course—am a gentleman." *A bit closer now.*

This close the shadows lifted from Seward's angular face revealing a scar-broken brow, a long mouth mobile with intelligence, and quiet, watchful gray eyes.

"Just what sorta deal is it you look to be strikin'? You wants a bit of the take? A little somethin' to turn the blind eye?"

"No," Seward said. "I want something you've already stolen."

"Oh." *What?* the thief wondered desperately, measuring the distance to the window, all the while still moving closer to Seward.

What could possibly be so important that Whitehall's Hound had been sent to retrieve it? Nothing taken had been priceless. Indeed, there were never any family heirlooms in the take, nothing anyone would bother to raise a sustained hue and cry about. No, nothing—*nothing*—justified the involvement of the War Office's premier agent.

"I told you to stop moving," Seward said, his gentle voice assuming a subtle mantle of deadliness.

The thief shuddered, a tincture of unhealthy pleasure spurring on a sudden, reckless decision. Lately, more and more often, audacity proved irresistible, the urge to give in to it irrepressible. Like now.

"Right you are, Cap." Nearly within arm's reach. There would be no second opportunity to catch Seward off guard. "But I told you, I ain't got no sticker. And we don't want the lads in the hall there to get wind of any deal we might be conductin', now do we? Pat me down if you don't believe me. Go on, satisfy yerself before we begins negotiations."

Seward's eyes narrowed at the same time his crippled hand shot out, seizing the thief's wrist. There was surprising strength in the twisted fingers. The Wraith jerked back, instinctively fighting the implacable hold until it became clear any struggle could end only with Seward the victor.

"I believe I will, at that," Seward murmured, pulling the black wool–clad figure against his hard chest and securing both wrists. Quickly and efficiently he swept his free hand down over the thief's shoulders and flanks, hips, thighs, and legs. He moved back up, his touch passing lightly over the thief's chest.

He stopped, pale eyes gleaming with sudden intensity, and quickly jerked the slight body forward by the belt. His hand dipped down, clamping hard on the juncture between the legs in a touch both violently intimate and absolutely impersonal.

"My God," Seward said, dropping his one hand as if burned, though the other still clenched the belt, "you're a woman."

She'd done it. She had him off balance and she needed desperately to take advantage of that fact. She gulped a steadying breath. "Your woman, Cap. If you want." She imbued the husky East End accent with low provocation, striving to keep the quaver from her voice.

She stepped closer and undulated against him, nudging her legs within the cincture of his rigid stance. His body was hard, like adamant. "We can come to some sort of an arrangement, Cap. One you'll fancy. I swear it."

"Arrangement," Seward echoed faintly, head dipping down and forward to better scan her face. His cheeks were lean. Hard lines of experience bracketed his mouth and marked the corners of his eyes. Eyes the color of some precious, abused metal.

Ah, yes, she thought, intoxicated by the sense of danger, disoriented by her very boldness, *tarnished silver.* Slowly he reached up to unmask her.

She could taste the flavor of his warm breath, feel the danger of his regard, the acute awareness arcing from his body, and she knew she was a second from having her identity discovered. Her heart thrummed in violent, fevered response.

She closed her eyes, knocked his hand aside, and wrapped her arms around his neck, drawing her body fully against his, crushing her breasts to his broad chest.

"I'm woman enough to pleasure a man like you."

"Pleasure." He spoke the syllables as if saying a foreign word, but he did not back away from her. His intense regard mutated, his curiosity swallowed by the need for some baser knowledge.

It was as if she embraced a razor-sharp blade, rigid, superbly balanced, lethal. With shivering fingers she combed back the clean, silky hair at the nape of his neck and guided his head to hers. He resisted. She arched up, standing on tiptoe to find his lips and opening her mouth over his.

Warm, hard. For three heartbeats he did not respond. And then it was as if something within him, something so long denied its existence had been forgotten, something waiting for release, abruptly found liberation. His passion spilled like acid over her body, bright, burning. He reacted instinctively, drawing her tight against his body, holding her to him by the belt he still clenched in his fist.

His lips softened. His free hand roved up her spine and cupped her skull. He bent over her, forcing her to flex backward and clutch his shoulders to keep from falling.

Too much. Unimagined. Unwanted. Feckless body. Treacherous mouth.

He was purely male, like every other male, being offered what all males seek. And yet . . .

And yet, dear God, it was so much more.

In the way he held her head to receive his kiss, he betrayed an awful hunger. His lust tasted like starvation, and behind it, in the pleasure—and Lord help her for that pleasure—there was hopelessness.

Worse, she recognized her own hunger in his and answered it. His lips roamed, his breath mated with hers, and she drank in his essence. Her thoughts swam with a hundred impressions: his hand fisted about her belt, holding her captive; the faint astringent aroma of soap beneath the wet scent of the fog drifting through the open window; the heat of his mouth; the slick slide of clean teeth against the tip of her tongue.

She wanted to lose herself in his seductive menace, longed to touch the darkest part of his need. She opened her mouth further, helpless to contain the surging desire created by each stroke of his tongue against hers. Her legs trembled weakly and she gave herself up to his strength, clinging now, wanting to surrender, to let him have her body, her life . . .

He tore his mouth free, his crippled hand still holding her head. "Bloody hell. Am I to take you on the desk and then, having spent myself in pleasure, let you go? Is that the trade?"

She could barely think. "Yes."

"I'd rather have you on a bed. Unmasked. Do you think Lady Cotton would mind?" The bitter bite of humor lay thick in his voice.

She shook her head. "Sorry, Cap. Here and now. That's the deal."

She twisted against his hold on her belt and he released her. She leaned against him, stood tiptoe, trailed her mouth lightly along his hard jawline. His skin was warm. The stubble of his beard abraded her lips.

"Almost worth it." He sounded breathless, damned. "Almost."

His lips were parted, his chest rising and falling in deep, silent breaths. He stared at her, his pale gaze holding her motionless in the moonlit-steeped room, something hard and angry and pleading in his expression.

"All right." He whispered the words and with them the promise of unimaginable pleasures. In his embrace she might finally lose every last bit of herself. She might forget . . .

She swayed back toward an embrace she knew would never release her and stopped. No. He was Whitehall's Hound. He'd use her and take her and do his duty. Heartless. Soulless. She should recognize his type; it was kindred to her own.

She clutched his jacket sleeves, jerking his arms down and driving her knee into his groin. He gasped, doubling over and dropping to his knees. He fell, reaching for her. She leapt clear of his outstretched hand and raced for the window. Before she heard his curse, she was on the sill, vaulting for the opposite roof.

She sprang too late, misgauging the distance to the building across the narrow alley. She landed on the eaves, slick with moss, then stumbled and fell. Frantically she clambered for a handhold, her nails gouging the wet, half-rotted shakes as she struggled to keep from plummeting to the ground.

With the last of her strength failing, she grabbed the lead drainpipe snaking beneath the eaves and fell. Her hands caught the full force of her weight, jerking her arms in their sockets. She hung, suspended fifteen feet above the ground. If she fell, she wouldn't die, but likely she'd break something and be caught.

Then she'd die.

"Hold on!"

From the corner of her eye she caught sight of Seward, half hanging from the window on the other side of the alley, arm outstretched, too far away to aid—or hinder—her. His expression was taut, only his eyes alive, filled with promises she could not name.

Terror gave her strength. With a grunt, she swung her foot over the eave and hauled herself back onto the roof. She scrambled upright and stood, panting and silent, regarding Seward across the eight-foot-wide gulf.

He gazed mutely back. Then, slowly, mockingly, he lifted two fingers to his dark, scar-traversed brow and saluted her. Even at this distance she could see the self-scorn blazing in his gray eyes, as if he had been retaught a lesson he should have learned long ago and appreciated her instruction.

"Until next time." Though she barely heard him, she understood the words to be a vow.

Next time? Why? Why had Whitehall's Hound been set on her trail? It seemed too extreme a measure to protect some wealthy aristocrat's baubles, no matter how expensive they might be.

She stared at him, a slow surge of triumph replacing her earlier fright. She'd been betrayed by her body, not only by her reaction to Seward's single, hot-mouthed kiss but by her desire to yield to him for the promise of a passion so heated it would sear the damning memories from her mind. Yet she'd won.

Across the narrow chasm, Seward inclined his head in gracious acceptance of his defeat. She could not let his gesture go unremarked.

Her smile was rife with anticipation as she snapped sharply forward at the waist, a perfect parody of an officer and a gentleman. Then she ducked back behind the chimney pot. She would disappear now. The paths open from here were myriad and secret and high above the plodding footsteps of guards and Bow Street Runners . . . and Jack Seward.

By morning the Wraith would be gone. In her place would be Anne Wilder, a wealthy member of the ton, a once-celebrated beauty now acting as a debutante's doyenne . . . a much-aggrieved widow. No one would ever suspect her.

Yet, even though Anne knew she was safe, she did not feel safe at all.

And, God help her, she liked the sensation.

Chapter Two

~~~~~~~~~~~~~~~~~

Sir Robert Knowles thumbed through the papers on his desk as Henry Jamison and the two other men in the room awaited his attention. He was being purposefully irksome, Jamison thought. But just whom was he trying to provoke?

An undistinguished and benign-looking man, Knowles's baby-pink scalp and the soft, pleated lines on his round face belied his character. Jamison knew he looked the complete antithesis: angular, imperious, and proud. It amused Jamison, during those rare moments when he allowed himself introspection, that such diverse looks could contain such similar personalities.

For thirty years Knowles and he had striven to best each other's equally powerful and equally nebulous positions on the Home Office's Secret Committee. Neither of them had a title for the posts they occupied, posts wherein they gathered information, thwarted certain plots, aided others, and gathered, manipulated, and manufactured information essential to the secret workings of the government.

Though Knowles currently held the upper hand, it would not last. It *could* not last. Because Jamison was destined for greatness. Not near greatness. Greatness itself.

Lately Jamison's political influence had faltered, the strength of his personality alone no longer sufficient to carry out his directives. He needed others to see that his interests were advanced, his power secure. He needed Henry John Seward—the most successful secret agent ever utilized by the British government.

"Have you discovered the thief's identity?" Knowles asked without looking up.

"No, sir," Seward said. "I have not."

Jamison pressed his liver-spotted fingertips to his lips. Wryly he noted how Knowles's purposefully intimidating desk did nothing to diminish Colonel Seward. He stood at spine-punishing attention before it.

"And why the blazes not?" the young Lord Vedder demanded. A precious little popinjay playing a far deeper game than he imagined, Lord Vedder had been brought into this meeting as the prince regent's representative and stayed at Jamison's sufferance. Popinjays, Jamison had long since learned, served their purposes.

"Because I have been occupied with other matters." Jack gazed passively at Knowles. "A fellow called Brandeth, a situation needing my attention in Manchester. And then there was the Cashman debacle." For a second, anger brushed Jack's words with coldness.

Knowles had recalled Seward from sabotaging the plots of the increasing number of angry political dissidents especially for the task of apprehending this "Wrexhall's Wraith." But if Jamison resented Knowles commandeering Seward, whom Jamison considered his personal agent, Seward resented being commandeered twice as deeply. Seward's words were a clear reminder—as if any were necessary—that he considered his current job trivial.

Brandeth had raised a small army on the Derby border, which Seward had anticipated. The Manchester affair had involved a far more ambitious plot, the storming of banks and prisons. Seward had infiltrated its leaders' coven, obstructing the plan before it could come to pass.

Seward had been violently opposed to Knowles's and Jamison's locating somewhat tainted evidence against Cashman, so violently that ultimately he'd refused to become involved.

Lord Vedder knew none of this. Jamison wondered if he would treat Seward quite so negligently if he realized that, if Seward so desired, he could engineer Vedder's death thrice times over—with little effort and less chance of being inconvenienced for it. Vedder adjusted his ridiculous chicken-skin gloves, sniffed imperiously, and embarked on a tiresome tirade about Seward's duty to his future king.

Jamison studied the agent's reaction to Vedder's harangue. Much as he expected, Seward didn't appear to have one. For nearly a quarter of a century Jamison had observed Jack, watched him develop from sinewy youth to densely muscled manhood, observed his violent passion become iron-controlled civility.

Perfect manners coupled with absolute remorselessness. It was a disturbing combination. Seward might stand with the military exactitude that attested to the success of a strict disciplinarian, but his face reflected only a polite interest in Lord Vedder's vitriol. An interesting creature, Colonel Seward.

Jamison, who'd a long history of manipulating others, had never known so enigmatic a man. It troubled him that he did not understand why Seward—the most effective agent he'd ever harnessed to his will—allowed himself to be used.

What would happen when Seward's interest did not run in tandem with the Home Office's Secret Committee? Or worse, Jamison wondered, his own?

"This is unlike you, Seward," Jamison muttered, cutting off Vedder's harangue.

The colonel's gaze swung smoothly about. He'd known all along that Jamison had been studying him.

"Is it, sir?" Perfect sangfroid. Exceptional address. Etiquette, Seward had once told Jamison, was all that mattered. Ideologies waxed and waned, religions developed and eroded, political parties rose and fell from power. Only courtesy remained one of the few things valued by all civilized men.

Seward had gone so far as to suggest that the reason so few of the men he commanded died was because it was the least wasteful way to arrange things, the least repugnant to the sensibilities, the best *manners,* in fact. A man like that was frightening.

"It is unlike you to be so incompetent," Jamison snapped, disliking this uncharacteristic alarm. "How do you propose to catch this thief if you cannot bring him in even after he steps into your own trap?"

Vedder slapped his gloves in his hand, demonstrating his ire. "He'll want more men assigned to him, I suppose."

"No, sir. Not a bit of it, sir."

Damn Seward. In spite of all Jamison's attempts to eradicate the last vestiges of his Scottish accent, he still clung to it.

"What then?" Lord Vedder asked.

"I would like entrée into the prince regent's social circle."

"What?" Lord Vedder's mouth dropped open.

"Be damned, one must admire your audacity," Jamison said.

"I have been pursuing this thief for six months, sir. By anticipating his choice of victim, I gave myself a chance to catch him. It was an easy enough deduction. The Marchioness of Cotton is well known for carting her gems about to house parties." His voice grew hoarser with each word. As a souvenir of having been hanged for two minutes by Napoleon's "patriots," Seward's voice carried a slight raspiness. Today the effect was pronounced. "But as you say, I failed to apprehend the thief."

Jamison noted the knuckles of Seward's crippled hand gleamed like marble beneath the skin. Interesting. His failure to apprehend the thief bothered him. More than interesting, useful.

An emotion—any emotion—might be honed, worked, used like a whip to drive him. And there were few enough scourges one found to drive the likes of Seward.

"I cannot predict the thief's next victim other than that he will most probably be, like his predecessors, an intimate of His Royal Highness," Seward went on. "If I am to catch this thief, I must be able to determine his victims. I will be better able to do so if I can observe who among the prince's friends attracts notice, appears vulnerable to a thief."

"Of all the gall!" sputtered Lord Vedder.

"What do you mean by entrée?" Knowles asked, entering the discussion for the first time.

"The crimes are aimed at the ton who are in London for the opening of Parliament, not the innermost circle of the prince's intimates," Seward said.

"You would need only attend the larger parties and entertainments?" Knowles asked.

"Yes, sir."

"I believe—"

"I cannot countenance such an imposition on His Royal Highness's friends!" Lord Vedder shouted. "This man is a bastard."

Knowles looked at him with distaste. "If the prince's 'friends' continue to be robbed whenever they attend one of his parties, His Royal Highness may soon find himself dining alone."

"You overstep yourself, sir," Vedder declared indignantly.

Knowles raked back his scant white hair. "His Majesty's demand that his friends no longer be targeted by this criminal was quite clear. Do you wish me to tell him you undermined our efforts to see this thief brought to justice because you objected to the circumstances of Colonel Seward's birth?"

With a sound of choked fury, Lord Vedder snatched up his cane from the table and stormed from the room.

Knowles released a small sigh. "A pity we must tolerate him, but tolerate him we must. He serves to mask our real purpose in finding this thief." He indicated a chair. "Won't you sit, Jack?"

"No, thank you, sir."

"Now, may I surmise that in addition to your failure to apprehend this thief, you have also failed to retrieve the letter?"

"Yes, sir," Seward replied.

"Dammit, we can't afford failure," Knowles said. "Most disappointing, Jack. You had the thief right in the room with you, is this not true? What happened? Did he overwhelm you?"

"Yes." The admission slipped out in a hushed, intense voice.

Jamison's attention sharpened.

"Are you getting feeble then, Jack?" Knowles asked in concerned tones. "Should I send some youngster with you to act as your strength?"

"For the 'youngster's' sake, I suggest not." Though the words were delivered quietly and an apologetic smile curved Seward's lips, the warning was clear.

Pride? Jamison thought in amazement. No, this was a baser emotion. Jamison leaned forward, every faculty focused on Seward. He considered himself a master of discerning another's heart, a skill he attributed to having no sentiment of his own clouding his judgment. Seward sounded . . . possessive.

"You *are* a bastard, Jack." Knowles relaxed, satisfied with Seward's response.

"Yes, sir. A fact Lord Vedder shall doubtless be tiresome in remarking."

"What do you think, Jamison?" Knowles asked. They might not like each other, but their respect for each other's acumen was extreme. Together they'd clandestinely orchestrated some of the Secret Committee's greatest coups and barely avoided as many catastrophes.

"I think," Jamison said, "it should have been done weeks ago."

"I might find it beneficial were I to know more of this letter," Seward said.

Knowles considered a moment before beginning. "This whole affair is most disconcerting, Jack. A while back I received a letter from Lord Atwood. In it he described how he'd come into the possession of a dangerous document. It had taken him quite some time to determine exactly what should be done with it and who had the proper authority to deal with such a sensitive issue.

"Apparently he'd already been in contact with Jamison here"— Knowles glanced at Jamison, who nodded once—"but wanted to reiterate to me the importance of this document he held."

"Yes," Jamison agreed. "He contacted me just before Knowles. An unnecessary redundancy. I'd already arranged to have the document delivered into our hands."

Knowles shot him a thoughtful look. "Yes. But it never was. The day before it was to have been delivered, it was stolen—along with the jeweled case that Atwood told Jamison he kept it in."

"And he informed Jamison of this theft?" Seward asked.

"Not Jamison, but an entire dinner party. The evening after the theft, he made a very public announcement that he was this Wrexhall Wraith's latest victim."

"Odd that he would have made so public a disclosure."

"Not so odd," Jamison disagreed. "He may have been telling the thief he knew his identity and giving him a chance to return the stolen property. This is one of the reasons we think the thief may be a member of society."

"Why didn't you ask Atwood who he suspected?"

"We never got the chance," Jamison said. "The next morning Atwood was killed. In a coaching accident."

"Accident," Seward repeated.

Knowles nodded wearily. "Just so."

Jamison waved his hand as if clearing a mist that threatened to obscure their real purpose. "The only questions that need concern you are these: Who was able to anticipate our last-minute arrangements for that letter's recovery? Who knew Atwood was our courier? Who was at that dinner party? *Who has that damn letter?*"

"Perhaps no one, sir," Seward said.

"Explain yourself," Knowles said.

"If this letter is as important as you say, it would have shown up by now. We may not have heard of it simply because the original theft was an accident and the thief only meant to steal jewels."

It was a plausible explanation, Jamison thought. "I agree," he said slowly. "If someone hired this thief to steal the letter, by now they would have either made its contents public or made some ransom demand."

"We can't be sure," Knowles said. "And we *must* be sure. That is why it is imperative you catch this thief and discover what he has done with that letter.

"Let me make myself clear, Jack." Knowles's grandfatherly mien slipped, allowing a glimpse of the calculating and ruthless intelligence behind his mild features. "I do not care what you do, or how you do it, but you will find that thief and you will ascertain from him what happened to that letter."

"And then?"

"And then," Jamison said, "you will act accordingly."

"Kill the thief?"

Knowles shrugged. "Well, I don't know what else you'll do with him. Not that anyone gives a bloody damn how many broaches and tiaras and geegaws he's stolen. But I will have that letter, Jack."

"Yes, sir, you will."

Jack stared out of the sitting room window of his rented town house, studying the low, jumbled London skyline. She was out there. Mocking him with her thefts. Uncovering for him in excruciating fashion a vulnerability he'd not known he owned—lust.

He'd never reacted thus before. He'd used sex; sometimes he'd enjoyed it. But he'd always known it to be merely another weapon in his arsenal, a weapon he used to control or manipulate another. Sex had never controlled him. He'd never become so involved in an encounter that he'd relaxed his guard or forgotten the purpose of the encounter—and it always had a purpose. Until now.

And with such scant inducement. A petite wool-covered body, dark eyes, the softness of a small, plump breast, the flavor of expensive burgundy still in her mouth . . .

Remembered sensation overwhelmed him, flooding every nerve ending with a physical memory of her. During the long months of his search he'd developed a certain admiration for his thief, the respect of one professional for another. Few had the wherewithal to evade his relentless pursuit.

He had come to look forward to the next move in the game they played. It was a challenge in a life that increasingly offered little recompense for the tiresome act of breathing.

But now—

Now they were involved in another kind of game, a baser form of stimulation. How brutally amusing that she should be the one who roused his sexual appetite from so long a dormancy. He could still feel her: the slight, accidental weight of her breast in his palm, the texture of her hair slipping through his fingers, the heat between her legs.

She'd gotten in beneath his guard. And in those few intense moments she'd fused herself into his nightly dreams. He very much looked forward to renewing their acquaintance.

The man behind him cleared his throat, and Jack unclasped his hands from behind his back. Vexed by his fixation, he turned away from the window, vaguely surprised to find the room steeped in darkness.

"You have news, Griffin?" he addressed the stout, middle-aged man by his side.

"Aye, Cap."

Jack had met Peter Griffin at a Parisian gallows a hundred years ago, when Jack had still thought—or hoped—dying would repay the debts he owed. A silly, naive notion and one with which he'd long since dispensed. Still, his willingness to trade his life for Griffin's and four of his compatriots had won him Griffin's loyalty, a loyalty proven a dozen times to be unwavering and fierce. After the war, Griffin had become Jack's most trusted subordinate.

"Do you have anything for me?" Jack asked.

Griffin pulled out a heavily scrawled over piece of paper and read. "Lady Houghton's maid was sneaking out to meet the footman. So it isn't her. The Frost woman might be interesting. Lady Dibbs's was a confidante of Caro Lamb. Might think of the whole thing as a bloody lark."

"Anything more?"

"Yes. The Wilder widow retires early every night and her young charge, the North wench . . . she's a heartbreaker, Cap. Dozens of laddies milling about those honeyed lips."

"Yes," Jack said, "but which of them had the opportunity on all occas—"

A tap on the door prefaced the entry of an anxious-looking youngster. He moved to Jack's side, murmuring his news into his ear. Jack nodded and the young man left.

"Minions," Griffin said with a sardonic grin.

"Excuse me?"

"I swear, I'm amazed at how many eyes and ears you have working for you. Children, old pikers, whores, and shopkeepers. Quite a network you have, Cap. Like the devil's minions."

"Ah, the tiresome devil appellation again, is it?" Jack said. *She'd* thought him the very devil; he'd no doubt of it.

"Some would say, Cap, and I'd not deny."

"Your Presbyterian antecedents are showing again, Griffin. At this rate, you'll be finding yourself in a pulpit renouncing your past. And you're much more valuable as an agent than as a minister."

"To whom?"

"Why, to me, of course. Too late to switch masters." Self-irony robbed the words of conceit. "Now, kindly tell me you were discreet. No one knows either the subject or the reason for your inquiries?"

"No one." Inspiration slowly filled his expression. "Bloody hell, Cap," he said, "you didn't tell your father who you suspect?"

"No," Seward said. Odd that so long into his life a reminder of his and Jamison's supposed relationship still had the power to prick. "I didn't tell Jamison."

"Nor Knowles." Griffin cocked his head inquiringly. "You didn't even tell them that their thief was a woman, did you?"

"No."

"And why not, I'm wondering?"

"Because"—though Seward didn't move in the slightest and his voice's modulation did not change one degree, Griffin stepped back—"they might interfere. And she's not their thief, Grif, she's mine. *Mine.*"

Chapter Three

Jack stepped over the threshold into Carlton House. The aroma of overwarm bodies and past-ripe fruit assailed his nostrils as the unchecked shift and press of bodies assaulted his eyes.

He slipped his greatcoat into the waiting hands of an attendant and asked after his host, the prince regent. He doubted whether he would be there. The six years since King George III had succumbed to madness and the prince had acted as his regent had proved unhappy ones. Reviled by the Parliament, despised by his subjects, and deeply depressed by the death of his beloved daughter Charlotte, the time the prince regent spent at his own parties had become increasingly short.

It was just as well, thought Jack. The prince regent could not be trusted to keep up a charade that had him suddenly befriending a base-born soldier.

After ascertaining from the page that the prince regent had, indeed, retired, Jack descended the stairs. A feeling of unaccustomed anticipation hurried his movements as he entered the crush.

From the first, he'd protested the assignment Knowles had given him. Knowles's only answer had been that finding this thief was more important than any other function Seward could serve. And because Jack had long ago made his pact with the devil, he'd acquiesced without further protest.

But now the thief had made the matter an intensely personal one. Far more than just his body, she'd aroused his imagination For the first time in his life Jack had become conversant with obsession. He wanted to possess her, all of her: her tensile strength, the exquisite tyranny of her submission, her fear, and her courage.

He took a deep breath and looked around.

Men clad in the universal uniform of the dandy slithered through the throng like black snakes through a field of blowsy feminine flowers. Saffron and ivory, silks and taffeta swept the marble parquet flooring as the women danced by, pale night moths beating powdery wings beneath the light of a thousand tapers.

He slowly searched their faces. He'd spent two weeks cross-checking various guest lists and had found four names occurring regularly: Jeanette Frost, Cora Dibbs, Anne Wilder, and Sophia North. He'd already placed surveillance on each of their houses, having taken for granted that his thief was employed by one of these ladies. But earlier this week, at a similar entertainment, he'd had cause to reevaluate this assumption. He'd been vividly aware he was being watched.

He'd felt her regard as keenly as any physical touch, as intimately as their kiss. Tonight he intended to speak with each of the four women. He smiled. If his thief were one of them, she'd appreciate the excitement of such a close pursuit. He'd felt her addiction to danger in the marchioness's bedchamber and recognized it immediately. It had been an unanticipated—and fascinating— addition to what he had learned of her.

Something more than monetary rewards drove her. It was the first discernible flaw in an otherwise meticulous career. And one he would use.

He started through the crowd, soon spying a familiar, properly bored-looking young rake—a Mr. Wells, if he recalled correctly— escorting Jeanette Frost from the dance floor. Smoothly Jack intercepted their progress.

"Mr. Wells, I beg you to do me the kindness of an introduction to your lovely companion," he said, bowing low.

Mr. Wells started but quickly recovered. He sketched a bow. "Course, Seward, old man. My pleasure. Miss Frost, I'd like to make known to you Colonel Henry John Seward. Colonel, Miss Jeanette Frost."

The dark-haired chit eyed him with a saucy smile, bouncing a little on her toes, causing the soft young flesh above her low décolletage to jiggle merrily.

"I am charmed, Miss Frost," Jack murmured, "absolutely—"

A red-faced man pushed his way between them. Miss Frost ceased her jiggling.

"Ah," Jack said smoothly. "Your sire, I presume?"

Miss Frost giggled. The father did not.

"You'll not know my daughter, sir," Ronald Frost said. "I don't care if the king himself claims you as cousin. I know what you are. I had a son under your command in the war."

"Really?"

"Yes, really!" Frost answered in a low furious voice. "He wrote me letters. I know what went on. What you did. Dirty tricks, assassin's work—"

"How indiscreet of your son," Seward murmured.

"Mock me if you want, but my boy died retrieving some useless bit of scut for you. You could have sent someone else. Some plebeian nobody. But you sent my *son*. May you rot in hell for that!"

"I wonder," Jack asked softly, "do you suppose the piece of hell I claim in your son's name would be so different from the one I would claim in a plebeian nobody's?"

"Damn your impertinence!" Frost hissed. "He was my heir!"

Jack inclined his head. "I grieve for your loss. Now, if you'll please ex—"

"The hell you do!"

Lost now to anything but his own grief and fury, Frost's voice grew louder. A few bystanders turned curiously. In a minute Frost would cause a scene. Jack could not allow that. He would do whatever necessary to prevent it. As he had always done.

"Your son wrote about his assignments, did he?" Jack heard his voice as if from a great distance. *Good.* He'd thought he'd lost that knack of displacement. He'd thought she'd stolen that from him, too.

"Yes," the man shot back.

"That"—Jack leaned very close, so no one would overhear his next words—"was not only indiscreet but possibly treasonous."

The older man's face suffused with an even more brilliant shade of red. His mouth compressed into a thin line as he realized the admission he'd made. Charges could be brought postmortem against his son and taint his family name.

"That's right, sir. You have a daughter to remember," Jack urged calmly, and then stepped back and made his bow. He was ruthless and he was callous. His job demanded he was both, but he could choose not to be brutish. That he could control. "Miss Frost, you have honored me."

Miss Frost, oblivious to the drama just enacted, giggled again. She was either an extraordinary actress or a very simple chit. No one, Jack concluded with a last look, was that good an actress.

"Sir, your servant." He inclined his head toward the lockjawed Mr. Frost and turned, already scanning the room for the next applicant to the role of thief.

Between the shifting bodies he spotted Malcolm North standing beside two seated women, one in an ugly cap, the other a fresh-faced beauty. North himself was a trim, nervy-looking gentleman with a ready smile and an opportunist's glib tongue. While his breeding was impeccable, his line of credit was not. He gambled deeply and lost often.

As Jack watched, North addressed the becapped woman—Anne Wilder—and took his leave.

Jack had observed the young widow a few days before, walking in the park on a particularly nasty evening. The wind had tugged a few strands of hair from beneath her hood and she'd stopped, lifting her face to the sky. Hidden from her view he'd watched, unaccountably stirred by the yearning expression that had traveled so openly across her face.

She was still hidden from him. But though her hair was concealed by an ugly cap and the lavender dress disguised her form, Jack read much in her posture: the graceful repose of hands, the downward cast of her eyes, the upward tilt of her chin. Here was a woman who'd learned patience late and perhaps too well.

Beside her sat North's daughter, the vivacious and petite Sophia, the sole reason the Norths were here—or anywhere in society, for that matter. Because Sophia was very young and very beautiful and the prince regent liked beauty and youth.

Candlelight danced in Sophia's burnished red hair, glowed on her pink skin. Her movements were artful, designed to attract the eye. She turned and their gazes met. A little frisson of excitement telegraphed itself in the agitation of the plump bosom displayed by a provocative neckline. The very tip of her tongue appeared and wet her lower lip.

A challenge? Jack wondered. Well, it would be rude to disappoint a lady.

He set his glass on a table and went in search of Giles Dalton, Lord Strand. It was Strand who was largely responsible for the smoothness with which Jack had been introduced into the prince's set. The marquis had considered the task hugely entertaining, "Rather like sneaking the wolf into the sheep meadow."

Jack finally found Strand bending the ear of some blushing pretty.

"Lord Strand," Jack said, approaching him.

"Ah, Colonel Seward." Strand straightened and greeted Jack. "Have you ever met a real live colonel, Miss—Miss?"

The plump beauty at his side pouted. "Lady Pons-Burton. My husband is Bertram Pons-Burton."

The knowledge apparently amused Strand, for he laughed. "Old Bertie? Be damned! Lady Pons-Burton, may I present Colonel Seward, my superior in every conceivable way?"

Without waiting for her answer he patted her hand, his face morose with feigned regret. "Now you've had your treat, darling. Begone. I've no desire to be called out by some ancient in breeches and powdered wig tomorrow. My club positively frowns on that sort of thing."

He turned her by the shoulders and pushed her gently away. She departed with a little huff of displeasure. "Forgive my interruption," Jack said.

"Nothing to forgive. I've no taste for servicing some old stud's filly," Strand said evenly. "Now, how can I be of use?"

"Introduce me to Malcolm North's family." The words sounded more an order than a request, but during the war Strand had worked for Jack as one of his agents and the habit of command refused to die.

"Little Sophia North, eh? Pretty, isn't she? I've thought of having a go there myself, but I am nothing if not consistent. I absolutely refuse to pursue a woman another man has not claimed."

Jack did not pretend misunderstanding. A few years ago Strand had discovered he loved a young lady—unfortunately for Strand he'd only made his discovery after she'd lost her heart elsewhere. That woman was now Mrs. Thomas Montrose.

"What more do you know of them?" Jack asked.

The looseness with which Strand shrugged suggested he was well into the wine. Pity. The man had much to recommend him.

"Girl's been keeping lads on tenterhooks all season," Strand said. "Her mother died last winter, I believe, and she's applied to her cousin's widow, Anne Wilder, to act as her companion and sponsor for the season. Sophia's something of a romp, I'm afraid. She's making her bow with a, shall we say, sophistication that is surprising in one so young."

A few of the prince regent's cronies sauntered past the North women, the gentlemen's heads craning as they looked over the beauty and to a lesser extent her chaperone. Like prime cattle at an auction, the women were being discussed, examined, their potential for amusement—all types of amusement—weighed.

"What about the widow?"

Strand's glance was sardonic. "Ah, you prove yourself a connoisseur, Colonel. An elegant and subtle piece of work is the dark and handsome widow. She has the most extraordinary eyes. Seasoned. Knowing," Strand said thoughtfully, "and yet she is now regarded as quite a saint."

"Saint?" Jack asked, amused. In his experience sainthood inevitably proved a guise for self-interest.

Strand's smile answered Jack's sardonic tone. "Oh, she wasn't always so. She made her come-out six, seven years ago. Indulged daughter of a widowed merchant. Only entrée to society was some perpetually rusticating grande dame on her mother's side. Father was knighted for his canny way with a coin during the war. Died a few years back. Yet in spite of her 'umble antecedents, she became a toast. Most definitely a toast."

"Really?" Jack invited further revelations.

"Yes. And a prime little hoyden she was, too. Surprised us all when Matthew Wilder, a fine and decent and noble—oh, the glowing adjectives grow too wearisome to recount—actually married the gel. But she settled nicely, I'll grant her that. Never made a cake or coxcomb of Wilder once he'd given her his name. Not that the marriage ever set well with Mama Wilder. The old biddy still won't have anything to do with her."

"How did Wilder die?"

"How did any of us die? In the war. Captained a ship, I believe. But from the way Anne Wilder acts, one would have thought *she'd* died. I've never seen a woman so greatly changed. I swear, I'm all agog to see who finally pierces her shell. I liked the hoyden, yet I admit—along with several dozen other fellows here, I'll wager—I quite lust after the saint."

"You keep saying saint," Jack prompted. "In what way?"

"As I said, she's just recently returned to society, ostensibly to chaperone Sophia. However, she spends a great deal more time eliciting funds for a charity she's founded than checking the teeth on Sophia's beaus. She calls it the Soldiers' Relief and Aid Something or Other."

Soldiers? "And you, of course, have contributed," Jack said.

"Of course. Her cause is quite the darling of society. Everyone donates to it or appears cursed tight-fisted. And you know how important appearances are in my little world."

Jack did not respond. Perhaps he should cross Anne Wilder's name from his list. A well-heeled do-gooder with wealthy sponsors for her pet charity would have little reason to clamber about roofs. Still, he reminded himself, the thief was not motivated by avarice alone.

"Have a care, Jack," Giles said. "She may surprise you. And not in an altogether comfortable way."

"Why 'soldiers'?" Jack asked, still pondering the widow.

"Oh, soldiers, sailors, any uniform will do," Strand said in bored tones. "I believe she feels she owes a debt to her dead husband's men. He wasn't a very good captain, I'm afraid. Got his ship shot out from under him. Lost a number of men. Or pieces of men. Anne Wilder takes care of them any veteran who can't quite remember who he was before the war. Lucky me, Jack, I remembered," Strand ended bitterly. "Even luckier you, the war never changed what you were to begin with."

"I daresay you're correct," Jack replied. "She doesn't seek to remarry?"

"No. There's not the least bit of coquetry left in her. I believe it was truly a love match." For a second Strand's face grew pensive, as if presented with a puzzle he knew he could never solve. "Matthew Wilder doted on her. I remember thinking how perversely in love he was, even after several years of marriage."

"And now the grieving widow has donned a cap and plays guardian dragon over Sophia," Jack murmured.

"What I would like to know," Strand said, "is who is going to play dragon for her? A nun with the eyes of a procuress." He began his own leisurely perusal of the widow.

"Will Malcolm North know me?" Jack asked.

"Hm? Oh. He jolly well had better. You're at Prinny's own party. Who would risk his wrath by snubbing you? Besides, the Norths aren't really of any consequence." Strand spoke the cruel words with the pragmatism of the elite. "No money, no property. North simply had the foresight to belittle Brummel when the rest of us were still sure he and the prince would patch things up. Prinny has proven a grateful sovereign."

Jack frowned. If the thief were Sophia North or Anne Wilder— though both seemed most unlikely—they might seek shelter in the prince's expansive arms, and he would be stymied. He could not allow that to happen.

"If you'd be so kind?" Jack motioned Strand ahead of him.

Chapter Four

Anne's gaze searched the crowd milling near the bottom of the staircase. She was almost sure she'd seen Jack Seward. Her pulse quickened with trepidation. That would be three times in the last week she'd seen him at the same entertainments she and Sophia had attended.

Perhaps she was mistaken, she thought. Perhaps her preoccupation with the austere colonel simply made her see him everywhere. She bit the inside of her cheek, willing the little pain to make her come to her senses. It didn't work, just as it hadn't worked for the last two weeks.

She simply could not forget his kiss.

Even the memory of it was enough to . . . to *excite* her, she admitted shamefully. She knew why—at least she thought she knew why. He'd awakened her basest appetites and introduced her to the temptation of pure physical gratification. His kiss hadn't meant "I love you, Anne" or "I adore you, Anne" or "Do you love me, Anne?" It meant "I desire you." It asked nothing of her but her body's involvement. And that's all she wanted—probably all she'd ever been capable of—animal rutting. She *should* be ashamed.

But she was tired of shame, exhausted by the knowledge that if she'd loved Matthew, truly loved him in the same pure, noble manner in which he'd loved her, he would be alive today. He wouldn't have volunteered for front-line duty, killing himself and condemning his crew along with him.

"Good God, Anne," Sophia said suddenly. Relieved to have a diversion, Anne looked around.

"Will you look at Lady Pons-Burton's bracelet. How deliciously vulgar." Sophia slanted a caustic look at her. "Do you suppose the gems can be real?"

Oh, undoubtedly they were real. Anne's father had taught her how to spot paste from real stones, even at a distance.

"I declare I will have one just like it when I'm wed," Sophia said, adding in a reverent voice, "It must be worth a fortune."

"Three fortunes," Anne murmured. Enough to keep a dozen families fed for a dozen years, she thought, recognizing anew the bitter disparity between these people and those seeking a night's refuge at the Charitable Society for Soldiers' Relief. With anger came a wave of disquiet.

She hadn't planned on becoming a thief when she came to London to act as Sophia's companion. The skills her father had taught her as a child had been games, a means of passing the time while her mother was away visiting her "top-lofty" relatives. The stories her father had told her about Blind Tom, Rum Mary, and the Prince of London's Thieves were just stories.

She hadn't found out they'd been real until the day she'd found her father's diary. Confronted, her father had sworn her to secrecy and then told her the truth; *he* was the Prince of Thieves. She'd been shocked, appalled, and, yes, thrilled. She'd begged her father to tell her more, teach her more. It had been such a lark to discover her own father had once been a notorious criminal.

Her father, perhaps a touch bored with life as a country squire, had happily complied. He'd taught her everything. It had been their secret, a wink between a father and daughter. She'd never expected to use the knowledge he'd imparted—

"Couldn't you?" Sophia demanded stridently. Anne looked over. Her husband's young cousin regarded her with palpable irritation.

"Excuse me?" Anne asked.

"I said that you are wealthy enough to buy a bracelet like Lady Pons-Burton's for each of your wrists. Though heaven knows why you would buy jewelry when you won't even buy yourself a decent gown." Sophia gazed with frank contempt at Anne's gown and looked away, clearly signaling she'd had enough of the conversation.

Anne did not look down at the muddy lavender gown. She knew its shape quite well, just as she knew she could have easily replaced it if she'd wanted. Upon Matthew's death she'd inherited a fortune, money she could not bring herself to spend on herself and for which she had no other purpose. She had no real home to maintain. The country manor where she had lived with Matthew had never been more than a way station in their pursuit of pleasure; she'd sold it soon after his death. So she'd decided to establish a fund for the men Matthew had misled so disastrously.

The estate's trustees decided she would not. They had, they informed her, a solemn responsibility to see that Matthew's fortune benefited Matthew's widow, not nameless, faceless ex-sailors.

But once the idea had taken hold of her, Anne was not to be gainsaid. She needed to do this thing—do something, anything—to help Matthew's men.

She'd begun by asking for donations soon after arriving in London. The ton had greeted her solicitations enthusiastically, impressing each other—and the popular press—with the enormous sums they promised.

But pledges and payments, Anne had quickly learned, were not always the same thing. And when confronted, those who promised money threatened to destroy the Norths' social position should Anne reveal their "economy."

So she stole what had been promised.

At first she'd robbed only those who'd pledged in public and reneged in private. But over the course of months she'd added others to her list of victims: dandies without occupation or conscience, ladies who squandered fortunes on the turn of a card.

Jack Seward had stopped her.

She resented it. She hated having to give up the night but she'd no choice.

He'd said she'd stolen something he wanted, but, try as she might, she could not think of what that could be.

And until he'd found whatever it was he'd lost, she needed to lay low. Reason demanded that she stop. She *would* listen to reason.

"Where's Father?" Sophia whispered urgently. "We can't be introduced if Father is not here."

"Introduced to whom, Sophia?" Anne asked, glad of the interruption.

"Good God, Anne. Will you attend to the conversation? I just told you. *He's* here."

"Another infatuation, Sophia?" she murmured. "Who this time? Lord Strand? Lord Vedder?" She frowned down at a button that had come loose on her long white gloves and began working the tiny seed pearl back into its satin loop. "Who is, Sophia?"

"Whitehall's Hound," Sophia said. "Some call him Devil Jack."

The seed-pearl button popped off Anne's glove and fell to the floor, skittering away beneath the sweep of a hundred skirts. A little tremor raced beneath her skin, a tingle signifying danger, disturbingly familiar and even more disturbingly gratifying. It was the same feeling she experienced when she donned a black mask and for a few brief hours became Wrexhall's Wraith.

She no longer fought against acknowledging the ruthless, rapturous sensation. It was only when she risked death that she experienced the edgy excitation that told her she was alive. After so many years of running from memories, she'd finally found a place where the past did not exist: London's rooftops.

There she'd become votary to the acceleration of her own heartbeat, to the laboring of her lungs as she flew, to the challenge of a hushed, locked room.

Her hands clenched in her lap. The echo of excitement died, replaced by a cold sense of foreboding. She'd been a fool to taunt him, with his wounded eyes and grave manner and gentle voice. She'd been a fool to kiss him. She was worse than a fool to want more.

"He's too delicious," Sophia whispered.

Carefully Anne lifted her gaze. There. Across the room, moving through the jostling company like the wolf Lady Sheffield kept. Just as contained and aloof, his demeanor as mild, his eyes, like the wolf's, those of a killer.

He searched for something. And Anne knew—far, far too well—for whom.

She watched him, praying Sophia would not notice her interest, praying he would not come closer, stimulated by the notion that he would, appalled at her reaction, helpless to look away.

He was transfixing, forbiddingly handsome with his rumpled golden hair, firm jaw, and piercing eyes. But something more than the arrangement of his features drew the eye. He had an indefinable quality of refinement about him, a gentleness of manner that, coupled with such predatory eyes, arrested the attention. Quite a few women followed his progress through the room with discreet and speculative gazes.

Anne unfolded her fan and hid behind it, watching him. She could not find a word for what she saw in Colonel Seward. She only knew that all the thousands of candles glowing in their silver chandeliers could not chase the shadows from his face, that the finest tailor in London could not lay a veneer of languor over that taut, hard figure, and that no dandy's slouch would ever bend that precise and curiously graceful posture.

As she watched, he bowed over Jeanette Frost's hand. The girl's father stepped between them, his color high. Whatever hard words he uttered had no effect on Colonel Seward. He simply leaned sideways, addressing Jeanette before calmly turning aside.

"I must know him. Such polish! Such address!" Sophia said in a breathless little rush. "He is fascinating. He was in the war, you know. They say he did terrible things there. Things no one else would do."

Terrible things. Elegant voice, compassionate, world-weary eyes. *Terrible things.*

"He's a bastard. Sir Jamison's get off a Scottish maid, they say. Never legitimized him. Wouldn't even give him his name. Though, to give the old man credit, he did raise him."

"Why do you know so much about this man, Sophia? It's unseemly."

"Oh, don't be such a prig, Anne. Everyone knows about him. He's rumored to be Prinny's new favorite"—she paused and let her gaze play over Seward's tall figure—"though he hardly seems Prinny's sort, does he? He's all the *on dit.* He and that thief." She released a rich trill of laughter. "Honestly, I don't know which would be the more exciting to meet, Devil Jack or Wrexhall's Wraith. What a delicious dilemma."

"Wrexhall's Wraith?" Anne asked, diverted. She had, of course, heard the name some wit had given her, but she didn't know her exploits had become public fodder.

Sophia spared her a pitying glance. "You really must try to be more *au courant,* darling. 'Wrexhall's Wraith' was so named because Lady Wrexhall was his first victim, and the old biddy swears she saw the robber disappear out of her third-story window like a ghost."

Anne did not reply. She'd believed her thefts were closely guarded secrets, that pride alone forbade anyone from admitting they'd been robbed. She should have known better.

Colonel Seward disappeared into the crush. With a sense of disappointment and relief, Anne closed her fan.

"Jeanette Frost is passionate that she should be the Wraith's next victim," Sophia stated nonchalantly.

"What?" Anne stared at Sophia, finding to her amazement that she had to quell the laughter bubbling up within. How long had it been since she'd been surprised into laughter? Years.

Sophia nodded sagely. "Both she and Lady Dibbs are rabid to be victimized by him. Many of the most fashionable ladies are. The Wraith has quite usurped Byron's place as 'mad, bad, and dangerous to know.'" Sophia smiled smugly. "But I do believe that given the choice, I'd rather the more . . . solid of the two. The inestimable Colonel Seward."

"If you're very lucky, given what you've said about this 'Devil Jack' fellow, you won't meet either," Anne replied, her amusement fading.

Sophia gave her a pitying look. "You have utterly lost your spirit, haven't you, Anne? When you married Matthew, I thought you the most dashing creature in the world. It's why I begged Father to invite you to be my companion." Her plump mouth pursed with distaste. "I must say, you've been something more than a disappointment. You're old before your time, prim as a nun, and have about as much spirit as my father's barrow pig."

"How kind you are, Sophia," Anne said levelly, meeting Sophia's caustic gaze with a direct one of her own. Sophia had once been a spoiled but harmless child. Her mother's death had made her bitter, and this in turn had made her malicious.

For a second the girl had the grace to look shamed but only for a second. She placed her hand on Anne's forearm, her expression earnest but her eyes hard. "I'm sorry, Anne. I only meant to point out that you didn't die, Matthew did. Life goes on. Just look what mourning has reduced you to. I am determined it will not happen to me. I will not run from life as you have chosen to do."

"I hadn't realized I might claim responsibility for your inspiring embracement of life," Anne replied dryly. "I must not forget to congratulate myself. When I catch my breath from running that is."

Sophia regarded her with faint appreciation. "I see you still have some wit to you."

"Sarcasm, do you mean?"

"It often passes as the same," Sophia said. "I intend to grasp as much out of life as I can and to steal what more I want."

Another thief in the family? Anne thought ruefully. Sophia knew so little and was convinced she knew so much. Unfortunately, time and experience had uncanny ways of snuffing out such brilliant self-confidence.

"I wish you well," Anne said.

Sophia's expression set stubbornly. "I'm not going to settle for lukewarm experiences and secondhand pleasures," she proclaimed. "I want passion. Not tame—"

"Tame what, Sophia?" North asked.

Sophia's head swiveled around, her expression woefully easy to read. Fear fought a losing battle with youthful defiance at her father's quarrelsome tone.

"That chestnut mare I bought at Tattersall's last week not spirited enough for you?" he asked.

"I . . . I was just—"

"No, Malcolm," Anne interjected soothingly, accepting the cup of punch he'd fetched. "Sophia was just favorably comparing the chestnut with one she'd ridden out of Lord Frost's stables last year."

North would beat Sophia purple if he suspected the unruly streak in her character, especially if it threatened his plans for her brilliant alliance. As much as Anne disliked the person Sophia had become, she would not willingly let her be abused by her father.

Satisfied, North nodded and retreated behind Anne's chair. On any occasion he'd little enough to say to either Sophia or herself. The only marvel tonight was he'd actually spent time in their company. The faro table must not have been set up yet.

They sat in such an uncomfortable pose for some minutes until Sophia dropped her head behind her fan. "He's coming over here!" she hissed urgently. "With Lord Strand!"

With a dull feeling of unreality Anne fixed a neutral smile on her face and faced the approaching men.

Lord Strand took the front position, his spectacular guinea-gold good looks marred by a heavy flavor of dissipation. Behind, with that military exactitude that made mock of all the dandies' posturings, strode Colonel Seward.

There was nothing dissipated about him but something both far more grave and far more subtle. He moved with the stiff grace of someone bearing a wound so old that he accommodated the pain without conscious effort. The shadows under his eyes and the pallor of his skin bespoke sleeplessness; the scar breaking his brow, the crippled hand and broken nose testified to innumerable confrontations—and the cost of as many victories.

Strand stopped directly before Sophia and made his leg. Colonel Seward waited at his side. This close Anne could see the color of his eyes. They were the cool gray of ashes from a long-dead fire. *Terrible things.*

"Mr. North, may I present Colonel Henry John Seward?" Giles drawled.

"Seward, eh? Delighted, sir. Heard of you. Prinny speaks highly of you."

"Honored, sir." His voice was the same as she remembered, smoke smooth, hot as embers.

Anne glanced at Sophia. Excitement related itself in the tilt of her neatly coiffed head, the glitter in her eyes, the slight opening of her lips. Without doubt Anne must woo Sophia from her infatuation. Seward would eat her alive with his gentle manners and ruthless eyes.

"Anne, m'dear, Colonel Seward," her uncle introduced them. "Sir, my niece, Mrs. Anne Wilder."

She swallowed, willing herself to act. She turned her head up, half expecting Seward to seize her wrist and drag her bodily from the ballroom. "How very pleased I am to make your acquaintance, Colonel Seward."

At her utterance of those few syllables, Colonel Seward's head snapped up from making a low, formal bow. His eyes narrowed on her.

She was caught.

Chapter Five

Jack carried Anne Wilder's gloved hand to his mouth and brushed his lips lightly over it.

"How very pleased I am to make your acquaintance, Colonel Seward," she said, and shivered. He could feel the alarm vibrating through her. Alerted, he looked up and found himself caught in her gaze.

She held him with a regard nearly masculine in its directness. Seasoned. Knowing. A touch of valiance. A portion of pain and much resignation. Hardly the eyes of a procuress, as Strand had suggested. Jack had procured much himself; he knew the look.

Rather, she gazed at him like a woman who sold her body might look at her buyer: with fatalism, submission, and a certain damning anticipation. It was an expression that said "Do it and be done." And it aroused him.

"Madam, I am honored," Jack said, taking a steadying breath. She, too, he noted, took a careful breath.

Small wonder Strand had sounded smitten. Individuality marked Anne's face with absolutes: wide cheekbones, square jaw, dark and unfashionably straight brows. Her nose was both bold and elegant, her eyes—a striking, night-devouring indigo—deep-set, the lids delicately stained with mauve. Her mouth alone was a subtle creation, tender and soft.

It disturbed him that a woman in widow's weeds should draw such a sexual response from him. But she was just a touch disheveled—a dark tress escaped from her cap, a wrinkle marred her glove—and a picture of her rising, blowsy and sated from his bed, crystallized in his imagination. He glanced away and heard her exhale with undeniable relief. He damned himself for being so obvious. The thief had done this to him, heated him, readied him for lust.

"Mrs. Wilder is acting as Sophia's companion this season," North said, recalling Jack from his preoccupation.

"How kind of you, Mrs. Wilder," he murmured.

"And this is my daughter, Colonel. Miss Sophia North."

Sophia tilted her small face, regarding him with supreme feminine confidence.

"Miss North, your servant."

"La!" the beauty said, snapping her fan open and dimpling. "I already retain servants aplenty, sir. Perhaps I can find another function you might serve?"

His smile feigned admiration. As sallies went it wasn't bad, but the determined brilliance with which she delivered the line suggested it had been used before.

"You're a friend of Prinny's?" the girl asked.

"I have a long-standing acquaintance with the prince regent."

"Oh." Her lips formed a plump and perfect circle.

She truly was an exquisite little creation, showy and kittenish, and she engendered in him not a whit of the confounding hunger awakened by his thief in her black silk mask and boy's breeches or the stab of lust awakened by a tousled-looking widow still clinging to half mourning.

He smiled ruefully. Had he grown so perverse that he needed a fetish to awaken his lust?

"Prinny rather dotes on my Sophie here," North said proudly.

"And does he dote on you, too, Mrs. Wilder?" Jack asked.

His query caught her off guard, though only someone observing closely would have seen the slight start of her hand, the tungsten brilliance flare in her dark eyes before she ironed her face smooth.

"As a fond monarch dotes on any of his subjects."

"Well, his interest in Sophia is hardly of a magisterial bent." North snorted.

"Oh, I don't know," Strand drawled. "Mrs. Fitzhubert claimed His Majesty's interest was every inch regal. And that his doting was daunting."

Malcolm North snickered and Sophia colored with scandalized pleasure. Jack glanced at Mrs. Wilder. She remained unperturbed, reminding him that before her marriage she'd run with loose company and was, as such, well acquainted with such heated quips. She was a woman with a history. Something he, too, owned in abundance.

"La!" Sophia laughed. "You are wicked, Lord Strand!"

"So they say, Miss North." Strand cast a sly glance in the widow's direction. "What a tolerant sort of doyenne you've found, North. You aren't being negligent in guarding this delightful young woman from my sort, are you, Mrs. Wilder?"

Anne lifted one brow. "A small child could identify accurately the warmth and wit in *this* conversation, sir. I'll save my warnings for subtler dangers."

Jack watched her with heightened appreciation.

"Ouch!" Strand said, his outward amusement belied by his eyes. "Did you hear that, Seward? She called me obvious."

"So she did."

"And I think she called me childish, too!"

"I believe so, yes."

"Anne!" North's face reflected his concern with such cheek. Small matter that she'd been impertinent to a man who'd been tainting his treasured daughter's young—and presumably virgin—ears.

Mrs. Wilder apparently appreciated the irony, too, but she killed the smile touching her mouth before it was fully born. Wit and subtlety. Discrimination born of experience. A woman who—if Strand was correct— had forfeited a hoyden's pleasures for a cherished husband's devotion. Yes, the widow was definitely interesting. But was she his thief?

"And you, Colonel Seward," Sophia said, recalling Jack's attention, "are you wicked, too?"

"Worse than wicked," Strand cut in before Jack could reply. "Nefarious. Have you never heard of 'Devil Jack'?"

Sophia nodded eagerly. Anne Wilder's brows dipped fractionally as if she scoured her memory.

She'd not heard his epithet before? Then she hadn't been listening. Whispers followed him into every drawing room, every opera house and gaming hell.

"*I* have," Sophia said, eyeing him coyly. "Is your reputation deserved, Colonel?"

He studied her a moment. He could easily see Sophia in the role of thief: her eyes avid with excitement, her little body tense with anticipation, her boldness its own reward.

"Well?" she demanded archly.

"How can I answer that, Miss North, when I know neither the author of that sobriquet nor the allegations that prompted it?"

"Ah," Sophia said with relish. "But you admit culpability."

"I admit only that if the neighbor's gardener named me Devil Jack, why yes, I do deserve the name, for I certainly denuded his orchard. When I was twelve." Anne laughed—an abbreviated surprised sound. Sophia pouted.

"Fa!" she said. "You tease, sir. A gentleman would give fair accounting of his character."

He tilted his head. "Can you not, Miss North, in your generosity, ask what I aspire to deserve rather than what I merit?"

"And what is that?"

Surprised, Jack turned his head at Anne Wilder's hushed query.

Sophia cut in before he could answer. "La! Worthy ambitions are not nearly so interesting as unworthy histories."

"Too true," Strand concurred sagely. "But Seward here is as tight-lipped as a clam where his past is concerned. He's devilishly proper."

"'The prince of darkness is a gentleman . . .'" Anne murmured, her extraordinary eyes lowered to her hands.

"What are you saying now, Annie?" Sophia asked irritably.

"Forgive my interruption. I just recalled a line from Shakespeare."

Annie? thought Jack. *Annie,* who read Shelley and who had, unless he'd lost his wits entirely, just called him a gentleman. How perplexingly imaginative of her.

"Won't anyone tell me about the colonel?" Sophia begged.

"I'm afraid that to hear the devil's résumé you'll have to ask his biographer," Strand answered.

"And that would be . . . ?" Sophia asked.

"Why, myself, dear child. By your leave, sir, may I partner your daughter in this dance? I have no doubts the chaperone will approve. It's a country set. Like myself, obvious and uncomplicated."

At North's nod, Strand secured Sophia's hand and whisked her onto the dance floor as a pair of gentlemen paused to speak to North. Jack ignored them, being absorbed by the spectacle Sophia North produced.

She tossed her curls, flashed brilliant smiles at her partners, and arched her brows in a manner both coquettish and worldly. A canny enough lass, Jack thought, though through the months during which he'd pursued his thief he'd conjectured for his adversary a real intelligence, not merely this vulpine shrewdness.

It was a few minutes before he realized he was no longer watching Sophia but instead studying Anne Wilder. She was so different from her charge, like the memory of a disturbing dream. She looked to be made of smoke, burned from within, a delicate vessel whose very core had been singed.

It would be hard indeed to reconcile Anne's frail-looking form with the lithe athlete who'd bounded from a second-floor window. Furthermore, Anne Wilder simply didn't have the Wraith's fevered hubris.

There was no anticipation in her gaze as she watched the dancers, no yearning. Everything about her bespoke exhausted passion. He could not imagine her offering him first her body and then violence. He should be so gifted. Anne appealed to him in more ways than he wanted to consider.

He was lost in such uncharacteristic musing when North cleared his throat.

"Annie, m'dear," North said. "These kind fellows have requested my company for a short while." He nodded at the men by his side. "Would you please—That is, when Sophie returns would you—Will you—"

"Yes, Malcolm," she answered.

"You'll join us in a friendly bit of cards, Colonel?" North asked.

"Perhaps later, thank you. For now I'll stay and enjoy Mrs. Wilder's company."

"Please, do not keep yourself from an enjoyable pastime on my behalf, sir," Anne said quickly. "I assure you I am quite content to watch."

"You wouldn't chase me away, Mrs. Wilder, when I can think of no better way to indulge myself than by staying?"

"That's decent of you, Seward," North said in relief.

Embarrassment flickered across Anne Wilder's face. "I assure you, I merely follow my inclination," Jack said, irritated with North's lack of sensitivity.

"Of course you do," North said. "So I thank your inclination." He laughed at his *bon mot*. "Won't be above an hour, Annie," he said, and promptly dove into the crush in pursuit of his departing companions.

"You needn't think yourself promised for the nonce, Colonel," Anne said, her gaze averted. "Time with 'the fellows' has a way of extending itself, and I am sure you have other people you must greet."

"If you mean to warn me against monopolizing your time, Mrs. Wilder," he said, "I assure you I have no intention of inviting unwelcome attention upon yourself. I know full well the tolerance practiced in regard to my presence here."

His words won a look of surprised speculation from her. She did not demur and for this he was grateful. Instead she said, "I have been the recipient of such tolerance myself and I assure you, I do not practice it. I meant what I said, Colonel."

"Are you always so honest, Mrs. Wilder?"

"Within my means, sir," she replied after a faint pause.

"Then, if I might be allowed a few more minutes of your company, I would count it a great favor."

She lifted her face and the golden light of the nearby candles edged one high cheek with gilt.

"If that is your wish, Colonel," she said, then fell silent, leaving him to assess her expression. He'd made his way by studying the subtle signs by which people revealed and concealed themselves. Surely one small widow could be no great challenge to his art. But she was. A great challenge.

Thus engaged he did not see Lord Vedder until he was almost to them.

"Mrs. Wilder." Lord Vedder bowed, ignoring Jack completely. "Once more we meet! What is this, the fourth time this week?

And you are here with your enchanting young cousin. How delightful to witness the past paragon present the new one. But tell me, will Miss North be able to keep up this breakneck pace of activities? Will you?"

Jack opened his mouth to give the insolent cur a dressing down, but Anne preempted him.

"How kind you are to concern yourself with us, Lord Vedder," Anne said calmly. "Yes, I fear Sophia is determined that no fête shall be spared her critique, no festivities suffer the lack of her praise, and no person shall be able to call her exclusive for the lack of her acquaintance."

"You are determined to disapprove of us," Lord Vedder said with a little fashionable sneer.

"Not I, sir. I critiqued, praised, and was available myself, as I'm sure you recall. Or so some men thought."

Vedder's heavy lids drooped over his eyes and in his silence and sudden rigidity Jack read the brief hard history of a young man, smitten and sure of his welcome, sent packing when he presumed his favors were as irresistible as his title. No, Mrs. Wilder had never been a saint. She'd been rarer, a woman sure of her value.

"Indeed, you are correct," Vedder said, sniffing and looking beyond Anne to the dance floor. "However shall we contrive to impress Miss North? Please, as one who has never been impressed, give us some direction. She already appears to *know* everyone."

"Oh, no, sir. There are at least two people here she's only just met."

Anne turned to meet Jack's gaze. An unexpected and thus unexpectedly charming dimple appeared in one cheek and self-mocking humor lightened her tone. "Colonel Seward here has saved society from becoming habitual by offering himself up as unknown territory."

"How obliging of him." Vedder's voice was chill.

"Ah," Mrs. Wilder started uneasily. "I have assumed too much. Do you not know Colonel Seward, Lord Vedder?"

"Yes, madam. I do."

They eyed each other with the formal antipathy of two strange dogs.

"Vedder? Is that you, Vedder?" a female voice demanded.

Jack turned his head to find a small flotilla of females bearing down on them. Their leader, a handsome, sumptuously clad woman in her late twenties, reached them first. Lady Dibbs. Her eyes swept over Anne and Vedder and found Jack.

"Vedder, cruel man," she said. Though she addressed the viscount, her gaze never left Jack's face. Was there some personal recognition in her eyes? "We ladies have depended on you to make the stakes at the gaming table interesting and yet you stand here. How so, sir?"

Vedder bowed. "I am remiss, Lady Dibbs. But I must beg your indulgence. You see, I found Mrs. Wilder in need of company."

The implication, Jack noted dispassionately, though meaning nothing to these late arrivals, was not lost on Anne Wilder.

"You are mistaken, sir." Anne's voice was rich and smooth as new cream. "Colonel Seward has been most charmingly attentive."

This time Jack's glance was startled, but, as her words made introductions inevitable, he had no time to consider why Anne should come to his rescue. Dutifully Jack bent over the other women's hands, taking the opportunity to study Lady Dibbs as he did so.

She had a small though ample figure. Like Sophia North, her expression had a bold and demanding quality to it. Dressed in gilt satin and lace, she moved restlessly, the gems draping her throat and hanging from her ears winking in the light with each sharp movement.

"Found Mrs. Wilder alone, did you, Colonel Seward? And you," she said, turning to Anne, "still soliciting for your soldiers, dear?" Her tone suggested that such petitions had resulted in Anne's solitary condition.

Even Anne's finely crafted repose was no match for such calculated cruelty. Rosy flags stained her cheeks.

"How fascinating," Jack said.

"Sir?" Lady Dibbs fell eagerly on his murmur.

"Well," Jack mused, "I have been wont to think of a certain number of those soldiers as *my* men. I know for a fact that Wellington thinks of quite a few as *his* and, well, the prince regent has proclaimed them *all* his men so I find it interesting you should choose to gift Mrs. Wilder with them."

A smile quirked Lady Dibbs's thin lips.

"Well, of course, they are, all of them, England's men and, as such, England's responsibility. Indeed, you remind me of my obligations, Colonel, and I thank you. I pledge you a thousand pounds, Mrs. Wilder. For our soldiers."

A little gasp of appreciation arose from the group.

"Another thousand pounds, that is," Lady Dibbs declared, her eyes glittering like the jewels around her throat.

Jack looked to see Anne Wilder's reaction to such munificence. She did not look particularly impressed.

"Then another thousand it shall be," she replied softly. And with barely a glance in Jack's direction, Anne excused herself to go look for her charge.

Chapter Six

The cold wind sifted through the hansom's floorboards, soaking through the thin kid leather of Anne's shoes. She ignored the discomfort, turning up the collar of her wool mantle and peering out at the wintry streets. Across the river the sun slowly sank toward the horizon. A few more streets and she'd arrive at the Charitable Society for Soldiers' Relief and Aid—or the Home, as the local denizens called it.

Anne settled back. She had much work to do there and she looked forward to it. For two weeks, ever since she and Sophia had been introduced to Colonel Seward—and he'd made his interest in them clear—she'd been plagued with anxiety. Each knock on the door brought her heart thundering to her throat. Each time the footman brought her his card—and there had been three such times—she'd gone to receive him certain he'd come to arrest her.

She wasn't sure she wouldn't have preferred that because she could not for the life of her determine if he came to call on the Norths because he suspected her or because he was as drawn to her as she was to him. And she *was* drawn to him. She found herself taking pleasure from his visits and looking forward to his company. Which was insane!

The carriage came to a halt and the driver opened the door. She hastened from the enclosed carriage and up the shallow stone stairs to a set of tarnished brass doors.

One swung open. A boy of twelve or so doffed his cloth cap and stepped back for her to enter. She halted inside the foyer.

"Hello, Will," she said, blowing into her hands.

The boy eyed her critically. She liked Will. Without his pragmatism and worldly advice she wouldn't have accomplished what little she had achieved here.

"You didn't show up none too soon, Mrs. Wilder," he finally said. "The weather turnin' nasty and we gots twice as many people in here as normal. We ain't gonna make any good impression on them lords and ladies lookin' like we do. You know religious types likes their poor folks in nice straight lines."

On some other day Will's jaded perceptiveness might have made Anne smile. Not today. Come early this evening, a group of sober and extremely wealthy patrons would arrive to tour the Home. If she could impress them with the good being accomplished there, they might donate more money. More important, they might donate their expertise. The people she'd invited had long experience with running charitable institutes, something she sadly lacked.

"We'll do what we can, Will. Where's Mr. Fry?" she asked, looking around for the administrator.

"In the kitchen," Will said. She pushed open one of the myriad doors leading to the main part of the building and entered, squinting in the dim light.

The Home had been a popular theater in a former incarnation. It still wore some signs of its former glory. Giant gilt pillars strained beneath the mostly collapsed balcony and chipped, garishly painted boxes hovered in the dark above a long-abandoned stage. The velvet curtains had long since come down and been slashed into squares to be used as blankets. All the chairs and most of the benches had been removed.

Now hundreds of people—more than she'd ever seen in here before—sat on the floor and leaned against water-stained walls, murmuring together in a low incessant pitch, like the ghosts of long-dead choruses. Their collective breaths created a cloud of vapor in the cavernous room.

It was cold and dark and dank, and in spite of all those crowding together in the room, it still seemed like an echoing, empty shell.

It never failed to depress her, yet she knew that for many it was a refuge of unparalleled comfort. So much want. So much need. Blank eyes followed her as she made her way toward the back of the room and the tiny kitchen. Occasional hands lifted, bestowing blessings and curses in equal portion. She couldn't blame those who cursed her. What right had she to wear a woolen coat, when they had no shoes?

"We must get mittens for the children, Will," she said softly.

The boy shrugged, matter-of-factly kicking out of his way a man reeking of alcohol. "If you be thinking to warm their hands, won't do no good. The mittens will be stolen within the hour and the yarn unraveled and sold for food. What's—"

"What are cold hands when you're starving?" Anne finished for him, fighting off a sense of futility.

"That's right, Missus Wilder," Will said cheerfully.

"I'm not very good at this, I'm afraid," she said apologetically.

"Aw, that's all right, Missus Wilder," the boy said magnanimously. "You gots too soft a heart is all, and them what has soft hearts don't think so smart." He tapped his finger against his forehead and Anne found herself wondering if Jack Seward had once been a boy like Will, tough and unsentimental and frighteningly able to deal with whatever horrors life handed him.

Jack with his stark, blasted archangel beauty and sharp, knowing eyes. She bit her lip, struggling to clear his image from her thoughts. She'd no right to think of Jack as anything but her enemy. In the past weeks she'd lost sight of that.

Will led her into the kitchen area. There were fewer people there. The stove squatting at the opposite end of the room did not heat this far, and its sullen glow was little augmented by the few tallow candles guttering noisily in wall sconces. Those near her huddled together, pooling whatever warmth their bodies could generate.

Rumor said Jack had spent his first years in a place like this. Only worse. Much worse.

"Where is Mr. Fry?" she muttered, scanning the room.

"Perhaps he went back up front," Will suggested.

"Find him, Will. Tell him I have to talk to him about the finances. Before these people arrive." Mr. Fry couldn't reveal how much money she'd given him. She hadn't the subscriptions to warrant such sums, and they would know it.

"Aye, missus." Will sketched a short salute and darted through the crowd, winning curses from those he stepped on in his haste.

"Mrs. Wilder?" An elderly woman plucked at her sleeve with gnarled fingers.

With a sense of despair, Anne looked down at the eager, attentive face turned up toward her. "Yes, Mrs. Cashman?"

Mary Cashman's son John had sustained a severe head wound while under Matthew's command. It had resulted in his discharge from the navy. His fate more than any other gutted Anne with guilt.

"Did you 'ear anythin' from the Admiralty Board yet, ma'am?" the old woman asked hopefully.

"Not yet, Mrs. Cashman. But we will not stop until we have your inheritance."

Cashman had spent two years hounding the Admiralty Board for his back pay so that his mother might no longer need to beg. Finally, angry, drunk, and frustrated, he'd stumbled into a rally of disgruntled would-be revolutionaries breaking into a gunsmith's shop. Too drunk to run, Cashman had been the only one apprehended.

He had been tried, found guilty of insurrection, and hanged. His last wish had been that his back pay should go to his mother.

"I'm sorry, Mrs. Cashman."

If John Cashman had not been on Matthew's ship . . . Pointless. Too bloody many "ifs" crowded her thoughts. If John hadn't been under Matthew's command . . . If Matthew had married his childhood sweetheart, Julia Knapp . . . If she'd been able to love him as he deserved . . . If Jack and she had only met earlier . . .

The elderly woman nodded bleakly. She was tired and beaten down and ill and she wanted only two things: her son exonerated and her inheritance.

"He weren't no traitor, ma'am," she said quietly. "He 'ad courage, Johnny did. 'The Gallant Tar' them papers called him, and I guess he was."

"Mrs. Cashman—"

"Hush, now, ma'am." Mrs. Cashman put a grimy finger over her cracked lips. "We won't rock the boat. Just hold the course a bit longer. All will come right . . ."

"Yes, Mrs. Cashman."

The old lady smiled. "Don't look so, missus. You have your own worries and frets. Losing a man like Captain Wilder. Johnny said he was the finest, most decent gentleman he ever served under."

"Aye, a true gentleman," a bleary voice behind her announced. "And a bloody awful captain."

A man clomped out of the shadows, braced up on a wood peg and supported by a rude crutch. He was missing both an arm and a leg.

Mary Cashman hissed at him. "What you want to be sayin' somethin' like that for, Frank O'Shea? After all Mrs. Wilder done for you."

O'Shea's lower lip stuck out defiantly. The scent of cheap whiskey blanketed him. "Got me worse than killed, your fine husband did. A gentleman playing at war!"

Anne had no reply. She stared at the ruin of a poorly severed arm, the peg where a leg should have been. Matthew had not only killed himself but sacrificed an entire crew with his inexperience and wanton courage.

She could have stopped him; she couldn't have. Her thoughts twisted together like snakes, venomous and corrupting.

Abruptly the fight went out of O'Shea. His eyes watered and he blinked. "Don't throw me out, ma'am. I don't know wot got into me. I h'aint got no other place to go. I only meant that the captain was too much the gentleman. He 'adn't the guts for war, if ye know what I mean."

"Yes," Anne replied faintly.

"See?" The drunk cast Mary Cashman a righteous glare. "Mrs. Wilder knows 'er 'usband 'adn't no place commanding a ship." His head bobbed on his thin neck like an overripe apple on a slender branch. "He shoulda been 'ome, pettin' 'is 'ounds and takin' tea with 'is lady wife."

His words fell on her ears like a curse. Anne stared at him as guilt welled and gibbered within her.

He swiped at his eyes with the back of his hand. The movement and drink served to unbalance him. His crutch clattered to the floor and he foundered on his one remaining leg.

Anne reached out to him just as he fell. He gasped, grabbing for her, his eyes widening with panic and embarrassment. She caught him. For a second his face, so near to hers, tightened with self-awareness and fury.

Why, Anne realized in startled despair, he was a young man. Probably not much older than herself. He'd once had prospects that war and Matthew combined had seen an abrupt end to.

"I 'ate being crippled!" O'Shea ground out through clenched teeth, tears streaming down his cheeks. "I *'ate* what I 'ave become."

"I know. I know," Anne murmured, easing him gently to the ground. Mrs. Cashman clucked her tongue and retrieved his crutch.

He snatched it from her and turned away. "Go 'way," he said sullenly. "Go the bloody 'ell away."

"You gots other things to worry about," Mrs. Cashman said to her. "I'll take care of O'Shea here. You gots all them noble people comin' to look at us, don't you?"

"Yes. Yes. I do," she said. She knew she was babbling but the words just poured forth trying to stop the inner voice that shouted condemnation at her. "I have to find Will and Mr. Fry. It's imperative that we make a good impression—"

A thick coil of hair suddenly slipped free of her careful coiffure and unraveled over her shoulder. She looked down. Her skirts spread over the floor, damp with stains. Her gloves were soiled and dirty.

Appearances meant so much to these people. A woman could fund a charitable institute, but she must never allow herself to become involved in the sordid workings of it. Only a coarse, vulgar woman would do so, and coarse, vulgar women did not get support from rich, well-bred ones. A tear slipped from the corner of her eye. So much for good impressions.

The simple fact that Anne Wilder roused a deep yearning in him did not exempt her from observation. So Jack had followed her to this tawdry section of the city where his thief had pawned her stolen goods.

He stopped a discreet distance from the converted theater that now acted as a charitable institute, and warmed his hands by a chestnut vendor's brazier, occasionally stomping his feet against the sloppy, ice-crusted mud. The rain began in earnest. He adjusted his collar time and again, but the water dripping from the brim of his hat still found a way to trace frigid rivulets down his back. He deliberated over whether he ought to go in after her. She might be meeting someone in there who dealt in stolen goods. Workhouses were a fine place to meet criminals. Still, he held back.

Because he didn't want to see her in that place.

Though it wore the tawdry air of an abandoned theater, the Home still exuded the aroma of a workhouse: sweat, gin, and desperation. He could smell it from here, nearly two blocks away.

Anne had probably never known the type of people who ended up there: men and women who experienced sex as nothing more than a bodily release because their minds and spirit were too numbed to partake of any other portion of it, children who would trade anything or anyone simply to live another day. People like he'd been.

As minute bled into minute he found himself growing anxious. She'd gone in there alone. Yes, she was their benefactress, but Jack knew firsthand how little that meant to a desperate man. What if she'd gone out a door leading into an alley and been accosted? What if she'd met someone in a lonely corridor in the building itself? What if—

He wouldn't rest until he saw she was safe. He crossed the sleet-blackened street, bracing himself against the scent and look of the place as he strode up the stairs to the front door. Twenty-five years ago he'd left a place like this. He'd never gone back inside another one. He didn't want to go now.

A pair of skeletal, rag-covered beggars shrank from his approach. He pulled open the door. A blast of stale, cold air kissed his face and coated his throat with its vile scent of desperation. Inside a baby screamed.

He loathed this. Yet he entered, keeping his eyes straight ahead, refusing to look at the specters from his youth. A hand brushed his leg in supplication. He jerked forward.

He spotted a boy whose sharp, clever face was turned with interest toward him. Jack motioned and the boy slunk forward.

"Where's the lady that came in here a half hour ago?" Jack asked.

"Mrs. Wilder?" The boy cocked his head. "What's it worth to you?"

"Half a crown."

The boy's eyes widened and then narrowed. He snorted and pointed at Jack's coat. "Your coat be worth ten times that. You can afford a bit more."

The coat was worth forty, but the boy would hardly know that since his own coat probably had been pilfered from a rag pile, or stolen from another boy.

Survival was all that counted here. That's all one asked of the next day, the next month, the next year. In a place like this anything could be forfeited in the endless barter for life.

Wordlessly Jack flipped a crown toward the boy. He snatched it out of the air, looking around to see what interested eyes had witnessed his sudden windfall.

"She be back here," the lad said, motioning Jack to follow. "In the kitchen here waiting fer the toffs to arrive."

"Toffs?" Jack kept his eyes averted from his surroundings. He kept his mind focused on the boy's words. He did not need anything freshening his memory of that place, the acrid stench of stale urine and ancient sweat. He did not want to *be* here.

"Aye," the boy said, pushing open a door tucked into the far wall. Jack followed him in, squinting as his eyes adjusted to the sting of smoke belching from an ancient stove. "She gots a bunch of gentlemen and ladies comin' down 'ere any minute now to see if we deserves their aid."

Jack wasn't listening. He spotted Anne just as a crippled man seized her around the shoulders. Jack surged forward but abruptly checked himself. The man wasn't attacking her. He was falling.

And Anne was catching him.

She clasped the filthy man tightly, easing him gently onto the filth-strewn floor and kneeling beside him.

Eyes riveted on her, Jack moved closer. Around him people parted before his advance. He heard her speaking. Something about making a good impression and then her hair fell about her shoulders and she looked down at it and began to cry.

She shouldn't cry.

He reached down and brushed her shoulder and she turned. Recognition and confusion filled her eyes.

"Let me help," he heard himself say. He held out his hand and she stared at it as if he offered her some devilish pact rather than his aid. Slowly, a bemused and helpless expression on her face, she placed her hand in his. He pulled her to her feet and led her toward the corner of the room.

There would be no privacy. Every act of procreation and survival was open for viewing in these places. But she wouldn't know that. She would never know that, if he could help it.

He moved nearer, using the breadth of his shoulders to block her from the others' view, creating a little space of refuge for her.

"Your hair has come down." He sounded breathless.

He could smell her, the warm, clean fragrance of her skin. It was as foreign and intoxicating as roses in January, and it was far too much to deal with in this place after all these years. He closed his eyes. The discrepancy between her and this place was too great. It disoriented him, past and present swirling together, desire and loathing running tandem in his veins.

He felt light-headed. He cupped her shoulders in his palms and bent his head, his lips inches from her ear. Touching her set off a molten wave of longing in him. He lifted his hand, brushed a knuckle against her small, squared jaw. A butterfly caress.

"Let me." He swallowed. "Let me help you."

Dear God, he had to turn her around. He couldn't stand looking into her clear indigo eyes a minute longer. He didn't know what he'd do.

He pivoted her gently about. "Bend your head."

She paused. Her head dropped forward.

He lifted his hand and touched her. Exquisite. Her fineness, her delicacy. He combed his hand through the thick dark mass of hair. It slid between his fingers like cool, resilient silk. He swept it up, exposing the nape of her neck.

Too vulnerable. Too tempting. Even in the shadows, the soft downy hairs gleamed. Her skin would be like plush, warm velvet. It would taste like soap or lavender water. His hand trembled.

"Are you done?" she asked in a whisper. She knew. She knew he trembled like a stable boy ogling the wet nurse's breasts.

"Almost." He twisted the glossy locks into a thick coil and untangled a tortoise-shell comb from near the crown of her head. He secured her hair and stepped back, aroused and haunted.

She turned slowly and looked up at him, her expression unreadable. Her mouth looked as soft and malleable as warm candle wax.

"Thank you, Colonel," she whispered.

"My pleasure, Mrs. Wilder." With supreme effort, he kept his expression simply cordial, his tone detached. But he feared his gaze would betray him, so he did not look at her.

And he missed the stark look of longing that she could not conceal.

Chapter Seven

Jack shed his coat and flung it over the chair outside the room Knowles had assigned for his use in Whitehall's labyrinth. Though he'd left Anne an hour before, he still felt muddled and inchoate.

She must think him mad, a satyr. He'd barely been able to keep his hands from her, and when the lords and ladies had descended upon them a few minutes after she'd thanked him, he'd practically run.

Jack pushed the door open and stalked into the small barren room. He didn't know himself anymore. This had to stop. He needed to focus himself, to wall himself off from all these distractions. He was losing himself, losing the control and distance that he so desperately needed to survive.

He turned around and started in surprise. Adam Burke stood behind him, waiting patiently. Jack bit down in frustration. He'd expected Burke, one of his better information gatherers. Indeed, he'd ordered Burke's appearance and then forgotten him. The knowledge incensed him.

"I want an accounting of all servants employed in each of these women's households," he said coldly. "I want to know where they sleep, with whom they sleep, who their parents are, and where they are. Can you do this, or shall I assign Griffin?"

"No, sir!" Burke said with alacrity. "No reason to bother Mr. Griffin, sir. I've got meself—myself—hired on at Frost's establishment, sir. You know how servants are. I'll be able to pick up any bits of gossip right away."

"I want more than gossip, Burke," Jack said sharply. "I want facts. Am I clear?"

"Yes, sir. Very clear, sir. You'll know the name of the tweenie's second cousin by week's end, sir!" The young man quaked visibly at Jack's tone.

Jack saw his shudder and forced himself to relax. His aberration wasn't the boy's fault. "Don't look so stricken, Burke. I'm in a foul temper. Excuse me. Didn't mean to bite your head off."

Excuse me? Burke's eyes widened with abject hero worship. Colonel Seward was the only man he knew who treated the enlisted men as courteous-like as he did the officers.

Burke had been in the army six years, half that time in "special service" to Colonel Seward. A fairer, harder, and more decent gent couldn't be found—on either side of the blanket. No matter what the gossips said about him being workhouse slag, Burke knew quality and the colonel was the standard for it.

"And the women themselves, sir?" Burke asked.

"Might as well make a start of it," the colonel answered. "I want to know any and everything pertaining to these four women. I want to know if their brothers have expensive habits, if their uncles have French mistresses. Anything."

"You'll have it, Colonel," Burke said, and then sobered. "I've only been there a few days, sir, but I have picked up some information. Mr. Frost, sir, the servants say as how he's kickin' up rough. Drinking heavy and talking wild. About you."

"Grief, Burke. He's lost a son."

"But he blames you, Colonel. He says that you, uh, that, um . . ." Burke fidgeted.

"That I threatened to publicly accuse his son of treason if he attacked my social status?" Jack asked mildly.

"Yes, sir."

"So I did." Jack leaned back in his chair, studying Burke impassively. "Do you have a problem with that, Burke?"

"No, sir. You always done what had to be done, no more, no less, and no pleasure in it for you. No, sir, I do not have a problem. But Mr. Frost does and I think I'd keep a weather eye out for him. He's the type what thinks a man don't shut up on the say-so of 'is inferior—not that you are, Colonel—and it eats at 'im something fierce."

"Your 'hs,' Burke," the colonel reprimanded gently. "Manner and deportment will ensure your entry anywhere, but only if you can eradicate any spore that leads back to your birthing den. Language is a telling spore."

"Yes, sir. But, ah, begging your pardon, sir, your own accent has a Scotsman's burr to it."

"Not always," Jack replied equitably, "and only because I choose it. It's my talisman, Burke."

Burke nodded though he didn't understand what the colonel was driving at. Still and all, Seward, having come from the meanest beginnings, was his model, and if the colonel wanted Burke's "hs" in place, in place they'd be.

"About Mr. Frost," the colonel continued, "I appreciate your concern and shall do my best not to test the gentleman further. Now, are there any other cautionary words you'd care to impart?"

At the mildly sardonic tone, Burke reddened.

"No, Colonel. I'll be on me way." Burke bowed smartly and left. On his way out he nearly knocked over an elderly, balding gent trudging purposefully down the hallway. Probably another of the colonel's useful old dodgers, thought Burke. The colonel had dozens of them, each working without knowledge of the others.

Burke grinned at the oldster. "Hope you got him somethin' useful. Looks like tryin' times our colonel's havin'."

The elderly man grunted noncommittally and ducked into the room.

Once inside, Sir Knowles cast an irritated glance over his shoulder. "Who was that impertinent young Adonis?"

"Adam Burke," Jack replied in a distracted voice.

"And Burke is . . . ?" Knowles pressed.

"Enlisted man. He is in constant demand as a footman in all the superior houses because of those Adonis looks. The more exacting employers demand servants not only serve but please the discerning eye while they do so. A good, sound man, too. He's recently been employed in the Frost household."

"I see," Knowles said, huffing slightly as he lowered himself into the leather chair.

"Forgive me my manners, sir. Can I have some tea brought in?"

"*Damn* your good manners, Jack," Knowles said equitably. "I've come to see how you progress and to inform you that some chap in the Admiralty received a rather strident demand for your head yesterday."

"Oh?" Jack asked.

"Frost charged in and began making all sorts of aspersions on your character."

Once more the damnable grieving father. "I hope they were accurate aspersions. It seems a waste of the language to pin imprecise adjectives to my name when there are so many applicable ones."

"Don't know. Don't care. He was sent on his way, of course." Knowles dabbed at his forehead with his handkerchief. "Still, can't have the ton racing around down here mucking about, getting in the way."

"No, sir."

"Good. Now then, Jack, you've been mincing about in the ton's drawing rooms for over a fortnight. Tell me what you've learned."

"I'm sure Jamison has shared my reports—"

Knowles broke in with a loud snort. "You're sure of no such thing. Jamison dribbles only the information he suspects I already have, or will have, and no more." Undoubtedly true. Jamison and Knowles played an endless game of Blindman's Bluff with each other, relating just enough information that the other might act in tandem with his own purposes. All other information they hoarded, intending that it should be kept for their own uses. Unfortunately, all too often the stakes were other men's careers, futures, and sometimes even their lives. As with John Cashman.

The thought sobered Jack.

"Jamison is adamant that once apprehended, this thief should meet with an immediate 'accident,'" Knowles said. "He insists that should the contents of this missive be leaked, the potential for disaster is enormous."

"So I've been told. Repeatedly."

Knowles bit at one of his nails and spat the little paring away. "I believe he'd like everyone who even knows of the damned thing to meet with an accident."

"Everyone?"

Knowles sighed. "Shouldn't be surprised. Jamison's loyalty to the monarchy grows extreme."

Jack digested these covert bits of information. The letter had some connection to the monarchy, and Knowles considered it a distinct possibility that once it had been recovered, or its destruction verified, Jack might be considered expendable.

Even more interesting was why Knowles had informed him at all. It bore careful thought . . . something he seemed incapable of lately.

"This thief, Jack—"

"The Wraith has disappeared since our confrontation. But I'm convinced that it will only be a matter of time before another robbery occurs. I intend to anticipate it."

Knowles nodded with satisfaction, heaved himself to his feet, and crossed to the door. "Very well. But let's do bring the thing to an end before Jamison has us all butchered in our beds for glimpsing his precious letter."

"Yes, sir."

Once more Knowles paused. "I know this is probably a waste of breath, but believe it or not, I am your friend, Jack, and will remain so should you ever need me."

"Thank you, sir," Jack said politely, waiting for a sign as to how Knowles wished him to respond. None came and the door opened and closed without Knowles uttering another word.

Confounded, Jack dropped into the chair. He couldn't begin to discern Knowles's motive in offering his aid, but then he could discern little enough lately. If it was possible, he would have suspected his mind had been poisoned.

Each night a woman-thief infiltrated his dreams to play out innumerable, erotic scenes. He awoke in the morning tense with sexual frustration and urgent with unfulfilled needs. Yet daylight offered no reprieve because with morning he incurred a subtler longing. By day Anne Wilder monopolized his thoughts. He enjoyed her unfashionable directness, her conversation, and even her oddly erotic and unconscious dishevelment.

The damnable part was he knew why. She might have married an aristocrat, but her antecedents were not so far above his own. Not really. Even more unforgivably daft, he suspected that deep within his black heart he harbored some dim aspiration, some flicker of impertinence that insisted she might not be appalled by his attention.

Absurd.

Anne Wilder, whatever her own history, had married a man whom all of society considered a paragon of virtue and loving devotion.

After such a union, what could she possibly find favorable in a man like himself?

Sweat covered Jack's body. His belly muscles seized in the painful grip of ungratified arousal. He rolled over, trapping the taut, slight body beneath him. The thief's thighs wrapped around his ribs. Her hands raked through his hair and dragged his head down to meet hers.

He covered her, entered her, and her hips pitched in a thick, slow roll, deepening his possession, establishing her own. He shuddered with the overwhelming heat of her and was welcomed by a deep, internal embrace.

He cupped her bottom and lifted, thrusting deep inside. She inhaled on a long, shuddering breath.

"Do you want me?" She gasped. He answered with a jolt of his hips, wanting more than simple words could express.

"Do you want me?" she insisted, her palms slipping down over his back to hold him deep inside her.

He wanted to drink passion from her lips, to feel her climax. The physical tension raked him with talons of need. His body thrummed with a desire for completion.

He heard his breath, ragged and laboring. His muscles trembled with urgency.

"Do you?" she whispered.

"Yes," he confessed. "Yes!"

She vanished. Dissolved. He flung back his head and howled with fury—and woke.

Disgust and sexual urgency greeted his waking state. He was taut and hungry, whipped to a lather of sexual frustration by these damned dreams.

It had been a month since his encounter with the thief, but in the last ten days these nightly encounters had increased. Each was explicit and erotic; each of them ended with an exacting lesson in sexual torment.

Not tonight. He reached down, closing his fist around his turgid member. He closed his eyes. He tasted the burgundy on her tongue, felt each supple line and soft curve of her body pressed to him. His hand moved.

Tonight he'd find satisfaction where he could. But, he thought as the rhythm and darkness worked a harsh release, for her sake he hoped that when he caught his thief, they were not alone.

Chapter Eight

Anne had been right. Vedder was a libertine. He was also a swine. Sophia stared angrily at her image in the beveled-glass mirror, daring tears to fall from her too-brilliant eyes. Well, she applauded Anne's acuity. May it bring her joy.

She picked up Vedder's note without glancing again at the boldly penned lines. She crumpled it in her fist and hurled it into the fire. It exploded into a ball of flame.

So, Lord Vedder had *never* loved her. But when she'd met him early those mornings in the park and followed him to that secret bower and he'd done all those things to her and taught her delicious secrets a woman could do to a man, he'd said he did. Thank God she'd never parroted that asinine sentiment. At least she could congratulate herself on that score.

She lifted her chin, staring defiantly at her image. Is this what a jade looked like? Then a jade looked fine to her. She ripped the delicate lace edge from the bodice of her new, expensive gown and threw it into the fire after the note. She supposed she might even thank Lord Vedder for his instruction, superficial though it undoubtedly had been.

There'd been much more pleasing Vedder than pleasing Sophia in their lovemaking. In fact, the "pleasures of the flesh" had been little more than pleasant. Rather like being offered milk when you expected cream.

But if even a selfish, tepid man like Lord Vedder could please, think how much better a man like Jack Seward would be. Her eyes narrowed thoughtfully. Vedder's note had made it clear he expected her to pine for him, shed tears for him, and make herself miserable for him. Vedder be damned. If, as he said, she was ruined, then she might as well enjoy it.

She smiled at her reflection. It was time she found out where they kept the cream. Tonight, at Lord Strand's musicale, she intended to find out.

The Norths arrived at the ball long before the fashionable guests arrived. But Malcolm had been determined he would not miss one hand of cards and Sophia was equally determined she would not miss one opportunity to dance.

"Hope that Seward chap don't come sniffing about Sophie again," Malcolm said from his position on the ottoman next to Anne. "Bastard, you know. Not very nice."

Anne could think of no reply. "Nice" and Jack Seward had no relation to each other. "Chivalrous," "grave," "polished," yes. But Jack Seward was, in no one's sense of the word, "nice."

"He's a smoky sort of fellow," Malcolm went on. "Don't see him anywhere, suddenly see him everywhere. Discourage him if you can, Annie. But do it discreetly. Fellow's got the regent's ear."

"I will try," Anne agreed, and prayed she would not see him and prayed she would.

Two days ago Jack had stood behind her and touched her hair and made her uncomfortably aware of his size and strength and masculinity. He played havoc with her emotions. She knew he'd trailed her to the Home, hoping to catch her in some criminal assignation, just as she knew his attention to her stemmed from suspicion. He was simply doing his job, and yet when he'd gathered her hair and looked into her eyes, she'd thought she'd seen something elemental there. Something akin to the fire she'd felt in Lady Cotton's bedchamber.

What was she thinking? She had seduced him from his purpose that night; he would certainly have done the same, using her attraction to him to his benefit. He could hardly fail to note it, she thought, or how susceptible she was to him. She wanted what he promised. She wanted to be gathered in his arms and lose herself in his passion—

"Oh, bloody hell," Malcolm suddenly exclaimed. "Clean forgot to tell you. Came upon Julia Knapp the other day. She sends her love."

Anne went utterly still. Julia Knapp had been Matthew's first love—his true love. As far as Anne knew, Julia had never married, remaining faithful to the man who'd abandoned her. Not that she'd ever faulted Matthew . . . or Anne.

She'd sent Anne a letter upon reading the announcement of her engagement. The heart, Julia Knapp had written, could not be ruled. If Matthew loved her, Anne could not be anything short of wonderful, and Julia wished them every joy.

Her subsequent spinsterhood had been like daggers in Anne's heart. But perhaps, if Julia had come to town now, she'd decided to reenter the marriage mart, Anne thought hopefully. If Julia had decided to pursue her own happiness, might not she do the same? A little surge of hope sped through Anne.

"Is she in town for the season?" Anne asked.

"Say, what? Julia Knapp you mean?" Malcolm said, scrunching up his face. "Couldn't say. Didn't ask. Can't think why she would be. Something of an ape-leader by now, I'd say."

"Oh, Malcolm. She's only a few years older than me."

"Exactly," said Malcolm, "and you're five years a widow."

No wonder Sophia had such a charitable nature, Anne thought sardonically. She came by it honestly.

Malcolm upended a glass of port into his mouth, placed the glass on the floor, and set his hands on his knees. With a grunt he heaved himself upward and peered around the salon until he spied one of his cronies. "I really should make the rounds, Anne. Remember to dissuade this Seward chap from bothering Sophie. Where is the chit, anyway?" And with that, he left Anne alone on the purple ottoman.

She stayed a few minutes longer but, as always, reminders of the past had sent little worms of tension crawling along beneath her skin. She wished she could quit this place, find a refuge from Julia Knapp and from Jack Seward. But in the five years since her widowhood she'd found only one place where guilt did not follow, and Jack Seward had seen that that refuge was taken from her.

She didn't dare go out on the roofs. He was having her watched too closely. She rose to her feet. Where had Sophia gone? Three quarters of an hour had passed since she'd wandered off on Lord Strand's arm.

She trusted Sophia's good sense less than that of her uncle's spaniel—who was presently in season. She quit the salon, heading down a corridor for the more remote and private rooms.

"Mrs. Wilder?"

His voice caressed her ear like silken sandpaper. Not until she recognized her relief did she realize how much she'd feared Sophia had been with him.

She turned and found him standing close beside her. His harsh, scarred face needed no mask. Who could read anything behind such unassailable politeness?

She tried to untangle her emotions. Apprehension, relief, and gladness all swirled together, confusing what should be a clear, single note of fear. But fear, she'd lately realized, had its own savage seduction.

Jack angled his head, trying to gauge Anne's expression. He'd been speaking with Lady Dibbs when he'd seen her disappear into this unfrequented passage. He'd told himself to ignore her, to stay and attend the rapacious Lady Dibbs.

But Anne had looked worried. He'd held to his resolve for five minutes before yielding to the impulse that had sent him after her.

"Colonel Seward," she greeted him.

Possibly he might believe in the relief conveyed by the smoothing of her brow, but the fleeting welcome that softened her voluptuary's mouth—certainly *that* must be a trick of light and imagination.

"I was just admiring Lord Liverpool's art collection," she said.

"May I escort you?"

She would preen now, he thought, like any handsome woman would upon suspecting a gentleman had abandoned another woman to pursue her. It was not vanity that caused him to entertain the idea. He knew his charms and understood that the greater part of them could be attributed to his being accessible and yet still taboo.

She did not preen.

She hesitated, as if unsure of what manners demanded. He could have told her. She should accept his offer. He was her superior, in gender, age, and rank, and she was no one, suffered here only by virtue of a dead man's wedding ring. But the thought of her accepting his company to appease etiquette pricked and this, in turn, confused him.

He waited, not helping her, memorizing the severe beauty and exotic angles of her face, knowing he would judge all future women against its watermark.

"I would not want to keep you from more agreeable company and I do not mind my own," she finally murmured.

"Is there more agreeable company?" he replied. "Perhaps *as* agreeable, but then as I have learned never to measure one pleasure against another, I couldn't say."

She smiled but it was just a social expression. "Prettily said, sir. I thank you and accept."

He held out his arm and she rested her hand on his forearm, so lightly he could barely feel her touch. He understood his mistake. Manners might have led her to accept his company, but they were not so good she could mask her aversion to physical contact with him.

Well, what could he expect after having taken extraordinary familiarity with her person just a few days before? That welcome smile—how right he'd been to call it imagination, he thought, and calmly drew her forth.

"Have you ever been here?" he asked after a long pause.

"Yes." She glanced at him. "A long time ago. Soon after my marriage."

"Surely it could not have been so very long ago. You are a young woman," he said gently.

Darkness moved beneath her smooth, surface calm.

"As years, perhaps not so great a number. But as minutes, a vast record, indeed," she murmured, and then, starting forward at a sedate pace, she said, "Forgive me for being tiresomely philosophic."

He studied her in surprise. Her gaze remained on him, a touch rueful, much overburdened, and suddenly he wanted to relieve her of those burdens, to prompt her tender mouth into smiles.

The concept fascinated him even as he recognized it as farcical. Bewildered, it was he who broke away from the silent exchange.

He lifted his head, scowling unseeingly at an alabaster vase balanced on a marble pedestal.

"It does not please you?" Though Anne's query was polite, her gaze continued searching the hall—looking for some excuse to escape his company, he thought soberly.

"No, it does," he replied dully. "It's one of a pair but one of them was broken in transit."

"How sad!"

"Yes," he murmured, watching her gaze fluttering about the empty corridor. "I told Thomas they were too fragile for transport."

"You were with Lord Elgin?" she asked, her gaze finally settling on his face.

"Yes." He did not elaborate by telling her he'd been in Greece arranging Napoleon's ignominious defeat at Alexandria.

"I should like to visit Greece." She said it unwillingly, as if manners forced her to trade conversation with him.

"You might have posed for one of their statues." Her laughter was sudden, rare, and delicious, a sound he wanted to hear again. "And which statue might that be, Colonel?"

Persephone. Wed to darkness, yearning for the light. "Oh, any," he said. "You have a classic countenance." Her eyes widened and she looked away.

"I should not have been so bold," he said, his halt enforcing her own. "Forgive my manners."

He cursed his clumsiness. Her cheeks wore a heated stain and she refused to turn back to him. She wanted free of him. It had been clear from the beginning. He could ignore her aversion no longer. Gently he disengaged her gloved hand from his sleeve—far too easy a task—and bowed.

"Mrs. Wilder, forgive me. Clearly your tour was intended to be a solitary one and I have interfered. I bid you good night."

Anne stared. She'd had to keep reminding herself to look for Sophia when all she wanted was to enjoy his company even though she could not find a way to reconcile her pleasure with her fear of him.

"You misunderstand my lack of composure, Colonel," she said impulsively. "I trust you will keep my confidence, sir, when I tell you that I do not regret your company but rather the absence of another's. Only because I fear the company *she* keeps. Sophia is gone an hour and I cannot find her."

He studied her for a moment. "Perhaps I can assist you in discovering her whereabouts?"

"I would appreciate that, Colonel."

Gravely he again offered her his arm, and now, his stride purposeful, he guided her through a dizzying array of corridors and halls, anterooms and chambers.

Though they searched rapidly, it took them another quarter hour before Anne heard Sophia's laughter coming from behind a closed door. She steeled herself to whatever spectacle might meet her eye.

Colonel Seward smiled down at her. "It will come right. I promise," he said softly, and she believed him. And in the midst of her anxiety she saw him clearly, understood his innate tact. He was a gentleman.

How odd to discover that Whitehall's Hound, a man who did "terrible things," had so much delicacy and comportment. Yet she did not doubt that he'd full well earned his sobriquet as Devil Jack.

For a moment, the sexual memory that needed only the smallest opportunity to reawaken was replaced by a feeling of kinship . . . of something like friendship. She'd never had a masculine friend before.

And she didn't have one now, she reminded herself sternly. She played at charades with this dangerous man. She could not afford to forget it.

Jack pushed the door open. Four men—Lord Vedder, Lord Strand, and two youngsters Anne did not know—sat around a baize-clad table, Sophia at the head.

The unchecked wicks of sputtering tapers sent black wreaths of smoke into the heavy, warm air. Coins glinted on the wine-speckled table linen. A bracelet topped an untidy pile of coins.

Sophia saw her first. Immediately a stubborn set hardened her face, defiance flashed in her eyes. Deliberately she turned her shoulder to Anne.

Anne ignored her, trying to estimate the harm to Sophia's reputation. It was not as bad as she'd expected. Many women gambled. True, not as young as Sophia and not in the sole company of gentlemen, but Anne would take whatever comfort she could.

"Sophia—" she started to say.

"Who will come to my aid?" Sophia declared. "Surely my kiss is worth the sum of one hand's stakes?"

Dear God, Anne thought faintly. The girl was utterly ruined.

"I'll play," Jack said.

Anne's head snapped around. He could not . . . He'd seemed . . . She was every kind of a fool. She moved forward and he caught her arm. Casually, with an easy motion that a viewer would have mistaken as her own, he turned her so that her back was to the table.

"A moment, gentlemen," he said. "Mrs. Wilder and I have our own small wager to settle." He plucked the hand carrying her silk fan from her side and raised it. His long fingers worked over her own stiff ones, prying the fan open between them.

"You will give them a story on which to dine for a fortnight if you seize your charge and drag her from the room," he said quietly. His mouth was all smiles, his eyes intense.

"She doesn't look particularly draggable," she shot back.

"Nonetheless," he said, "you must trust me in this as you trusted me with the reason for your traveling these halls. Please, Mrs. Wilder."

She did trust him. The very quality that demanded she fear him made it impossible for her to do anything *but* trust him. Once he set himself to a task, he would not fail.

"Affect disinterest," he said, bending his head as though studying the fan. "Absolute, yawning disinterest."

"Impossible."

For an instant the smile touched his gray eyes. "For Miss Sophia's sake at least try for insouciance." He released her hand and straightened. "You are correct, Mrs. Wilder," he stated clearly. "The scene is definitely in Hogarth's mode."

He approached the table and indicated an empty chair. "Miss Sophia, gentlemen, may I?"

Vedder opened his mouth but before he could speak, Strand, his gaze amused, said, "Of course, Colonel."

"Thank you." He took his seat, crossing one leg over the other.

"I doubt you've the blunt to play this table, Seward," Vedder said, his gaze raking Seward's attire.

For the first time, Anne found herself looking at Seward's clothes rather than Seward. Though well cut, they bore no ornamentation, nor did they exaggerate the male figure, a hallmark of the consummate tailor's creation. Seward dressed soberly, as would a man of limited means.

"I'll voucher Colonel Seward," Strand drawled. "Though I won't stay in the play to let him estrange me from my money. I fold."

"You are too generous, Strand," Seward said.

"I only seek to disprove Mrs. Wilder's unhappy opinion of my maturity. What say you, madam? Is not refusing the pleasure of a wager a mark of maturity? Damme, I'll bet it is." The gentlemen burst into laughter but Anne would not be distracted from Seward's actions.

"Now, Miss Sophia," Strand said, "would you shuffle?"

The play went slowly. Each bet and raise caused Anne's pulse to jump. Sophia, a dazzling smile pasted on her face, appeared completely unaffected. Only the hectic color flagging her cheeks evinced that she'd begun to realize the gravity of her situation.

More and more coins covered the table. With each card, more sweat beaded the younger men's brows. They splashed wine down their throats, dividing nervous glances between Lord Vedder's sneering visage and Colonel Seward's cool, politely interested mien. Finally one, then the other of the pair dropped from the game.

It did not take much longer for play to end. Vedder assumed Jack's raise in answer to an audacious bet was a bluff. He assumed wrongly.

Jack's hand won easily. Vedder had no recourse but to accept the defeat with as much dignity as possible. And that was scant enough, Anne noted. He shoved himself back from the table.

Wordlessly Jack pushed the coins across the table to a now white-faced Sophia. The two youngsters snickered from their position near the sideboard.

With his peculiar rigid grace, Jack rose from his seat and approached Sophia. She gazed up at him.

He would kiss her now, Anne thought helplessly, and she would be ruined. Even if Jack did not claim his kiss, the others would only tell how Sophia had made the offer but had been refused. Then not only would her reputation be destroyed, but she would be ridiculed.

Poor Sophia, thought Anne. Poor, wretched, confused little beast. But beneath her sympathy another emotion rasped her conscious thoughts, clamoring for expression.

Sophia would feel Jack's kiss, the pressure of lips Anne all too clearly recalled. Sophia would know their warmth and texture . . . *Sophia.*

"Miss Sophia, may I have my kiss?" Jack withdrew a handkerchief from his vest pocket and with an elegant bow presented it to Sophia. His aplomb was absolute; not a flicker indicated he'd ever any other notion than this.

Sophia gazed at him with wide, disbelieving eyes. Gratitude surged through Anne and the breath she'd held released itself in a soundless rush.

Take the handkerchief, Sophia! she implored silently, and slowly, as if in a dream, Sophia secured the snowy linen and brushed a gentle kiss on its length. Smiling, Jack retrieved the scrap from Sophia's limp hand.

"I will treasure this, Miss Sophia. Lord Strand, too, I believe, has one of these sweet mementos from another lady."

"Aye," Strand drawled. "A lady of incredible refinement and impeccable taste."

"Seems a bold gesture," one of the youngsters remarked.

"Don't let anyone hear you say that, m'lad," Strand said with a laugh. "Should my lady ever hear her gesture had been misconstrued, I've no doubt she'd react very poorly. As would her husband. A fine duelist."

"I would not like to think *anyone* would misconstrue a lady's whim," Seward said. The gaze he turned on the lads was as harmless yet potentially dangerous as an unsheathed blade.

"Of course not!" one avowed quickly.

"Only the veriest blackguard would misread a lady's intent," the other added sententiously.

With a sigh, Strand hefted himself to his feet. "I believe the entertainment for the evening is at an end, sirs. Shall we find ourselves some nourishment?"

The two younger men agreed immediately, exiting the room hard on Lord Strand's heels. Vedder followed them out, inclining his head only as he passed Anne. "Your servant."

Sophia, color returning to her face, bit hard upon her lip and rose from the table. "Thank you, Colonel. I am in your debt."

"Miss Sophia, you owe me no more than your good opinion," he said, looking past her to where Anne stood motionless, her eyes brilliant and burning, like stars in a midnight sky.

Chapter Nine

It took most of the rest of the night, but Sophia finally managed to lose Anne and go in search of her erstwhile savior, "Devil Jack" Seward. He was in definite need of reward.

It didn't take long to find him. He was alone, standing beside the door leading to the dining room. Several popularly acclaimed beauties paraded slowly by him, but they did not draw his interest.

Sophia had no intention of being subtle; she would—as she'd told Anne—take what she wanted. And she wanted Jack Seward. She walked up to him, opening her fan and brushing the soft plumes across her décolletage.

"Ah, Colonel Seward!" she said.

His glance was speculative but his manner faultless. He bowed his head in recognition. "Miss Sophia."

"You aren't enjoying any of the entertainments our host has so kindly provided."

"It is kind of you to concern yourself."

"How could I not?" she declared, folding her fan and sweeping it down his broad chest. "La!" she said, "'tis too hot in here. I fear I shall be overcome if I don't get some air."

The corner of his long mouth quirked with amusement. His hooded gaze grew lazy. "By no means can we allow that," he said. "May I escort you to Mrs. Wilder?"

"Oh, no!" Sophia declared with a laugh. "I wouldn't want to alarm Anne. I fear I've done enough of that for one evening. If I could just find some fresh air . . ."

"Allow me to accompany you," he said suavely. Silently he drew her out into the deserted corridor and down to its end. The window there had been cracked and the cold air stirred the drapes.

She glanced at Jack. He smiled politely and cocked his scar-traversed brow. "Are you feeling more revived?" he asked sardonically.

"Oh, yes. Thank you," she said, stepping closer to him. She bit her lower lip, knowing it to be provocative. "I must thank you properly for coming to my aid earlier this evening. I see now that my actions were impulsive, certainly ill-considered. Some might think hoydenish."

He did not deny it.

"But then, I fear I am hoydenish." She inched closer to him and placed her fan back on his chest. The feather tips touched his strong, dark throat. "You saved me from the effects of my misjudgment. I want to"—she spread her fingers across his chest; it was hard and the skin beneath his waistcoat was warm—"demonstrate my appreciation."

He looked down at her. "That isn't necessary, Miss Sophia."

"Oh, but I want to."

He shook his head, his smile rueful and apologetic. "I'm old enough to be your father."

"I already have a father." She put her hands atop his shoulders, rose on tiptoe, and pressed her body against his.

"You are too kind, Miss Sophia," he said. "But this is not the time, this is not the place, and I, I fear, am not the man you think."

He reached between them and gently traced her jaw with a crippled finger. The movement, though tantalizing, effectively broke her contact with him. She dropped flat to her feet, thwarted and unhappy.

"Are you feeling quite recovered?" he asked mildly.

She might not have made her bold advance for all the effect it appeared to have had on him. He must have enjoyed any number of extreme encounters to be so blasé. The thought titillated her.

"For the moment, Colonel," she said, allowing him to turn her around and lead her back. "For the moment."

Anne Wilder moved slowly past Lady Dibbs, craning her head surreptitiously as she scanned the crowded ballroom.

"Have you lost your charming young relative, Mrs. Wilder?" Lady Dibbs asked with amusement.

"Dear me, no. I just wished to see that she is enjoying herself."

Anne contrived to look unconcerned, but Lady Dibbs could see her words had struck a nerve. Satisfaction spread through her.

Seven years ago Lady Dibbs had been the reigning toast of the London season—for all of two weeks. That was when Anne Tribble, a pocket-size nobody from nowhere, had arrived and promptly taken the ton by storm. Not only that, but she'd managed to snare Matthew Wilder, a man who had, for that same two weeks, shown definite signs of succumbing to Lady Dibbs's attractions.

But that was not the primary reason Lady Dibbs disliked the dark widow. She disliked Anne Wilder for the simple fact that she alone of their peers knew that Lady Cora Dibbs, the wealthy wife of an ancient, bedridden baron, recanted on her donations.

Every time she saw the widow, she was reminded that she was a fraud and a sham. Yes, she definitely loathed Anne Wilder.

"Where ever do you suppose she could have got off to?" Lady Dibbs asked innocently.

"I believe she's dancing. These young girls can dance for hours."

"Dancing?" Lady Dibbs echoed. "I thought for sure I saw her leaving the room with Colonel Seward." That sharpened the interest in Anne's thin face.

"I know that in your youth you allowed yourself to be familiar with those others would have chosen not to know, but I feel you really should warn your young relative off."

"Do you?"

Lady Dibbs could not help her sliver of admiration for Anne's cool expression. Too bad her eyes ruined the effect. They were quite, quite hot.

"Yes," she said, adjusting her gloves. "I know for a fact that Colonel Seward is quite base and"—she looked to either side before bending closer—"he seeks the company of the lowest type of woman."

"You don't know that." Anne's voice was taut.

Good Lord, Lady Dibbs thought in amusement, she has developed a *tendre,* an honest-to-God *tendre* for him! Several women she knew had declared their interest in Devil Jack, but interest of a purely physical nature. None of them would seriously consider him anything more than an exciting diversion.

"But I do, my dear. He's been seen procuring their company."

"I can't think why you would be telling me this, Lady Dibbs," Anne said stiffly, thereby betraying herself.

Lady Dibbs laughed. "Why, my dear! Because of Miss North, of course. Why else?"

Ruddy color rushed to Anne's wan cheeks. She lifted her chin. "I thank you for the advice." She looked beyond Lady Dibbs and her features flooded with relief. "There is Sophia now," she said triumphantly. "With Lord Strand. If you'll excuse me?"

"Oh, yes," Lady Dibbs said contentedly.

Sophia laughed gaily at a young officer's comment and tossed her head, catching Strand's eye to make certain he noted the admiration being showered on her.

He noted it and gave her the appreciative glance she sought. He glanced at the standing clock. It was well after one in the morning. Bored, he wandered into the antechamber. It, too, was overflowing with flushed-faced guests and frenzied servants.

He'd just decided to quit the party and find his club when he spotted Anne Wilder sitting on a velvet-upholstered bench, squinting down at a piece of paper. Above her a long line of Lord Liverpool's ancestors sneered in eternal disdain. Not that she noticed.

Strand smiled at her concentration, but his smile slowly faded as he considered her.

He'd long been attracted to Anne. At first, he'd explained his interest as being simply another of his self-defeating infatuations. Other men's property always attracted him. But now Anne Wilder belonged to no man and her attraction only grew more potent. Which was odd, Strand thought as she raised her head and light spilled across her face. She was not the beauty she'd been during her first season.

Mauve shadow stained her lids. Her pale skin cleaved too tightly to her fine-boned skull, and the shallow indentations over her temples looked fragile. She was too thin. No, she was no longer a toast, but there was something in her that stirred him far more than beauty.

Perhaps, Strand mused leaning against the door jamb, his attraction to Anne was in keeping with his past behavior, after all. Because ultimately Anne belonged to someone he could never usurp, never wrest dominion from: herself.

She was so uniquely and wholly her own creature.

Though he'd tried his best, he'd no idea how to charm her. His address and repartee, which, vanity notwithstanding, were formidable enough to have toppled many citadels of virtue, did not impress this one slip of a widow. He alternately hovered over her and ignored her, treated her with hauteur and courted her with attention . . . all to no avail. She simply did not *see* him.

Why?

He pushed off the doorway, angling through the jostling crowd and approaching her obliquely.

"I say, Strand."

Strand silently vcursed as Ronald Frost cut across his path. The whites of his eyes were pink and watery. A cobweb network of veins mantled each of his cheekbones.

"Your servant, sir," Strand said, and made to step by him. Frost clasped his forearm.

"I say, Strand," Frost repeated.

Drunk, Strand surmised, well familiar with that too-careful diction.

"Always thought Liverpool was a chap who only tolerated the best of everything: food, wine, company."

"And so he is." Strand beckoned for a footman, noting Lord Vedder standing nearby watching them with a sardonic smile. "Here, Frost. We must get you a glass of wine. Liverpool has some Puligny Montrachet that merits a connoisseur's approval."

Frost ignored him. "This affair has the stench of the stable about it."

"Must be my boots, old man," Strand said, trying to extricate himself from Frost's grip.

"'Tisn't your boots," Frost said, "it's that fellow, that Colonel Seward. Wouldn't have him in my house."

"Ah," said Strand, prying Frost's fingers loose. "Well, what can one do seeing how he's so chummy with Prinny and all?"

Vedder abandoned his post and sauntered nearer.

"Still wouldn't have him under my roof." Frost puckered his lips disapprovingly and swayed forward on his toes. Vedder caught his arm, steadying him.

"Thank you, Vedder," Strand said.

"My pleasure."

"Get Mr. Frost here a bottle of the Bouchard," Strand said to the footman who'd finally made his way over. "Frost, my dear fellow, this wine is superb." Far too good to waste on a man half sunk, but even drunk Frost would know if second best was being foisted on him. "You must give me your opinion."

"Damn fine vineyard," Vedder drawled. "Wouldn't mind tasting that meself."

"Yes. Splendid idea," Strand said.

"Come on, Frost, old horse. I'm convinced we share similar tastes . . . and distastes." Vedder secured Frost's elbow, gently nudging him after the departing footman.

Terribly obliging of Vedder, Strand thought, and terribly out of character. Still, he must remember to warn Seward of Frost's growing antipathy. He started through the crowd again, anticipating his opening salvo to Anne Wilder. It would be something clever and sophisticated and provocative. She'd pay him attention tonight, by God—

Strand stopped. Jack Seward stood before Anne Wilder. Her face was radiant with interest. The expression on Seward's hard, scarred face . . .

Carefully Strand edged back toward a marble pillar. From here he would be hidden yet could still clearly hear their voices. Feeling despicable, he leaned the back of his head against the cool stone, begging for the integrity to walk away and leave them. He closed his eyes and listened.

"—you enjoyed the museum?" Seward's voice held real interest.

"Yes. Though I don't know much about art."

"I thought ladies learned painting and artistic things from birth," Seward said.

Anne was silent a few seconds. "I'm not really a lady, Colonel Seward. But I'm sure you know that."

"I know nothing of the sort, Mrs. Wilder," Seward responded gravely. "You are every inch a lady."

"No," she insisted softly, as if it were a matter of importance to her that she convey this to Seward. "I am not. I did not have a formal education. Or much of any education, for that matter. No governess or tutors. Only the vicar and only when he was desperate to settle his grocer's bills."

Seward laughed. Strand started. He'd never heard Seward laugh before.

"My parents tried to convince me of the merit of book learning," Anne said. "I was not very receptive to the idea." Strand could imagine her lifting her dark eyes to Seward, daring him to match her honesty with his own.

"You were far more interested in . . . ?" Seward invited her confidences. She did not disappoint him.

"Running wild, I'm afraid." A thread of feminine laughter played like music in Strand's ear.

"Tell me." Seward's rough, low voice was warm with encouragement.

Strand pushed himself away from the pillar, walking sightlessly through the other guests. He'd asked himself why Anne Wilder did not seem to see him. He had his answer.

He'd always measured the success of his love affairs by gauging the effect he had on a woman. Had he ever considered asking a woman how she'd spent her day or what occupied her thoughts? Had he ever considered *any* woman's day worth discussion? No. Only their nights. And only if they spent them with him.

The unfamiliar act of self-scrutiny bludgeoned him with reality. He'd never married because he'd always cast his nets too deep. Henceforth he'd only play the shallows . . . where he'd lived all his life.

For it had only taken a few seconds to recognize the lure Seward held for Anne: Jack cared more about Anne's words than his own.

Jack was supposed to have passed through that rare stratum of society as a transient interloper in pursuit of a thief. That was no longer true. Because she was here, occupying that rare atmosphere, making it rarer still, and so he wanted to be, too.

He shook himself from his reverie and looked down at her, perched on the bench. He was uncertain what to say next. The sensation unsettled him. He'd always known exactly what was expected of him, exactly how to give satisfaction. With her, he was lost.

He should have been pursuing Lady Dibbs or even the unlikely Jeanette Frost, not spending time playing uncle to Sophia to win a few minutes in her chaperone's good graces. He certainly could no longer tell himself he stayed close to Sophia out of suspicion. The girl was clearly not his thief.

His thief.

It angered and confused him. In a life singular for its lack of attachments, to become obsessed with two women at once was lunacy.

"And you, Colonel," she said, breaking the too-long silence, shifting her gaze away from his. "Do you enjoy the museum?"

"I've had little opportunity to learn about art or music." He crossed his hands behind his back and looked beyond her. There'd been no music in the workhouse but the songs of unremitting hunger. There'd been no art in Jamison's house unless you counted the human spirits he twisted to his own designs. He could hardly tell her that. "But I confess I do like a landscape and I've a fondness for sweet sounds."

"'The man that hath no music in himself, Nor is not moved with concord of sweet sounds, Is fit for treasons, stratagems and spoils,'" she recited softly, her expression gentle.

"You'll find yourself labeled a bluestocking, Mrs. Wilder. Beware of bedazzling poor regimental officers by quoting Shakespeare at them."

She laughed again. She was beautiful. "Colonel, my days of fretting over whether I reveal too much or too little are long gone. And you simply cannot be offering yourself as an example of this 'poor regimental officer' I am to have bedazzled." Her lovely mouth softened on a wistful note. "We both come here by way of the back door, don't we, Colonel?"

"Yes, Mrs. Wilder," he heard himself say. His heart beat heavily in his chest. With so few words she bound him to her.

"Like yourself, my father had scant opportunity in his youth to pursue learning for pleasure. Music was one of his primary indulgences and my mother's, too."

"You were . . . much involved with your parents," he said.

Memory lent her severe beauty a gentleness he'd not witnessed in her before. "We *loved* one another."

The tentative bond he'd felt snapped. Her innocent words created an unbreachable gap between them. Try as he did, no matter how relentlessly he scoured his memory, he could recall no mother's voice, no tender hand, nothing that provided incontrovertible proof that he had not one day simply appeared, hunger and rage and a tenacious, unreasonable desire to survive having pooled together in the workhouse corner to form him.

She'd known love. It had shaped her from her earliest years. Thus, she would always be unfathomable to him. How could it be otherwise, given his history?

"You are fortunate, Mrs. Wilder." He bowed his head and left her.

"You'll dance again, won't you, Miss Sophia?" The red-coated officer was as smitten with her as a hummingbird with nectar. It really would be impossible to refuse him.

"All right, sir. Only give me five minutes' rest before I join you." Having sent him on his way, she looked about for Colonel Seward, preparing to amuse and captivate . . . and tease him a bit.

She'd no intention of letting go of her fascination for Colonel Seward. Fantasizing about him was enough to make her flush with discomfort. Her body ached with the yearnings roused by hot-handed young men in dark corners and despicable viscounts in other, more private places. Roused but never quite satisfied. She needed satisfaction.

She spied him sitting alone, one long leg casually tossed over the other, his arm outstretched along the back of the couch he occupied, the picture of desultory interest. Even his crippled hand had its perverse fascination, and his thighs stretching the tight fabric of his breeches looked hard and muscular. She started toward him when something in his expression arrested her.

Though his posture bespoke nonchalance, his eyes were riveted on some unseen target. His regard was so fixed he did not blink, so painful she could feel the tightness in his throat as if it were her own. With a sense of inevitability, Sophia edged through the crowd to see what held him rapt. She stopped.

Anne was speaking to some older woman, her hand raised in illustration of some point. She was dark and small as a goblin, her dress priggish and severe; even her damn cap was ajar. And he stared as if she were a goddess. Jealousy and confusion fought for precedence in her hard little heart.

"Come, Miss Sophia," Lord Strand drawled softly in her ear. "We are both *de trop*. But I promise to find you a place where you can be sure of a most ardent welcome."

Chapter Ten

The next few days seemed interminable. Though Anne fought to keep her thoughts from Jack Seward, he possessed her days and haunted her nights. She stayed in her room pleading a sick headache, but each time a visitor called she found herself straining to hear Jack's soft-hoarse voice. At night she woke to the memory of his mouth on hers, his body hard and tensile beneath her hands, his hunger feeding her own. Her obsession frightened her.

Nothing could come of her association with Jack Seward except perhaps her own death on the Tyburn Tree. She was the thief he'd been sent to capture. That knowledge alone should have killed her fascination for him, but it didn't.

Each day her room seemed smaller and her nerves stretched tighter. She paced restlessly, measuring the corridor with her steps time and again. The walls seemed to be closing in on her; even the air seemed thick and hard to breathe. She wanted to escape to the rooftops but she knew that Jack had someone watching the house.

Finally she could tolerate her self-imposed incarceration no longer. One evening she snatched her wool capote and headed for the park where the dark evergreens glowed in the twilight. Her pace slowed as she entered through the gate. She closed her eyes and gulped the chill, moist air, lifting her face to the sky. Overhead, a few stars burned dimly. The air frosted with each breath she took. The sounds of traffic grew dim, muffled by hemlock and yew.

"There now, sweetling."

She recognized that quiet intonation and faint burr. *Jack,* she thought without surprise. But yes, he would stand watch himself.

"You're a pretty little chit, aren't you?"

He seeks the company of the lowest class of women . . .

Dear Lord, he was with some doxy. Mortified, she cast about, looking for some other path to travel. There wasn't one.

"Let me pet you a bit more. There. Not so bad, is it? Gently, darlin'," he crooned, his voice mesmerizingly tender and amused.

Did he caress her roughly or tenderly? Could she taste the flavor of his breath?

"I've half a mind to take you home with me—"

She froze where she stood.

"Mrs. Wilder?" he called.

She forced herself to turn around.

He was holding a cat. A little shivering gray cat. He scratched her chin and she purred contentedly. Slowly Anne became conscious of the fact that she was smiling foolishly at him and that he returned her smile with a slightly bemused one of his own.

"Good evening, Colonel Seward."

"Good evening, Mrs. Wilder." He inclined his head and the cat crawled up his coat, pushing her small angular face beneath his chin. He gently unstuck her claws and resettled her in his arms.

She stared at him, her earlier near panic dissolving in wonder. "You like cats, Colonel?" she asked.

"Yes." Her astonishment amused him. "And I like dogs, too."

"Do you own one?"

"No," he answered, "but someday I will. Two or three dogs, and a stableful of cats."

"Someday? Why not now? It's a simple enough venture," she said, as surprised by the teasing quality in her own voice as by the subject of their conversation. "You pick one up, as you've just done."

"And put it down where?" he rejoined in a likewise cajoling tone. "I don't own a home, Mrs. Wilder. I rent apartments."

"I'm sure your staff would set out a dish of cream."

"I don't have a staff. Just a cook and a daily housemaid." Though his voice was mild, his eyes were careful.

She blushed, embarrassed that he should have had to remind her of his straitened circumstances.

"But there'll be a day I retire to a house in the country. My kitchen door shall stand open all summer and hounds and cats will trespass at will."

"And what will you be doing while the wildlife makes free with your cupboards?"

"I'll be watching them, Mrs. Wilder." The gray cat batted at his chin with a velvet paw. He covered her head with his big hand and stroked her. The cat purred. Envy pricked Anne, envy of a cat.

"Just watching them?" she said.

"Yes," he answered simply, intentionally standing motionless, hoping to lure Anne closer.

And she had moved nearer during their conversation. His breath grew shallow as he waited.

She peeled off one glove and tentatively reached toward the cat. Her hand brushed against Jack's crippled fingers. She did not look up; he could not look away. Sensual awareness shot through his ruined hand.

He watched, mesmerized by the slow motion of her slender, elegant fingers burrowing through the cat's thick pelt, massaging it with sure, deft strokes. His body quickened with arousal at the sight as he imagined her hand on him. His body went tight with urgency.

The intensity of his reaction caught him off guard and he lifted his chin above her head, staring out at the twilight. She was so slight, so small. He could hold her without much more effort than he cradled the cat.

Standing this close their joint body heat created a bell jar of warmth in the cold air. He imagined he could smell the faint perfume of feminine skin, the same elusive, maddening fragrance he had scented at her charity house.

"I still think you should take her home, Colonel," she said softly. He looked down into her dark eyes. The tabby lifted her delicate face as if in agreement. "Cats don't require much care."

He shook his head. "No. She's a street cat, used to roaming at will. She would only howl for freedom if I locked her in my apartments."

"But then again, she might curl up beside your fire and be content never to leave. Perhaps she's had enough roaming, Colonel." A small line appeared between her brows. She withdrew her hand and replaced her glove.

A wave of longing and emotion swept through him. Everything he wanted stood before him and if he did not soon find something that proved his presence here was profitable, he'd be sent elsewhere. Away from her. She would never know that she meant something to him, something significant because it was so bloody, bloody rare. It seemed important, vitally important that that didn't happen.

Carefully Jack set the cat down. It stared up at them with an impoverished air until the distant bark of a dog sent it darting into the thick yew hedge. He offered his arm. "May I escort you back, Mrs. Wilder?"

"I thank you." She settled her hand on his forearm, allowing him to lead her down the path and out of the park gate. Darkness had settled rapidly. The lamp-lighter had already lit the streetlamps, and the road was empty.

Silently Jack escorted her across the street and down the abandoned walk to Malcolm North's town house. At the bottom of the steps, he paused, looking about with a disconcerted air. Finally he drew her to the side of the stairs, into the warm shadows and away from the cold night breeze that had picked up.

"Mrs. Wilder, I will not be here for the season," he finally said, looking straight ahead.

"Not here?" Anne asked, unable to keep the distress from her tone. He spoke too carefully, too seriously. Her earlier pleasure receded before an encroaching sense of apprehension. "Why?"

"You are an intelligent woman, Mrs. Wilder, and an acquaintance of Lord Strand's. Have you not wondered why Strand has promoted my presence in society?" His face flushed. "I presume too much. You would hardly concern yourself with my presence or absence."

All the time, she thought numbly. *Every second you are gone I note the vacancy. When you are here, I am far too involved with you. Disastrously so.*

She gazed into his beautiful, troubled gray eyes. She should agree with his assessment, confirm that she spared him little thought. But she couldn't.

"No," she said aloud, "I have noted you."

An enigmatic smile flashed across his stern features. "Yet you have never evinced any curiosity."

She held her breath. *He knew she was his thief.*

All his attention, his courtesy, his regard, had been circling before the kill. She could not care. She'd suspected as much from the start. Her soul felt held in abeyance.

"You accepted me even though you must have suspected I'd covert purposes here, among such society." Dread filled the vacuum.

"I am looking for the person known as the Wrexhall Wraith."

This was worse. So much worse than having him take her prisoner. He cared for her enough to trust her. "I have thus far met with no success."

"I'm sorry." He would never know how much she meant those words.

She wanted to sob, bury her face in her hands, and cry. She didn't know, hadn't realized he cared. "I'm sorry," she whispered again.

"If I do not apprehend the thief soon, my employers will assign me to a new duty. One far from here. I . . . I will miss you, Mrs. Wilder."

Imprisonment was child's play compared with the punishment of his trust, trust she would betray. She looked away, the movement small, her gaze frantic.

He hesitated and then set himself before her, his stance wide, his hands crossed in military fashion behind his back. "Mrs. Wilder?"

"Colonel?"

"May I make an incredibly bold request?"

Her gaze lifted to his. She felt emptied from within. "Ask, Colonel."

"Would you," he said, "do me the kindness of speaking my Christian name?"

He petitioned her for more than a few syllables. He requested an intimacy greater than a lover's verbal caress. He asked her for acknowledgment, for recognition.

A gust of cold wind teased an errant strand of hair across her mouth. The hard line of Jack's mouth abruptly softened, his eyes grew gentle. Carefully he reached up and brushed her hair away. He'd moved closer. A matter of inches separated them. She could feel his warmth and she longed to lean into it, become enveloped by it.

"It is John, is it not?" she asked in a hushed voice.

"No," he replied with quiet intensity, "Jack."

They regarded each other gravely. The chime from a distant church bell tolled the hour. A night bird fluttered across their path. He skimmed his thumb gently along her bottom lip before dropping his hand. His head bent down, her face tilted up.

She heard herself sigh, the faint soughing of her soul. His mouth touched hers, so delicately, so softly it might have been a butterfly's wing. She couldn't deny him.

"Jack," she whispered into the promise of his kiss. "Jack."

For a second his lips hovered above hers and then he stepped back. She heard him draw a shaky breath.

The front door opened and the footman appeared in the bright rectangle of light.

"Thank you, Mrs. Wilder," he said gravely. "I will see you tomorrow evening."

"Tomorrow," she repeated tonelessly, and wished with all her heart for yesterday.

"Strand says you think this thief is a woman." Jamison inched the leather-bound edition of Plato's *Republic* into perfect alignment with its mates. "A woman could complicate matters no end. People are so cursedly sentimental about women. If it is a woman, she must be dealt with summarily. There must be no trial, no opportunity for her to reveal the contents of that letter."

"Strand told you I believed the Wraith a woman?" Seward asked.

"Seward, do not dignify this creature with a sobriquet. And as for Strand, yes. Why shouldn't he? Did you imagine he had some loyalty to you?" he asked, walking stiffly to his desk.

Strand had told Jamison nothing; one of his other toadies had given Jamison the clues that had led him to make such a supposition, but Seward would not know that. It was best to keep Seward isolated, away from attachments. It made him sharper and warier and, thus, more effective.

"No, sir," Seward said blandly.

Jamison lowered himself into his chair, congratulating himself. He'd taken a boy with the rudest of skills and molded him into this splendid, remorseless, and analytical being. Looking at him now, so polite and ruthless, one could even give credence to the rumors that Seward was his natural son.

He pinched the bridge of his nose, choosing his way carefully. "I will be blunt. If you find this thief, man or woman, kill him. Do not ask questions. Do not attempt to divine the whereabouts of this letter."

"May I ask why, sir?" Seward asked. His lean face masked whatever surprise he felt. "If this letter's return is so important . . ."

"Its return is not as important as its destruction and the destruction of any who may have read it. I have come to believe, as you, that the thief either doesn't have the blasted thing or doesn't realize the importance of it.

"It's probably been burned as trash," he went on. "*But,* should the thief someday remember what he read . . . Well, the effects could be disastrous. So he—or she—mustn't live to remember."

Seward did not evince a modicum of aversion. And why should he?

"Your presence among the ton has only sent the bastard to ground. There hasn't been a robbery in six weeks, and the prince is once more happily gobbling marzipan kingdoms with his ridiculous friends. Perhaps the thief is dead. Perhaps one of his cronies killed him. We all know how some betrayals lead to death," Jamison said meaningfully.

Seward remained impassive. Jamison did not like it. Seward, always a puzzle, grew ever more enigmatic.

"I really should recall you from this assignment," Jamison said.

Seward's brow furrowed. Jamison leaned forward, immediately alert. "What? What is it?"

"The thief is not a fool, sir," Seward said. "He won't attempt a robbery while I'm looking for him, not as long as he can help it."

"This has been a waste of time then," Jamison said, relaxing, "and any further effort would be senseless."

"Not necessarily," Seward replied. "I said 'as long as he can help it.' But I don't think he *can* help it. Not for much longer."

"Whatever are you talking about, man?"

"I believe that money isn't the sole motive for these robberies. I believe the thief feels compelled to commit them."

"Nonsense," Jamison said, plucking his walking cane from beside his chair and bouncing the heavy silver head in his palm. "He'd be a madman."

"Perhaps. But I would like to wait a bit longer, sir."

"There are more important things to do than chase after some thief who is not thieving. We'll put someone else on it." Someone Jamison could be absolutely certain of controlling.

"No." The hard note in Seward's voice took Jamison aback.

Jamison's eyes narrowed. "I've a dozen other matters that could benefit from your skills," he said tightly. "Or have you developed a taste for snuff and punch, Seward?"

"I'm sorry, sir," Seward said more calmly, "but in this matter I'm not yours to direct."

Jamison caught the cane's head and held it. "What did you say?"

"Lord Knowles does not feel I am wasting my time. As he is the man who initially involved me in this affair, I will continue my investigation until he relieves me of the assignment."

Jamison stared at him stonily, unwilling to believe his ears. Seward was his creation. *His* creature. How dare he forget that?

"I work for the government," Seward went on. "I am—excuse me for pointing it out—a club hound, sir. I work for whoever holds the leash."

"Is that supposed to be humor?" Jamison asked coolly.

"I've never thought it particularly witty."

With a sudden violent movement, Jamison slashed his cane across the desktop, sending paper flying. "Did we not just discuss betrayals, sir?"

"Not to my recall. Sir."

Like sand suddenly blanketing a blaze, Jamison's expression mutated from violence to blandness. "I will see the leash returned to its rightful master."

"As you will," Seward replied.

"If I do not have the letter within two weeks, I will speak to Knowles and you *will* be removed from this assignment." With a short impatient flick of his hand, Jamison dismissed him. Seward started out, carefully avoiding stepping on any papers as he left.

Jamison sat silently for a long time before reaching for his pen and a sheet of paper.

"Come in."

Griffin entered the colonel's bedchamber. The colonel looked up from studying his image in the looking glass. "Do you think a simple silver stickpin, or something with a jewel for the Norths' fête?" he asked.

Griffin blinked, sure the colonel was having him on. Blimey, he was serious. Jack Seward, who cared about fashion about as much as a cat cares for swimming, was asking for advice on stickpins. "The silver is nice for the daytime, I'd think. But for night, I'd say a touch of flash."

The colonel nodded. "A diamond. Right."

Griffin eyed him. "I haven't decided whether you are playing fond uncle to the young lady or reticent suitor to the widow."

"The widow," the colonel said, "mistrusts me." It did not seem to give him offense, Griffin noticed.

"Must be a lady of taste," Griffin said silkily.

"No." The colonel studied the cravat a second before emitting a sound of dissatisfaction. He dragged it from his neck and flung it onto the pile already occupying the bed. He held his hand out for another. Griffin obliged.

"She has no taste at all," he said softly. He finished tying the new cravat, gave a satisfied nod at his reflection, and tucked the ends inside his waistcoat. "If she had taste she wouldn't accept the company of the likes of me. And she does. But she's perceptive, my dark widow. Watchful and uneasy as a fledgling peregrine."

"Be wary her talons, sir," Griffin said, troubled. "I don't like women. Don't trust them. They complicate matters."

"Don't they though?" the colonel murmured, affixing his fob to his waistcoat. "Now what news do you have for me?"

"Miss Sophia goes to manteau makers and libraries, adding occasional unchaperoned visits to Lord Vedder's town house and not-so-respectable coffee houses. With quite a variety of gentlemen, too. Mrs. Wilder has been keeping close to home, though she regularly visits that charity haunt she set up."

"Fine," the colonel said. "What of Jeanette Frost and Lady Dibbs?"

"Jeanette Frost giggles. Her father drinks more each day. Vedder's his favorite companion. He is also Lady Dibbs's newest lover."

"Vedder?" The colonel's interest sharpened.

"Aye. But don't get your hopes up, Cap. They don't go wandering over the rooftops when they're together. Besides, Lady Dibbs is too plump to fit through some of those windows the Wraith must have entered."

"Yes," the colonel agreed. "There has to be something to go on, somewhere."

"Jamison been at you?"

"He's given me a fortnight to find the thief." The colonel frowned. "Something's more to this letter than I understand and that I do not like, Grif. Jamison became nearly apoplectic when I reminded him I am under Lord Knowles's directive." He worked the fingers of his gloves on. "What *is* in this cursed letter that has him so deviled?"

"I'll find out, Cap. I'm making some progress. I discovered that the letter originally came from Windsor."

The colonel paused and looked up. "That's interesting."

Griffin frowned. The set of the colonel's jacket didn't look right. "Where in the palace?"

"Don't know yet." Griffin tugged the offending lapel straight. "But I have a man there that's good at ferreting things out."

"There's no one even *in* residence there now. Except the old king," the colonel said. "And he ceased to be a political factor long ago when he went mad and his son became regent."

Griffin stood back to survey his attempts at valeting. "The diamond was definitely the right choice, Cap."

Anne sat staring stonily at her image in the mirror. Her dress was new, the product of a rare free afternoon and a canny shopkeeper's window display. It had been delivered this morning, along with crystal-studded shoes, delicately embroidered silk stockings, and a net shawl sprinkled with tiny gold beads.

Against the rich Forester's green, her hands looked interestingly pale, ivory instead of their usual waxen shade. Gold silk edged the hem and piped the low décolletage and short puffed sleeves. Yesterday the dress would have pleased her. Today it might as well have been sackcloth.

Could she love Jack? Ever since that horrendous idea had arisen, she'd been unable to think of anything else. And it was absurd. Love? What did she know of love? she thought bitterly.

She'd once been "in love." She'd married the man and spent the next two years being taught the deficiency of her heart, because her love had withered even as Matthew's had grown. Try as she had to love him, to give back to him some part of the enormous burden—*gift*, she thought wildly, the enormous *gift* of his adoration—she hadn't been able to do it. And he'd died because of it.

In his last letter to her he'd made it clear that he was freeing her from their marriage in the most complete way possible. By dying. Only she wasn't free, was she? She'd never be free.

She swayed forward, her head throbbing, and pushed her fingertips into her temples. She wouldn't call this thing she felt for Jack love. She wouldn't.

How dare she think of loving Jack? When he discovered who she was, he would despise her.

Her head snapped up and she stared at the woman in the mirror with brilliant, burning eyes. That was it. Jack Seward was an opiate, an addictive peril, like leaping across ten-foot spans a hundred feet above the ground. Loving Jack simply raised the stakes, made it more stimulating, more perverse, more dangerous.

No! From within something struggled to repudiate the ugly accusation, but she would not listen. Self-loathing and hopelessness spurred her on, away from the avalanche of loss threatening her.

She no longer knew what she did or why. From the spinning, disconnected thoughts jumbling for expression in her mind, only one emerged clear and imperative: She had to escape from him.

Chapter Eleven

Chinoiserie vases brimming with Michaelmas roses cluttered the tables. Polished sideboards reflected the buttery glow of beeswax tapers and the sweet strains of a string quartet drifted from upstairs. The Norths' fête had begun.

Only a dozen or so guests had arrived, Jack Seward among the first. He went in search of Anne. He needed to see her, speak to her, find out what he had done with his impulsive kiss. Though, he amended wryly, that faint meeting of lips, that brief exchange of breath would hardly qualify as a kiss, yet it had stirred him more deeply than any other such exchange had ever done. Except perhaps one. And that had stirred him in another manner altogether.

"Colonel Seward!" Sophia had found him. She bore down on him, shepherding a tall, brown-haired woman before her.

"Miss Sophia."

"Julia, dear." Sophia secured the arm of the gentle-faced woman. "This is Colonel Seward. Colonel, our good friend, Miss Julia Knapp."

"A pleasure, Miss Knapp." Jack inclined his head.

"I can't think but there must have been some sort of accident on one of the main thoroughfares," Sophia said, looking around. "So few people have arrived."

"Undoubtedly," Jack agreed. The party was light on guests, Jack noted, and of those present not a duke or earl among them. Poor Sophia had been mistaken in her self-assessment. In someone else's home she might be flirted with as a comely wench. To accept an invitation to dine in hers would declare one's willingness to take her aspirations seriously.

"Have you been in town long, Miss Knapp?" Jack asked. The necessity of making idle conversation chafed. He wanted to see Anne.

"No," Miss Knapp replied. "I came down with my brother's family last week. I met Sophia at the museum yesterday. She kindly invited me here tonight. My brother and his family had prior engagements."

Her gaze slid away from his. So, Miss Knapp had not been invited to join her brother, Jack thought. "Have you known Miss North long?"

"Since she was a child and spent her summers at Mill End."

"Mill End?" Jack asked.

"My cousins', the Wilders, country house," Sophia answered for Julia. "I spent summers there. The Knapps own the property adjoining Mill End. They've been neighbors for generations."

Julia had known Matthew Wilder, Jack thought. Just what sort of man was his dead rival? What about him was so exceptional that Anne had prolonged her mourning so far beyond what decorum demanded?

"Then you are acquainted with Mrs. Wilder," Jack said.

"Oh, yes, Julia knows Anne," Sophia said with a purr.

Julia shook her head and her soft brown ringlets bobbed lightly. "Not so very well, Sophia. I met Mrs. Wilder the year of her come-out. She was so spirited and self-assured. We all strove to emulate her." Her voice reflected only the sincerest admiration.

"Yes," Sophia said in a pensive voice. "Anne was splendid. I thought her the most fascinating creature on earth." Then, unwilling to be caught in so unfashionable a mood as sentimentality, she opened her fan with a snap. "I only meant she once had a fine sense of style. But she's forsaken style for all those tiresome gray things."

"Oh, dear," Julia said. "Do not tell me she still mourns?"

"I suggest you ask her. Colonel Seward, punch?" She did not await his answer but beckoned a servant over.

"I'm sorry." Julia colored. "I have been forward." She darted an apologetic glance in his direction. "Forgive me. I had . . . It is just that I hoped Anne had found peace."

"Not at all, Miss Knapp," he said. "Your concern does you credit."

"Ah." Sophia's expression intensified, her smile grew tense. "Lord Vedder has arrived. I must go greet him." She swept by them, her chin high, her eyes glittering.

"Sophia has certainly grown up since her mother's passing away," Julia said, watching Sophia greet Lord Vedder with a high, artificial laugh.

"You were telling me about your friendship with Matthew and Anne Wilder," Jack responded casually.

"Oh, yes," Julia said. "I was a childhood friend of Matt—of Captain Wilder's."

Matthew, Jack thought. "Then you lost a friend of long standing. My condolences." Odd. He'd never offered Matthew's widow condolences. "What was Captain Wilder like?"

Julia paused, not giving him the quick response to a simple conversational gambit that he would have expected but framing her response carefully. She *wanted* to talk about Matthew Wilder, Jack realized, and so knew that the past at Mill End had contained more than simple friendship, at least on her part, and that in speaking of Matthew Wilder, Julia Knapp made him live again if only in her memory.

"He was exceptionally handsome and dashing, and yet not at all self-conscious about his looks. He was warm-hearted, gregarious, and generous. He was not clever in the way of Brummel, but he had charm. Great charm."

She tilted her head, as if picturing him in her mind. The image brought a smile to her plain face. She'd been in love with him.

"Warm-hearted, generous . . . a most worthy man," he said.

His tone must have lacked some quality of appreciation because she darted a reproachful glance at him. "He must sound dreadfully proper to someone like yourself, Colonel Seward. But it was not a fault of his, only my lack of ability to describe him."

Damn. Even if he was jealous of a dead man, he needn't advertise the fact. "He won your approval, Miss Knapp. That is high recommendation enough."

She smiled. "Thank you. It wasn't just me, you know. I used to accuse him of quite ruthlessly seeking adoration." She laughed. "The truth is Matthew made people strive for the best in themselves. He would accept nothing less."

"A great gift," Jack said.

"Yes," Julia said slowly. "Except when people did not live up to his expectations. He hated that, as if failure or indifference in any form somehow reflected on him. It wounded him gravely."

"He must have spent a great deal of time hurt then." He should not have spoken so cynically. He could not remember ever behaving so boorishly.

Julia took no offense. She merely shook her head. "That's just the thing of it, Colonel Seward. He rarely was, because, overwhelmingly, things and people *were* better for his association with them."

"Even Mrs. Wilder?" Once more, even though he knew his probing was vulgar, he could not help himself.

Her gaze lifted. "Matthew loved Anne. He—" She looked away as if something in his face reminded her of a past hurt. "From the moment he met her, from the first time he saw her, Matt *adored* Anne."

He waited.

"She wasn't of his class, you know. She was quite open about it. Not that it mattered to Matthew. He wooed her as if she were royalty. And yes, to answer your question, she was better." She spoke with a certain defiance.

"In what way?" he asked, keeping his tone smooth, his manner interested but noncommittal.

"Anne was"—she scrunched up her face, searching for the right word—"restless when she first came out. She shone almost too brightly. It was like watching a flame consuming a brand."

"I should have liked to have known her then," Jack mused.

"We, I confess, thought her perhaps a shade too wild, too spirited, but Matthew would have none of it. He thought she was perfect. She declined his hand at first. You didn't know? He was determined though. He said that only if Anne agreed to marry him would he be complete. Perfect."

A servant stopped by their side, offering them punch from a silver tray. Julia Knapp accepted a cup, raising it daintily to her lips and sipping.

Could this be the cause of the pain he saw in Anne? Had she fallen from Matthew's pedestal? It puzzled him that Matthew Wilder, with no real naval experience, but with family and wealth and charm—and Anne—should have volunteered for such hazardous duty.

Had Matthew, finding himself not married to a fairy-tale princess but a mere mortal, chosen to throw his life away rather than live less than a "perfect" existence?

And if Jack was right, what of Anne? Had she felt the slow development of his disenchantment? Had she asked herself what she lacked, what quality Matthew imagined that she'd not in actuality owned? How would it feel to be so well loved and then find, through no fault of your own, through no device you can fix, that you no longer inspired your spouse's affection, perhaps not even his regard?

He had to know if he was right.

"I have never been married, but I would assume that the ardency of their courtship must eventually have been tempered with the familiarity of marriage."

"I'm a simple country woman, Colonel Seward. I assume that love, once given, grows. And certainly I saw nothing in their marriage to dissuade me from that opinion. Not that I saw them very often. Matthew loved taking Anne to new places, exotic locales. He had a huge appetite for travel and meeting new people."

"So he was as fond a husband as he was a suitor?"

She nodded and gave a little sigh. "Oh, my. Yes. Matthew loved Anne more with each passing month, each year."

He cast about for some different answer to the enigma. "Surely a rarity. And the jealousies that such ardency produces in this case never arose?"

The idea clearly surprised her. "Perhaps some were jealous. But then, who would not be jealous of living a fairy tale come true?" She ended with a small apologetic smile.

But all fairy tales have an ogre, Jack thought. *What, or who, was it in Anne's story?*

"Matthew wanted her happiness above all things," Julia said softly, looking about for a place to set her empty cup.

"Then why did he ask for a command he was unfit for?" Jack murmured. Julia looked up, long years of confusion marking her countenance. Clearly she'd asked that question of herself many times.

"I . . . I do not know." The silence between them stretched into a long, empty moment and then many more as they stood together until Sophia found them again.

"Look who I found," she said. "And she's not in gray!" Her laugh sounded brittle.

Anne stepped from behind Sophia. Jack stared. She took his breath away.

He had prepared himself for her effect on him, but no preparation would be adequate enough to temper the thick acceleration of his heartbeat. His senses heightened all at once, as if all of him were attuned to her, opening to her, thirsty to drink in every element: the look of her, the sound of her voice, the scent and heat of her.

She wore some shimmering gown the color of pine boughs shot over with gold. Framed by the rich hues, her beauty was even more arresting, stronger and yet, conversely, far more vulnerable.

She did not look at him. He would have wagered she did not even realize he was there. For an instant she stared at Julia Knapp as if seeing a ghost. Then the expression faded, replaced by irony and finally, fatalism.

"Miss Knapp," Anne said. "How wonderful to see you again after so long."

Julia came forward in a rustle of taffeta, her easy welcoming smile so at odds with Anne's expression that the contrast could only hurt those who witnessed it. "My dear Mrs. Wilder! How fine you look."

Anne hesitated one telling second before embracing the much taller woman. "Malcolm said you were in town. You must have only recently arrived?"

"Last week. I've been—"

"—busy. Of course! Isn't the season always just so? Has Sophia offered you punch? But I recall you disliked punch. Lemonade, perhaps?" Anne said, her words coming rapidly. Her eyes glittering. Her smile brilliant and false and heartbreaking. We must—" She spun away from Julia, turning directly to face him. She froze. "Jack."

He barely heard her. It was not even a whisper. More an exhalation. A sound of finality.

"Good evening, Mrs. Wilder." He bowed.

"Good evening, Colonel Seward. How pleasant you could come to our party." Her tone was as sweet and unsubstantial as meringue. He'd never heard such tones from her before. "But you must meet Miss Knapp, Colonel. Oh, you already have? Ah! Excellent." Something was terribly amiss. He stepped forward. She backed away from him. A constriction began in his chest, like an iron fist closing about his heart. Her gaze pulled away from his, like an animal dragging a trap, painful and awkward.

He frightened her. He'd seen the look in her eyes far too often to mistake it. She had gone to her room last night appalled at his boldness and her submission to it. She wasn't Lady Dibbs. She would not be well versed in averting unwanted attentions. He'd taken advantage. He felt ill.

"Miss Knapp is residing with her brother," Sophia said, her gaze darting between Anne and him.

Anne smiled even more brightly, a pathetic eagerness in her expression. "Oh? For the season?"

"He has kindly asked me to make my home with him," Julia said. "My father passed away early last year."

Anne paled. "I . . . I am so sorry."

"Thank you," Julia answered graciously. "Simon and his family have moved into the manor. He has kindly invited Mother and I to stay on. I can't tell you how delightful it is to hear children in the house again."

"Miss Knapp is in the excellent position of being a doting aunt to her brother's five children." Sophia's tone quite clearly told Jack that it was not an excellent position. "How are they all?"

"Well," Julia hastily assured them, "they are all very healthy. Thank you. But you, Mrs. Wilder, I hear you are doing wonderful things for our soldiers and sailors. A relief fund of some sort?"

"Yes," Anne replied, shifting uncomfortably.

Julia caught her hand in both of hers. "How fine! How very, very fine. Mother and I did some nursing when they first were bringing our soldiers home," she said, her eyes glowing. "We opened the house. It was quite satisfying."

She gave Anne's hand a squeeze, her face wreathed in approving smiles. "If Matthew were alive I'm sure he would have encouraged you."

"Would he?" Sophia did not look convinced. "But that would mean Anne wouldn't be able to spend every waking moment with him."

Julia laughed. Anne, Jack noted, did not. "Oh, Sophia, still such a tease! But really, Anne, I am jealous of you, having something so rewarding to occupy the long days—"

She stopped abruptly, suddenly mindful that her words revealed a loneliness and aimlessness in her life that might make her companions uncomfortable.

Anne rushed to fill the awkward gap. "How are you enjoying the little season, Miss Knapp?"

"Oh," Julia answered easily. "I'm not here for the season. My brother's eldest daughter will make her bow in a few months. We're visiting dressmakers and such."

"But Julia," Sophia protested. "You must allow yourself a little fun."

"I'll be gone by week's end, I'm afraid," Julia said quietly. "I've no reason to stay."

"We will miss you," Anne said in open discomfort.

"Colonel Seward was asking about Matthew, Mrs. Wilder," Julia said a shade too brightly. "He wondered what sort of man he was."

Anne's head swung up. She pierced him with an indecipherable look, tragic and bitterly alone. "Oh. The very best, Colonel Seward," she declared. "The very best."

Chapter Twelve

O h, dear," Julia said, gazing anxiously at Anne. "I am so sorry.
I hadn't thought it would still be so painful for you to speak
of him. Please forgive me."

Her distress cut Anne with a thousand little blades of guilt.
"Please don't apologize. I'm fine," she answered.

Julia was the most decent woman in Anne's acquaintance. She'd
never accused Matthew of abandoning her or Anne of pursuing him.
And she could have been so accused. She *had* pursued Matthew
Wilder, with all the skills and determination at her command.

"Colonel Seward was going to tell us about Scotland," Julia
said, casting about for some topic of conversation.

"Was he?" Anne asked. She glanced in his direction, barely able
to bring herself to look at him, it hurt so much.

He was frowning at her.

"I think Scotland a fiercely romantic place, don't you, Julia?" Sophia gushed. "Especially the mountains. Did you come from the Highlands, Colonel?"

"No. Edinburgh."

That's right, Anne thought, her gaze fixed on Julia, her every other sense attuned to Jack. They said Sir Jamison had found him in a workhouse in Edinburgh. She'd forgotten. As she'd forgotten she was a thief.

"Mrs. Wilder?" Julia's low voice took her by surprise. "Might I have a word?"

Anne nodded numbly. With a light touch, Julia drew her aside, leaving Jack and Sophia together. "I should not speak here, but I feel I must. I doubt whether I'll have another opportunity and I feel I owe it to Matthew," Julia said softly.

Anne went still. "What do you owe Matthew, Miss Knapp?"

"He loved you so very much."

Dear God. A deep, acid pain spiked through her stomach. How many more reminders must she bear? How many times must she be reminded that she'd been loved . . . no, *adored,* given the sort of affection most women only can imagine? The love Julia Knapp should have had.

"From your reaction to my mention of Matthew's name, it is obvious that you still mourn. You shouldn't. It isn't right. Matthew would have been appalled."

Matthew would have loved it. The thought bubbled up inside with unexpected vitriol. Aghast, she bit her lip.

"I grieve, too," Julia said earnestly. "Matthew was my friend. And though I haven't experienced the loss that a"—she paused— "a wife would, I know he wouldn't have wanted his memory kept in a shrine of unhappiness. 'When Annie laughs,' he once said to me, 'I cannot help but smile.'"

"Please don't."

Julia secured one of Anne's chill hands in her own, rubbing it between her palms. "Dear Mrs. Wilder, begin again. You're young. Your whole life is before you. Begin once more to enjoy it."

"As you have?" Anne asked in a hushed voice.

Julia smiled. "But I have none of your resources, my dear. If I could find something to give myself to . . ." She shook her head ruefully.

"I could change that," Anne said, and heard the pathetic eagerness in her tone. "You could come and stay with me. Be my companion. We could—"

"Live in Matthew's house? Eat from his table?" Julia shook her head. "I could never accept anything of Matthew's from you." There was no spite in her refusal, just a deep and ineffable pride that refreshed Anne's knowledge of how profoundly Julia had been hurt by Matthew's abandonment.

How stupid of her to suggest such a thing. To be made the companion of the woman who'd stolen your future, your life? She could add callousness to the list of her transgressions.

"That was insensitive. I apologize."

"There's no need." A sweet smile lit Julia's plain face. "But please, try to put the past behind you."

She nodded, knowing herself to be a liar. The past would not stay behind. It stalked her on a peg leg, reproached her in an old woman's voice, and in Matthew's mother's accusing letters. It came dressed in taffeta to dine. It would always be with her.

Her gaze fell on Jack Seward's dark-gold head bent close to Sophia's. Why had he kissed her and torn open her well-guarded heart, exposing her to this pain of wanting something that could never be? Is this how Matthew had felt? No wonder he had chosen death over such pain.

Why had Jack done this? What did he see when he looked at her? She closed her eyes. Her head thrummed with pain. Her heart felt near to breaking.

Bitterness came to her aid.

Jack saw a grieving widow. A woman with no illustrious name to protect, a woman who'd once married above herself. He saw a woman who'd won a saintly man's adoration.

He didn't see *her* at all. He glanced up, his expression tense and seeking.

The thief. That was who she was. He should learn. He should know.

If only he would not look at her with such frowning concern, as if he would find her demons and excise them for her. If only he were not ever present, besieging her with his grave courtesy and warm eyes, his rare laughter and strength, maybe then—God help her—she could make herself stop caring about him.

She laughed, the sound small and brittle. The laugh turned into a sob. And she caught it back.

Jack stepped forward immediately, leaving Sophia's sentence hanging unfinished between them. Anne held up a hand, fending him off. Julia's worried gaze fell on her.

"I must have taken a chill this afternoon," she heard herself say as if from a distance. "Sophia, you will entertain our guests? You'll forgive me if I retire? Miss Knapp?"

"Certainly, Mrs. Wilder."

"Colonel?"

He inclined his head and she fled.

The Norths' party ended an hour later. Unfashionably early but far too long for Jack. He walked from Mayfair to his address near the wharves, replaying Anne's expression as she'd fled the room and—he could not help but think—him.

The chill rising in misty sheets from the riverbanks swirled lazily about his legs. It was too cold to be out drinking, too late to be working. No one manned the flickering barrel fires.

Griffin and a boy materialized from the mist as he reached his door. "I stayed awake the whole bloody night," the boy said without preamble. Griffin stood by silently. "Just likes you says to. The kitchen maid's a right doxy, sneaks out 'alf the nights, but she ne'er climbed no roof."

Jack nodded. It was as he'd expected. He'd misplayed this from the beginning. He'd depended on the thief's recklessness and audacity compelling her to act in defiance of him, in spite of—or perhaps because—she knew he was close.

He'd been wrong. She'd disappeared.

He fished into his pocket for some coins and tossed them into a grimy waiting hand. "Keep watching."

"Right-o, Cap." The boy slunk away.

The thief had called him Cap, too, but her coarse Dockland accent wasn't a native's. She'd learned it either secondhand or later in her life.

For days he'd neglected her pursuit, bent on another pursuit altogether. But now time grew short and he needed to return his attention to the thief. Only in finding some trail to follow could he buy himself more time. Time to solve the riddle of this letter.

"Give me some news," Jack said. "What have you heard from Burke?"

"Nothing," Griffin said in disgust. "The boy gave his notice to Frost and hied off up Sussex way on some mad chase."

"And what have you found? I need a trail to follow. I need it *now*," Jack demanded tersely.

"I think Atwood had the letter for some time before he told Jamison about it," Griffin said. "My lad at Windsor said how Atwood was a regular visitor until April, when he made his last visit."

"Who was Atwood visiting?"

"This is what surprised me, Cap. He was visiting the old king."

"*What?*" Jack asked incredulously. Griffin nodded.

Could there be something there? Had the king in his madness disclosed some scandal, some information that could be used to blackmail the regent?

"And speaking of strange bedfellows, I've had Lord Vedder watched like you instructed. He's getting chummy with Frost who—not to pretty it up none—hates your guts, Cap. And Vedder paid another visit to your father night before last. Knowles wasn't invited."

"He's probably demanding Jamison have me beheaded for my impertinence. Still, he bears watching," Jack said, then without further comment climbed the stairs to the front door and let himself in.

"You'll be ruined if you stay," Strand cautioned in his laconic manner. He lifted his candle, shedding light over the heavily swathed figure of his late-night visitor. "Haven't you heard about men like me?"

Sophia North dropped her cloak's hood, exposing a glorious mane of red-gold ringlets. "Ruin me? Aren't you rather assuming too much?"

His face grew still. She tossed her head and the red gold shimmered in the soft candlelight. He'd always been partial to red-headed chits.

"What do you want here, little Sophia?"

She arched her brow playfully. He almost laughed at her. She'd been a warm armful in the conservatory and a most willing pupil, soft and fragrant and filled with urgency. Too much urgency. The girl had no finesse.

"I've come to finish what we started." She pointed to the back hallway where he'd uncovered her breasts and kissed her small nipples as she'd panted appreciatively while a few feet away his other guests had chattered and laughed. It had proven a stimulating seduction.

"I doubt your father would approve."

"Probably not." She'd begun to untie the silk frogs at her neck, but now she hesitated. Just as well, he thought with a small inner sigh. He'd had a few too many bottles to drink this evening, and lately, even when sober, he'd little enough self-restraint. This, while it held a certain appeal, simply could not be a good idea.

"And what of Mrs. Wilder? She can't be aware of your whereabouts." Mrs. Wilder of the dark and magnetic gaze and the wise and worldly mien. Now, there was a woman to spark a fire in a man's loins and heart. If he'd had one.

He smiled at Sophia, prepared to send her on her way and find himself a woman of talent to bed. A woman who'd make him forget that other lovers found more in bed than wetness and heat, flesh and blood. He gestured for Sophia to depart through the back door whence she'd come.

She didn't move. Something he'd said or something she'd read in his face had tipped fate's balance. Defiantly she loosed the last silk fastening. The cloak dropped from her shoulders, pooling around her feet.

She was naked. The guttering candlelight hungrily licked her pink and ivory flesh, glinted in the red-gold thatch between her sweet thighs, flowed over twin plump breasts even now peaking in the chill hallway.

"Teach me what a man likes, Strand." Her voice was low, hypnotic. "Teach me what a woman likes."

Strand smiled, his gaze sweeping her flushed face, the brilliant excitement in her eyes, the bravura humming in her vibrant, abominably young body.

"You aren't thinking of using me, are you, little Sophia?"

In answer, she reached out and clasped his hand in hers, lifting it and sliding his knuckles against her lips. Soft and silky smooth lips.

"Yes," she whispered, pressing a moist kiss on the back of his hand. "But won't you be using me, too?" How charmingly ingenuous of her. Of course he would be using her. To forget Cat Montrose and Anne Wilder and all the Anne Wilders who promised to bring repletion to a man's soul, not merely a temporary depletion to his sexual drive.

Yes, he thought, she might make him momentarily forget the little matter of being so damn alone.

She moved within arm's reach and placed her hand not on his chest but on his thigh. He swelled. She smiled knowingly. "We can use each other."

Perhaps she was not so innocent after all.

And, really, he thought, his own hands moving up to pet her breasts and flanks and soft rounded little belly, she couldn't have asked for a better teacher.

Chapter Thirteen

The night was sky, all sky. If she lifted her arms, closed her eyes, and leaned out, she wouldn't fall. She would dissolve into its vastness or rise like smoke and be tattered in the high, clear winds that scoured heaven's underbelly.

The earth below was the more ephemeral element. It crouched beneath the fog like a leper hiding beneath his shroud. Up here her nerves were attuned to every nuance and her senses quivered in voluptuous surrender to her compulsion.

She glanced back through her bedroom window. Behind the frost-rimmed glass, a single candle glowed on a side table. Crumpled sheets twined across the bed and the silk puddle of a cast-off nightgown shimmered on the carpet.

Peering in like a secret spectator on her own life, Anne thought the room unfamiliar. She fancied that if she stood outside long enough gazing in, she would eventually see its exhausted tenant cross the room with a cup of warm milk.

The thought petrified her. So like madness, fancying two people inhabited one life.

Too little sleep, she thought, rubbing her fists into her eyes. Too much wine. Too many memories and obligations, too many regrets and wishes crowded her thoughts, her heart, her soul. She wanted freedom from them all.

She wanted to shed her humanity, abandon it to the animal prowling within her, that blessed conscienceless creature without past or future, just the single focus of its intent: Jack Seward, who courted her in one world and hunted her in the other.

She pulled the black cap down over her hair and readjusted the silk mask over her eyes. The length of rope draped across her chest felt awkward, and the pistol jammed beneath the waistband at the small of her back dug into her flesh.

The sky was black, the air was frigid, but at least it was hers. Tonight she visited Devil Jack, Whitehall's Hound, a man who did terrible things—but none so terrible as making her believe she might have loved him, returning to her that destructive illusion, that killing hope. With a man like that, one didn't take chances.

The cold penetrated her joints and stiffened her fingers. It would have numbed her heart if that organ hadn't already been deadened.

She needed this to awaken it, these intense and empowering moments when she risked nothing more important than her life, when she belonged only to herself and the night and the cold distant stars.

She trotted sure-footed along the rime-frosted roof. Her senses swam under a deluge of stimuli. Sound was a forest, color a feast, breath and muscle and movement an orchestration. And she reveled in it.

Damn Sophia and her father. Damn Julia Knapp. Damn Matthew's crippled soldiers and Mrs. Cashman huddled on some foul street corner. And damn Jack Seward.

She peered over the eaves. A youngster by the park gate across the street lifted his clever face and searched the rooftop. Another of Jack Seward's lackeys. Let him search.

She ran lightly, her breath making fog. The steep-pitched surface was not so easily navigated as the flat broad peak, but her figure would be hard to pick out against the black background. She did not consider the danger of unsure footing. She did not care.

She only wanted one thing from this night, an end to dreams and resurrected pain.

She went on, her direction unerring, her flight straight as a nighthawk's. She knew where he lived, an unassuming address in an unprepossessing area of town, where the landlords catered to impoverished second sons and debt-ridden fashionables.

She came to a chasm demarcating a street far below and flung herself into the emptiness above it. She laughed as she landed on the far side, pushing herself to go faster, quicker than her betraying mind could form Jack's face. Only exertion touched her now, dampening her skin with equal measures of sweat and pleasure.

Another street, another leap. Her muscles stretched and quivered, her pulse raced like a rabbit's, and every pore of her skin breathed exhilaration. Heart pounding, she scrambled up the steep slate shakes to the top of the town house.

She was there.

She caught her breath. Beneath her Jack slept and dreamed and plotted her capture and her capitulation. He was too much involved with her, she thought grimly. He pursued the woman *and* the thief, and now he'd pay for that error.

A vague premonition tightened her mouth with pain and challenged the feral light in her eyes. She shivered, breaking free of its petrifying hold. Hadn't she always taken what she wanted? Well, now she wanted Jack Seward.

She crept to the edge of the roof and hung over. Directly below a window gleamed blankly, its ledge no wider than a man's hand.

She snaked over the eaves, balancing on her hips, and released one hand to search the top of the window frame for a hold. Mortar crumbled beneath her fingertips. She dug into it and pivoted out and over, swinging onto the ledge.

She peered in on an empty room as she wiggled a thin sliver of metal between the casements and loosened the catch. Then she slid the window open and slipped inside, looking about. She was in the bedroom of a small town house, like hundreds of its neighbors, neither character nor charm distinguishing it, merely convenience. She'd been in its like before.

Through the open door to her left would be one more bedchamber and a dressing room beyond that. Below this would be a formal dining room and a salon, maybe a library, and on the ground floor the kitchen and pantry and servants' quarters.

She moved cautiously to the open door and peered in, giving her eyes time to adjust to the darkness. She was right. It was a bedchamber—Jack's. She could just make out his long body stretched over a narrow bed. She moved into the room, cataloguing the contents.

It had to be something mocking, threatening. Something to make him aware of his own exposed position, to make him feel anger, frustration, and loss. Something to make him renew his efforts to find her.

She searched among the impersonal collection of toiletries, books, and unassuming possessions that lined his bureau. There was nothing except . . .

The idea took hold of her imagination, refusing to be shouted down. It would be so easy, so perfect. And afterward he would hate her, rising to her provocation like a hound to the scent.

He would become single-minded in his pursuit of her and thus—oh God, she nearly laughed with the bitter humor of it— his attention turned once again toward the thief, the widow would fight free of his fascination. That's all she needed. A bit of space.

But first he had to lose his composure, be provoked beyond his ability to resist giving chase . . .

With a small sleek hiss of steel she pulled his ceremonial sword free of its ornate sheath. To use his own weapon against him would be a good start.

Jack's breathing hitched, but in this man's dreams such a sound was a boon companion. Steel, the smell of gunpowder, the call of dying men, all were too customary to call him back to the sentient world. She recognized the truth of her intuition beyond question and the recognition stopped her. He was no longer a stranger to her. She knew him.

And *he* thought he knew *her. Fool.*

The slender sword still in her hand, she padded to the window. Carefully she drew back the drapes, letting in a weak illumination. She peered down, frowning at what she saw. His window backed against a cramped alley thirty feet below. Black with soot and unadorned, there were no easy handholds. A brick watercourse no more than a few inches wide was all that broke the sheer expanse.

She leaned farther out. One other window gave out from his apartments. Set catercorner six feet below and four feet over, it was too far away to be useful. She returned to his bedside, lifting a light wooden chair on her way and carrying it with her. She set it down beside his bed, keeping her eyes averted from him. A man like Jack would feel himself being watched even in his sleep.

She swung a leg over the chair, settled lightly on the edge, and lifted his sword. It glinted in the moonlight. She pointed its tip directly at Seward's throat and, taking a deep breath, nudged the bed with her foot.

He came awake without movement, only the sudden silence that his exhalation should have filled alerting her that he was conscious.

"Yer awake, Cap. Dinna take me fer a fool," she whispered roughly.

His eyes opened, clear and so utterly alert she wondered if he'd ever been asleep at all. His pupils reflected back a darkness as clear and brilliant as any color.

"My thief." The soft, rich tone held a greeting. His gaze traveled to the point a few inches from his neck. Even in the shadows she could see the bitterness in his smile. Without asking her permission he sat up. The bedsheet slipped to his waist. The collar of his nightshirt had come unfastened during his sleep and twisted. The opening was pulled wide across his upper torso, exposing his chest, shoulder, and upper arm. The sight brought the blood racing to the surface of her skin.

The muscle of his biceps bunched. Gilding him like a statue in moonlight, what light there was clung to the powerful swells and tensed, flowing lines.

"Put yer arms up. Yer not thinking to pitch yerself at me, are you? I'd pith you like a toad."

"Would you?" His tone was no more than curious, but his muscles relaxed and he eased fractionally back into his pillow.

She trusted his relaxation less than his tension.

"And why wouldn't I? Yer become problematic-like and yer interferin' with me lay."

"Lay."

"Me job. Me scam. Me livelihood."

"Forgive me for importuning you," he said. "But all you have to do is give me back the letter you stole from Lord Atwood."

What letter? she wondered. Atwood had no letter. He—

Jack edged forward and her attention snapped back to him. The movement had further exposed his chest. Not that it mattered to him. He took no more account of his partial nudity than if he'd been fully clad. She was not so fortunate.

His bones carried the weight of his heavy musculature with clean and elegant ease. His skin looked dark against the white sheets, taut, fine-grained, and smooth. A light furring of dark hair glinted on his chest and a night's worth of stubble further shadowed the hard angle of his jaw. Lying recumbent in the dim room, he looked incredibly, hypnotically masculine.

Latent sexuality stirred in the air between them. She could nearly feel his tongue against the seam of her lips, his hands on her . . .

She did not want to be overpowered by this. Too much in her life had already overpowered her, left her spirit scattered on an ocean of regret. She was in control now. She would have mastery here.

"You've annoyed me!" Her voice sounded weak and petulant, mewling like a weak, spineless creature.

"Once more, I'm sorry." The whiskey-smooth apology mocked her, yet uncertainty kept his gaze vigilant.

How far would she go? he was asking himself. Of what was she capable?

She needed him to be more than uncertain of what she might do. She wanted him to think she was capable of committing any crime, any act. And wasn't she? Didn't she shed the widow's fretful life when she took to the rooftops?

He'd hounded her thoughts and her person. He'd followed her into her dreams and into her world. He'd harried her and cornered her and now she'd turned on him.

And she *wanted* to do this. She wanted to own all the power he represented.

"'Sorry' won't do, Cap. Maybe I should just ends it now. With you out of me way, I'd have a fair clean go of things."

"Murder? My, what a wee bloodthirsty thing you are."

She cocked her head. "I wouldna 'ave to sully me immortal soul with murder, now would I? I'd just have to cripple you like." With a short, savage stab, she speared the sheet, pinning it an inch from his side. He emitted a sharp, involuntary hiss. She smiled.

"Fascinatin' feelin', ain't it? Not knowin' if the next minute will be yer last. Knowin' yer enemy holds yer fate in 'is hands and there's naught ye can do about it." She leaned close enough so that she could see him breathe in her scent, trying to place it and name her. Even now, even here, he still pursued her.

She drew back, furious she'd been unable to instill in him any of the fear he awoke in her. "'Ow does it feel bein' the 'are rather than the 'ound?" She jerked the sword, wrenching the sheet off him.

He surged forward, his face breaking free of the shadows, for a moment clearly illuminated in the light from the window. But she'd already swept the sharp tip of the sword back, denting his dense pectoral. "Sit back!"

For a second a nerve twitched beneath his fine, clear eyes then he slouched back into the murky half-light. His chest rose and fell in deep controlled measures. Heat and a tingling abrasive sensation rode over the surface of her skin, into her belly and breast and thighs. She'd stopped him. She'd bent him to her will.

For a long minute they stared at each other.

"Up, Cap," she said, and rose from the chair. She pulled the pistol from her belt, holding both the sword and gun level on him.

"And if I refuse?"

"Ever seen a stallion gelded, Cap?" The sword tip dropped, lightly flirting with the linen covering his groin.

Their gazes locked for the space of a heartbeat. Without a sound, Jack backed away from the implicit threat and hefted himself from the bed. He was tall, so much taller than she was, and yet—dark sensuality shivered in her veins—she had power over him. Even at the distance of two yards, he stood towering over her, his stance relaxed, his gaze watchful.

She returned his sword to the level of his throat, refusing to back even an inch from him. A fragrance of sleep and musk and something indefinable and stimulating filled her nostrils.

"And where do we go from here?" he asked.

She indicated the chair. "'Ave a seat, Cap."

"Before a lady? I think not." He bowed, mocking her yet again.

"I'm no lady. I'm a thief. Your enemy. But tonight you're mine."

His gaze sharpened, his face set in lines of intense concentration. Too late she realized she'd spoken without the masking benefits of her father's accent.

"Sit, damn you!"

He sat, his shrug declaring her small victory a matter of the most banal import. She moved behind him and pressed the barrel of the pistol to the side of his throat.

"'Ands behind yer back, Cap," she commanded hoarsely, slipping the rope from her shoulder. He submitted and she grasped his crippled hand first, unwillingly noting the painful assemblage of knuckle, tendon, and sinew.

He'd sustained damage. He'd been wounded. God knows how many times, and yet he'd fought on. He'd survived it. More important, more fascinatingly, he'd survived his own actions. If only she could make such a claim. She hesitated.

"I'll catch you, you know," he said, turning his head and slanting a vicious look at her.

She noosed his wrist, snapping the rope tight before catching his other wrist and lashing his hands together. She circled back in front of him and raked his trussed figure with an insolent gaze.

It had no noticeable effect on him.

"And now?" he asked.

"Now I play with you, Cap. Like you been playin' with me. And you gets to wonder, 'Is this where I buy it? Is this me end?'"

"You won't kill me."

"Won't I?" Her voice was harsh, demanding. "If it comes to choosin' between me life and yores, I'll choose mine, Cap. Have no doubt about it. I done it before. I'll do the same today."

"You've killed a man?" he asked, watching her carefully.

"Yes!"

"Well, if that's your intention, please do so quickly. I don't wish to spend my last minutes trading confessions with a thief and a murderess and a cowardly, masked one at that." He evinced not a shred of fear, not hauteur or disdain. He simply stated a fact.

"I don't care what you wants," she spat out. "I care what *I* want. Don't you know that about thieves, Cap? They only wants what they can't have and once they gets it, they only wants more."

"You don't want to kill me. You want me to stop hunting you. But I won't. Not now. And you know it."

"Shut up!"

He cocked his head, his gaze speculative. "You might have had freedom if only you'd waited a bit longer. But you didn't. Why?" The question was sharp, intent. "Why, when you must have suspected that you only needed to lay low for a short while longer and I'd be recalled, why did you do this now?"

His words pounded at her, threatened her. *"Because I wanted to!"*

"Do you know what I think?" His voice was cool and remote and tempting.

"No." She jerked the sword up and placed the point against his breast. Ruthlessly she ran the sword tip down his chest until it caught at the end of the nightshirt's collar. She did not stop there. She sliced through the linen material, exposing the hard ladder of his flank, nipping each rib as she drew the blade down over his corrugated belly to the jut of his hipbone.

She'd found a way to make him stop talking.

His gaze fixed on her face with regal imperiousness. Only the darkness suffusing his throat and jaw betrayed that he felt anything. That and the retribution promised by his soul-eating eyes. They gleamed in the shadows like a wolf's.

She would not swallow. She would not stop. She'd begun this. She would finish it. And this, after all, is what she wanted, had wanted from the first. This was the reason she was here, no matter what lies she told herself tomorrow. Because this was all she would ever have of him.

And she'd steal it, too. Even against his will. She sliced through the last of his nightshirt.

"Well, now you'll have to kill me, thief," he said, his tone conversational, his eyes branding her. "Because I won't stop until I find you. I won't stop until I have you. No matter how long it takes me, no matter how far it takes me."

She dropped the sword. It clattered against the hardwood floor. Her heartbeat thundered in her throat. Deliberately she stepped between his knees.

"Yes," she said. "But right now, *I* have *you.*"

Chapter Fourteen

He worked his thumbs into the small easement he'd made in the bonds when she'd strapped his wrists together. A few more minutes and he'd be free. Fury fanned his resolve with a white-hot flame.

He should have called her bluff, but this was not the same woman who plagued his dreams. His thief had changed. She wore desperation like a mantle and walked some thin line of self-control. "Beauty—a deceitful bayte with a deadly hook," Lyly had written, and so she was.

He'd seen its like before in men who'd pushed their own limits too far and finally left them behind. She had their look. It declared itself in brisk, inelegant movements and in the sweat trickling down her throat and soaking her dark shirt. Her smile cleaved her face with razor sharpness, dying only to be reborn seconds later as if in answer to some taunt only she could hear.

And looking at her, reckless and cursed, he realized they were as mated in spirit as fire and ash. Anne Wilder was a dream, an aspiration, a portrait of what love should be. The thief was his reality.

At their first meeting—perhaps even before, perhaps when she'd challenged him with her cunning and her audacity—he'd taken her like a bullet in the chest. And like that bullet, the right touch could remind one of its potentially fatal presence.

"I have you," she repeated in that tough little whisper, nudging herself between his thighs in a parody of a lover's more intimate stance. He could barely make out her features in the darkened room. He heard her breathing and felt her warmth. Awareness skittered over his skin . . .

Abruptly he realized what he had sensed in her from the moment he'd opened his eyes. *Sex.* It rolled off her in waves: carnal, potent, and intense.

He named it and like tinder to a sea of grass, her arousal set him on fire. Swift and hard, his body stiffened with readiness and a familiar, violent longing.

He wanted her. Not her capture or the damn letter. He wanted to be in her with a desire so intense that it felt like need.

"You know what's so bloody funny, Cap?" She leaned close to him. Her words pattered like warm rain on his mouth.

Her eyes glittered from behind the black mask. He couldn't speak. He wanted too much. She'd tied him to this chair and forced him to taste his lust as well as his powerlessness. But worse, in a life singular for its lack of illusion, she'd made him cede the one illusion he wanted to believe in. She forced him to cede Anne Wilder.

"I don't even 'ave yer bleedin' letter," she said, her voice raw, her lips inches from his. "You did this to us for nothin'!"

Her mouth came down over his. She clasped the back of his head with one hand and spread the other flat against his chest.

Her tongue stroked the seam of his lips with dark, warm intoxication. A river of sensation swept down his body, pooling in his groin. Dear God.

He forgot freedom, forgot revenge in the face of this far greater need. He heaved himself forward, straining against the ropes holding him, seeking a more intimate contact.

She gave it to him. She moaned deep from the back of her throat as his tongue came alive in her mouth. She crumbled between his knees, clutching at his shoulders. Her hands played down over his chest to his stomach, her nails lightly raking his belly and moving lower.

He squeezed his eyes shut. The back of her fingers brushed against his swollen member. He ground his teeth together, refusing to give her the victory of his gasped pleasure, and then her hand closed over him with white-hot delicacy. A sound of pleasure rose from his throat. His neck arched, his hips lifted.

Desire burned to a cinder all of his plots and strategies and tomorrows. One thought drowned him with its imperative: He wanted what she alone offered—she alone of all the women he'd ever known offered: an end to longing.

Whatever price she demanded, he'd pay.

She trembled against his chest while her hands hungrily explored him. He angled his head to kiss her again. Her eyes were closed.

"Open your mouth." He instructed in a hoarse whisper. "Give to me. Let me—"

She broke free of his kiss and tumbled backward, catching herself with her hands. Her eyes widened. Like a starving man watching a feast snatched from before him, he roared his fury.

She skittered away from him. He flung himself against his bonds, wrenching his arms, following her with fierce determination. She whimpered—sweet sound of abandonment!—and like an addict to the opiate, crept back to him. Her eyes searched his. Her deliciously vulnerable mouth trembled beneath the black silk mask. She settled her hand on his thigh. He ground his teeth in frustration and closed his eyes.

"What do you want?" he demanded. "Whatever the bloody hell you want, just finish this!"

Her gasp jerked him back to reality as no word could have done. He felt the ropes cutting into his wrists, heard his breath laboring like a beast's, smelled the sweat and musk of his own arousal.

She wasn't going to satisfy this primitive need. He could see fear rising in her, overtaking her desire.

She needn't fear him. God, he'd have fallen like a supplicant to his knees for her touch, for her kiss, and her body. Would have—

Too late he realized his admission and recognized what she'd done. He'd have traded all the long years he'd spent fighting for a portion of control, a particle of expiation, just for the chance to rut with her. Damn her!

Savagely, silently, he wrenched against the ropes. He was a boy again, a starving workhouse roach chained by ignorance and desperation to a life of squalid imprisonment. He was a boy hurling abuse on every other tenant of that rotting hell, hating them all but none more than himself for he couldn't stop fighting. And fighting the inevitable only made the pain worse.

The lashes the workhouse guards had used were nothing to the pain of simple want. He could shut himself off from their brutality. He could use that pain, work it, and learn from it. He'd never learned anything from the pain of wanting but to want more. Until he'd finally damned himself with it.

She bloody well should shrink. She should run. Hide in hell if she could—for what little good it would do her. He'd find her. "Let me go!"

She fumbled on the floor behind her for his sword and found it. She shoved herself to her feet and pointed its tip at his throat. "No."

The rope scoured his wrists; warm liquid greased the hemp. His blood.

"Stay there!" she commanded, her voice shaking as much as the sword's madly wobbling tip. She craned her head around, looking for escape.

"Why don't you make me?" He twisted his crippled hand and yanked it free. He surged upward and the chair crashed to the floor behind him. His ruined nightshirt fell open at his side. Her gaze fell upon his arousal and for an instant her eyes fluttered shut.

He took advantage of that improbable maidenliness. He seized the blade in his hand, ripping his palm open on it. More blood.

She panicked and grasped the hilt with both her hands, trying to wrest it from him. With his free hand he seized the back of her neck and toppled her against him. She fought desperately as he pulled her into his punishing embrace, absorbing each blow.

Anne panted. She could not think. He was too big, too strong, and far too angry. Dear God, she thought hysterically, twisting madly, had she really thought to control him?

Tears coursed down her face as she fought him, but beneath the tears desire, like a ravening animal, still clamored for satisfaction. God help her, it had been so long and never like this: so elemental, so raw.

Some deep-buried part of her not only wanted this struggle and this fight but wanted his victory, wanted the smell of him hot and angry inundating her senses, the slick slide of his belly muscles against her own. His dense masculine form straining above her—

"No!" She went limp. For just an instant his hold loosened on her wrists. She skewed violently and jerked her head up hard beneath his chin. She heard his teeth crack together and wheeled the sword hilt around, smashing it into his temple. He fell back a step. It was room enough. She twisted, sprang free, and raced for the window.

She heard him behind her and then she was through the opening and swinging down past the sill. Her hands flew over the brickwork and found purchase in the crumbling mortar above the frame as her toes scrabbled for the watercourse. Her heart pounded in her temples. Her legs flayed wildly, frantically. She couldn't find the watercourse.

Her weight began dragging her fingers from the shallow, grout-filled gully. Her feet beat like a chimney-trapped bird against the brick. Her hands cramped. She slipped. Blackness yawned greedily beneath her, pulling her—

Her wrist was seized in a viselike grip.

She stared up. Jack leaned half out of the window, his chest and arms cording with muscle and sinew, his teeth set as he struggled to pull her up. But his hand was slick with his own blood and weakened by the deep gash across the palm. Even as he lifted her she felt his grip loosen. He would drop her thirty feet to the cobbled pavers below.

"Swing me through the window below!" She gasped.

"No!" he grated out.

"Swing me through! Or I'll die!"

Indecision, pain, and fury writhed across his fierce countenance and then, with a grunt, he leaned farther out. His torso gleamed with sweat in the cold moonlight. His face was rigid with concentration.

He gripped the sill with his good hand and heaved her sideways, pitching her away from the window, using her momentum to swing her out and away from the building. And then she was arcing back in.

The window loomed like a black flat lake of glass. She cried out once and closed her eyes. A thousand prisms exploded about her as she broke through the window and pitched into the room among a fantasia of broken, crystalline shards.

She landed tucked, rolled, and regained her feet as she'd been taught. And then she was through the archway into the dark hallway and running for the front door, her thoughts racing.

She slowed, her pulse thrumming in her throat, her chest heaving with the stimulation of having cheated death—and him. He'd saved her.

Tuning her ears for the inevitability of his chase, she slipped into a dark alcove by the front door. The beat of his footsteps raced down the staircase and past her hiding place. She heard his soft curse as he stopped before the front doorway. The glow of the streetlamps outside attached to his long, hard body.

She stepped silently behind him, filling her eyes with the sight of him: the span of his back, the straight line of his shoulders, the narrow hips, the hard buttocks tapering into long thighs and calves.

She touched the barrel of her pistol to the small of his back. He swung around and she dipped beneath the clenched fist flying above her head. She shoved the gun into his hard abdomen and wrapped her free hand around his neck. Surprise and anger flashed in equal measures across his face.

For the second time that night, she kissed him. She opened her mouth against his hard, chiseled lips and felt him swell against her. With a sound like a growl he crushed her in his embrace and lifted her against him. Heedless of the gun pinioned between their bodies, he propelled her back against the wall. Ravenously he angled his mouth over hers as his hips pinned her to the wall. His shoulders broadened as he bent over her like a falcon above its kill. He enveloped her in his masculinity.

Surrender. He's won, she thought, drowning in sensation and need.

"Damn you!" He muttered, the curse lost and furious and hopeless with self-loathing and awful longing.

He wants this, she thought dizzily. *He hates you. He'll kill you.*

She shoved him away and stumbled back. Still holding the gun on him, she groped behind her for the door handle. He stepped forward.

"No!" Her voice sounded frantic, near to shattering. He stopped.

"I'll find you wherever you go," he swore grimly. "However long it takes. You can't run far enough."

She bolted. Light and fast as a greyhound coursing over the wet, cold cobbles, she fled. She gained the rooftop and pitched herself recklessly through the night's mocking stillness, her breath coming in sobs because she knew he was right; she'd never run fast enough or far enough again.

Chapter Fifteen

The prince regent was having a dinner party. He'd planned it for weeks. Carlton House was to be filled with sumptuous food, beautiful people, and witty conversation. Afterward they would dance and gamble and then have a midnight refreshment.

The prince regent never made it to the dancing.

The weather and the renewed activities of Wrexhall's Wraith conspired to keep many of his guests at home. Feeling put upon and unappreciated, he'd cried off directly after dining, leaving his company to look after themselves.

Those who remained were stalwart revelers, determined not to let any happenstance interfere with their pursuit of pleasure in all its forms. The Norths, along with Anne Wilder, were among their number.

Brilliant blue-white light filled Carlton House's huge windows. The brief flash went unnoticed by the revelers. Except Anne. A few seconds later the floor beneath the crowd vibrated. She lifted her head and watched the chandeliers dance in time to thunder so low and deep it hid beneath the chattering of human voices. The storm grew nearer.

Anne gazed down into her punch and swirled the ruby liquor in the glass, creating a tiny whirlpool in the center. Each day, it seemed to her, spun by as uncontrollably as the fleck of cork spinning madly around her glass. Ever since Jack—

No. Not Jack. She wouldn't think of Jack. She looked around, hoping to seize upon some distraction, and a short distance away saw Sophia with Lady Dibbs, Lady Pons-Burton, and Jeanette Frost. They slowly wended their way toward her. Sophia, she would think of Sophia.

Anne had heard rumors lately, from concerned acquaintances, helpful dowagers, and knowing gentlemen whose words had commiserated but whose eyes told a different tale.

"High spirits, Mrs. Wilder," they'd say. "I recall you kicked over the traces when you were that age, too, didn't you? Didn't hurt you any though, did it?"

The little whirlpool in the middle of her glass grew deeper as the wine swirled faster. Oh, yes, mustn't pass any opportunity to extract a bit of late payment from the merchant's daughter for having tricked a peer into marrying her.

Their graceless innuendos simply did not hurt her. They had no subtlety to them. Jack Seward would have killed her with courtesy. He would have—

No. Sophia. Three nights ago she'd gone to Sophia's room and discovered the girl missing. Sophia had returned just before Malcolm arrived home.

Poor bit of luck for Sophia, Anne thought. He'd shouted abuse at Sophia and the servants and most especially at Anne herself. Fearsome sight, if you were capable of caring. But wasn't that her stigmata? The inability to care deeply enough or love? That's what Matthew had said. And he should have known.

Sophia and her coterie stopped a few feet away, their conversation humming like the buzzing of bees in a hive. Yes, Anne thought, studying Sophia's low décolletage and practiced smile, she'd done a fine job of guiding Sophia. With any more of her guidance, Sophia would end up in a brothel.

She'd tried. She had honestly tried. Just as she had tried to love Matthew.

Rain began pelting the glass panes. The cold water against the heated glass caused fog to mist them over. The thunder crackled closer now, interrupting the conversation of the four women.

"Ghastly weather," Lady Dibbs said when it had ceased. "And me in new shoes. But where was I?"

Sophia smiled politely as her gaze wandered freely among the men. *Poor Lady Dibbs,* thought Anne. *She doesn't even realize she's been preempted.*

Just a short while ago Lady Dibbs had ensured Anne's silence regarding her debt to the Home by threatening to have the Norths ostracized. She didn't have that power now. Sophia had decided to see to that task herself.

The girl's smile deepened. Anne looked over her shoulder to see who now had attracted her attention. Strand stood a ways off, Jack by his side. Anne's pulse quickened at the sight of him. His gaze touched her and moved on.

She'd wanted Jack Seward to abandon his courtship of the widow in favor of his pursuit of the thief. Her desires could not have been better realized. He no longer sought her company. He avoided even looking at her. He gave her only the barest minimum of what his exquisite manners demanded.

She should smile. She should feel triumphant. After all, her plan—her oh-so-clever plan—had worked, hadn't it? Her throat closed on the welling pain.

It had been five nights since she'd gone to Jack's room. On each subsequent night she'd gone out and stolen gems and baubles, trinkets, and heirlooms, growing bolder with each theft. She simply no longer cared.

What did it matter now? She made herself one with the role. She relished it, reveled in it. She *needed* it because the only thing she would ever have of Jack Seward was his pursuit. The widow wouldn't have his regard; the thief wouldn't know his passion.

Sophia would never suffer from Anne's acts. They were related by only the most slender of associations. She was Sophia's cousin's ill-bred wife. Indeed, society might offer sympathy to the poor girl who'd been so taken in by—

"The Wraith forced himself on me last night."

Anne's head snapped around. Stunned attention met Jeanette's hushed statement. She might as well have dropped a dead cat into their midst.

"He stole my broach and then he . . . he kissed me."

"My dear child!" Lady Dibbs cried, her eyes alight with speculation.

"How exciting!" Sophia said. "And terrible, of course. Do tell us what happened."

"Yes," Anne urged dryly, "do tell us so we can contrive to escape your fate."

Jeanette needed no further prompting. "Well," she said, "the clock had just struck midnight."

Midnight? It had been three hours shy of dawn.

"I awoke to the feeling of a shadow passing over me. I opened my eyes. He was bending over me. I was terrified."

"I should say," Anne said. Jeanette Frost had been snoring like an asthmatic mastiff during the entire time Anne had rifled through her drawers and jewelry boxes.

Jeanette clasped her hands to her bosom. "'Blackguard!' I shouted. He leered down at me, a tall broad-shouldered brute of a man, and said, 'Aye, wench! And since I'm a blackguard I may as well take the blackguard's portion.' He seized me and kissed me and laughed again when I slapped his face." She giggled.

"Is that all?" Sophia asked.

"Oh!" Jeanette's maidenly gasp didn't come accompanied by the slightest of maidenly blushes. She glanced about her audience, undoubtedly deciding what ending would lend her the greatest cachet. "But of course that's all."

The other women's faces collapsed in disappointment.

Cowardly, Miss Frost, Anne thought. But definitely the wiser course. She looked over at where Jeanette's red-eyed father divided his glowers between his daughter and Jack. A ravished daughter in the Frost household might as well be dead.

"One kiss?" Lady Pons-Burton asked, her plump cheeks distended in a pout.

"Just one kiss." Jeanette nodded, her eyes straying toward her father.

"How awful for you, Miss Frost," Sophia said, and Anne had the disturbing notion Sophia wasn't consoling Jeanette on her adventure but on its tame ending.

"I must tell you all something," Jeanette said, looking about. "I don't think the Wraith is a commoner."

"And why is that, Miss Frost?" Lady Dibbs asked.

"I can't exactly say. He just had such an air about him. And he was well spoken, if gruff. I should think he may well be some"— her voice dropped as her gaze slanted to where Jack's broad back stood against them—against her—"nobleman's by-blow."

"Well, we know how interesting they can be." Lady Dibbs bit her lower lip provocatively.

"A lot of commotion about nothing if you ask me," Sophia replied blandly. "Or wishful thinking."

"Why, Miss North," Lady Dibbs said, glancing at her companions to see if they shared her feigned amazement at the unsolicited opinion of so young and—ostensibly—inexperienced a girl. "Whatever are you referring to?"

Jeanette and Lady Pons-Burton snickered.

"I'm speaking about Colonel Seward, of course," Sophia said, her eyes narrowing slightly. "I don't think the man nearly as transfixing as the stories about him."

"But how would *you* know, child?" Lady Dibbs purred. She looked over Sophia's head directly at Anne.

She blinked as if she'd forgotten she was there. "Perhaps dear Mrs. Wilder here is better qualified to tell us about Colonel Seward, seeing how he quite shadows her. Or did. I thought you'd adopted a new pet there for a while, Mrs. Wilder. But then, they call him 'Whitehall's Hound,' don't they?"

The four ladies dipped behind their fans and tittered.

When Anne didn't respond, Lady Dibbs turned her bright gaze back on Sophia. "And then what with the two of them having such similar histories and all . . . Oh, dear! I haven't offended you, have I, Sophia?" Lady Dibbs's bright-red mouth dribbled artificial laughter. "I mean, it's not as if no one knows, is it? One must be apprised of what and with whom one associates. And Mrs. Wilder never did care who knew how . . . unassuming her ancestors are."

Despicable woman.

"It's his manner," Jeanette broke in, utterly oblivious to the byplay. "Such a violent history and such refined manners. The combination is simply galvanizing."

Anne refused to look at him. It would be as if she'd never mated her tongue with his, as if she'd never strained against him, stroked the warm, hard wall of his chest, felt his pulse thundering in the silk-hard manhood.

God help her, when would she forget? She bit the inside of her cheeks as hard as she could until she tasted the metallic tang of blood. In the last days she'd resurrected a specter of the girl who'd once dazzled London society. No one seemed to mind that her laughter sounded brittle, that her sharp wit had no kindness, and that the promises she made with her eyes were empty.

She bewitched and teased, nearly manic in her determination to fill the emptiness. The gentlemen flocked to her, their expressions avid and speculative, eager to see what this newest incarnation of Anne Wilder might allow. She'd tried so hard not to remember. It had been futile. It was futile. He possessed her—

"Mrs. Wilder." Lady Dibbs's tone suggested she'd repeated Anne's name more than once.

"Yes?"

"Surely you could entertain us with some interesting information about Colonel Seward?"

Damned if she wouldn't give the woman a subject to coil that venomous tongue around, Anne thought. She'd already lost everything important. Nothing Lady Dibbs took from her mattered anymore.

"I don't know any stories about Colonel Seward, Lady Dibbs. I do know some interesting ones about you, however."

Lady Dibbs stared at Anne in disbelief. Her mouth dropped open and snapped shut and then opened again. "Really, Mrs. Wilder, I don't think—"

"All too obvious," Anne said. "But let me clarify. The donations, the thousand pounds you pledged to the Soldiers Relief Fund on two separate occasions? I never have received a single penny of them."

The women around them fell abruptly silent. Lady Dibbs drew herself up. "Transferring sums that large takes time," she said coldly, warning in her voice.

"Certainly no longer than the time it took to acquire that necklace," Anne replied calmly, her gaze touching lightly on the pearl and diamond pendant. "I believe you were telling some of the ladies it is new, isn't it?"

"Are you insinuating that I reneged on a pledge, Mrs. Wilder? I advise you to think carefully before you answer." If Lady Dibbs thought to set Anne's knees to trembling, she'd far misjudged her woman.

Anne's smile burned to ashes all signs of the humility and submissiveness Lady Dibbs and her sort demanded as entry fee to their exalted realms. Lady Dibbs stepped back. Anne stepped forward.

"Insinuate, Lady Dibbs?" she said clearly. "The facts speak for themselves. You *pledged* two thousand pounds; you *gave* nothing. Except a very public demonstration of your munificence."

Lady Pons-Burton snickered. Lady Dibbs quelled her laughter with a vicious look.

But Anne wasn't done. "The only reason I brought it up at all is that being such a champion for veracity, so adamant that people's lives and histories be opened to your scrutiny, I felt sure you'd jump at the chance to make your own known."

"I think you're done now, Mrs. Wilder," Lady Dibbs said tightly.

"Do you really believe so, ma'am?" She looked around at the ladies who stared at their erstwhile leader with undisguised embarrassment. "And here I thought you were."

"Oh, brava, Anne." Sophia had caught up to her by the time she'd reached the door into the ballroom. Her tone brought the heat to Anne's cheeks as none of Lady Dibbs's barbs had done.

"If you want to be blacklisted, fine," Sophia continued. "But since you've spent the past two months lecturing me on the importance of society's approval, I must own I'm puzzled. Or did you not think how your actions would reflect on me?"

Anne's patience with Sophia was at an end. Whatever course the girl was set on, she'd started long before Anne's arrival. "You've been testing society's tolerance all season, Sophia," she said. "You should be glad I've given you an excuse to tell your father why you'll not be accepted into the better salons and homes."

Instead of taking offense, Sophia laughed. "I daresay you're right. Besides, I don't need Lady Dibbs's approval any more."

"What do you mean?" Anne asked.

"Just what I said, Anne. I merely took a page from your own book. You had the right of it when you came out: Ignore the ladies and concentrate on the gentlemen."

"I did no such thing."

"Come, Anne. You did. The gentlemen still talk of you. And it's apparent that Lady Dibbs harbors no fondness for you. I suspect her enmity might have developed its roots a few years back. Don't look so stricken, Anne. I'd be proud of it, if I were you."

"Where did you hear this twaddle?"

Sophia gave a gentle snort of derision. "Lean your ear in any corner and you hear it. Admit it, Anne. You don't give a fig for these women. And Matthew didn't either. You were completely wrapped up in each other."

"Sophia," Anne said, "you don't understand. You've never understood. My marriage was—"

"—made in heaven," Sophia said in a suddenly hard voice, her smile still painted on her face.

Anne shook her head, her heart going out to the confused, bitter girl. "No. It wasn't."

But Sophia wasn't listening. She fell back a step. "The whole bloody world knows what a wonderful, perfect marriage you had. Well, I'm not looking for perfection. I'm looking for position. And power. And pleasure." She lifted her hand and hailed a rakish-looking gentleman on the far side of the room. "And not necessarily in that order."

Chapter Sixteen

J ack watched.

Purposefully, utterly, serenely, Anne drove him mad. It wasn't only the dress, though the Lord knew it made no pretence at decency, Jack thought sardonically.

Apparently she'd suddenly considered her debt to widowhood fulfilled because the gown she wore celebrated a man's every carnal dream. The top of her breasts swelled above the embrace of luscious mandarin-red silk. The shimmering material flowed past her waist and swept like a current down over the curve of her hips.

She danced like a bacchanalian bride. A challenging light made her eyes brilliant. A ribbon at the nape of her neck made frivolous work of containing her cloud of dark hair. A loose tendril caught in her dance companion's coat and played intimately among the folds of his cravat, the sight filling Jack with jealousy.

And he'd no right to be jealous. He'd yielded that right when he'd plundered a thief's mouth with his tongue and had been made a beggar by the lust she inspired.

He had expected to feel regret at having to relinquish his *tendre* for Anne but not this bottomless ache, this feeling that a hole was being torn in his heart. She was beautiful and cruelly abused and defiant, and she burned his eyes. She spun amid the crowded dance floor like an exotic nighthawk.

He frowned. Where had that thought come from? Why give Anne Wilder the predator's role when she was so achingly vulnerable? Hadn't he proven that? Hadn't he exposed that in her?

She deserved to be—how had Julia Knapp put it?—*adored*. His adoration began in his loins. The thief had demonstrated that. He lusted after her—Anne? the thief? both?—like the basest animal.

He didn't know himself anymore. Love was a fiction fashioned to drive him crazy with the wanting of it. But now, having realized it *was* a fantasy, the widow should have ceased to fascinate him. Instead, she attracted him even more.

The dance ended and she curtseyed to her partner and prepared to quit the floor. As he watched, Lord Vedder approached her. He held out his arms, she walked into them, and the music began again.

Lord Vedder's hand moved too intimately on her waist. He bent his head too near to hers, as if he might lick the salty moisture from her temples. Jack's body tensed. He made himself watch. She radiated vibrancy and self-assurance, drawing gentlemen like moths to a flame, creating a wall of suitors between them.

This is how she'd been that first season, when she'd reigned over all the ton, he thought. This is who she'd been before Matthew took her, tamed her, and left her crushed under the weight of his death. What a fool the man must have been.

"Good evening, Colonel."

Jack looked around to find Strand standing beside him. His father's latest informant. He'd been honest when he told Jamison he expected no loyalty from Strand. But he would have liked it. "Lord Strand," he acknowledged.

"You're not dancing?" Strand asked.

"No."

"You really ought to. I know you're not officially a gentleman, but what with all your so-exacting manners, I'd never have thought you'd knowingly disappoint a lady."

"What lady is that?" Jack asked incuriously.

Strand's smile was slow, ripe with genuine amusement. He laughed. "Oh dear. This is so rich! I swear, I am diverted beyond my imaginings."

"If I've been able to relieve your ennui, Strand, I'm honored to have been of service. Perhaps you'd best find another remedy, though. I have other matters to attend."

"Ah, yes." Strand nodded, setting his finger alongside his nose. "The investigation. How goes it, Colonel? Have you discovered which woman is your thief?"

"No."

"Are you getting closer?" Strand asked.

"Perhaps."

"Dear me," Strand mocked, his expression sharp with interest. "So reticent. Don't tell me it really is a member of the ton?"

"I'm not telling you anything," Jack said mildly. "I would like to know, if you'd be so kind, what led you to believe I thought the thief a woman?"

"How did you . . ." Strand shrugged. "I deduced her gender from observing where you focused your attention and who you questioned."

"I see."

Strand looked very at ease. Perhaps he assumed Jack knew he reported everything to Jamison. But then, Strand also knew Jack disliked having information he'd gathered reported to others.

"I shall have to be more careful," Jack said blandly.

Strand sobered. "Puzzling. I thought we . . ."

Whatever he had been about to say, he thought better of it. "Of course not. I'd see this thing to a quick resolution if I were you. Jamison came round to see me the other day."

"For any particular reason?"

"He wanted to know what you were doing." Strand paused and when Jack did not respond he laughed again. "Damme, Seward, if you aren't the most uninquisitive inquisitor I've ever met. Probably why you ferret out so many secrets. You make people so bloody uncomfortable standing there so stiff and sententious that they panic and start babbling, filling the disapproving silence with all sorts of indiscretions."

"Forgive me. I didn't mean to give the impression I was uninterested."

Strand's gaze sharpened. "Let me be blunt. Jamison wants the thief dead and her lodgings and belongings burned to a cinder pile. For whatever reasons, he doesn't trust you to do the job."

No one was going to kill the thief.

"Then," Jack said, "Jamison will have made arrangements with others. They'll already be looking for her."

"He's never been one for sitting on his hands," Strand agreed.

"Interesting," Jack allowed, his mind working over his father's obsession to have the thief murdered. He had to catch the thief before Jamison. She'd committed three thefts in five nights. The last time she'd been spotted by a footman and nearly cornered in the stable yard. With each theft she grew bolder and sloppier—nearly indifferent. It was only a matter of time before she made a fatal mistake. He needed to spread his net wider, faster, and farther. He scowled.

"Pray don't waste your frowns on me, Colonel," Strand said. "There are women present who simply pine for the opportunity to swoon when you scowl."

"Hm? Excuse me, Strand, I wasn't attending."

"Part of the enigmatic appeal, no doubt."

"Say again?"

"Nothing."

"I should leave," Jack said. He glanced toward Anne, still in Vedder's embrace. Strand followed the direction of his gaze. "Your servant, sir."

"Not my servant, Colonel," Strand said. "And not, apparently, the lovely widow's either."

Jack, in the process of turning, halted. "What do you mean?"

Strand tilted his head in Anne's direction. "The rather fiercely elegant little widow doesn't look satisfied. I'll allow she looks a bit disheveled, but that doesn't necessarily imply satisfaction." He sighed noisily. "She simply must be satisfied. She's Prinny's guest, after all."

"You're speaking in riddles, Strand. I'm not in the mood."

Strand's voice became tinged with resentment. "You ignore her and it hurts her. I'd rather she wasn't hurt."

"Since when are you an expert on Anne Wilder?" Jack tried—God knows he tried—to keep his tone remote, casual. He knew he failed.

"Since when are you so obtuse? Nothing could be more obvious. She follows your every move. Only look at her reflection in the window here. Her face is turned this way even now."

Unwillingly Jack studied the images moving across the black surface of glass. Anne appeared, riding through billowing rapids of lace and flounce like a crimson flower carried on a current of white tulle froth. And yes, she gazed in his direction—until Lord Vedder drew her closer.

She did not struggle, but her arms braced against his, a telling movement. Vedder did not back away. Jack swung around. Her expression was strained.

"Yes," Strand said, his words mimicking Jack's own thoughts, "she needs a spot of rescuing. Did you know Vedder pursued her quite assiduously when she made her bow? Made a pest of himself. And he wasn't looking for an honorable attachment, as I'm sure you realize. Appears he's renewing his suit. Has the look of a weasel in musk, doesn't he?"

"Help her, Strand."

"Not I," he said, looking at Sophia North and drawing Jack's momentary attention.

Hectic color stained the girl's cheeks. Her father stood behind her. As Sophia began moving away, her father caught her arm and jerked her back to his side. Though she struggled, he kept her by his side. Even from here one could see how his fingers dug into her arm's flesh.

"It seems I have my own little pigeon needs rescuing." A fine undercurrent of pain belied Strand's light tone.

"Needless to say, my pigeon arrived in the wolf's maw quite through her own devices. The threat to her is not nearly so severe as the one to me should I actually take it into my head to do something. And without doubt you can take for granted that her needs are but a dim approximation of your lady's, as is her grace, her spirit, her wit . . ." Strand fell silent, then his mouth twisted ruefully.

"But she *does* need rescuing," he said, "and I've never indulged such an impulse before. Damned if you're not right, Seward. It's time I did something about this infernal ennui." He bowed low. "And I strongly suggest you do something for that other lady. Would that I could." With a small smile, he sketched a bow and left.

Jack made no effort to resist her need. He went to Anne's aid with as much resignation as gratification. He'd no choice here. It seemed in the past few weeks he'd become a creature living solely on impulse and vagary, incapable of navigating beyond the treacherous waters of his own desires. He stopped on the periphery of the line of dancers, directly before her.

The dance ended. Anne backed away from Vedder and curtseyed. Vedder followed her withdrawal, whispering something that caused the color to climb her throat. She turned. Vedder grasped her hand. She tried to pull—

"Good evening, Mrs. Wilder," Jack said. He stood before her, unaware that he'd even moved.

"Colonel," she answered coolly.

"You're hopelessly *de trop,* Seward," Lord Vedder said, securing Anne's elbow.

Jack ignored him. "Am I, Mrs. Wilder?"

She hesitated.

"It occurs to me, Mrs. Wilder, that in the course of our short acquaintance, we have never danced," Jack said. "I will never forgive myself if I don't remedy that oversight."

It was as if she drew in on herself. A social smile clicked into place on her face. Her eyes grew distant and dull.

"Please, Mrs. Wilder?"

"I really—"

"Listen, Seward, lest you forget, you're not here to dance," Vedder broke in. "I've had just about enough—"

Jack's harsh gaze cut off Vedder's words with an undeniable and terrifyingly gentle promise of violence. "Forgive me for being so ambiguous, Lord Vedder. I was asking *Mrs. Wilder* if she would care to dance, not you."

Rage stained the viscount's ears purple. "You go too far, you insufferable—"

"I should like to dance, Colonel," Anne interceded hastily. Jack blessed Vedder, for without the excuse of keeping the two men from coming to blows, he doubted whether Anne would have accepted his invitation.

"Mrs. Wilder—" Vedder sputtered.

"Thank you for the dance, Lord Vedder." Anne lifted her gown's short train. Jack inclined his head toward Vedder, took her hand, and led her out onto the floor.

The maestro proclaimed a waltz. She stepped close to him. He rested his hand just above her waist, on the fine-boned ribs. Warmth permeated his palm. He took her other hand high in his.

She averted her face, unwilling to meet his gaze, and after the first few strains of music, she made no attempt to keep her artificial smile on her lips. Indeed, they trembled and lost all hint of pleasure, mirroring her distress far too clearly. They had been soft beneath his kiss, soft and tender and, for the space of a heartbeat, yielding.

He wanted her. He wanted her as much, no, *more* than he had wanted the thief. Which was impossible.

Pain washed through him, pricking him with the knowledge of his inconstancy. He pulled her nearer. Her gaze flickered to and from his face and she recoiled from his embrace.

He would not let her. He would never hold her again, never have her in his arms, never touch her, and he would not—not for manners' sake, not for her sake, not for his own peace—let her rob him of even one short moment.

Lithe and supple as a willow, she moved in his arms and beneath his hand. Her body was unlike those of other gentlewomen; no softness padded her slender form. Indeed, her fragile appearance belied her tensile strength. He could feel smooth muscle beneath his palm, the strength in the fingers grasping his hand so tightly in her futile attempt to hold him distant.

It intoxicated him. It bewildered him. It set him on fire.

She speared him with a look of distress and anger. She did not want to be here. Too damned bad.

He closed his eyes and pulled her closer still and breathed deeply. She smelled warm and angry and clean, devoid of any masking properties of perfume or soap—

His eyes opened slowly, like a man who knows he will witness some horror. His breath grew shallow. *Strength and passion, no betraying scent. Dear God, no.*

She stumbled in the steps of the dance, falling against him. He caught her body against his. So intimate, so familiar. She pushed her hand flat against his chest, in the same place she had five nights before.

She jerked back.

Somewhere, Jack thought dully, Satan laughed.

Jack's body shook. He had never been closer to losing every aspect of self-control. How fortunate for her that they were not alone. Because, just at this moment, he was not at all certain he wouldn't have killed her.

He grasped her shoulders and stared down at her. She gazed up at him defiantly, with eyes lit up like a midnight pantheon of dying stars.

"My thief," he said.

Chapter Seventeen

"Did you think I wouldn't know you? That I don't carry the imprint of you burned into my skin?" he demanded in a low, furious voice.

"You're hurting me," she said softly.

His hands dropped from her shoulders. A couple nearby stared at them and, with a sound of frustration, Jack guided her back into the steps of the dance.

"God help me, I can taste you. My body knows yours. There's no escaping such recognition." His silky-rough voice had never been silkier or more deadly. She'd thought she was beyond fear. She wasn't.

She could feel the blood draining from her face. Play the game to its end. Pretend he referred to his gentle kiss outside the Norths' town house.

"Colonel. Please." She did not have to feign acute discomfort. "I am not as wanton as my actions the other day proclaimed me. I can only plead that your . . . your kiss took me by surprise."

His lips curled. "You don't want to do this."

"Do what?"

"Play these games with me." His grip must have tightened once more because she realized that her fingertips tingled.

Lightning flashed, thunder boomed, and the rain sheeted the glass pane with coursing water. The room closed in on her. Her head spun.

"It's over," he grated out. "Accept it. You're mine."

"Is this some sort of flirtation? Though I accept responsibility for seemingly encouraging your advances, I . . ." Her voice faded, a dim buzzing had begun in her ears. Hurt rolled over her in waves. *No more Jack. No more tenderness. She'd already lost it all.* "I must protest. I was caught off guard being unfamiliar with the ways of . . . your sort of men and—" Pain flickered in his gaze like a moon shadow crossing the luminous gray of his eyes. *Say it.* "I wish to remain unfamiliar with them."

His head snapped back as though she'd slapped him. His lips parted and he drew a sharp breath. "You are lying."

"Please, Colonel," she said softly. "I find this conversation highly repugnant. Perhaps we should quit the dance?"

His eyes narrowed. A second passed and his expression smoothed, fury banked beneath the cool ash of his gray eyes.

"Oh, no, madam." His tone was diamond hard and diamond polished. "I most humbly beg your pardon and beg you to finish this waltz."

She should leave him. He'd given her more than ample cause. But she could not force the dismissive words from her throat, could not compel herself to abandon him on the dance floor. He did not await her answer.

They described a slow, elegant arc around the room. The music joined them in rhythms as austere and intricate as the game they played. Even through the thin silk tissue of her dress she felt the impression of each of his fingers, the breadth of his wide palm, the curve of his hand riding her flank. The feeling intoxicated and bewildered her, stunned her with sensual provocation, set her afire, and she thrilled to it.

This was self-immolation. Madness. She had to get away.

"Are you certain this is what you want, madam?" he asked.

He gazed unwaveringly on her as if he would read her thoughts from the fluctuations of color in her skin or the steadiness of her gaze, things she could not control.

"You do not appear to be a fool, Mrs. Wilder," he continued tightly. "Yet the course you have set yourself on can only have a tragic outcome."

There was an odd air in his last words that in a less self-possessed man might have verged on a plea. Ridiculous. He would think that she had used his interest in the widow to conceal her identity as the thief. He would feel betrayed and duped. He must hate her. But if he looked at her much longer like that she would surrender—

"You are speaking of my less-than-stellar performance as Sophia's chaperone," she said. "Have I really been that poor a doyenne? I know Sophia may be a bit strong-headed, but what girl of spirit—"

"You purposefully misunderstand me."

She sighed. "I constantly disappoint you, Colonel." He did not disagree.

"Then let us find another topic of conversation. How goes your search for the Wraith?" She forced a mocking tone to her voice, certain it was better to reveal his hate rather than torture herself with illusions.

For a moment she'd thought she saw concern in those cold eyes and heard regret in his hard voice. That couldn't be. It was another fairy tale. She'd lived a fairy tale once before. It had nearly destroyed her. Perhaps it had.

As if in answer, an angry drumroll of thunder shook the house. "Not that the poor fellow is likely to be out on a night like this," she said brightly. "He'd have to be desperate indeed. Though there are certainly temptations aplenty here tonight." Lady Dibbs twirled by in the arms of an aging roue. "Lady Dibbs is sporting a fine new necklace. And Lady Pons-Burton's tiara would make a plum prize."

She glanced up. He was watching her carefully now. "You must be horribly frustrated not being able to catch him. But you mustn't feel badly," she said. "Who could possibly anticipate the movements of a criminal? Their thoughts can't follow the same pattern as normal people."

She angled her head back. His expression was devoid of emotion. "I hope I'm not boring you, Colonel. Or should I call you Jack?" She said his name defiantly.

He would not be indifferent. Hate was preferable to apathy.

"Oh, I assure you I am not in the least bored," he answered. His smile was a mere matter of muscular contractions.

God, he must hate her. Hysteria brushed the little burble of laughter that broke free of the pain choking her throat. She could not control the trembling that suddenly seized her. She misstepped and stumbled, seizing his crippled hand to keep from falling. He grimaced.

"Oh!" she cried. "I've hurt you."

"No," he denied softly. "I won't give you quite that much of an advantage ever again, my dear."

His thief. Fragile preoccupied widow merged with lissome audacious thief. Lust and tenderness. Desperation and pride.

She taunted him. She flung his illusions in his face. Not that it mattered. His desire for her enraged him far more than her open ridicule.

His breathing labored. She'd played him, allowed him to court her, reveal himself to her, and trust her. That knowledge could not kill his desire.

He pulled her nearer and put his lips near her ear. "Forgive my familiarity, Mrs. Wilder."

She flinched and his lips opened on a feral smile. Beneath his hand she felt delicate and slight. Her fragile, otherworldly pallor and her dark haunted eyes had duped him, but his body knew hers. Oh, yes. He'd never experienced such visceral recognition. Nothing so intense and elemental had ever touched him before.

The waltz ended. They stopped, neither making any move to step away from the other. Her gaze lifted to his.

"Anne—"

"Don't be familiar," she said in a panic-stricken voice. "What gives you the right to be so presumptuous? You don't know me. You don't know me at all." She lashed out at him like the threatened wild thing she was. And like a wild thing, he'd catch her. Anger burned white hot in his veins, distilling into savage resolve.

"Do not test me much further," he said.

"Go find your thief, Colonel Seward." Beside them people began to turn in response to her rising voice.

"I already have. You are my thief," he muttered thickly, securing her wrist and dragging her arm over his. She was insensible to her surroundings. At any minute she could reveal herself. He would not allow that.

"Calm yourself," he said harshly. "You don't want to draw any more attention than you already have."

Her frantic gaze wavered from his, passed over the interested and amused faces nearby.

He raised his voice. "If you wish to find Miss Sophia we will, of course, do so immediately, Mrs. Wilder."

Her feet dragged as he propelled her before him. She held her head high, like someone going to the gallows. Dark circles stood out beneath her eyes like coal marks. At the far side of the ballroom, he led her into the hall and ushered her ahead of him. "Come with me. We need privacy."

"No. We do not." She had regained her calm. The hectic fever in her eyes had died away, leaving them opaque and unfathomable. "If you think I am your thief, you are mistaken, Colonel Seward." Her voice was calm, too calm.

"Don't push me any further," he suggested grimly.

"If your attentions to me have been because you thought I was this Wraith you seek, I am sorry you wasted your time."

Very nice, he thought approvingly, furiously. The angle of her head, the slight quiver of her lips, the timbre of her voice, all bespoke her offense and pain.

He wouldn't let her mock what he'd felt for her. It did not deserve to be used like this.

But hadn't he used others just as cleverly, just as ruthlessly as she had used him? The unbidden question arose from nowhere. Hadn't he preyed on others' illusions and weaknesses to gain him what he wanted?

He refused to consider such matters. Rage owned him.

He grasped her elbow. She struggled against him as he drove her out into the shadows. In the hall, he claimed her hand and held it up between them like a challenge. He grasped the edge of her glove, peeling the fabric from her forearm. She realized his intent then. A flicker crossed her face, a momentary and harsh, self-mocking humor. Their gazes locked and strove against each other. He stripped the glove from her fingers, exposing her bare flesh. Little half-healed cuts covered her forearm.

"You received these crashing through my window, shielding your face," he snapped out.

"Pruning the holly into floral arrangements," she shot back.

"You have a scar. On the bottom of your little finger."

Her eyes widened. "How could you—"

"I felt it." He turned her hand over and, without breaking eye contact, traced the ridge of raised flesh. "When you put your hands on my bare skin. I can *still* feel it." The words were an accusation.

She swallowed. "You're mistaken."

Her words touched off a bonfire of anger in him. "Do you think that you only have to say 'It isn't me' and like some poor besotted fool I will simply doff my cap and stammer, 'Beggin' your pardon, ma'am, I must be mistaken'?"

She tried to bolt. He yanked her back and dropped his face within inches of hers. He spoke, keeping the words soft and low. "I'll be paying you a visit tomorrow, Mrs. Wilder. I suggest you be at home. Alone."

She shook her head. Thunder rumbled ominously above and without.

"You'll be at home." He forced the words between his teeth. "If you aren't, I will—" A woman knocked against him, upsetting his balance. He spun angrily. Lady Dibbs blinked up at him.

"Oh! Excuse me, Colonel Seward." She saw Anne and her eyes went hard with enmity.

Lady Dibbs's companions appeared behind her. They stood in a little queue, like sheep before the pasture gate, all fluffy and white, eyeing him as if he were some wolf.

They looked beyond him to Anne and their faces hardened. She'd donned a remote expression. Her bare hand was safely hidden in her gloved one. Unfortunately Lady Dibbs had sharp eyes and a sharper desire to find fault.

She spied the glove he still held. Playfully she flicked it. "Mrs. Wilder!" she said. "You appear to have lost your glove. Don't tell me . . ." She pressed a hand to her heart and turned to the other two women. "My dears! We have interrupted a tête-à-tête!"

Avid glances darted between Anne and him. They were rehearsing their stories even as they stood. Jack could hear it now: The little Sussex nobody having already acquired position through an incomprehensibly brilliant match could now afford to indulge the base side of her lineage by dallying with a bastard.

Lady Dibbs smiled, toying with the gaudy necklace draped around her plump throat. Anne's gaze fixed on the movement as if hypnotized.

"Tit for tat, Mrs. Wilder," Lady Dibbs finally said in a quiet, deadly voice. "I hope your charity's generous and elite patrons are also . . . open-minded, shall we say?"

Anne regarded her blankly. She seemed to have drawn in on herself, like a little hedgehog, playing dead. Certainly her eyes looked vacant, hopeless.

He jerked his gaze away from her. He would *not* have pity on her, he thought savagely.

"And fancy this," Lady Dibbs went on triumphantly. "I have been talking to some of my friends and we've discovered a rather interesting fact about your little charity. Did you know that the majority of people robbed by Wrexhall's Wraith are those who've donated to your cause? It quite concerns us. You don't suppose the thief is one of your destitute soldiers, do you? I mean, we cannot be asked to support people who victimize us, can we?"

Anne turned her head slowly toward him. "You'll excuse me if I leave you, Colonel? I must see about getting Sophia home. There's so much to do." Her tone was indifferent; her gaze returned to the trio of ladies. "Lady Dibbs, have I complimented you on your lovely necklace? Ladies, I bid you good evening."

With a dignity he could not help but admire, she curtseyed and brushed past Lady Dibbs.

Anne had ended the interview and spiked his guns. He could not follow her. To do so would be to invite comment, and attention was the last thing he wanted.

But he watched her until she disappeared.

Chapter Eighteen

The storm gathered power as the night continued. It came
from the coast and when it found London, it hunkered down
as if to stay. Adam Burke had arrived on the early mail coach from
Sussex and walked the four-mile distance to the address the colonel had given him. By the time he'd arrived, his boots were soaked
through. Now every time he moved he made squishy sounds. A
special agent assigned to Colonel Seward oughtn't make such un-
dignified noises, Burke thought.

He crushed his soft cap in his hands and waited for Colonel
Seward to stop thinking and start speaking. Another clap of thunder shook the rafters, rattling the bric-a-brac. Burke looked around.

Not much of a place the colonel rented. Adequate and clean but
not much in the way of creature comforts. Even the bric-a-brac

turned out to be nothing but an empty glass set too close to a decanter.

Burke glanced at the colonel. This matter was playing hard with him. His hair was rumpled as if he'd run his hands repeatedly through it, and his jacket was off. In the six years Burke had worked for the colonel, he'd never seen either. Added to that, he looked bone-tired. But seeing how it was two o'clock in the morning, weren't they all?

Burke had spent nearly a month following a fascinating paper trail. He'd finished reciting his findings, and mighty interesting findings they were. He couldn't figure out why the colonel wasn't clapping him on the back and saying "Good work, Burke lad, and thank you for comin' out this god-awful night" instead of staring into the hearth like a cat mesmerized by the firelight.

"Tell me more about Anne Wilder's father and Jamison." The colonel's sudden question caught Burke off guard.

Tribble and Jamison? He tried to remember everything he'd learned about the odd association between a thief and a . . . a Jamison. He didn't know what to call Jamison's position, just as he really didn't know what to call the colonel, who worked directly below Jamison or the dozens of others—himself included—who worked for the colonel.

"I started with the banks," Burke said, "trying to get a handle on who needs money. Well, the answer is they all do or did . . . except Anne Wilder's dad, Sir Tribble. He had money."

The colonel nodded encouragingly.

"But on looking closer, I found something odd. Tribble's money doesn't come from any investments; it comes in regular payments from someone in London. And I can't get no further than that. So I visit Sussex and talks with them what served Tribble before he died. They tell me how he came up from London with a Dockland accent and a trunkload of money. He bought himself a manor and married into the local gentry."

The colonel turned away from the hearth and leaned his shoulders against the mantel. The light coming from behind him made it look as if he'd walked straight out of the fire. The notion was unsettling.

"This is all fine, Burke," the colonel said, "but it doesn't explain Tribble's association with Jamison."

"Well, soon the Tribbles have themselves a daughter. Mr. Tribble dotes on the girl. Won't have her out of his sight, not even when the missus goes off to visit her folks in Bath, which she does thrice yearly. Mr. Tribble doesn't go with his wife, in spite of them being what you call a devoted couple. Fact is, Mr. Tribble never leaves Sussex."

"Go on," murmured the colonel.

"Now things start falling into place. The servants say that as soon as the missus is gone, Tribble's got his kid up to all sorts of outlandish tricks. Tree climbing, opening doors without any keys, walking on a rope strung between two trees, tumbling . . ."

The colonel looked up sharply, his attention finally engaged.

"Yeah, and it gets more interesting. As I said, Tribble never leaves Sussex. *Never.* He doesn't even go to London, where he comes from. It's as if he was afraid he'd be recognized. Or"—he laid his finger aside his nose—"he'd been told *not* to come to London. Except . . ."

"Except what?" the colonel demanded.

"Around 'bout the war starts—and soon after Anne Tribble become Anne Wilder—Mr. Tribble suddenly starts traveling, staying away for weeks, sometimes months. Then the war ends and Mr. Tribble comes home to find his daughter a widow and all but thrown out of her own home by her husband's mother."

"*What?*" The colonel stepped forward.

Burke shifted uneasily on his feet and nodded. "The old bitch don't want nothin' to do with the younger Mrs. Wilder. Blames her for her son's death. Real vocal about it, too."

"*Was* she to blame?" the colonel asked in a low, tense voice.

"Huh?" Burke squinted at the colonel.

"Was Anne Wilder to blame for her husband's death?" the colonel repeated.

"Oh! No, sir. Leastways no one else thought so. Not the gentry or the servants." Burke shook his head. "By all accounts a perfect marriage. Mrs. Wilder's maid swears he'd have given her the world if she'd asked. Can you imagine loving a woman that much?"

The colonel did not answer. He simply turned his attention back to the fire. Not that Burke thought he would reply. He smiled at the notion of the colonel trading romantic musings with him. He smiled even more broadly at the notion of the colonel *having* romantic musings. The colonel, fine and decent as he was, was the most pragmatic man he knew.

"They did say as how Mrs. Wilder changed a great deal after she married Mr. Wilder."

"In what manner?"

"Well," Burke said with a knowing smile, "she was something of a firebrand, you know. Always getting up to some mischief, and with what we now know about her dad's child-rearin' technique, is it any wonder?" Burke chuckled. "Anyway, she was a cavalier sort of gel. But after she married Matthew Wilder, she settled right down. No more havey-cavey shenanigans and not an ounce of scandal attached to her name.

"Nope." Burke shook his head. "Mrs. Wilder had no call to say bad things about the young Mrs. Wilder, and when Mr. Tribble came back from his journeys he was fit to be tied at the way his daughter had been treated."

"Unpleasantness?"

"Nah," Burke said. "Tribble was too canny to fight the old biddy openly. When all is said and done she's quality and he ain't. But a few weeks later Mr. Tribble is *Sir* Tribble and the old bitch is eating crow at his knighting. Next day she has an interview with 'unknown persons.' Thereafter, old Mrs. Wilder shuts up."

"Is Jamison the 'unknown persons'?"

Burke's face crumpled dolefully. "I don't know," he admitted. "I tried but I couldn't find out."

"No matter."

Relieved by the colonel's mild tone, Burke ventured on. "But aren't you interested in what turns a plain, rich Mr. Tribble into a 'Sir' Tribble? I'm *real* interested specially as to why the finance minister recommends him for knighthood when he don't have no financial interests."

"Good question. I take it this time you found an answer?"

"Yes, sir. I got chummy with the finance minister's secretary," Burke said. "We gets talking about all these merchants getting knighted, and I mention Tribble's situation and he says, 'Oh, Tribble weren't knighted by my gentleman. He got knighted at the request of some old cager my gentleman owed a favor, a chap named Jamison.'"

For a moment the colonel stood motionless. "I see." He pushed himself away from the mantel and walked over to the window. He drew back the curtain. "So her father wasn't just any thief. He stole things for Jamison. Probably information. First as a young man in London and later in France."

"That's what I think," Burke agreed. "And Tribble taught his daughter his skills and maybe told her about his London connections who might be interested in a 'sensitive article.' Appears Annie Tribble is putting all that information to good use . . . or bad, depending on what view you take."

"So it would seem."

Burke, amused, shook his head. "Who'd a thought? A member of the ton, Wrexhall's Wraith. Think being widowed deranged her?"

The lines around the colonel's lips deepened. "Have you reported any of this to anyone else?" he asked sharply.

"No, sir," Burke answered, slightly affronted. The colonel had never questioned his loyalty before.

"Good. Don't."

"Very well, sir."

"Had anyone else been asking questions? Have Jamison's agents entered the race?"

Burke shrugged. "It didn't occur to me that anyone else would be looking, sir. I never thought to ask." He wriggled, brutally aware of the disappointment on the colonel's face. "I mean, he set you on the case. I never thought he'd take it into his head to set someone after you."

"Of course not. No reason you would," the colonel replied. He looked back out of the window. Lightning danced in the sky, a fireworks display that would have put Covent Garden in its prime to shame. "Find out who else is looking, Burke. It's probably too late already."

A rap announced the old Scot, Griffin. He poked his head in the door and eyed Burke malignantly. "Finished your pleasure trip, have you?"

"What is it, Griffin?" the colonel asked.

"Boy to see you, Cap. Says it's urgent."

"Send him up."

"Already up, Cap." Griffin turned and waved his hand.

A small sodden figure slipped into the room and headed for the fire. He lifted his raw hands, rubbing them vigorously. Steam rose in fragrant clouds from his mismatched clothing.

"Get him some hot tea," the colonel said, sending Griffin on his way. "Now, what's so important?"

The boy's eyes slid warily toward Burke.

"Go on," the colonel said.

"She left."

"What?" the colonel shouted. Burke started in shock. He'd never heard the colonel even raise his voice before. In ground-eating strides, the colonel swallowed up the distance between himself and the boy. The lad cowered back toward the fire. Abruptly the colonel stopped, his hand clenched at his side.

"Tell me," the colonel clipped out.

"She snuck out 'alf an hour ago," the boy said gruffly. "I wouldn't 'ave seen her but lightning flashed just as she was creepin' across the roof. That's how she's been gettin' by me. She stays off the peak and waits for some fog to come up then blends in with the roof. Lord, it must be a slippery go."

Lord of Mercy, Burke thought, staring out at a sudden burst of manic lightning dancing across the sky. She'll be burned to a cinder out there.

"Where did she go?" the colonel demanded.

"Don't know." The boy cringed again. "Couldn't see. It's somethin' wicked out and what with the way she's dressed and tryin' to stare into the rain and all, I didn't catch more than a glimpse of 'er. She headed northeast, though."

"Northeast? You're sure?" the colonel asked.

"Pretty sure," the boy said. "I tell ya, she's like some bleedin' shadow."

Griffin pushed the door open and entered carrying a tray laden with a pot, cups, and a plate heaped with bread and cheese.

The colonel raked his hair back with both hands. "Where in blazes would she—" He stopped suddenly.

He's figured it out, Burke thought. He knows just where she's heading. *If she makes it there.*

The colonel headed toward the door. "Griffin, feed them and get them out." He grasped the boy's shoulder in his hand. "You've always known enough to keep mum. This time it's doubly important. Not a word of who and what you did or learned this night. Not one word. Do you understand?"

The boy met the colonel's gaze with a level one of his own. "I'll consider me life to be worth the price of me silence."

"Wise lad," the colonel murmured, and then looked at Griffin. "Give the boy here two crowns." He glanced at Burke. "You, do as we discussed," he said, and left.

The boy bolted after him, heading toward the kitchen.

Burke met Griffin's eye. "Is she really up there? In this?" he finally found the voice to ask. "She really must have gone mad."

Chapter Nineteen

Her foot caught and she sprawled on the ancient shakes, slipping toward the edge. Driving rain sheeted her face, blinding her. She gouged her nails into soft, wet wood trying to arrest her fall. A foot from the edge of the roof she stopped. Laughed.

Gasping for breath—or was she sobbing?—she scrambled to her knees and pitched herself up the steep incline. She patted the bag laced to her side and smiled in relief at the reassuring weight of tiara and bracelets and money purse and broaches and ear bobs . . . and Lady Dibbs's necklace.

Tell your friends, Lady Dibbs, thought Anne. *Tell them how you suspect someone from that dreadful nobody's charity was using the donors' list as a sort of criminal guidebook. Convince your peers to rescind on their pledges and turn their backs on their promises, because by tomorrow it will be too late. At least for you.*

Anne laughed again and lifted her face into the weather. The rain stung her chill cheeks and lips with icy needles. Lord, she was cold. Cold was good. Numb was better.

Just a little farther and she'd be to the rain barrel where she'd stashed her clothes: an overlarge skirt that slipped easily over the thief's close-fitting stockinette, a heavy coat that hid her soaking shirt, and a bonnet.

The lightning rent the skies and heaven loosed its latest volley on her. The sound enveloped her, resonating in her heart, stomach, and blood. She gasped and when it was over, she smiled and looked down.

"Where are you, Jack?" she called softly. Home in bed if he'd any sense. But he didn't, did he? He'd trusted her and that meant he had no sense at all. No one trusted a thief. Not with their hearts, not with anything.

Another flash of lightning. Bright this time. Nearer. She straightened, standing in the buffeting winds, concentrating on the electric promise tingling over her flesh, building toward the crescendo—

Boom!

She gasped with the elemental thrill of it. So close! Any closer and she'd become part of the storm itself, she'd meld with that exquisite white fire. She laughed again before fleeing along the aerial highways.

The lightning erupted into a blinding tapestry, lacing the sky with brilliance. Jack forced himself to squint against its glare. There she was. Lithe as the wind, lean as a winter sun, she sprinted high above him, heading toward the park. He closed his eyes, breathing deeply. God alone knew why she hadn't been hit. It could only be a matter of time. No one challenged the elements like that and lived.

He started forward again, keeping one eye on the tops of the black rain-washed buildings and the other on the narrow streets. He'd been over this route any number of times, having weeks since picked out the easiest paths a rooftop traveler might take from Lady Dibbs's house. He'd marked such routes for all the wealthy ladies and gentlemen who frequented Carlton House.

He should have realized her intent earlier; she'd all but boasted of her plans. But he thought he'd scared the hell out of her. *He'd* left the party last night confident of his power to intimidate her. *She'd* left the party last night and taken immediate advantage of his hubris. She'd simply outmaneuvered him. And how ravishingly well she'd done it, he thought angrily.

Jack sneered. How many times had he consoled himself with the thought that the men he'd sent into danger had been cautioned never to underestimate the enemy? Yet he'd underestimated her five times over. A warm flood of harsh anticipation, of near gratitude, washed through him.

So she wanted to play, did she?

Well, they'd play then, and when he won—and he fully intended to win—he knew just what trophy he would claim.

His lungs labored now and his legs ached. The rain grew heavier. His coat's sodden weight hung on his shoulders like lead, slowing him down. He wouldn't risk losing her. He shed the wool greatcoat, dropping it to the flooded streets, and ran in his shirtsleeves, impervious to the cold, biting wind or the drenching rain.

A lorry driver cursed him for a lunatic when he bolted in front of his cart. A pair of prostitutes huddled in the doorway of a church shrank from him, hooting when he passed.

He saw her twice more. Each time her silhouette grew smaller against the sheets of lightning, as if she were slowly disappearing into the very center of the storm. East over the exchange offices she went and then a perilous drop to the slate-covered roof of an Episcopalian church. South now, coursing over the stable roofs of countless town houses until reaching the park. There she'd no choice but to alight, his little bird. And he'd be there waiting.

The breath whistled in his lungs, burned in his throat. Two more streets. She *had* to be coming from one of the buildings on the next street. He sprinted around the corner and collided with a girl in a light-colored coat. His hands shot out to keep her slight body from pitching into the wall, righting her before shoving by. Her voice stopped him.

"Why, Colonel Seward! Can that be you?" He spun. Anne Wilder stood before him in a prim, fawn-colored coat. Neat gloves encased her hands. A fashionable bonnet covered her hair. *Impossible.*

"How?" he demanded. "How did you get dressed like that?"

She laughed with odd and inappropriate pleasure. She sounded feverish with excitement. Her eyes gleamed like wet, blue-black ink. The rain tangled in her thick lashes, studding them with diadems of water.

"Why, Colonel, you're soaked through!" she exclaimed. "You'll catch your death out on a night like this without a coat. Whatever could you be thinking?"

His temper snapped. He grabbed her by her shoulders. "How did you do it? Where are your clothes?"

She laughed again, making no attempt to break free. "My clothes? I am wearing clothes, Colonel, and a good deal more of them than you."

He stared at her. With awful clarity he recognized the expression in her eyes. She was beyond his ability to influence by threats or reason. She'd been to Lady Dibbs's and she'd stolen her jewels and she didn't have them on her. Jack read it in her unbridled excitement and fevered laughter.

She'd gorged herself on the elixir of victory and now she felt invincible. Like the soldier whose entire regiment is wiped out in a charge yet somehow remains personally unscathed, she reeled with guilt and power and a horrifying sense of her own invulnerability.

He took her arm and wheeled her around. With his touch her bravado shattered. She stumbled in his grip.

"No!" she said, setting her heels. "What are you doing? You can't just—"

He ignored her protest, dragging her out of the alleyway and onto the street. She threw her weight back against his, but this time the hand holding her wasn't slick with blood or weakened by a cut and his clasp did not loosen in spite of her best efforts.

"Are you insane?" She gasped, clawing at his fingers.

"I must be."

"Let me go, Colonel," she said. "Have you lost your senses? You can see I'm not your thief. You're deluded."

He hauled her to his side and hailed a cabdriver lounging beneath the shelter of a tree on the far side of the street. The cabby's eyes widened at the sight of him clad only in a soaking shirt, a woman struggling in his grip.

Jack cursed roundly. Anne slipped on the slick cobbles underfoot and fell to her knees. She tore at the hand clasping her wrist. Her skirts soaked up the water streaming in the gutter. Her face, turned up into the driving rain, was frantic. God help him.

"Me wife's been taken with a fit!" he bellowed above the din of sudden thunder. "Five quid to get us 'ome!

The man stared a second more as Jack hefted Anne into his arms and secured her thrashing body against his own. With a nod, the cabby began a slow climb to the driver's seat.

"Are you mad?" Anne gasped, gulping on her sobs.

"Am *I* mad?" he shot down at her. "What are you doing out here, Mrs. Wilder?"

"I . . . I . . . the Home . . . I went to see—"

"You haven't been anywhere near there. You've been stealing Lady Dibbs's jewelry, and tomorrow morning I'll have the square mile around here turned over leaf by leaf to find it."

"You won't find it. You won't find anything." She stopped struggling. "You can't prove anything," she said. "Let me go."

"No."

The hack lumbered to a stop before them. The driver clambered down to open the door.

Jack tightened his hold on Anne. "Do not make a scene," he said in a hard voice filled with promise. She must fear him, realize he would commit any act he deemed necessary. And wouldn't he? He could not ever remember being so angry.

He forced the cold implacable words from his mouth. "If you do, I shall strip you right here and now to discover your secrets."

She blanched and went utterly still except for the shivers racking her body. He swore savagely, low vehement words learned in a Scottish workhouse. Her shivers turned into shudders. He thrust her into the cab and climbed in after her. Already she'd scooted across the seat and grabbed the handle on the door opposite.

He grasped her around the waist and hauled her back onto his lap. Her sopping skirt soaked through his trousers. The brim of her bonnet smacked into his face. Holding her tightly around her middle, he loosed the ribbons of her hat and jerked it from her head. Long silky black ropes of hair uncoiled down her back. Wet silk.

"Amazing how your hair is wet, considering the lining of your bonnet is still nearly dry, isn't it, Mrs. Wilder?" he asked.

In answer she redoubled her efforts to escape. The sweet, taut swell of her buttocks wriggled against his groin. Rolling shock waves of pleasure rippled through him, surprising and infuriating him. Even here, even now, even knowing how she'd played him, he wanted her.

"Be still," he said with a growl, willing himself to ignore the feel of her strong, supple little form.

She went limp and roughly he pushed her from his lap. Immediately she scrambled into the corner of the cab and turned to stare at him like a feral cat.

"Where's the letter that you stole from Lord Atwood's room?" he ground out. "The one in the silver jeweled chest."

She blinked. "I don't know what you mean."

He grabbed each side of her collar and jerked her from her corner. He heard her knees bang against the floorboards. He dragged her up so her face was level with his. Pitifully easy to do. She weighed next to nothing.

Terror declared itself clearly in her expression. Her lips trembled. God help him, he wanted to taste them, to stop their soft quaking with his own mouth.

Why not? Why the bloody hell not?

He yanked her forward and covered her lips with his. He angled his head, forcing hers to arch beneath his onslaught, opening his mouth in a rough demonstration of his power, forcing her to accept his tongue. She whimpered far back in her throat. He could taste the salt of her tears. That was all she needed to do.

With a sound of rage he tore his mouth from hers. He'd never forced himself on a woman before. It did nothing, *nothing* to satisfy the lust careening wildly at the back of his black thoughts. Indeed, it sickened him, and this in turn infuriated him.

He would not let her do this to him. He would not let her overwhelm him. He shook her and she cried out, a small, involuntary sound.

"Not to your taste, Mrs. Wilder? I thought you liked a bit of roughness to your amorous sport."

"Please."

"Oh, no. Not yet. Later. Right now I want answers, not you."

Liar!

"But I don't—"

"I've had enough denials, Mrs. Wilder. They begin to pall." His voice was stiletto sharp, thin, and lethal. He was good at this. He was the fucking *best*. He pulled her a few inches closer, letting his gaze travel with deliberate leisure over her face and throat and bosom. "Now, let us try again. Where is that letter?"

Her hands flew up and circled his wrists, trying to stop him. *Useless act.* His thumbs brushed against the cool damp skin of her throat. If he wanted to, he could snap her neck like a twig.

"I don't know what you're talking about," she pleaded. "There wasn't any letter in that jewelry chest."

"At least we've progressed to a tacit agreement on your identity," he said. "But you still aren't quite complying with the spirit of the game, Mrs. Wilder. I ask a question. You answer. Stop shaking, damn you!"

"I can't help it!" A sob broke from her throat.

"Where is that letter?"

"I told you," she said. "I never saw any letter. There wasn't anything in Lord Atwood's chest. It was empty!"

"A secret compartment," he said impatiently. "It was in there."

Her face mirrored a confusion that looked real. If he'd interrogated her as a stranger, he would have sworn she told the truth. Being able to gauge if someone lied or not had been his bread and butter for more than a decade. But he couldn't trust his judgment where she was concerned. He was far too involved and in far too many ways.

He had no concept of what she felt or thought, where her allegiances lay or even if she was capable of having any.

She was staring at him. "There wasn't any secret compartment," she whispered, as if afraid of provoking him.

He laughed, a bitter sound that made her wince. He'd been far more than provoked, as she'd soon learn. "Am I supposed to believe a thief of your skills didn't check a jewelry chest for a hidden drawer?"

She swallowed. Twin lines appeared between her straight dark brows, and in spite of himself he longed to smooth them with his fingertips. He dropped his hands abruptly. Traitorous things, they might soothe when he needed them to terrorize.

"I didn't search it thoroughly, but I did look," she said rapidly. "There wasn't a catch or a lever. If there was a drawer it must have been a very small one."

He considered the possibility that she was telling him the truth and decided it could make no possible difference. He couldn't trust her. He couldn't believe a word she said. And damn it, it *hurt*.

It was so impossibly stupid he nearly laughed. He still wanted her. Any part of her he could have.

She was lying to protect whomever she'd sold that damn letter to. Either she *wanted* to protect him, or she feared this person more than she feared Jack.

Silly girl. He was the biggest bad wolf in her particular little story. She was about to find out how bad.

"Where is the chest now?" he asked.

"I fenced it. As soon as I . . . I stole it."

"Convenient."

"It's true! Did you think I would keep something so easy to identify lying about my uncle's town house? I sold it to an old man on the docks. I used an intermediary."

"Better and better," Jack said grimly. "And what was this old man's name?"

"Blind Tom."

"Tom." His voice was ripe with mockery. "Should be easy to find. What about this 'intermediary'?"

"I . . . I don't know."

He smiled. She flinched as if warding a blow. "Perhaps one of your charity cases knows. Perhaps that brat. What was his name—Will?"

She went still, like a deer caught in the beam of a lantern. "Please," she whispered forlornly.

"Very nice. Now, let's talk about the name of the intermediary."

Tears welled in her eyes, overflowed the cradle of her lids, and splashed down her cheeks. "I don't know his name. I don't even know how to contact Blind Tom. He contacts me. Through different people. Children mostly, carrying notes they can't even read."

"Amazing man, Blind Tom, to be able to write with such a handicap."

"I don't know. Maybe he uses a scribe." She was pleading with him now. In her extremity she'd abandoned the corner and leaned toward him. She plucked at his sleeve. Her skin shimmered like fresh milk in the dark carriage interior. Her hands, even gloved, electrified him with their touch.

Lust and fury pumped in his veins. God, she had him tangled in a web of desire and hopelessness so complete he doubted he'd ever escape.

"Please leave Will out of this. He doesn't know anything about this. He's just a boy. I'll help you find it. I swear."

"Oh, we'll find that chest, all right. But it will take time." *Time during which my father will be searching for you, and when he finds you he will kill you. And that I will not allow,* he silently vowed. *No matter what I have to do.*

"Whatever you want."

"I want you to marry me," he said coldly, watching her intently.

She stared at him, more horrified than she'd been at any point that night. "Marry you? I can't marry you."

"I beg to differ. You can. I assure you arranging for a special license will be one of the easier tasks I've had to accomplish."

She shook her head back and forth in violent denial. "No. I can't. I couldn't!"

"You can," he bit out. "And you will. Or I will have that boy arrested as Wrexhall's Wraith."

Her eyes widened. "But he couldn't have done it. No one will believe you."

"On the contrary"—he kept his voice level—"they shall believe the evidence, and I shall make certain there is plenty of it. Irrefutable evidence."

"You'd fashion false evidence to convict an innocent boy?"

"My dear," he said softly, "you are stunningly naive for a thief. It's been done before, many times. Nothing could be simpler."

"I'll confess."

"No one will believe *you*. You'll simply be thought a brave if stupid young woman. Besides, who would believe that Wrexhall's Wraith is a female? Jeanette Frost may look foolish claiming she was kissed by a boy, but better that than a woman or, even worse, letting society know she wasn't attacked at all and is a liar."

"You can't mean to do this, force me to marry you."

His voice hardened. "But I do."

"Why?" she pleaded helplessly. "I don't understand. Why would you want to marry me?"

"I hunted you. I tracked you. I trapped you. And now, by God, I'm going to keep you."

Chapter Twenty

"I don't believe this." Jamison slammed his fist down on his desk. "He'd never have done something like this without my approval."

The man, shielded from view of the door by the wings of the oversize chair, shifted in his seat. "He's done it. Married her by special license two nights ago."

"Why?" Jamison demanded. His visitor didn't respond, which was just as well. Jamison didn't expect, or want, speculation from this man. He was a drone carrying information.

Jamison did not like his information. It supported a fear—no, he would not call it "fear"—a *misgiving* he'd had for some time that Seward's allegiance to him was eroding. Seward on a tight leash was one thing; he was quite another as a free agent.

"I don't see that there's much to be done about it," the man said.

Jamison spared him a contemptuous look. There was *always* something to be done. He'd begun his association with this aristocratic little drone years before by proposing a solution to his approaching insolvency. Since then Jamison had fixed far more than financial worries for him. In return, Jamison demanded only very occasional but utter obedience from him.

It had proven a useful relationship. The man had some intelligence and a knack for surreptitious observation. That he moved in the most exalted circles of the ton also had its benefits. But he was nothing compared to Seward.

None of the agents Jamison directed could take Seward's place. There was no way to tally what such a loss would mean to Jamison. He would be without his premier weapon, a man who commanded respect and fear, who could discover not only his enemy's weaknesses but his strengths, a man of intelligence and intuition.

"I will not allow it!" The words burst from his lips with insuppressible vitriol.

The man in the shadows of the chair looked startled.

Jamison folded his hands on the desk. Calm replaced his rare outburst of passion. A man who made emotional decisions made bad decisions. He refused to lose the use of Seward's many talents, but retaining them would demand careful planning. Seward married, for God's sake. The thought repelled him.

"*Why* has he married her?" he asked.

The man in the chair lifted his hands. "I don't know. He's been favoring her with his attention for weeks. But I thought he suspected she was Wrexhall's Wraith. I told you he'd been with her."

"You did no such thing," Jamison corrected. "You reported to whom he spoke at these parties and where he sent what agents you knew to be his. *I* put together the pieces of the puzzle. *I* told *you*."

The man shrugged. "Regardless of that, from the way Seward sticks to her, I was sure she must be the Wraith."

"Who the bloody hell *is* this woman, anyway?" Jamison said.

"No one," his visitor declared. "She caused a minor sensation when she came out some years ago. Dark creature, a certain degree of dash to her. But other than that . . ."

"Come man, there must be something," Jamison said coldly. "I can't see Seward marrying someone for her 'dash.'" He sneered the last word.

His guest's expression wrinkled with distaste. "She runs a charity for soldiers, solicits donations from the ton, but she's *no one*, I tell you," he declared. "Her mother was just country gentry. Her father was nothing but a merchant from Sussex—I think he was knighted a few years back—but *everyone's* knighted these days—"

"Knighted?" Jamison leaned forward, suddenly alert. "What was this merchant's name?"

"Let me think. Tristham? No, no, it was Tribble. Yes!"

Jamison leaned back in his seat. It couldn't be the very same thief he'd employed all those years ago. That upstart piece of rabble from the docks who insisted he be knighted so his daughter's way in society would be clear. But of course it was. Tribble had been the most useful and skilled thief Jamison had ever used. His daughter would be no less.

If he'd been of a humorous bent, he would have laughed. "Well, you may have earned the money I pour into those empty pockets of yours. I believe Seward's wife *is* Wrexhall's Wraith."

"But why would Seward marry her?"

"He hasn't got the letter," Jamison said. "Rather than kill her as I commanded, he has married her to keep her under his control until he finds it."

"Then he might already have it."

"No," Jamison replied. He shifted the papers before him into straighter alignment. "So, Seward thinks to outmaneuver me, does he? I expressly told him I wanted that thief dead. I see I'll have to handle that task myself."

"You can't mean to kill your own son's wife?"

"Developing sensibilities rather late in the game, aren't you? Before you decide to wallow further in such sentimentality, I suggest you remind yourself of all the creature comforts you so well love and the title you so esteem and remember how you came by that title—through the fortuitous death of a distant relative." Even in the shadows, Jamison could see the man pale visibly.

Jamison's lips curled. "Besides, she's not Seward's wife. She's a bargaining chip that he's keeping under his thumb in the simplest and most convenient way possible."

"I don't know," the man said. "There's something more there, I'll wager. You haven't seen him. He looks . . . smitten."

"I raised him, you'll remember," Jamison said. "If he's smitten it's only with his physical response to her. His head isn't involved."

"What of his heart?"

"He hasn't got one. Still"—he pleated his fingers together and tapped the index fingers thoughtfully against his chin—"he *has* cut himself off from me. He might resent my killing her. I don't want that. I want him back under my control."

"*I'm* not killing her."

Jamison's eyes glittered. "Probably not," he said calmly, "but make no mistake, should I say so, you *will* kill her."

The man hesitated before jerking his head once in assent. Jamison studied him narrowly. His visitor knew enough to realize there would be no alternative should Jamison give him that order. He was, after all, not a stupid man.

"How are you going to do it?"

"So rash." Jamison clucked disapprovingly. "I must study the situation first. It may take some time, working the finer details out. But she'll be dead soon enough."

"What if she tells him where the letter is?"

"But she won't," Jamison clipped out.

"But how can you know she won't—"

"You may go now," Jamison dismissed him.

With a sound of relief the man rose and picked up his coat. "What about Frost?"

"Stay close to him. Keep him unhappy and drunk. He may just be your means of keeping your conscience clear, Lord Vedder."

As soon as Vedder left, Jamison rose and made his painful way to the bookcases. He selected a volume high up and pulled it down. Without bothering to look around—no one would dare enter his sanctuary unannounced—he ruffled the pages. They fell open on a thick sheet of thrice-folded vellum with a broken wax seal. A royal seal.

The Tribble chit wouldn't tell Jack where the letter was because she didn't know. Only Jamison knew where it was, and he intended it to stay that way.

A week before his death, Atwood had come to him with the letter. From some friends in the Admiralty, Atwood had learned how Jamison, along with Sir Knowles, handled "matters of political delicacy." Jamison, immediately recognizing the letter's importance, had happily unburdened him of it. That should have been the end of it.

It hadn't, of course. Jamison shut the leather-bound book and replaced it. For whatever reason, Atwood wrote Knowles and described the contents of the letter and his discussion with Jamison about its importance. Luckily, Atwood didn't mention that he'd already given the letter to Jamison. Perhaps he assumed Knowles already knew Jamison had it. They were reported to work in tandem.

Knowles immediately wanted to know when Jamison could expect to secure this fascinating letter. Jamison, caught unawares, told him he'd already arranged for its delivery.

He'd been trying to determine how to handle the situation when a stroke of fortune in the guise of this little thief provided him with the answer. She stole Atwood's jewelry case.

Jamison had taken immediate advantage of the opportunity this presented. Atwood himself had helped Jamison's cause. The night after the theft, he'd gone to dinner and regaled his friends with the story of his victimization at the hands of the notorious Wrexhall's Wraith.

Jamison wiped the dust from his fingertips with a clean kerchief and smiled. He could almost let the thief live if only for that. Almost.

Unfortunately for her, she was the only person besides himself who knew for a certainty that Atwood had not been in possession of that letter at the time of his death and that it had not been in the jeweled chest as Jamison had claimed. He might have even let her live then, except for Knowles's interference.

Jamison wadded the handkerchief in his fist, his expression growing grim. Though Jamison had told Knowles that he would handle the situation personally, *Knowles* had appropriated the task. *Knowles* had decided who was to be sent. *Knowles* had picked Seward, knowing Seward was Jamison's agent, going over Jamison's head and gaining authorization to do so. Jamison's clenched fist trembled.

Such affronts would not be tolerated once he regained the advantage in their relationship. Knowles would be the first to know it, and Seward would quickly learn afterward the wages of betrayal. How dare Seward disobey his orders to adhere to those given by Knowles?

With an effort, Jamison calmed himself, returning his thoughts to the matter at hand. As soon as he'd learned that Knowles had set someone on the thief's trail, Jamison had decided the thief must die. No one must ever learn he had that letter. It must be kept secret, especially from Knowles, until such a time as he could use it to expand his own power. At just the right time, in just the right circumstance, a letter such as this might greatly enhance his influence.

All he needed to do now was to arrange an accident for her before Jack—or Knowles—put the pieces of the puzzle together. An accident like the one he'd arranged for Atwood. He smiled, his good mood restored. Even that had played in his favor. Knowles saw Atwood's death as part of a political conspiracy revolving around the acquisition of the letter.

Jamison's small smile turned to a speculative look as he hobbled back to his desk. His troubled expression cleared.

Let her try to gain Seward's trust and convince him she didn't have the letter. He'd raised Seward, shaped him, *created* him. He didn't trust anyone. Not even himself.

The small figure ran across the bridle path. Strand watched Sophia with mixed feelings.

She was so damn young. Young enough so that his formidable status—hell, he thought irritably, his nearly *venerable* status—as one of the ton's most eligible bachelors didn't impress her. In fact, the only thing that did impress her was his lovemaking. And even that was subject to debate.

"Giles!" she said, flinging her arms around his neck. Mete from habit than any real concern for their good reputations—he, after all, had none, a state she was well on her way to emulating—he gently untwined her limbs. She pouted. Adorably, he supposed.

"Don't you like me anymore?"

"Of course I do, puss," he said lightly. Tucking her hand in the crook of his arm, he led her down a deserted footpath he'd discovered, oh, probably the year she was born. "Now, what is this all about?"

Her tongue flicked out to damp the very center of her upper lip. A very nice and exceptionally provocative affectation. One that had him growing hard in response.

"I just wanted to see you," she said, nuzzling him.

"I see." He didn't believe her for an instant. Had she wanted a sexual liaison, she would have come to his house at night as she had before. Or, he thought, she would have claimed his attention for one of the brutally quick and rough encounters that invariably took place in a back hallway while a party progressed around them.

Strand's smile was jaded. It wasn't much his preference, but his little Sophia had a taste for such settings. And he was, after all, a gentleman.

She glanced at him out of the corner of her eye. He could read her so easily.

"I had a note from Anne today," she said.

His attention sharpened. "Yes?"

"Seward really did marry her. She says so in her note."

"Really?" He tried to keep his tone careless. "What else did she say?" *Is she happy? Does she love him? God, if he hurts her . . .*

"Oh, a lot of drivel about how it wasn't as precipitate as it seems and how their elopement was for the best because she didn't want to burden everyone with a formal wedding." Sophia's little mouth turned down petulantly. "A fat lot of thought to the burden she handed me! Leaving me without a chaperone and the season not even begun."

"Poor puss," Strand responded tonelessly. Anne had married Seward. *Good luck to them.*

Sophia halted in the shadow of a huge yew. Its ancient branches sagged beneath the weight of their greenery. With a quick guarded look around, she led him behind it. He went with her indifferently. Doubtless she planned another dangerously staged seduction.

It hardly mattered to him. His body, well conditioned to the act, had already made it clear it would be happy to comply. If he thought about it, it rather amused him that he, who'd used so many women before, was now used so thoroughly by a chit barely out of the schoolroom.

Predictably, as soon as they'd rounded the tree, she shoved her hands beneath his coat and under his shirt.

"My fingers are cold," she murmured. "Are yours?"

"Oh, yes."

She withdrew her hands and slowly unhooked the silk frogs holding the front of her pelisse together. Beneath her coat she wore a gown more suited to a brothel than a walking path in February. Her little breasts were squeezed together in the constriction of the tight, low-cut bodice.

She took his hand and placed his gloved fingertips between the soft, warm mounds. "Isn't that better?"

"Yes. Much better."

"I have even warmer places," she breathed, standing on tiptoe and running her tongue along his throat. She began backing beneath the yew's branches, guiding him through the thick limbs until they stood beside the trunk, shielded in a tent of living green.

Idly, he wondered who'd introduced her to this dark bower. He'd never asked her about her other lovers. He knew they existed and she made no real attempt to make him think otherwise, but they didn't overly concern him, especially not while her fingers were working nimbly over the fastenings of his trousers. His hard member sprang free, and she gave a little sound of pleasure as her hands closed over him.

Clever hands. He closed his eyes and leaned back against the gnarled trunk. He supposed he ought to be thankful he had the ability to really enjoy the physical side of love since he'd apparently never experience any other aspect.

"Do you like this?" she whispered.

"Yes."

"I do, too."

"Aren't we fortunate?" If she heard the irony in his voice she ignored it, redoubling her efforts to please.

"I'm in some difficulty." He heard her voice as if from a long way off. His concentration was completely focused on her fingers, sliding up and down, tugging expertly.

"I'm belly full, Giles."

Well, yes. She was a young healthy woman and she'd been very active.

"Am I the father?"

She hesitated but her hands didn't. "You might be."

He broke out in laughter. God bless her, the girl might be a tart and a cunning romp but she wasn't a liar. He could respect that. He opened his eyes and stared down at her. She gazed back, a look of slight irritation on her oh-so-pretty face.

"And what do you want me to do?"

"I need to get it fixed."

The laughter died from his throat. Carefully he reached down and secured her wrists. Just as carefully he held them away from him. It didn't matter now anyway. His erection had left.

"I don't know who 'fixes' these things," he said, looking at her face. Her skin was like cream, her green eyes clear, and her hair like a flame. So young to be so old. It didn't seem right.

"But you can find out."

"No."

She pulled away from him, irritation fully marring that pretty face now.

Why not? he thought. *Why the bloody hell not?*

"You know," he said, "it occurs to me there are better ways of dealing with this than subjecting that pretty little body to butchery."

"Really?" She sneered over her shoulder.

At least he would have the distinct pleasure of surprising her. Who would expect that a man with his reputation . . .

He laughed and she turned around, looking clearly puzzled. "Why, you can marry me, puss."

Chapter Twenty-One

I hunted you. I tracked you. I trapped you. And now, by God, I'm going to keep you.

Anne stared listlessly out between the grillwork covering the bedroom window. Freedom taunted her beyond the iron tracery. Jack Seward taunted her with his absence.

She hadn't left this room for two days. Not since Jack had dragged the young rector at Saint Bernadette's from his bed and forced him to marry them. He'd returned her here, escorted her to this room, and left.

Within minutes she'd discovered the barred window and the jammed lock on the only door. The exterior bolt thwarted her every attempt to slide it back.

She'd huddled on the bed all night. The next morning that dour-looking Scotsman, Griffin, entered, followed by a wiry boy lumbering beneath the weight of a battered trunk. Under Griffin's silent and forbidding supervision, a middle-aged maid, Spawling, arrived and unpacked her clothing.

Jack had appeared while they were there. He was as somberly and immaculately groomed as ever, and she'd felt keenly her own soiled and disheveled condition. His blank gaze had swept over her. In a voice that could have been commenting on the weather, he'd asked her for a description of the boy who'd carried her last message.

He'd been flawlessly polite. There was nothing in him that she recognized as "Jack," and it frightened her far more than his anger and brutal kiss of the night before.

She pleaded with him to let her go. He'd ignored her and left with the suggestion that she write and inform Malcolm and Sophia of her marriage.

The only other time he'd come near her had been late last night. She'd lain sleepless on the bed, staring into a black corner and imagining any number of fates that awaited a thief who'd challenged and debauched and betrayed Whitehall's Hound, a man noted for doing terrible things.

She'd heard the bolt on the door slide back and held her breath. Soft footsteps crossed the room and came to a halt beside the bed. For long, tense moments she'd felt him standing over her. And then he'd gone.

She didn't know what he intended to do with her. It could be anything. She'd been a fool to think she understood the smallest thing about Colonel Jack Seward. She didn't. He was as terrifying and incomprehensible as the lightning she'd taunted atop the roofs. And God help her, just as seductive.

Below, the front door creaked open. She rose and padded to the door and pressed her ear against the oak panel. Footsteps climbed the stairs.

Her heartbeat skipped lightly in her chest. Anticipation and fear shivered through her body. He would come in now. He would introduce her to her fate.

The footsteps slowed. She straightened, lifting her chin and preparing to face him. He paused outside the door. She took a step back. The silence extended into long seconds and then the sound of footsteps resumed, grew faint, and disappeared altogether.

Tears flooded Anne's eyes, broke over her lids, and washed down her cheeks. Maybe this was her fate. To be kept locked away from sight, alone with her mad passion her only company. Was that his punishment? Did he know how she'd felt? How much she wanted him?

God, you're a fool, Anne! she thought violently. *How could he not know? You took any opportunity, any excuse, to touch him, to taste him.*

Of course he knew.

She banged her fists against the door. "You can't keep me in here forever! You can't!"

No one answered her shouts. She drummed harder, her tears came faster, sobs breaking her voice. She shook the knob, pounding again and again. "Damn you, let me out! You can't keep me like this! Jack! *Jack!*"

She beat against the door until her hands ached, called until she was hoarse. Her head fell against the hard wood panel.

He couldn't be so cruel.

He could be anything.

She pushed herself away from the door and looked frantically about. She had to get away. Once more she studied the barricaded window for some weakness, and once more found none. The spacing between the ornate fretwork was far too small to wriggle through. One would have to be a child . . .

She spun around, ran to the hearth, and knelt down in the cool ashes. The fire had died earlier and no one had come to relight it. She angled her head under the chimney and looked up into a small, dark tunnel. Big enough. She could escape up the flue. She jerked her head back.

And then where? She wouldn't think past the moment of escape.

She grabbed handfuls of ashes and darkened her face and arms. The dress she wore was far too narrow and confining to climb in. It would have to be sacrificed. With a penknife she sliced away half the length of her skirts and most of the sleeves.

She snatched a light cloak from the wardrobe and wrapped it into a tight narrow roll, planning to use it to cover her destroyed dress once she was on the streets. Then, taking a deep breath, she crouched down and crawled into the center of the hearth.

The acrid smell of smoke permeated her nostrils and coated her throat. She lifted her face, blinking as a fine mist of soot and ashes rained down on her.

She stood up in the narrow channel and lifted her arms, groping blindly for the perimeters of her escape route. Tight, very tight. Bracing her back against the brick wall, she jammed her feet against the opposite side. Slowly, foot by painstaking foot, she began crab-walking up into the narrow, black channel.

It took forever. Each increment was an agony of black darkness and choking coal dust. She scraped her hands raw on the uneven surface of brick. Her legs cramped in the tiny hole. Tales of climbing boys—children apprenticed to sweeps at the age of four or five—caught in passages too narrow to go either forward or backward haunted her.

She came to a sharp turn in the flue. Only by twisting and scrambling was she able to squeeze around the angle and continue. Sweat coursed down her face. Her muscles trembled on the point of exhaustion.

Finally, mercifully, she felt the brush of cold air fall like a benediction upon her face. She redoubled her efforts. Minutes later she straggled from the tiny chimney pot like a bedraggled phoenix. She fell panting on the rooftop and lay for a few minutes, letting the sweet, icy air revive her. She couldn't stay there. Any moment he could discover she was gone.

She clambered to her feet, unfolded her bundle, and wrapped the thin cloak around her shoulders. She looked around in despair.

She knew these unmarked highways. They could take her away from here, away from Jack. But not tonight.

Tonight the fog was as thick as clotted cream. She simply could not see well enough to make the leaps these airy byways demanded. But she'd no time to waste in regrets.

She scrambled lightly down the side of the building, the descent as easy as the ascent had been hard. The streets below were deserted. Fog and cold made it too uncomfortable for any to be abroad but those with the most imperative reasons.

She kept close to the buildings. Before and behind her an occasional figure appeared like a phantom, only to dissolve a second later into the murky whiteness. She went slowly, disoriented in the fog, unfamiliar with these earthbound passages. Sound expanded around her, amplified by the wet air.

Gradually Anne became aware of a faint echo to her footsteps, as if someone followed her and was carefully matching his gait to hers. She looked over her shoulder and squinted, uncertain whether a figure hovered just beyond her ability to make it out.

She stopped, listening intently, all her senses focused out into the dense, churning soup. Nothing. Just an ominous watchful—

"Dear God!"

The sleek little form sliced through the mist, darting across her feet. She jumped back. *A cat.*

Her breath came out in a rush of nervous laughter. "Poor cat," she murmured. "You look as nervous as I—"

The man was on her in a second. His shoulder rammed her into the wall, banging her head against the bricks and stunning her. His hands found her throat, closed savagely around her neck, and squeezed. She hung helpless in his grasp, choking, tearing at the hands throttling her. Fireworks exploded in tiny starbursts behind her lids.

Suddenly his hands were snatched away. She fell heavily to her knees, gasping for breath. A few yards away, half hidden by the mist, two dim figures swirled in a mute, violent dance. She heard the sharp, savage sound of flesh hitting flesh, a whispered groan, and then silence. One of the figures slipped down and was swallowed by the thick blanket of fog.

The other figure turned and came toward her.

Jack. And Jack meant safety.

He is not your savior. He loathes you. Her heart mocked her thoughts, but then her heart was an idiot, incapable of being trusted.

She skittered away from him on her hands and feet. His jaw tightened and he reached down. She blinked up at him, uncertain what he meant to do. He grasped her upper arm and pulled her upright.

"If you want to live, stay right next to me," he clipped out, drawing her near.

"But how—?"

"Griffin discovered you missing." His gaze raked her dirty face and disheveled hair. He lifted her hand and turned it over. Blood seeped from her raw, dirty palm. "We didn't think of blocking the chimney." He dropped her hand, spun her about, and shoved her, propelling her ahead of him.

"That man tried to kill me." Her voice came out in a shaky whisper.

"I know. But he didn't. No one will kill you."

She stared at him in amazement. His face was turned in profile to her. A small cut marked his cheek. He refused to look at her.

He'd saved her life. Again. She'd done nothing but betray him and hurt him and use him, and he'd saved her life.

Not that it made any difference to him. He'd removed himself from her as completely as if he inhabited another sphere. He may as well never have asked her to say his name. He would never make the mistake of exposing his vulnerability again. Perhaps she'd killed the last of it.

"He won't be the last one who'll try, however," he said, eyes still fixed ahead.

"What?" she exclaimed. "He was just a—"

Jack stopped, grasped her upper arm, and spun her around. He pinned her against the wall and moved in close. His coat brushed her breasts. His warm breath fanned her brow. He sounded winded. He looked angry and cold.

"That man wasn't 'just' anything. You were no chance victim in a street attack." His voice was tight, urgent. "He'd been sent to kill you. *You.*"

His gaze pierced hers. His body was warm; his hands pinning her shoulders to the wall were rough. For a long, tense moment he stared into her face, his expression damned and damning, his gaze roving over her features as if confronted by a mystery without answer. Finally he snatched her from the wall and pushed her forward again.

"Now," he said, "if you want to live—which I begin to doubt—you will do exactly as I tell you to do."

"I want to live," she said.

"Good," he replied. "That ought to make it easier."

"But why did he want—"

"Later. When we're in the house." His expression brooked no argument.

At the corner he stopped her and went ahead.

Quickly he studied the street in front of his town house before returning. "This way, if you please."

She followed him across the street, noting how he kept her purposefully to the inside of his figure, shielded from any traffic or eyes. The door to the house opened onto a black hall as they started up the stairs. Once inside, Griffin pulled her to the side. Jack slammed the door behind them.

"Where's that maid?" Jack asked.

"Spawling, sir. I be here, sir," the thin older woman said, coming down the stairs, dispassionately eyeing Anne's filthy face and shredded clothes.

"Send the boy from the kitchen to me. He'll need to take a message immediately. And Mrs. Wi—" Jack stopped. "She needs a hot bath. And something for the cuts on her hands." He looked down at her. "But first, we will talk."

Chapter Twenty-Two

J ack handed the boy the note he'd written Knowles just as Anne entered the small sitting room. The thin cloak still covered her slight shoulders. Even from across the room, Jack could see her shivering. The black witch locks hanging wildly about her shoulders trembled and her lips quivered.

He pulled out a battered chair by the fire. She blinked at it suspiciously.

"Please," he said.

She nodded and sat down, regarding him steadfastly. Such a dirty face, so solemn and sincere. One would think he'd be comfortable with street urchins with earnest faces and black hearts. He smiled grimly. He couldn't remember the last time he'd so misjudged a person.

Apparently, where the lovely and treacherous widow was concerned, his cock had taken over making decisions. Even now he felt himself growing hard. Sex. Who'd have thought sex would control him so utterly? Or try to control him.

He moved to the far side of the room and lit the candles on the side table. Best to keep as many obstacles, tangible and otherwise, between them.

"There's a man," he began without preamble. "His name is Jamison."

"Your father?" she broke in.

He looked at her sharply. It didn't matter that she knew his possible parentage.

"Yes, he could be my father. He is involved in politics." He paused, uncertain how to explain what Jamison did, what *he* did. "In the least conspicuous aspects of politics but, in many cases, the most important." Though she nodded, her expression conveyed confusion.

"Jamison is interested in the letter you stole." He held his hand up, forestalling her predictable protest.

"More than interested," he went on. "Originally he wanted it returned. Now he wants it destroyed—and anyone who's seen it. He'll do anything to accomplish that end. He owns"—he looked around as if hoping to find some way to emphasize the gravity of her situation, the enormous power of the man who sought her destruction—"*lives*. He doesn't have employees or agents; he has men and women in his thrall."

She'd started shaking her head as soon as he'd mentioned the letter and continued shaking it stubbornly. Her dark wet locks writhed like Medusa's snakes around her grimy face. He wanted to haul her from the chair where she sat perched like a recalcitrant child and beat some sense into her.

"I've told you, I don't have the letter," she said. "I never did. What can I do to convince you?"

"Whether I believe you or not is no longer the point. *Jamison* doesn't believe you."

What skin was visible beneath the layer of soot paled as the implication of his words sank in.

"I don't have the letter."

He took a step forward and stopped. She tested his patience and his self-control as no woman had ever done before. "I can't guarantee your safety. It's only a matter of time before he gains access to you."

"Access?" she echoed blankly. "You speak as if I'm a thing."

He looked away from her. "It's simply a way of speaking and it's hardly the point."

"What is the point?" she asked.

He slanted a savage look at her. "The point is you'll be dead very soon unless that letter is retrieved." She stared at him mutely. He wasted his time trying to read anything from her expression. She was, after all, a consummate actress.

"Whom did you steal that jewelry case for?"

"Myself."

"Don't ask me to believe in a coincidence that has you stealing a jewelry case holding such an important document," he said tiredly. "Especially considering your father's connections."

"What connections?" Her surprise looked genuine.

"Well," Jack said in a dangerously gentle tone, "he was knighted for stealing things at Jamison's behest. In addition to the names of good fences, I'm sure he also told you the names of men who would pay enormously well for sensitive missives."

"No." She shook her head once more—in response to his charge or her father's history he could not tell.

He masked his growing frustration. "Perhaps I should clarify our respective positions. *I* do not believe one single word you utter—"

"Why would I lie?" she exclaimed plaintively. "You tell me if I don't give you this letter, I'll die. Why would I possibly try to keep the truth from you?"

"Because you are more afraid of whoever you sold this letter to than Jamison. Which is a very grave, a potentially fatal, mistake."

"I'm not lying," she said piteously, stretching out her hands in supplication. The skin of her palms was torn and filthy. He nearly went to her.

A very nice pose, my dearest. One's heart bleeds. My heart would bleed if you hadn't already drained it so utterly. The theater had lost a star when Anne Wilder had taken to treading the rooftops rather than the boards.

"Fine," he said, his tone disinterested. "You are not lying. You don't have the letter. The jeweled case had no secret compartment."

She could not completely mask her relief. But it was premature. He would have his answers. He'd spent a lifetime refining the skills to discover secrets. She was afraid of him, yes, but she also wanted him. The combination of fear and lust made for a particularly potent combination, one he would use ruthlessly. In fact, he would use any means at his disposal to unravel the mystery of Anne Tribble Wilder Seward.

She shifted uneasily beneath his gaze. "We'll concentrate on finding the jewelry chest," he said mildly. "Perhaps if the letter is still in it, we'll be able to convince Jamison you know nothing of its contents."

She opened her mouth to protest again, but he forestalled her.

"Towards that end I want as complete a description of that chest as possible," he said. "I want to know the names of every contact you have ever heard about who is associated with the criminal underground. We might as well start with what you *are* willing to admit."

"*We?*" She seized on the word, and he cursed himself for handing her this leverage and himself for giving it to her. "Why should you care? Why should you help me?"

"Why, because, my dear," he said, his voice ironed of any intonation, "you are my wife."

It was an unfashionable hour in this least fashionable of London's coffee shops and the place was nearly empty. A pair of merchants with gentlemanly pretensions crowded the front bow window. Their new top hats sat prominently displayed on the marble-topped tables. Their posture was as stiff and artificial as their newly acquired accents.

God, Knowles hated a cit. Nearly as much as an aristo. Troublesome children, the lot.

He stirred another lump of sugar into the thick black brew before him and waited. He'd arrived early for this meeting Seward had insisted upon, expecting the man to have beaten him here. But Seward had new distractions to impair his efficiency.

An interesting enigma, Jack Seward, one with which Knowles had never been completely comfortable and, therefore, one he valued. Too many men became complacent as they got older and more entrenched in their positions. They took their power for granted. One would never make that mistake with Jack Seward.

Jack had always been something of a dark horse. His inscrutable loyalty to Jamison manifested itself at the strangest times and in the oddest manners. Yet, at other times, his actions proclaimed him an avatar of remorselessness, with no agenda but his own.

And, too, Knowles thought, reaching for a little sugared cake and popping it into his mouth, aside from his usefulness, Knowles rather liked the man.

"Do you suggest the almond or honey cakes?"

Knowles wiped his mouth and glanced out of the corner of his eye at Jack. He returned his gaze to the plate before him. Jack looked awful. His eyes appeared cavernous in his lean face. An incipient beard shadowed his jaw and chin. But the most telling point was the disarray of his cravat. In all the years Knowles had known Jack, he'd never been less than impeccably dressed.

"Honey," he answered as if he'd been pondering the query. "The almond is a touch off."

Jack motioned for the servant to bring him a pot of coffee and took his seat. "I need your help, sir," he said without preamble.

Good, Knowles thought. Helping Jack could prove of lasting benefit. He said nothing, however, merely sipped his coffee and looked askance at the man.

Jack leaned forward. "Jamison is trying to kill someone. I don't want him to succeed."

"I see. Do have a cake, Jack. You look positively undone." He held the plate out invitingly. Jack shook his head.

With a sigh Knowles replaced the plate. "I may be able to obstruct Jamison's plans for a while," he said. "Perhaps even until this person's usefulness to you has spent itself, but beyond that . . ."

Apparently this was not the response Jack sought. He ran his hand through his hair, as if in need of restraining his emotions. Odder and odder. An emotional Jack Seward. He'd seen it all now.

Knowles shrugged apologetically. "You know how tenacious Jamison can be when he's set himself on a course."

"Yes, I do, and that's why I want this person's welfare assured, sir, and not merely for a day or a week. Forever."

"Ah!" Knowles laced his fingers across his stomach and smiled sadly. "Who of us is assured a healthy 'forever'?"

Jack did not return his smile. "I want hers to be."

Hers? The interview could not possibly get any more interesting. "Are we speaking of your new bride, perhaps?"

Jack nodded curtly.

"I see." Knowles pursed his lips, giving the matter his full attention. The waiter brought a fresh pot of coffee and disappeared.

In truth, he saw a great deal more than even Jack would surmise. He had agents no one even knew about. Secret people whose sole job was to keep him informed about the nuances in the lives of certain people whose job was to keep a finger on the movements of even more important people and so forth and so on, up to the mad old king himself.

Jack's bride and her propensity for heights had only recently come to his attention. Knowles applauded Jack on his ability to discover Anne Wilder's interesting talents before he had. But he knew now. Just as he knew Jamison wanted her killed. What he did not know was *why*. Jamison's insistence that the thief must be killed on the supposition that she had read the letter seemed extreme behavior even for him. Atwood's description of the letter, a description related in a note Atwood had sent Knowles shortly before his death, had certainly been interesting, but enough to warrant bloodshed? Knowles began to suspect he didn't know all this letter contained.

He reached out and selected another sugar cake from the plate. Fascinating, he thought, popping it into his mouth. The entire affair was fascinating. He couldn't remember being so diverted.

"Jamison and I have a tacit agreement," Knowles finally said. "We do not interfere with each other's business. You're asking me to break a rule which has stood us both in good stead for decades."

"Spare me the demurrals, sir. You told me once if I should ever need anything, I should come to you. Well, I need something, sir. And I'm here."

Knowles wiped his fingertips on his napkin and nodded gravely. "I will see what I can arrange. But nothing will be accomplished quickly, and during that time I suspect more attempts will be made on your, er, wife's life."

If Seward were the sort of man who sighed in relief, he would have sighed then. As it was, Knowles watched the slight ease of tension in the set of his shoulders. Not that they could be said to have unbent. *Really,* he thought in grim amusement, *what had Jamison used on the boy to achieve that punishing posture?*

He lumbered heavily to his feet, a portly old man with a waist-coat dusted in sugar powder. With the conscious penuriousness of the merchant class, he carefully counted out the coin for the coffee and cakes. He did not pay for Jack's untouched pot.

He placed his hat upon his balding pate and looked down at Jack before leaving. "I will, of course, expect something in return."

"Of course," Jack replied.

Chapter Twenty-Three

They kept bringing hot water, buckets and buckets of steaming-hot water. And when the soot and grime from the chimney flue had soaked off and floated on that water, they'd emptied the hip bath and filled yet another one. Anne drifted in the steaming liquid. The hot soapy water stung her lacerated hands and penetrated her aching muscles. Physically and mentally drained, she allowed herself to be scrubbed by Spawling.

She had nothing left to fight with. Someone wanted her dead, and the only one who stood in his way was a man who had every right to hate her, who'd already stated—and with every justification—that he disbelieved every word she uttered. She should fear for her life, and she did, but the fear lay buried deep beneath a glacier of pain.

It was Jack's enmity that kept rising in her thoughts, like a bubble of acid, destroying the blessed numbness. His hatred alone had the power to wound her profoundly, where the last of her heart survived. The combination of hurt and fear finally depleted her, consuming the last of the fevered energy she'd been existing on.

Jack might be keeping her safe for some future revenge, or to be used as leverage, or as a show of power to his father, or for any number of reasons that she could not discern. All she could do was wait and see what he would do with her . . . to her.

Mechanically Anne lathered her hair and waited while Spawling silently rinsed it with ladles filled with clear, warm water.

"Thank you," she murmured, and allowed the maid to help her out of the tub and into a thick, Turkish cotton robe. Anne sat at the dressing table while the woman started working through her tangled knot of hair with a fine-toothed comb.

"Do you ever speak?" Anne asked.

"Aye."

She glanced at Spawling's closed, tight face reflected in the mirror. "Have you been with Colonel Seward long?"

"Two months. Mr. Griffin hired me."

So much for insights into Jack, Anne thought tiredly. A knock at the door sent the maid to answer it. She returned a minute later.

"The colonel be wanting to see you, ma'am."

Anne quelled the temptation to refuse. What would it accomplish? She had nowhere to go. Her parents had died, her dead husband's mother hated her . . . she had no home of her own.

She could refuse Jack nothing. She relied on his sufferance just to draw breath. She rose. The maid had already opened the wardrobe and withdrawn a gown.

"This 'un, ma'am?" she asked, holding up a bright-orchid *robe de chambre*. It was Sophia's. Her maid must have packed it by mistake.

"Yes," Anne replied listlessly. "Fine."

Fifteen minutes later Anne followed Griffin to the little room where Jack had interviewed her before. He held the door open and closed it behind her.

She didn't see Jack at first. Only the weak glow of the fire and a poorly trimmed lamp offered illumination. The heavy drapes had been pulled tight against the night . . . or whatever else might seek entrance.

The thought chilled her and she rubbed her arms. She turned to go, unwilling to wait in this inhospitable room, and saw him. He sat in a chair pulled deep within the shadows. His elbows rested on the arms and his hands were steepled beneath his chin. His head was lowered but his eyes were raised, watching her. She started, confused that she'd not perceived his presence.

She'd developed a sixth sense, like the sleeper's awareness of another's regard. It had never failed her before.

She moved away from that relentless, inimical regard. His gaze tracked her with the calm purposefulness of a predatory animal. He was in shirtsleeves, the cuffs rolled up his forearms. Against the pristine white, his skin appeared dark. His wrists and forearms were elegant and strong. Not all the darkness on his lean face was due to shadows; he looked in need of a shave.

She suddenly realized she'd been staring at him and, disconcerted, glanced away. His intense stillness was not the result of camouflage. Nor did she sense that he achieved it by drawing in on himself, burying the essence of himself so deeply it couldn't be found.

On the contrary, she felt as if she were looking at a man whose soul has been caught in a hurricane, each layer ripped from him, piece by piece, until his soul had become diffused, so thin as to be imperceptible.

He was neither darkness nor light, but he was perpetually haunted by the potential for both. A twilight man, existing in some slender moment of glimmering darkness. *My Lord,* she realized, *I have never seen him in the daylight.*

She had to say something. He unnerved her.

"You wanted to see me?"

"Yes. I wanted to *see* you." Only his lips moved. A brand popped in the hearth and a shower of embers reflected against his clear gray irises. A fanciful mind might think they revealed a fire deep within the man. She was not of a fanciful nature. She swallowed.

"Why do you do it?" he asked.

It would be futile to pretend she didn't understand the question. But how could she explain what she didn't understand herself? So, as she didn't have any answer, she gave him the thief's flip retort.

"Haven't you ever stolen anything, Cap?"

She was unprepared for his response. He surged forward then jerked to a halt as if caught on the end of a barb hook. She backed away. Her pulse kicked into double time.

An evil smile crept over his lips. "Nothing compared to what you've stolen."

She knew he was speaking of the night she'd tied him up and done the unimaginable.

His smile became knife sharp. "I see you understand me. Did you think I was bluffing when I promised I'd have you? Or did you think that when I discovered that the woman who fondled my body with such enthusiastic eroticism was the modest and digni-fied widow, I would renege? I won't. I never break a promise."

Her knees went rubbery and her hand shot out, searching for support. He rose, coming to her as gracefully and attentively as a court swain to his lady's aid. He took her arm and led her to the small, straight-backed chair she occupied earlier.

"Here. Sit by the fire." He held it for her. Confused by this com-bination of suitor and enemy, she obliged. He took a position looming unseen and silent behind her.

"I think I deserve a little compensation for that evening, don't you?" he asked softly.

His hands came down on her shoulders. She jerked half out of her seat. He pressed her back down.

"Easy," he murmured, as if gentling a horse. "You're cold. Your hair is still damp. Let me help you."

His voice rippled over her like rough silk. He threaded his fingers through her hair and slowly separated the thick mass into dark strands, spreading it like a net over her shoulders and breasts, his knuckles brushing lightly over her bosom as he worked. His hands were beautiful. Even the ruined one had a certain tortured grace.

It disconcerted her, having him standing behind her, as she was unable to see him. He touched her familiarly, almost casually. She wanted to read his expression but could not bring herself to turn. It would be too intimate.

More intimate than this? She caught back a burble of laughter. Her head swam with fatigue and increasing tension.

He ran his thumb lightly along her neckline and dipped it beneath the laced edge. She went as still as a hind in a woodsman's net. She shivered. He'd sworn he'd have recompense. Fear added its unique flavor to her tumultuous emotions.

"You really are exquisite." He might have been a sightseer commenting on a particularly nice vista. His voice was detached. Idly he pushed down her gaping neckline, revealing her breasts nearly to their tips.

If he heard her slight gasp, he ignored it.

"One cannot help but wonder how someone so exquisite, with so many advantages, decides to take up thievery as a pastime."

She could barely think. His hands flowed down over her. The heat from his broad palms penetrated through the silk, warming her flesh. He cupped her breasts and massaged them, testing their texture and weight with ruthless gentleness.

Tongues of firelight flickered over her skin, bathing her in stripes of light and shadow. He scared her. She couldn't remember a time when her body had been caressed so deliberately and with such obvious intentions.

"Was it boredom?"

"What?"

His thumb had found the peak of one breast beading beneath the tissue-thin silk. "Was it boredom?"

"No." She sounded breathless. She *was* breathless. She started to rise but he abandoned his languid fondling of her bosom to push her down into her seat again. She began to turn but he braced her head gently between his hands, keeping her facing forward and away from him.

"Stay there," he whispered, his warm breath rushing over her ear. She could judge nothing from that soft, rasping voice. "A few touches. Surely you had more of me."

He set her hands carefully on the arms of the chair and covered them with his own. "Hold on. You aren't required to do anything, to acknowledge anything. Just feel." His low voice hypnotized her with unspoken promises of a dark knowledge she longed to share; it sucked her will from her.

She looked down. His dark hands were casually fiddling with the satin loops decorating her neckline, his knuckles rubbing artlessly against her nipples.

"Well, Anne? Why do you steal things? Just blood running true?" His voice held a trace of amusement or pain, impossible to tell which one.

"No."

He quit playing with the satin decoration. Disappointment and relief flooded her in equal portions until she heard him move. He'd knelt behind her chair. She stared straight ahead, unsure and apprehensive of what he planned.

He reached around her and slid the back of his hand down her skirts to her knee. Slowly, incrementally, he crumpled the material in his fist until he'd exposed her calf. His fingers slipped behind her knee, making small, delicate little circles on the too-receptive flesh.

"Relax," he whispered in her ear. "There was a night when you wanted me. Do you remember? I do."

Her face and body flushed with mortification. "I'm sorry."

His hand stopped for a heartbeat. Then he began touching her again. The laughter fanning her cheek held no amusement. "Liar. You are not. But I am."

"Please."

He drew lazy designs on the soft downy flesh inside her thigh. "You never allowed me to participate. Unkind. One might say discourteous. I would have been happy to oblige you. Service you. But you know that." For an instant an edged note penetrated his languid tone. "You demonstrated quite clearly just how willing I would have been."

Yes. Her eyes fluttered shut, reeling beneath the casual assault he made on her body. *Yes.* She'd wanted him. Wanted to control all that masculine power and sexuality. From the start she'd been drawn to his strength, his power, his control. It had been such a contrast to her own lack of power, her own lack of sexuality, her own lack of control.

"I want to oblige now. Let me pleasure you."

Pleasure? The concept beckoned her. She'd never been allowed pleasure for pleasure's sake, uncomplicated and in its rawest form. No man had ever done things to her just to gratify her senses. The idea enticed her.

She wanted him. Like a moth to fire, his ability to destroy her bewitched her. His free hand lifted her heavy mantle of hair and swept it aside. She felt his open mouth on the nape of her neck. Her head fell back, her throat arched, offering itself to his exploration. Warm lips brushed feathery kisses at the corner of her eye and on the curve of her chin.

"Let me service you."

"*Yes.*" She breathed the consent in surrender. She no longer cared what he sought from her, revenge or shame.

She felt his smile against her temple. "First, explain to me, Anne," he said. "Tell me why you stole."

She started to lift her hands in a gesture of defeat. He caught her wrists in midair, returning them to the arms of the chair.

"Keep your hands there." His voice held no cajoling note, and for the first time she understood that in teasing her, he teased himself. The thought occurred and disappeared, drowned in sensation: moist kisses and featherlike caresses, darkness and heat, an unseen figure pleasuring her with casual disdain. She clenched the rounded knobs ending the chair's arms.

"I'm waiting, Anne." His hand moved higher and higher up between her legs. Her pulse raced. Her nerve endings felt charged with an electrifying jolt as his fingertips brushed between her legs.

"Well?" he asked.

She didn't have an answer for him. She couldn't explain it herself. She fumbled around, trying to find the answer he wanted. Anything. She shivered, stretched on tenterhooks of sensation, needy and gasping.

"They deserved it," she said at last, gulping.

He laughed gently in her ear, a warm and unconvinced sound. "Try again." His fingertips returned to the juncture of her thighs and lightly caressed the swell of female flesh.

She gasped, heeling back. His teeth nipped her ear, a salt of pain seasoning the growing pleasure. "Why?"

"I needed the money for the Home."

"No."

With one hand he clasped her knee and spread her legs wide. Without strength, her thighs fell apart, allowing his careless exploration. With his other hand he dipped beneath the swell of her right breast and lifted it above her neckline, freeing it from her bodice. She looked down at herself: legs wide, Jack's hand fondling her sex, one breast pulled above her bodice that his other hand might play with her nipple.

She tried to find the will to move but couldn't.

"Pretty Anne," he murmured.

He withdrew his hand from her breast. She made a sound of protest. She heard a sleek suckling sound and then his hand was back, tanned and strong against her white skin, and he was stroking the areola of her exposed breast, anointing it with the moisture from his mouth.

The firelight glistened on the dampened tip. His breath grew deeper, harsher. Idly he rolled her nipple between thumb and forefinger. "A pretty thief and liar."

"I'm not," she whispered hoarsely, arching into his touch, her bottom lifting from the chair to afford him better access.

Uncomplicated pleasure? There was nothing uncomplicated about this.

"A thief? Or pretty? I disagree." He nuzzled beneath her ear, his tongue drawing a slow moist line down her throat. Her head rolled to the side.

"I'm not a liar," she whispered.

He ignored her. "I have my own theory, you know. Would you like to hear it?"

God, how could he sound so unaffected, so casual? Her body ached with tension, quivered like a bow strung too tautly.

"Would you?" he asked.

He sucked gently on her earlobe. His fingers between her legs worked as delicately and thoroughly as a watchmaker's. She closed her eyes and heard herself moan.

"May I take that as a yes?"

Her heart trip-hammered in her chest. Waves of pleasure rolled through her like distant thunder, centering at the point between her legs that he teased.

"You do it because you enjoy it." His voice was as smoky and seductive as vice, so low it seemed an extension of her own thoughts. "All of London spread beneath you. No skirts binding you. No restraints. Nothing to tie you to the past or the future."

Warlock. Sorcerer. His words echoed in her mind with an opiate's allure while he played with her body, searing her with need. She turned her face and his silky, fine hair rubbed against her cheek. "Jack—"

Abruptly he slipped a finger deep inside her, stretching the tight closing. She bucked against the sudden invasion. He looped his arm around her waist, imprisoning her against the chair as his finger toyed with the opening to her body. Slowly, purposefully he eased another finger in. Surely she would die. She gulped. "Please—Jack—"

"Quiet." A fine note of tension had crept into his voice, a razor's edge of steel. "You steal because it excites you. Don't you?"

His fingers within her flexed. The heel of his hand rubbed hard against the mound. "Don't you?"

"Yes." The admission came on a sigh.

He stopped. She would go mad. "Please." He withdrew his hand. She sobbed, wrenching her head around.

For the first time since he'd begun his tormenting seduction, she saw his eyes. A few inches away from her, they blazed, afire with pain and desire, stark and brutalized with need.

"Wrong," he said savagely. "You did it so you would be caught. Because you wanted to be punished." She stared at him, stricken by the anguish in his voice.

"Tell me, Anne, did you imagine I would be punishment enough?"

She shook her head so violently her hair flailed his face and spilled over his hands and arms. He caught her by the shoulders, stilling her.

"Well, madam," he said grimly, "let's find out."

Chapter Twenty-Four

You were never my punishment," she said in that naked voice, and he wanted to believe her. *Too bad.* What he wanted made not the least bit of difference.

"No?" he said carelessly, as if her words couldn't matter to him, didn't mean pain or pleasure. "Well then, perhaps you're mine."

She just stared up at him, damn her pretty eyes. She looked so uncomprehending, so lost. Her hair fell in a dark cloud about her shoulders; her one breast swelled sweetly above the tight edge of her neckline; her long legs had fallen apart in sumptuous relaxation.

He could feel his careful, monumental detachment crumbling as he stared into her blue-black eyes. He resented the fact that though she looked like a lovely, sated demirep she still inspired such tenderness in him. Touching her was like touching a raw, exposed nerve. Yet—God help him—he couldn't leave her alone. Just as he couldn't let anything happen to her, had to keep her safe from Jamison.

But who is going to keep her safe from you? He ground the thought down. She didn't need saving from this. She wanted this. She sought sexual pleasure like an addict seeks its opiate. She melted into each stroke, arched into each caress, quivered for the release he withheld.

He strove to regain some control. The control she'd stolen from him in that upstairs room, tied to that damn chair, sobbing with desire for her.

"Isn't this what you want?" he asked. He rounded to the front and loomed above her. She gazed up at him helplessly.

He wanted her frightened.

He wanted to make love to her.

She angled her head up. Her hands still clenched on the arms of that damn chair, just as he'd told her. Damnation, it was like looking at a child's flip-book: the thief merged into Anne, Anne became the thief, both mingled together until he could not say what was real and what was a construction.

"What?" She sounded disoriented. Her pupils were dilated. She looked heartbreakingly vulnerable.

"Moments existing alone," he replied tonelessly, "unconnected with one another. No guilt. No consequences. Just sex."

He knelt down before her. Heated by the fire, the perfume of her arousal filled his nostrils. He closed his eyes and breathed deeply, opening his lips just a little to taste her spice.

Dear God, he must have her. He would do whatever was necessary to seduce her. He would offer her respite from whatever demons plagued her, promise her pleasure without accountability. Pretend he raped her if that's what she needed to enjoy this.

"Freedom is an illusion, Anne," he said. "You can truly separate yourself from your actions only if someone else accepts liability for them."

He'd begun stroking the side of her face and throat with his knuckles, unable to keep from touching her. She shivered uncontrollably.

At least her body possessed a certain honesty. Even the most consummate actress couldn't feign responses like these. It was the only advantage he had in a wholly mismatched encounter.

"I'll accept the liability," he said, slowly rolling her skirts up her lax legs. "I'll take the blame. But that means that I take control."

He dipped his head down and pressed little kisses along the inner curve of one breast while his hand slipped up along her thighs. Smooth, firm muscle lay beneath the silky skin. *The legs of an athlete. No, a thief.*

He roved higher and, finding her heated core, began lightly fingering her. Her breath hitched . . . as did her hips. He withdrew his hand. His fingertips gleamed.

Holding her gaze, he slowly lifted his fingers to his mouth. Languidly, deliberately, he lapped the moisture from his fingertips. Her eyes widened in shock. He sucked the tips of his fingers, letting her see how much he enjoyed her taste.

There. He saw the suggestion blossom in her thoughts, disturbing her, shaming her, and exciting her. She wanted him to taste her, deeply and completely.

He would happily oblige. But not yet. Not until he had her complete submission.

His gaze feasted on her face. She squeezed her eyes shut, all her concentration centering on hoarding the sexual sensations. He eased two fingers into her. Her face lifted and her lips parted as if in supplication.

Others accounted him a powerful man, yet he'd never felt it so. He'd never felt strong until now, when he had the ability to bring Anne to climax. He stretched his fingers a bit within the sleek, heated channel. Her breath hitched again.

"Think of it," he whispered against her velvety throat. "Perfect freedom. Unaccountable. Exempt from whatever happens. An innocent bystander. My victim." He scraped his nail against the sleek nub. She moaned. Her eyelids trembled.

He withdrew his hand. Her eyes flew open and she stared at him in pained accusation. She reached out, grasped the edge of his shirt in her fists, and ripped it open. Lust jolted through him.

"Keep your hands on the arms of the chair," he said, struggling for a dispassionate tone. "You can't be victim and villain, Anne. Only one role per person." He wouldn't be able to continue if she touched him, wouldn't be able to wrest from her some small portion of what she'd taken from him. And that was important.

He clung to the concept, unsure now why, only knowing he wouldn't give this to her too, when he'd given her so much. He had to keep some small part of himself inviolable.

Hesitantly she complied. "But—"

He leaned over her and stopped her words with a deep, rough kiss. He lined the seam of her lips with his tongue.

"Open your mouth," he muttered. She complied like the good girl-child she looked, and his tongue swirled deep within, feeding on the sweet taste of her.

She gave to him willingly, too willingly, arching up trustingly. He pushed the self-loathing away, clinging instead to the sensation of her mouth pressing against his in a long, passionate kiss.

Finally he broke contact. She looked as dazed as he felt. He wanted one more thing from her. He tipped her chin up with his index finger and bent down, flicking his tongue along her throat and collarbone, tasting her fresh, slightly soapy, slightly salty flavor along with that of his own damnation.

"Say 'Please, Jack,'" he whispered.

"Jack." There would be triumph in his gaze. She didn't know why, she was beyond thinking, but she'd expected triumph. He wanted to hurt her, that much was clear. But there was no triumph. There only was pain. He flinched at the sound of her entreaty.

"Please." She bowed her head, feeling stupid and frantic and desolate, struggling to give him whatever he wanted so he would end this torture . . . for both of them.

He lowered his head to her bare breast and tongued her areola with deep lush strokes, finally taking the nipple into his mouth and suckling until she was lost in the rhythm. His head shimmered like molten gold against her white skin. Even the cool silky texture of his hair chafed her oversensitized skin.

"Please." Her body felt as if she were staked in the center of a delicious conflagration, conscious thought burned to an ash, her very will swirling away in a maelstrom of want. "Jack?"

"I'm here." His hands and mouth flowed over her, touching areas she didn't have names for, moving with shattering intimacy and devastating knowledge. And when he took them away she thought she would dissolve, sucked down into an endless vacuum of need.

"Don't stop!"

"I'm not going to stop," he reassured her. He sounded almost gentle. Ever since he'd begun this, though his touch had been excruciatingly gentle, his tone had not.

He lifted her skirts, bunching the crumpled red-violet silk around her waist, exposing her to his impartial gaze. He looked up.

No. Not impartial. Something burned deep behind the glacial coolness, like the fluid heart of a volcano beneath a lake of ice.

"Why are you so damnably beautiful?"

He couldn't tease her anymore, couldn't torment her with promises.

He could.

He lowered his head between her thighs and harrowed her a thousand ways. Each flick of his tongue stoked the fire that threatened to consume her. Each brush of his lips turned pleasure into exquisite pain. Everything he did to her promised, none satisfied. Her breasts felt swollen, her nipples ached. Every inch of her flesh felt abraded and tender.

She bit her lip. She did not want to sob. If she had any pride, any decency, she'd get up. She'd leave. But her limbs were liquid and impotent; all her energy was concentrated on what he was doing to her with unimaginable skill.

That was what this was all about, wasn't it? she thought. A demonstration of his power and her powerlessness.

"Give in to it, Anne." Sorrow laced his seductive voice. Sorrow and regret. "You aren't accountable."

His tongue flickered over the threshold to her body, swept within the folds of her femininity, and touched the heart of the ache. A small strangled sound rose from somewhere. Her own throat, she realized dimly.

His breath was warm, a sigh that stimulated. "Just take the pleasure and leave the rest behind."

But that wasn't what she wanted. That had never been what she'd wanted, despite what he thought. She wanted him. She tried to find the breath to form words between her shallow pants.

"Please." She reached down and grabbed fistfuls of his silken hair and forced his head up. He stared up at her with the face of a fallen angel.

"Be there with me, Jack," she pleaded. "Don't make me do this alone."

He wouldn't be able to do it.

One look into her stricken face and he felt himself breaking apart, his every intention destroyed and shredded in the face of her need. No matter what he knew, how many deceits and crimes he could prove in a thousand ways by a thousand witnesses, he loved her.

His heart had performed an act of sedition, a revolt against reason, a mutiny against a lifetime dedicated to his own survival. He was powerless. She'd only to offer the plea of obsidian eyes and he shattered before her.

"Please," she whispered again.

He groaned and surged to his feet, scooping her up into his arms. Her body was as light and tempered as an épée. Yet strong as she was, he could kill her without any effort. Her fragility confounded him. Her strength abashed him.

He carried her the few feet to the desk and lowered her to its edge. She clasped the edges of his torn shirt and peeled it from his shoulders. She stroked his arms and his chest with a shaking hand, as if she were afraid he would stop her and she needed to collect as many sensations as quickly as possible.

She needn't have worried, he thought, his mouth twisting. He wouldn't stop her if a gun were held to his head.

He pushed her bodice down around her waist, a little too rough in the execution of the act, tearing the sleeves. *A little eager, Jack?* he taunted himself. He needed to go slowly, to be gentle. He had to make it good for her.

Lord, he should be used to restraint by now. He'd become a disciple to perpetual arousal, disciplined to months of unappeased longing. It didn't seem to matter.

She touched him, her fingers fumbling inexpertly at his trousers— sweet agony-dealing incompetence—and closed about his erection with unskilled ardor. Her touch unleashed upon him a torrent of sensation.

"Jack," she whispered, nearly undoing him. Her eyes were closed. The pale lids looked brushed with light, like a mist of pearls. "Jack?"

There was that lost sound again. He knew better than to believe in it. But there was nothing left for him to believe in and, God, at least he could choose his illusion.

"I'm here."

He hooked her legs around his waist, planing his palm down the long, smooth line of her thigh and calf to the delicate arch of her foot. She wriggled, trying to get closer, desperate for the climax.

"Please, Jack."

When had the words meant to punish her become a benediction?

He rucked up her skirts, cupped her firm, rounded bottom in his hands, and lifted her.

Her arms twined about his neck, pulling his head to meet hers. Her body shuddered, raked with need. He reached between them to give her the end she sought.

Her eyelids drifted open. Beautiful eyes. Tragic eyes. "No!" she whimpered. "Please, Jack. *With* me."

His mouth came down on hers and he enveloped her in his arms, holding her body as close as he could—breast to breast, belly to belly, each inch of flesh struggling to absorb her.

"Jack?"

"I'm here." There was nothing he would deny her.

And then he was inside her, drowning in her embrace.

He moved with violent elegance, a big man, a strong man. She clung to him, absorbing his thrusts, passion tumbling her like a pebble caught in the ocean's undertow. Wave after shattering wave rolled through her body, each one pitching her higher than the last.

"Jack?" She sought him now, needed him now more than ever. She clung to the anchor of his big body. Pleasure seared her. Not yet there . . . not yet . . . "Please, Jack!"

"Anne." Her name on his lips finished her.

Chapter Twenty-Five

A nne rolled over in the bed and opened her eyes. She was alone and the perception left her bereft. She was in Jack's room.

She recalled her shattering climax and the slow spiral back from ecstasy. Three times the entire cycle had begun anew with the touch of his lips. Finally exhausted, finally sated after years of thirst, she'd drifted on a warm sea of languor while strong arms had cradled her and the sound of a heart beat steadily beneath her ear.

Too exhausted to open her eyes, she'd murmured a protest when he'd lain her on the bed. The last thing she remembered was the warm wall of Jack's naked chest beneath her head and the soft fur covering his chest tickling her lips.

She wanted to see Jack. Now. She had to see him. She believed she—her brow furrowed in an expression of pain—she loved him.

A sliver of light outlined the single window. She raised herself up on her elbows and the thick blanket slipped from her shoulders. Cool air streamed over her bare flesh. She shivered and swung her legs over the edge of the bed.

A dress hung neatly over the end of the bed. Hastily she donned the soft wool gown and had just finished rolling her stockings on when there was a knock.

"Madam?" a muted male voice on the other side of the door called.

"Yes?"

"The colonel said as how you'd need breakfast. I brought it."

"Oh." She slipped on a shoe. "Will he be joining me?"

"No. He's gone."

She slipped the other shoe on and stood. "When will he be back?"

"Didn't say." The man sounded impatient now. "Shouldn't expect the colonel, if I was you. You'd waste a good part of your life if you did."

Jack had left her. Well, what had she thought? As much as her body pleased him, there could be nothing else of *her* that he would want. "Come in," she said listlessly.

The handle turned and Griffin backed into the room carrying a tray laden with food: steaming, fluffy biscuits and a jar of honey, fragrant rashers of bacon and fried kidneys, a pair of boiled eggs and a pot of coffee. A dark shape darted between his legs, nearly upsetting him.

It was the gray cat from the park. Jack had given her a home after all. The sight of the small, undernourished feline filled her with unaccountable gladness.

"Ah, she's dear," she exclaimed as the little cat approached her with fey and unwise confidence. It butted its tiny head against her skirts and slithered sinuously around her ankles. "What's her name?"

"No name," Griffin said gruffly, setting the tray down on a table before the hearth. "Just 'Cat.'"

He held a chair out for her. Gladly, she took it. She'd not eaten much in days. Her mouth watered. She broke open a biscuit, slathered it with honey, and had devoured half of it before she realized that Griffin still stood there—like a guard.

She set the partially eaten biscuit on her plate. "Am I allowed to leave?"

"No, ma'am," he said impassively. "The colonel hasn't changed his orders since yesterday."

"The colonel." She cracked an egg against the side of her plate. The gently cooked yolk wobbled in the center.

"Aye, ma'am." The Scottish burr did little to mask his animosity. "Your husband, such as he is."

"You're not a valet or a butler, are you, Griffin?" She scooped out the rich, golden yolk and plopped it on her teacup saucer.

"No, ma'am."

"Where are the servants?" She set the saucer on the floor. The gray cat darted from under her skirts and settled like a tiny glutton over the plate, noisily devouring the egg.

Griffin clasped his hands behind his back. "The colonel doesn't employ many except the maid and Cook. No need for more. No need for a valet."

"Why is that?" she asked.

"The colonel doesn't own a house. Or carriages. Or horses. Or anything besides the clothes on his back, for that matter." His pleasant smile related anything but pleasantness. "You've not married a man of property this time, madam."

"I see." Jack owned nothing. The implication troubled her, but she couldn't identify just what it implied or why it bothered her. "Where does he live when he isn't in town?"

"Wherever he's sent."

"Sent?" she echoed.

"Wherever his skills are most useful."

Terrible things. The words spun through her thoughts. She

reached for her half-finished biscuit and thought better of it. She'd lost her appetite.

"What skills are those?"

The smile hardened on Griffin's face. "Whatever no one else has the guts to do, whatever no one else can do. Whatever, almost certainly, will get a man killed."

She couldn't seem to take a deep enough breath. "Who does he do these things for?"

"Jamison, mostly," Griffin said without expression. He bent over the tray and dusted the crumbs into the napkin. "You done here, madam?"

Sent by his father?

She'd realized before that Jack was a stranger to her but not to what extent. "What sort of man sends his own son into one potentially fatal venture after another?"

"A monster, madam." He straightened and eyed her with ill-concealed amusement. "Nice family you've married into, ain't it?"

"Why does Jack do it?" The words were out before she could recall them.

"Because that's what he's been trained to do, ma'am. That's what he is, that's what Jamison made him. He took that boy out of a workhouse." With each sentence his voice grew thicker and his expression grew harder. "He took him and set to tempering him in the furnace of his own blasted heart. He set his hammer to him and struck each soft part of that child until nothing soft remained. And when he was done"—he stopped, his lips compressed into a line of anger that only the need to speak could pry open—"when he was done, he'd wrought himself a weapon to set at the throats of his enemies."

His words struck at her with the force of a heart blow. Dear God. *That poor child. That poor little boy.*

"That's not the worst Jamison did to him."

She swallowed and shook her head in negation, against Griffin's revelation or against Jamison, she could not say.

"He made the boy think he was damned. Consigned to hell for the crime of having been born. The colonel believed it just as strongly as you and I believe there's earth beneath our feet. I'm not sure he still doesn't."

"Why would Jamison do that? Why would you do that to your own child?"

"Because he could. With a man like Jamison that's all the reason you need."

"Why are you telling me this?" she asked, wanting to stop her ears against any further horror. "Why?"

He didn't answer her, only fixed her with a black look and went on. "The colonel isn't a devil. He saved my life and the lives of four other men, men he didn't even know, willing to sacrifice his own to do it."

He moved closer to her, his voice intimate, his eyes hard.

"We were all working for Jamison then," he said. "Not that we knew it. We gathered information on the inside, information against Napoleon's troops, relaying it through different channels back to London. We got caught"—he shrugged—"and the Frogs made plans to string us up as spies. Jack heard about it and he offered them a trade: His life for ours."

Griffin smiled. "Oh, they leapt at the chance, let me tell you. Jack Seward had been a thorn in their sides since day one. There was a reward on his head that would have ransomed a prince." The pride in his voice made her flinch.

"So they agrees to terms and Jack has it worked out that they can't crib on the deal, and in he walks and out we walks."

"What happened next?" she asked.

"They hung him." The insouciance disappeared from his voice. "They *hung* him. We couldn't get through that damned front gate fast enough. One hundred fifteen men against twenty and we couldn't bleeding make it through fast enough." He stared at her as if she held the answer to that mystery and deliberately withheld it.

"Why?" he demanded. "They knew they were outnumbered. They planned to surrender all along, and yet they strung him up anyway. Didn't you ever wonder where your husband got his interesting 'accent'? For two bloody minutes he hung there before I cut him down."

His teeth bared in anguish. Only the sound of her own shallow breath filled her ears.

"*Why* am I telling you this?" he threw back her question. "I'm telling you as fair warning. Jack Seward has somehow managed to hold on to his humanity. There's something decent in him that his father couldn't kill, couldn't touch, no matter how hard he tried.

"I think you could, though," he said, his eyes hardening on her. "I don't want anything more taken from that boy. And if you do, ma'am, I'll kill you myself."

Ever since Griffin had hurled down his threat and walked stiff-legged from the room, Anne had been beset by horrifying images: a man choking on the end of a rope, a boy brutalized by an adult's mad schemes.

Dear Lord, to call what Jack had lived through "childhood" was an abomination.

Fate or chance or mad design had wed her to a stranger, and no matter how short-lived she knew this marriage was fated to be, she wanted it. She wanted it for as long as she could hold on to it. And Jack's past held the key to her future.

She moved restlessly about the room. The gray cat lying on her pillow watched her with knowing golden eyes. She held back the heavy curtain, peering anxiously outside. A grim specter flashed through her mind: Jack, hurt and alone, lying in an alley.

That way lay madness. He wouldn't be hurt. Far more likely he'd dispatch anyone sent against him as easily as he'd dealt with that ruffian last night.

She let the curtain drop and looked around the room. For the first time she realized how lacking it was in personal possessions. On the bedside table lay a short stack of books. A tortoiseshell brush and comb occupied the marble-topped dressing table along with a neat, unpretentious shaving kit. A few pieces of good, moderately expensive jewelry lay inside a velvet-lined box: several stick pins and a set of ivory collar stays. On the wardrobe shelves were stacked well-cut, unexceptional clothes.

There was nothing else that proclaimed the character of the room's occupant and when these few items had been packed away, there would be nothing to suggest Jack had ever lived here at all.

When Jack left her would he carry any sign of their association? Would she affect him, or was she like this room—a way station in his life, another empty room he left behind?

The idea plagued her and she fought it as an unworthy thing. She would carry the memory of Jack for the rest of her life. And she wanted him to remember her as more than just a thief and a liar and a good tumble in bed. She wanted to be important to him. She would not examine why.

"Ma'am?"

"Come in." Anne recognized Spawling's voice and turned eagerly. Jack might have returned.

"Pardon, madam"—the maid bobbed a curtsey—"but there's some people downstairs what come to see you."

"People?" A thrill of fear brushed her spine. Someone sent into the house to strike at her?

"Lord Strand." Spawling's brow beetled with concentration as she ticked off his name on her finger. "A Sir Pons-Burton and his lady, a Lady Dibbs, a Mr. North and Miss North, and a Miss Knapp."

Hearing only familiar names, Anne relaxed. She'd forgotten about Sophia. Shame burned in her cheeks. "Please, tell them I'll be down at once."

The maid hurried off, leaving Anne to drag her hair up as best she could before splashing her face with water and straightening her gown. She started down the narrow hallway. Long before she reached the stairs she heard the murmur of voices.

"What a dreary little domicile." *Lady Dibbs.* Anne's footsteps faltered.

"Apparently Seward hasn't pried the treasury keys from her yet," Malcolm said, and laughed.

"Naughty, Father." Sophia sounded bored.

"It's only true," her father protested. "Matthew left her filthy rich. Can't imagine they'll want to live like this when they could live in splendor."

"What good is living in splendor if society won't know you?" Lady Dibbs inquired dryly.

"What makes you think they won't be acknowledged?" That was Lord Strand's smooth voice.

"You think they will?" A vaguely familiar man's voice spoke.

"I do hope so." Dear Julia Knapp, Anne thought. So fretful and for no cause.

Whatever her future held, Anne had no intention of living in society again. Her value as Sophia's confidante and guide had been virtually nonexistent. The girl held her in no esteem or affection— but if Anne were honest she would admit that Sophia had neither esteem nor affection for anyone—and openly resented her.

No, no one in society would miss Anne and she would not miss them, either. In fact, she realized as she started slowly down the stairs, she hadn't had a friend, not a *true* friend, since before she'd married Matthew.

There had never been time for friendships. Matthew had filled her days with a whirlwind of activity and pursuits, with fêtes and romps, with European travel and ocean voyages. He'd cocooned them in a world of sumptuous pleasure-seeking.

There'd been people, of course. Hundreds of people. She closed her eyes and she could see a sea of admiring faces. With each new season, with each new port of call, with each new city, the faces changed but the smiles, the looks of approval and—and *envy* stayed the same.

She frowned. The doorway to the tiny sitting room stood ajar.

"—blood runs true," someone said.

Envy? Why did that word seem to hover around some yet to be perceived insight?

"I'm sure there were reasons for the elopement," Julia said.

"Oh, my, yes!" Lady Dibbs's vulgar trill of laughter drove Anne from her preoccupation.

She opened the door. Lady Dibbs and Lord Strand stood together before the mantel. Malcolm was pouring himself a drink from the sideboard while Sophia sat on the only couch beside Julia Knapp. They were speaking to a young horse-faced woman Anne recognized as Lady Pons-Burton. Her husband, a much older, pock-faced gentleman, stood behind them.

Julia spotted her first and swiftly rose, coming to meet her.

"Dear Mrs. Wilder—" Her eyes lowered modestly. "But it's Mrs. Seward now, isn't it? I do hope this isn't an imposition. I had thought there would only be myself and Sophia but—"

"Not nearly the imposition that leaving me unchaperoned during the beginning of the season might have been," Sophia spoke from the couch.

"I'm so sorry, Sophia," Anne said earnestly.

Julia captured Anne's hands and squeezed tightly. "I *so* wanted to wish you happy, my dear."

"Oh, you needn't turn that alarming shade of red, Anne." Sophia's haughty tone drowned out Julia's soft voice. "It appears I won't need you anyway. Or anyone else for that matter. Tucked away in all this"—she waved her hand disparagingly about the shabby room—"connubial bliss as you've been, I'm sure you haven't read the papers. Let me tell you myself. Lord Strand has announced our engagement."

"Lord Strand?" Anne said. The man had always been most amiable to her and if his wit was sometimes too sharp for her taste, he'd always been a gentleman. Unkindly, the thought flashed through her mind that Strand deserved better than Sophia.

But perhaps he would curb her impulsive nature. Perhaps she would teach him compassion. Perhaps cows would fly.

"Yes, Mrs. Seward." Strand stepped forward. "I have that honor." *Mrs. Seward.* The name brought the blood rushing to her cheeks.

Julia, darting a nervous glance at him, melted back.

"Quite the *coup,* eh?" Malcolm crowed, rocking proudly back and forth on his heels, the ruby port sloshing over the edges of his glass. "Er. For Strand, that is."

Strand's expression grew sardonic.

"My congratulations, Lord Strand," Anne said. She turned her head toward Sophia. "I wish you happy, Sophia."

"I intend to be."

"Oh, news abounds in society these days." Lady Dibbs had apparently had enough matrimonial felicity. "Little Sophia here catches the perennially eligible Lord Strand, you run off and elope with the enigmatic Colonel Seward, and I—" She paused and looked around to see whether she had the room's attention. "*I* am set upon in my own boudoir by Wrexhall's Wraith."

"Really?" Anne asked.

"Yes." She managed to shiver. "A huge brute of a creature. I fear Jeanette Frost is wrong. There was nothing refined about the primitive brute in my room. He was more like a . . . warrior."

"Oh?" Anne said lightly.

"Yes. But then, some women have the misfortune to rouse those baser elements in the male of the species. Through no fault of their own."

"I'm sure," Anne remarked. "You weren't *offended* by this beast, were you?"

"I . . ." Lady Dibbs touched the back of her hand to her forehead. "I don't wish to talk about it." A little sigh escaped her mouth. Lord Pons-Burton broke from his torpor and shuffled quickly to her side. Lady Dibbs waved him away with an impatient flap of her hand.

"But we've come to wish you well, Mrs. Seward, and, dare I say it?" She cast a flirtatious glance around the room. "Steal a march on the rest of society. We're all simply dying to hear your fabulously romantic tale. You must have been more captivated by the forbidding colonel than I'd suspected."

Forbidding? Though she'd applied the word to Jack herself, she disliked hearing it from another. "I do not find Colonel Seward forbidding," she said gravely. "Everything about him recommends itself."

His severity. His grace. His bravery. It wasn't that she mistook him for a fairy-tale hero. She knew full well that he had indeed done terrible things, and yet he was *not* a terrible man. Perhaps— the thought came with a rush of urgency and power and hope— perhaps she was not terrible, either. A feeling like her soul was sighing rose in her.

"But I mean, who would have expected it?" Lady Dibbs continued. "I cannot envision a man less like your former husband. Can you, Miss Knapp?"

"Perhaps the colonel is a private gentleman," Julia offered doubtfully. She plucked at her lace mittens as her expression grew distant. "Few men are as open, accommodating, and genial as Matthew."

"I should say so!" Lady Dibbs said with a laugh. "He accommodated any number of ladies in their belief that he was a demigod."

Sophia joined her laughter. "How true."

Julia's face lifted. "That's unfair. Matthew never sought adulation. He sought only the happiness of others. He did not seek adulation," she repeated.

"He would stand for nothing less," Sophia said in genuine surprise.

"I'm sure you are wrong." Julia spoke through tight lips. Her usually gentle face was set in stubborn lines.

Sophia and Lady Dibbs traded knowing glances. Anne should have come to Julia's rescue, but she was transfixed by the conversation. For the first time, she heard Matthew spoken of with less than veneration. Or, she thought, perhaps for the first time she listened.

"My dear," Lady Dibbs said calmly, "we all loved Matthew quite well. But we watched him work his way through several fields of adoring young debutantes. He made a career of being worshipped. Only Mrs. Wi—Mrs. Seward here gave him a proper run for his money."

Lady Dibbs cast an appraising glance at Anne. "Yes. She proved quite a challenge to Matthew. She wouldn't fall on her knees like the rest of us—of you—did. I shudder to think what Matthew would have done had Anne refused his hand. It would have quite put his nose out of joint."

"I'm sure you believe your impressions of Mr. Wilder correct, Lady Dibbs," Julia said in as cold a voice as Anne had ever heard her use. "But I, who was acquainted with him his entire life, can assure you that he had no such sense of himself. And it offends me that you should taint his memory with such talk. As it does, I am sure, Mrs. . . . Mrs. Seward."

But it didn't offend her. It startled and confused her.

She was so used to thinking of Matthew as perfect and pure-hearted, that now to hear Lady Dibbs accuse him of consciously encouraging women's infatuations . . .

"If you say so, Julia," Sophia said flatly, and turned her attention to Lady Pons-Burton. The others in the room shifted about uneasily and returned to their private conversations.

"I say, Strand." Malcolm beckoned his future son-in-law to his side. With a rueful twist of his lips, Strand left Anne with Lady Dibbs.

Casually Lady Dibbs linked her arm through Anne's and drew her aside. Anne eyed her warily. The woman wanted something.

"I think we ought to call a truce, Mrs. Wilder, I mean Mrs. Seward."

Anne kept her face ironed of expression. "Are we at war, Lady Dibbs?"

"We might be. Warning shots have been fired. Now we must be careful. Let me be frank. Wars are often costly. I'm sure neither of us want to beggar ourselves unnecessarily."

Lady Dibbs's presence here finally made sense to Anne. Lady Dibbs was afraid.

Three days ago, Lady Dibbs had held the upper hand. She'd known that she'd only to exert her influence to damage Sophia's chances of a brilliant match or to spread her theory that one of Anne's charity cases was Wrexhall's Wraith, a rumor that would have economically ruined the Home. But now Lord Strand, far and beyond her social superior, was marrying Sophia, and Anne, too, had wed a powerful, if base-born, man. Lady Dibbs had lost her leverage.

In spite of her bravado, she did not want her name being made the object of derision. She would not willingly bear the ignominy of being mocked by her peers as a common piker.

"I'll see my pledges carried out," she said in a low voice, "but you must not on any account mention how long it took for me to honor them."

Anne studied the gorgeous woman. Lady Dibbs's pride had suffered mightily. She hated this interview, hated having to seek anything from Anne at all. Her face betrayed her loathing of the obsequious role she played and the tension she felt awaiting Anne's answer. She licked her lips. "Just tell me when you want the money deposited and it will be done."

Lady Dibbs, by freeing Anne from her belief in Matthew's saintliness, had pointed Anne toward a future. True, she'd done so unwittingly, but that didn't matter. The future had never been anything but a bleak, endless black tunnel. Today Anne thought she just might find her way out of the shadows.

And Lady Dibbs, Anne thought, had nothing. She was married to a man she never saw, spent money she didn't have, lived in a house she didn't own, took lovers who didn't wake in her bed. Everything else that mattered to her had been bartered away for her position in society. It was all she had left.

Anne took pity. "I'm sure that anything you arrange will be satisfactory."

Chapter Twenty-Six

J ack heard the strangers' voices when he opened the front door
to the town house. It was an unfashionably late hour. The afternoon sun had long since melted into the horizon, leaving only a
thin slice of magenta light behind.

He faced Griffin, standing a few feet behind him, and pressed
his index finger to his lips. His heart thudded in his chest. He
entered the house and listened.

A burst of male laughter drifted down the narrow hallway, followed by its feminine counterpart. From the sounds of it a half-
dozen people occupied the sitting room. No one posed a threat to
Anne then. He did not relax completely, however.

An assassin would have to be bold to visit the house of his
victim, but what better way to scout the area and look for

weaknesses? Were Jack in a similar situation, he would certainly consider doing the same.

Quietly Jack shrugged out of his coat and moved to the door. Unseen by those within, he tallied the names of the guests: Pons-Burton and his young wife, Malcolm North and Sophia, Julia Knapp and Lady Dibbs.

And Strand.

Like sudden impact on a bruise he didn't know he owned, Strand's presence hurt. Jack smiled bitterly.

It was so bloody logical. Indeed, it was obvious that Strand had been sent by Jamison. But Anne's culpability had doubtless been obvious, too. Indeed, to one not so involved, her duplicity probably would be stunningly clear and her lies would be as blazingly apparent as Strand's function as Jamison's spy. Just because he couldn't see them didn't mean they weren't there.

Jack could see only the back of her head. A lock of hair had escaped a thick plaited coil and trailed down her back. Such a small thing to stir him. A rueful smile turned the corners of his mouth. He'd gained too much knowledge last night. He knew the texture of that soft mass, the cool brush of it against his chest as she moved above him.

For the thousandth time he cursed himself for a fool. Despite what he knew, he wanted to believe in last night's passion. He had wanted to hear honest desire and, damn him, something more in Anne's haunted voice as she'd begged him to be with her in those shattering moments of ultimate surrender.

It was senseless to wonder at the vagaries of his heart. It didn't matter. He wanted to believe in Anne. He wanted to believe Strand was his friend. Well, he'd once wanted to believe in a benevolent God, too.

He had other matters to concern himself with now, the most important being how to put the current situation to the best use.

If Strand was Jamison's agent, Jack could send a clear message of warning to Jamison. Or to anyone else who threatened Anne.

"Good evening, ladies."

Jack entered the room tugging his gloves from his hands. He looked about with a polite smile, as if he'd expected them. Which, Strand conceded, he may well have. The man's intuitions were uncanny.

I wonder if he intuits that I yearn after his wife? Strand thought, schooling his face to an attentive expression as Lady Dibbs droned on in his ear about some triviality. *But then less than two months ago I told him I lusted after her.* Not the sort of thing a man forgets.

But lust is not the same as pining, is it? he asked himself. *Really,* he thought, *I must desist from revealing so much, especially to myself.*

"Have you been fed?" Jack asked, smiling like the perfect host into the uncomfortable miens of the Pons-Burtons. He wandered to a position behind Anne. "May we offer you dinner?"

The Pons-Burtons hastily muttered their thanks and refusals. Obviously they'd not expected the husband to arrive home while they were still busily gathering the sweetmeats of gossip.

One look at his future bride and Strand knew to whom this piece of misinformation could be attributed. Sophia did not look in the least disconcerted. She looked amused. His little darling exhibited the most unusual of humor.

"At least let me ring for some refreshment," Jack suggested, for all the world as if this was a palace rather than a second-rate rented town house and he its luxury-loving potentate, rather than a hardened soldier.

The man's élan was alarming, Strand thought admiringly. He—

The thought died as it was formed, because as Strand watched, Jack reached down and lifted that damned loose lock of Anne's hair. Idly he toyed with it. Strand's mouth went dry. The intimacy and ownership implicit in the gesture was unmistakable. He willed himself to breathe evenly. She was his wife, after all. She was his.

"I must apologize for having stolen Anne from you, Mr. North," Jack said easily, looking past North directly into Strand's eyes.

Damn the man for a mind-reader.

"I hope you do not find yourself unduly inconvenienced?" Jack asked.

North squeaked, his eyes riveted on Jack's hand caressing Anne. He coughed and tried again. "No. No. We were just telling Annie here the happy news. Lord Strand has announced his engagement to my dear little Sophia."

"Dear little Sophia's" eyes narrowed on the sight of Jack's dark fingers amid Anne's shimmering tresses. The tip of her tongue peeked out and wet her lips. Strand almost pitied her. She wanted that hand on her.

"Ah. My congratulations, Lord Strand." Jack's eyes were like coins on a dead man's eyelids: flat and unrevealing. "I know you will be as"—he paused tellingly—"*satisfied* in your marriage as I am in mine."

The others in the room were making a halfhearted and ill-fated effort to drag their gazes from the private bed play being enacted. Jack brushed Anne's hair away and caressed the skin at the nape of her neck with his thumb. His fingers curled lightly around the front of her throat and began proprietarily massaging the tender skin.

The color fled Anne's face. She lifted her chin bravely.

"I am sure I will be," Strand answered stiffly.

Jack's behavior was unconscionable, fitting only for the lowest classes. Strand had always assumed Jack's quality. He'd never seen him treat anyone, man or woman, villain or peer, like this. He might as well have marked Anne with a brand of ownership.

Damn him, married or not, he'd no right to exhibit his appetite in such a bold and vulgar fashion. Lady Dibbs's mouth looked fit to trap flies, and the others were trading scandalized looks.

He had to stop this.

"Colonel," he said. "I have an interesting bit of news regarding that horse you were interested in finding. That racer from Atwood?"

"Oh?" Jack murmured indifferently, his attention obviously elsewhere. He continued stroking Anne's throat. And Anne? Anne's chest rose and fell in a deepening cadence as Jack's gaze bent on her. Far from being blank now, his eyes blazed with ardor.

"I wouldn't want to *offend* the ladies with indelicate details so"—Strand ground out meaningfully and took a step toward the hall, extending his hand—"if you would be so kind?"

Jack looked up. "I'm afraid I'm not much interested in horses right now, Strand, old chap," he said calmly. "Really, man, your timing is ill-planned. I'll have you remember I'm newly wed and all afire to enjoy my wife . . . my wife's company, that is." He bowed his head near the back of her neck. His lips hovered a few inches above the creamy flesh.

Strand, a stranger to embarrassment for nearly two decades, felt his face grow hot. "Jack—"

With a sigh of exasperation, Jack straightened. "No, Lord Strand. I'm not in the market for horses. You couldn't get me out of this house to buy the crown jewels for a ha'penny or Plato's hand-written letters for a song." He weighted each word with subtle yet deliberate emphasis, and Strand realized the message Jack was giving him.

Jack had quit his mission. He no longer concerned himself with the missing letter, the jeweled case, or, by extension, Wrexhall's Wraith.

Suddenly Anne reached up and slipped her hand into Jack's. She trembled slightly, from passion or some other, less obvious emotion, Strand could not say. And then she laid her cheek against the back of Jack's hand. Her eyelids shut. Her thick, dark lashes delicately swept the brown skin of Jack's hand. The emotion springing starkly in Jack's eyes hurt Strand to witness.

This time Lady Dibbs's gasp didn't feign shock. "I think we have overstayed our welcome."

"Indeed!" Pons-Burton said. "Come along, Treacle-buns."

"Treacle-buns" giggled as he hauled her to her feet. Pons-Burton's face clenched into a tight fist of outrage as he shepherded his wife ahead of him and out the door. They did not pause to take their leave.

Lady Dibbs nodded in their general direction and hurried after them.

"I, er—" North's gaze darted between Jack and Anne. His sudden grin was lechery itself. "I wish you happy, Anne," he said. He bowed sharply and hastened after the others.

Sophia alone of the group did not look pleasurably scandalized. She looked nearly sick with jealousy. Strand doubted anyone else would have suspected it from the bland expression on her beautiful face, but then, he had the advantage of being in the throes of the same emotion.

Poor girl. They would have to find succor where they could.

Anne rose too, but she did not move away from Jack's touch. Indeed, her eyes barely broke away from her husband's visage. She looked besotted.

Julia, looking flustered and unhappy, came to Anne's side. "All the best, Anne," she said softly, and then, bobbing her head in Jack's direction, hastened out of the room. Sophia took her place at Anne's side.

"Good-bye, Anne," she said, leaning over and tapping her cheek briefly against Anne's.

"I wish you every happiness, Sophia," Anne said sincerely. Her dark gaze moved from Sophia to briefly touch Strand. "And you, Lord Strand," she said softly, and with a sad little smile.

"Yes. All the best," Jack said, his arm curving around Anne's willowy waist. She canted back into his embrace. Not really moving at all, almost as if her spirit surged to meet him.

"How kind of you." Sophia turned and looked at Strand.

He knew he was being weighed against Jack Seward and that he did not bear the comparison well. He smiled at her. "Come along, Sophia." Strand tucked her hand into the crook of his arm and led her out of the room. He would not look behind him. Not now. Not ever again.

In the hall, he silently wrapped Sophia's cape around her shoulders. With inbred courtesy, he escorted her down the steps to where Julia and his future father-in-law waited. North's brows wagged suggestively. Dutifully Strand handed first Julia and then Sophia into his waiting carriage before ushering the older man in and following him.

Inside, Strand took pains to tuck the Kashmir lap robe around Sophia's and Julia's legs, offering the other to his future father-in-law. Then he settled down on the seat opposite them and rapped on the carriage roof with his cane. It lurched forward. For long minutes no one spoke.

"Do not look so put out, my dear," he said finally, silently congratulating himself. There was not a hint of the bitterness he felt in his voice. "I have no doubt we are even better suited than Seward and his bride."

Chapter Twenty-Seven

The door swung shut behind them and Anne looked up at Jack from within the circle of his arm. Her face was so close he could see little violet flecks in her irises, arranged like a corona around the pure black of her pupils. Her brows were sable and sleek and as emphatic as her nature.

"Thank you," she said, confounding him. At the least he'd expected her to react to his public pawing with disgust, certainly with hostility.

He withdrew his arm from around her waist. She did not step away, and for a second he felt an undeniable rush of pleasure. But then cold suspicion blackened his enjoyment.

He studied her face, searching for some clue as to her honesty or perfidy. She suffered his intense inspection bravely. But then, why would she concern herself over his ability to read her? He'd never yet been able to see anything in her but what he wanted: courage, gallantry, and wisdom.

Anne knew full well how susceptible he was to her. Did she hope to distract him from his investigation?

The little fool, it would only get her killed. He would not allow that, not while he drew breath. He did not trust her, yet he would willingly die for her. Because he loved her.

He broke his gaze away from her and stepped back. "My pleasure, ma'am," he said. "Might I ask how I earned your gratitude?"

"All that nonsense about horses and jewels and letters; clearly you were telling someone in that room that you considered me under your protection."

Ah. But he shouldn't have been surprised. As thief or widow, he'd never doubted her intelligence.

"I thank you," she said once more, her eyes lowered in a lovely aspect of shyness. God, if he could only believe in it.

He'd spent the day collecting rumor and intelligence. He had planned on retiring to the library to devise a strategy to keep Anne alive. But he didn't have all the necessary information yet.

He'd had no word from Knowles and Burke had seemingly disappeared. Now, looking at Anne, he could not think of any reason why he shouldn't stay with her. God knew how long he'd be able to do so.

"Have you eaten?"

She raised her head, smiling into his eyes. "No."

"I'll have Cook prepare something. May I . . . may I join you?"

"Certainly."

He relaxed, unaware until then that he'd feared she'd refuse his company. He glanced down at his attire. He must look windblown and shoddy.

"Excuse me while I make reparations. I shall tell Cook to serve us in the sitting room in—" He raised his brows, looking to her for an acceptable time.

Her smile widened, lighting her entire face with vitality and warmth. He'd never seen her smile so unguardedly before. He shook off the mesmerizing effect it had on him. He couldn't stand here like a besotted boot boy ogling the dairymaid.

"Half an hour?" she suggested.

"Half an hour, then. In the sitting room?"

"Yes."

"We'll dine."

Her smile flickered across her mouth like a prism, its quality changing, lightening and deepening with subtlety and beauty. "Yes."

"Well, then . . ." He bowed as she'd moved past him into the sitting room, and when he went up to his room he took the stairs two at a time.

Anne set her spoon down beside the *pot de crème*. It was not very good *pot de crème*. In fact, the entire meal, from watery consommé, to soggy vegetables, to overcooked mutton, had been mediocre. The company, however, had been fine.

They'd dined under the banner of an unspoken truce. Neither of them mentioned the letter, Wrexhall's Wraith, or last night. But every time Anne looked at Jack she remembered their lovemaking. *Lovemaking.* The word was infinitely beautiful and gorgeously evocative.

Jack had set out to make her comfortable. And since he was easily the most gracious and attentive man she'd ever met, and since he endeavored not only to please but charm her, by the time the *pot de crème* arrived she had been thoroughly beguiled. She'd forgotten, in the light of their recent passionate encounters, that for the space of a few short weeks, they'd been friends and that they'd enjoyed each other's company.

He'd provoked her smile with his subtle and surprisingly gentle irony and invited confidences with his attentiveness. And while in his easy company she'd found a remnant of that vivacious girl who a decade earlier had charmed society with her candor and cheek.

Until she remembered that he distrusted her and thought the worst of her.

"You look pensive."

She glanced up. She hadn't realized he'd been watching her. But then, Jack had been some sort of secret information gatherer. He'd made a career out of discovering the weaknesses of his enemies. She didn't want to be his enemy.

Was this entire evening—the genial conversation, the focused interest, the charm—simply a way of ferreting out the information he wanted from her? If it was, she commended him. He was damned good at this. In its own way this seduction was nearly as powerful as last night's.

The memory caused fire to smolder in her throat and cheeks. The dark fingers toying with the stem of his wineglass had toyed with her most intimate parts. The lips that curved now in such a guileless smile had fed with concentrated lust on her body—

"Anne?"

She started, blowing a little gust of air out between her lips, reining in her wayward thoughts. What had he asked?

"Excuse me. I was woolgathering."

His slow smile called her liar. "I said you looked pensive."

"Did I? I was thinking of"—she threw out the first thing that came to mind—"I was thinking of the past." His smile fled. His expression grew subtly distressed. "Your marriage?"

"No." For some reason it was very important that he not be allowed to think Matthew had been there, either last night or during their dinner. "My family."

"Tell me about them."

She relaxed. "My father was as common as gorse on the moor, though I should probably say 'common as a beggar at St. Paul's.' He came from the docks."

Jack nodded thoughtfully.

"You know he was a thief. Well, he gave up the game and retired to Sussex. He met my mother and they fell in love. Times being what they were, her father, my grandfather, didn't object too strongly when Dad asked for the privilege of my mother's hand . . . and paying my grandfather's debts."

Jack laughed. The corners of his eyes crinkled in deep lines and a long dimple creased his cheek. She leaned over the table, drawn to the magnetism of his smile like a sunflower to the sun's first rays.

It felt good, telling someone about her father. Not Sir Tribble, the upstart London thief who'd married above himself, but her father, the retired cracksman who'd wit enough to quit the game before he was caught.

"Then what?" Jack asked.

"My mother died of the influenza," she said, sobering. "A few years later I came to London and made my bow. I met Matthew and we married." How simple it all sounded.

"Pleasing your father very much, I'll wager." Jack reached across the table and poured her a glass of sherry.

"Oh, yes. I suppose." She frowned in concentration. "I didn't see my father much after Matthew and I married."

Her father had watched her proudly as she stood at the altar. After the wedding breakfast, he'd embraced her and then gone. Disappeared from her life, it seemed.

"Why is that?" Jack prompted softly.

She looked at him, her face troubled. "There never seemed to be a good time for him to come to us or for us to visit him. You know how it is. Matthew would promise us elsewhere in the fall, or he didn't want to impose on Father with our entourage. Then the season would begin and there was a staff to hire, carriages to order, and clothes to fit. In the winter, Matthew loved taking people sailing around Italy . . ." She trailed off. "And then, soon after he was knighted, my father died."

"I'm sorry."

"Yes," she said softly. "I know you are. Thank you."

She had the uncanny notion that Jack braced himself. "Tell me about Matthew."

She sighed. "Most people thought he was a saint."

"Impossible," Jack said firmly.

"Oh, no," she insisted tiredly. "He was generous and considerate and honest."

"But there speaks a fond and loving heart—"

"No!" she snapped sharply. Astonishment flickered over Jack's face. She forced herself to speak calmly. "No. Ask anyone who knew him. Matthew was exceptional."

"He treated you well."

"He treated me like a queen. My every wish was granted." Her voice sounded flat. "I had only to admire a painting and within hours it would be mine. If I praised a book, Matthew would read it so that we could discuss it. If he saw me laughing with a new acquaintance, he would invite them to dine."

With the recitation of each loving deed, Anne could hear her voice grow more artificial and strained, but she could not help it. The words, so long kept inside, tumbled out.

"Why, if I expressed an opinion, he would adopt it as his own so that no one would doubt he supported me. He did all these things because he loved me. He told me over and over again how much he loved me. He told me over and over again how all these things proved that he loved me more than any man had ever loved before."

And he'd also told her how her reception of these wondrous gifts proved that she *hadn't* loved him. She had tried. She'd labored for years to give him the love he so desperately craved. She'd done everything in her power to prove to both him and herself that she *did* love him, but ultimately his doubt had proven stronger than her effort.

She'd been incapable of returning one tenth of that horrifying, choking emotion. And the disappointment had killed Matthew. How could she tell Jack that?

She looked at her wineglass. The ruby liquid shivered in her hand.

Jack regarded her closely. "He would have made a doting father. I'm surprised you didn't have a houseful of children."

How she would have adored having children.

Immediately Jack reached across the table and took her hand. "Forgive me. How unconscionably rude."

She stared down at the linen. It had been the only thing Matthew had categorically refused her. And now she thought she knew why. He'd always claimed he could not bear to share her with anyone else for too long. She'd thought he'd been joking. But what if he'd been telling her the truth?

Images from their past, images she'd spent five years trying to bury, struggled to be remembered: Matthew crying bitterly because she'd forgotten to tell him she'd loved him that day; Matthew on his knees at a crowded ball, laughing and declaring he would do anything for her and she, embarrassed and disturbed by his show; Matthew in despair because she'd gone to the public library without him; Matthew coming to her bed like a supplicant in the temple, touching her with numbing reverence; Matthew savagely declaring her base blood made her incapable of his higher form of love.

A year ago she had believed Matthew, that she wasn't capable of real love. He had, after all, spent three years telling her so. Now she wasn't so sure.

Jack's fingers curled around her wrist. He rubbed his thumb comfortingly across her skin, pulling the words from her. "I . . . I wanted children but Matthew thought I should be older first."

Jack's expression was grave, concentrated.

If she could see the thoughts roiling about that clever mind, she'd no doubt they would weave a dark and tangled skein. She was not sure she wanted to know the verdict all that careful deliberation must necessarily entail because what had begun in passion last night had ended somewhere else. She'd never felt quite so vulnerable in her life.

She was not sure any longer if Matthew had been right about her, but she wasn't willing to let Jack judge. She couldn't survive it if he found her wanting.

She cast about for a safe subject of conversation. "Turnabout is fair play, Colonel."

His head snapped sharply up at the sound of his title.

His predator's eyes abruptly went blank. But she knew him now, recognized the protective shield he threw up whenever she came too close to something he didn't want revealed. She did not look away from that forbidding blankness. "Tell me about yourself."

Tell me about yourself. She didn't ask easily. She knew what she asked and she asked all the same; and she was willing to wait for her answer.

Jack gazed down at the delicate wrist he clasped. Carefully he turned her hand over and studied the healing gashes on her palm. Somewhere in those bloody scrapes lay the answer. If he only knew how to read them.

Loving parents and idyllic childhood, a spectacular London season as an acknowledged toast, a brilliant match, a fairy-tale marriage, and then tragedy. And Anne Wilder starts risking her life for a few thousand pounds' worth of other women's jewels. But was that the correct sequence? Something in the manner in which she'd described her former husband's adoration had hinted at monstrosity. Matthew's love had sounded devouring rather than adoring.

"Colonel?"

He slowly released her hand and looked up. She regarded him with brilliant, demanding eyes.

"I have told you about myself," she said.

And far more than you realize, m'dear.

"Now it's only fair that you give something in return."

"What would you like?" he asked smoothly.

"Griffin told me about"—she hesitated but plowed on—"about Paris and what you did."

"He did, did he?" Jack murmured. "How enterprising of old Grif."

"And something of Jamison. Tell me more."

She wanted to know about Jamison.

He'd never spoken about Jamison. For that matter, he'd never talked about his past. He knew what the rumor mills churned out about him. Whether they were lies or truth made no difference to him, but now *she* asked. She asked and that made all the difference in the world.

He pushed his chair back and crossed his legs, gazing levelly into her inquisitive, midnight eyes. If this was what it took, this is what he would do. If she wanted his heart dissected on a platter, so it would be.

He hadn't meant to care for Anne Wilder. He hadn't meant to lust after the thief. To find that the two women were one and the same only compounded both desires. The damnable thing was that if what he'd begun to suspect was true, a declaration might well send Anne racing out onto the rooftops for good. So he would do what he could.

He smiled ruefully. After all, he wasn't looking for a miracle; he was looking for something much rarer—love.

Chapter Twenty-Eight

I do not know who my parents are," Jack said. He sounded calm and unaffected. *Good.* "Jamison claims he might be my father, but that depends on his mood and what he wants."

He took a sip of sherry and replaced the glass. "He found me in an Edinburgh workhouse where he was looking for his bastard off a Scottish maid. I volunteered for the position. He accepted. Terms were drawn up to which we both agreed." *There. That hadn't been so very hard.*

"How old were you?"

He shrugged. "They assumed I was somewhere near seven. Eight? Maybe nine."

For a second a shadow of horror appeared through her carefully maintained mask of politeness.

"I'm sorry," he said. "The records for those places aren't well maintained. Those on me were lost. If they'd ever had any."

"But what about your mother?" she said.

"I think she died giving birth to me. I'm not sure. I don't recall any women but those from the workhouse."

"No one?"

Maybe this wasn't going to be quite so easy.

"Who took care of you?"

He gazed at her helplessly. Hadn't her father told her what life for beggars was like? "I'm sorry."

Anguish shot across her face. She looked away as if the sight of him were painful.

"I am sorry," he whispered again.

"Please, don't." She looked so damn miserable and he hadn't told her anything. Not really. He couldn't stand having her look so. He started to rise but she turned back to him, her expression fixed.

"So Jamison may actually be your real father?"

"No. I don't think so." He took a deep, steadying breath. "There was another boy at the workhouse, a sad half-witted creature who carried the name Jamison looked for. I think he may have been Jamison's real son."

"But why didn't he rescue the boy if he was his own child?"

Jack's lips twisted with something like pity. "Jamison did not have any use for a slow-witted child. So he asked if any of us would take the boy's place, if given a chance. I said yes." The confession fell like a death knell. Anne's hand covered her mouth in the ancient, intuitive sign of aversion.

Well, yes, Jack thought wearily. *What else would she do?* He'd stolen another boy's birthright, perhaps even his life.

It was over. She would get up now and leave the room. Whether she allowed him to protect her or not, she would be forever beyond him. His hand trembled as he reached once more for the wineglass. His mouth felt unusually dry. He splashed down a mouthful of wine. His eyes closed.

"But you don't know if he was Jamison's son."

Still here? But for how much longer? He wouldn't lie to her.

"I don't," he agreed. "I never will. Though it wouldn't make any difference. I looked for him once, years ago. He'd disappeared. Died, most likely."

"No," she said quietly, as if speaking to herself. "You'd still see it the same way, wouldn't you?"

He tried to read her expression and couldn't. "We had struck a bargain, Jamison and I. I would get a clean home, regular meals, and an education. He would have my every effort to please him, and later my talents would be at his disposal."

"You must hate him." Her voice was low and vehement.

"Hate him?" Jack asked in surprise. "No." At her shocked expression, he felt suddenly embarrassed. He supposed he *should* hate Jamison.

"But why not?" she asked. "He was never a parent to you. He took you and blackmailed you and made you think—"

"Anne," Jack broke in quietly. "Jamison made an offer. I accepted it and his terms. *I* am responsible for who I am."

"Don't tell me you love him?"

Exasperated, Jack combed his hair back from his temples. "Love? Yes. No. I don't know." She stared at him in confusion. "The heart doesn't ask permission. It is singularly unconcerned with the qualifications of those it chooses to love. It mocks the intellect, it subjugates reason, and it holds hostage the will to survive." He was speaking of her as well as Jamison but she wouldn't know that. Her expression was intent as she listened.

"Jamison never showed me any affection," he admitted. "He was brutal and harsh. He manipulated and used me for his own ends. But he was all I knew, Anne.

"He may not have had any affection for me, but he *valued* me. Anne"—he held out his hand, palm up, silently pleading for her understanding—"no one had ever valued me before. No one had seen anything in me but a bit of gutter trash that they could ill afford to keep alive but that stubbornly refused to die."

His mouth twisted ruefully. "Do I love Jamison? I do not trust him, I do not expect anything from him, nor would I want anything from him. I fear him, I disapprove of him, and I abhor the devil's bargain I made with him, but still, yes, I suppose you might say I love him. Can you understand that?"

He held her gaze, his empty hand still held out to her. She glanced down at it, at him. "No, I don't understand."

His hand curled into a fist and he withdrew it. How could anyone understand something so alien? He didn't understand himself, and he'd failed to explain it to her.

"What does Jamison have you do?" Her tone begged him to be subtle and creative and to sugarcoat those things he'd done at Jamison's behest. He'd not come this far to compromise the truth now. He never would have anticipated she would still be here asking questions. Hope fluttered restlessly in his heart.

"Jamison and a man named Knowles are responsible for the actions of people who work behind the scenes in matters of a political nature. I am one of those people."

"What does 'working behind the scenes' mean?" she asked cautiously.

"Arranging things, collecting information, making sure that certain eventualities occur, that others do not. Necessarily, most of these actions take place outside the aegis of government approval."

"You're a spy."

"Sometimes." He shifted in his seat. *Honesty,* he abjured himself. "Yes."

"And that's why you were sent after me. Because this letter that you were told I stole is important." Her brow furrowed in concentration. "If it weren't supremely sensitive, this person Jamison," she fairly spat his name, "would not want everyone dead that he suspected of having seen it."

"Yes," he agreed quietly.

She raised her eyes. "I don't have the letter, Jack," she said. "I never did. No one hired me to steal it." He'd no reason to believe her. She was a thief and a liar. She'd encouraged his regard so that she might keep abreast of his movements and distract him from his goal. She'd used his body to pleasure her own. She honored the memory of a sainted husband by pitching herself from rooftops and stealing from his friends.

And he loved her.

"Yes," he said. "I know."

Her eyes fluttered shut as if she were hoarding some emotion.

"But as I've already explained," he went on, "it's Jamison's beliefs that concern us. You never needed to convince me. What I believe does not make the least bit of difference."

She opened her eyes and regarded him with brilliant constancy. "It makes all the difference in the world to me."

He uncrossed his legs and began leaning across the linen. Hope seemed perilously close to undoing him. If he didn't control himself, he'd pitch the bloody table out from between them.

He could see her recognize the passion in his expression. It intimidated her. He saw it in the watchful way she studied him and in her slight withdrawal. How hellishly amusing. She didn't even realize the power she held over him.

"What is it?" she asked. She sounded a shade breathless.

He cast about, uncertain what she was speaking about.

"The letter," she explained. "What is it that's so important no one else must see it? A record of baptism? A marriage license?"

Her words recalled him to the very real danger they lived under. Even as they spoke Jamison would be putting into action his next attempt on her life.

"I don't know."

"Love letters? A confession? What does it look like? Is it a copy of something or a page from a book?"

He shook his head. "Once more I don't know. I never saw it. Lord Atwood is the only one who had. He was to be the courier."

Her brows puckered with concentration. He wanted to stay with her but he couldn't. He rose, catching her attention.

"I'm going to Windsor Palace. I think that's where this letter originated. If I can discover the letter's author, I will be better able to follow its trail. There have to be footprints leading somewhere, Anne. I'll find them." He moved behind her, heading for the door.

"Jack?"

He stopped with his hand on the doorknob. "Yes?"

"I want you to be careful."

He mustn't read anything into that. "Yes," he said, enforcing the casualness in his tone. "I shall certainly do my best."

Griffin let him back in the house just before dawn. Jack shed his coat and ordered the sleepy-eyed maid to bring him coffee. Sleep would be impossible after what he'd learned that evening. All and nothing at all.

The king's attendant met him at a secret entrance and led him to a high-vaulted room. Inside awaited an ancient blind man, his shriveled body buried beneath the weight of his bedrobes. A single instance when he'd glimpsed this elderly man from afar allowed Jack to name the frail old man.

"Your Majesty." He'd bent low and swept his arm out in the grand manner of a bygone age, hoping fervently he did it right. Apparently he had. Over the course of the next few hours, Jack had learned that the fire of the king's tenacious but unfocused spirit belied the frailty of his appearance.

"Anything new, Cap?" Griffin asked.

"The rumors about the old king are true," he answered.

"He isn't mad then?"

"Oh, mad he undoubtedly is, but his madness is an inconstant thing, interrupted by moments of lucidity. The king wrote that letter, Grif. He writes a lot of letters. His Majesty once had deeded Atwood all of Scotland."

Griffin snorted. "Who'd want it?"

Jack smiled. "But there was one particular time the attendant remembered Atwood taking pains to see that the letter His Majesty wrote was sealed with the royal crest. The attendant didn't think much of it. He thought Atwood was humoring His Majesty."

"And what did he say in this letter he wrote that has Jamison sitting on coals?" Griffin asked sardonically. "Denounce Prinny as a bastard? Should think he might be, hating him as he does."

"I don't know, but I doubt it's anything quite so dramatic. Every time I asked His Majesty what was in the letter he wrote for Atwood, he started ranting about the moral leprosy that has infected the nation since being led by that 'fat disgusting creature.' I believe he was referring to his son."

"What about the servants and like?"

"They substantiated what the attendant said."

"I say it would be justice met if the old king disowned the prince regent—where are you going?"

"I need to send for Burke," Jack said, his hand on the study door. "I want him to go to Atwood's and chat up the servants."

"She's in there," Griffin said.

Jack withdrew his hand and looked around in surprise. "Anne?"

"Yes." Griffin's expressive face had gone flat.

"What is she doing up at this hour?"

"I wouldn't know. She never went to bed as near as I can tell."

Carefully Jack turned the handle and eased the door open. Without turning he said softly, "Thank you, Grif. Get yourself some sleep."

"But you should have something to eat," Griffin protested, his voice sharp with disapproval. "You shouldn't be getting so involved with that woman, Cap. She'll get you—"

"That will be all, Griffin." He stepped over the threshold and closed the door behind him.

A few remaining embers suffused one side of the room in a soft, soporific light. Anne lay curled asleep in one corner of the faded sofa. The gray cat had tucked itself behind her knees. Sleep had smoothed a brow too often of late lined with worry. The lace covering her bodice rose and fell in a slow, hypnotic tempo.

He circled around her, careful to move quietly so as not to disturb her slumber. He considered her as she slept, piecing together the riddle of her past and present, seeing hints of enlightenment where before all had been dim.

Her eyelids drifted open. She saw him and she smiled as if waking to a pleasing dream before promptly turning her cheek into her hand and closing her eyes again.

His heart beat thickly in his chest.

"Hello, Jack," she murmured.

"Hello."

"I was dreaming about you." She sounded hazy and melodic. She was still half asleep.

"Were you now?"

"Umm-hm. You and I. We were standing on a ledge so high you couldn't see the ground below. It was coming night and everything was turning black. You took my hand and told me to fly. I said I couldn't." Her voice faded away and for a moment he thought she'd gone back to sleep but then she began again in that drowsy voice. "I was afraid. But you took my hands and you drew me to your side and told me to look into your eyes. I did and I wasn't afraid. And when I looked down I realized we were moving through a silver sky—silver like your eyes, Jack—and that we'd come all through the night into the dawn."

"And so we will," he murmured, and, unable to resist, he sat down on the sofa by her side and brushed the silky hair from her temples.

Her eyes opened. She reached up and cupped his jaw in her warm palm. There was no hesitation in the gesture. It was altogether unselfconscious. Her thumb lightly brushed his lower lip. "Jack, I do so—"

A sudden disturbance in the outer hall interrupted her. Jack's head snapped around and he listened. Griffin had probably fallen over pressing his ear to the door.

"Grif?"

"Aye!"

Damn the man. He carried loyalty to extremes. Jack surged to his feet, strode to the door, and threw it open.

Ronald Frost stood in the doorway, his eyes red and glittering, his jaw clenched with fury, the primed pistol in his hand aimed straight at Jack's heart.

Who will take care of Anne? Jack thought in despair as he stared at the weapon. Who would guard her when he was dead?

"Now you'll see how it feels to have your own taken from you!"

The meaning of Frost's words penetrated Jack's brain as the gun barrel swept by his chest and toward the couch.

"No!" He leapt forward. The ball caught him in the head, knocking him back. Pain and light erupted in his temple. And then darkness.

Chapter Twenty-Nine

The explosion catapulted Anne fully awake. Her eyes flew open as the cat streaked away. A shadow moved in the hall. Her head snapped up. Jack lay on his back on the floor.

She scrambled from the couch and dashed across the room to his prone figure, dropping to her knees beside him.

"Jack?" Blood masked half his face, flowing thickly and pooling beneath his head.

"Jack!" She slipped her hands beneath his head, cradling him. He did not move.

"Griffin!"

She crouched over him and pressed her ear to his chest. He still breathed. His heart still pumped. Tears sprang to her eyes and ran down her cheeks. She tore the lace inset from her bodice.

"Griffin!"

Footsteps pounded on the floorboards overhead. Anxiously she swiped the blood from his eye. He groaned, twisting about.

"Dear God, please, Jack—"

The door burst open and Griffin hurdled in, swinging the pistol in his hand around the room. When he saw Jack, a muffled curse sprang to his lip. He hastened over and knelt down. Snatching the blood-soaked lace from her trembling fingers, he began efficiently clearing the bloody sheath from Jack's face.

"Who did this?"

"I don't know. I was just waking and I heard Jack say 'Frost' and then 'no' and then—" She bowed over Jack's form.

Once more Griffin swore. "Burke told him Frost was nearly mad with rage. Why wouldn't he listen?"

Anne did not understand. "Why would Frost want to hurt Jack?"

Griffin pressed the red wad to Jack's temple and glowered at her. "Because he holds the colonel responsible for his son's death," he said. "But then people are always placing blame at the colonel's feet, so they don't have to trip over it themselves." He looked down. "The bloody fool. He should have taken measures to control the man. And he would have"—he speared her with a look of condemnation—"if he hadn't been distracted by you. Get out of my way."

He slid his arm under Jack, shoved his shoulder beneath the colonel's arm, and then, with a grunt, struggled upright. Jack flopped over his shoulder like a barley sack. Griffin lurched unsteadily across the room.

With another grunt, he heaved Jack from his shoulder onto the sofa. Jack fell like dead weight and lay motionless. Griffin turned the wick up on the lantern and lifted it high above the unconscious man. With his free hand, he probed some unseen wound.

"Will he be all right?" Anne asked, her voice quavering.

Griffin speared her with a contemptuous look. She didn't care what he thought of her, she had to know.

"Will he live?" she demanded hoarsely. He *had* to live. She'd give anything—

"I'm no bleedin' leech." He set the lantern down and turned toward the door. "Spawling!" he bellowed.

"What can I do?" she asked helplessly. The contrast between dark blood and white skin scared her. Jack had never been a pale man. Right now he looked like alabaster.

"Haven't you done enough?" Griffin spat out with controlled ferocity. "The colonel's always been awake on every suit. Until you. Were it not for you he'd be breathing easy now and not lying unconscious and God knows what else. Get out! That's what you can do."

The sob caught in her throat and she choked it down. She rose to her feet. Her vision swam as she made her way unsteadily to the door. She met Spawling halfway up the stairs.

"What ever is the—good God," Spawling said. "What's wrong? What's happened?"

"Griffin needs you. Bandages. Water. Get them." She climbed by the maid. Each step felt as if she was being sucked down toward hell. "The colonel has been shot."

The day passed in a nightmare of endless minutes. At noon Anne crept down to the study and cracked the door, peering in like a dog at the stable door.

Griffin had stayed by Jack's side, tending him with an efficiency and expertise Anne could in no way emulate. He was there now, dribbling liquid from a spoon into Jack's slack mouth.

A light blanket had been spread over Jack and a white bandage encircled his brow. But he hadn't woken and to her eyes his flesh looked nearly as white as the linen. She left without making herself known.

Later in the afternoon she ventured from her room once more, drawn by the notion that she might be of some use, some comfort to Jack. She entered. Griffin was asleep in the chair, his head resting on his chest. She picked her way silently to Jack's side and looked down.

His breath came in shallow pants. A fine mist of sweat sheathed his skin. She looked around for a cloth with which to sponge his skin. Beside the sofa sat a tray containing a pitcher of water, bandages, and a corked half-empty brown bottle. She'd no idea what form of medicine Griffin was giving Jack, and she doubted he'd tell her.

The Scotsman came awake suddenly. Seeing her there, he clambered to his feet and began stalking from the room.

"Wait!" she whispered. He stopped, eyeing her with intense dislike. She couldn't do anything for Jack but Griffin could. She wouldn't let pride or personal desire interfere with Jack's welfare. "Stay. I'll leave."

She'd returned to her room and a book she couldn't see and a pain that would not ease. Her fear grew with each hour. Finally she gave up trying to concentrate on the book and stared outside. The sun hung above the horizon like a yellow pearl pendant on evening's throat.

Please, Lord. Let Jack live.

A light tap sounded on her door. "Ma'am? There's a gentleman to see you," Spawling whispered urgently.

"Who is it?"

"He says he's the colonel's dad. A Mr. Jamison."

Jamison. Come to finish the task himself? Anne wondered bitterly.

She doubted he would come openly to murder her. Besides, if the man was willing to kill her by his own hand in Jack's own house, a simple "go away" wasn't bloody likely to stop him, was it? And if Jack died, well then she didn't have anything to lose by finding out if he would.

"Show him up."

"The maid tells me Jack has been shot," Jamison said, entering the room.

"Didn't you know?" she said tightly, coming to stand in front of him. "I thought you were responsible for it."

"I?" he queried evenly. He placed his walking stick across the table and began withdrawing his gloves. He frowned as if scouring his memory. "No. I assure you, my good woman, there are plenty of people who seek Jack's death with no encouragement from me."

The cold gray light made a silhouette of his bony face. In the British Museum she'd once seen an ancient gold coin bearing an elderly Caesar's profile. His skeletal face had been disdainful and exalted. Jamison could have posed for it.

"So you are Jack's bride." He studied her with an impersonal gaze. "Do you know the weapon you've wed, young lady?"

There was nothing in him warm or humane. He'd come here and it could be for only one purpose, to push forth his own hidden agenda. She needed to know what it was. This, at least, she could do for Jack.

"Of course you don't," he said. "But I do. I fashioned it, I cultivated it, I polished and honed it."

"It?"

His smile conceded her points. "Seward then. He's my creation and you've stolen him from me. I do not easily give things up. Particularly the creation of a lifetime."

"He's not a weapon; he's a man." Restlessly she paced the floor in front of him.

"Please, have a seat." Her movements, her lack of focused attention on him, on his words, annoyed and irked him.

"No." She circled the sofa and stopped.

Jamison sighed. "I am well aware Seward is human. It is what makes him so deadly. A weapon does not see the shadows behind the target. Seward does. He knows shadows intimately. He's lived with them all his life."

"You've seen to that, haven't you?" She refused to back down from this man's mocking hauteur. She began circling the room again.

Peevishness marred his regal countenance. "I really wish you would stay put and, yes, I have. To provide myself with a weapon. A dutiful son must be willing to sacrifice himself for his sire, don't you think? And Seward has ever been dutiful. You won't mind if I sit, will you?"

She flung her hand mockingly at the couch. "By all means."

"So gracious," Jamison purred. His gaze grew flat and reptilian. He settled himself delicately on the cushion. "But you are not, it would seem, without your own talents. Tell me, are you willing to barter your soul to save your husband's life? His soul, I'm afraid, is already spoken for."

"What do you mean?"

"No matter." A fractional lift of his shoulder bespoke his boredom with her query.

"Explain yourself, sir. How has Jack bartered his soul?" Jack had told her of the choice he'd made in that workhouse and she'd seen the horrible, nearly fatal wound it had caused him. It had healed—God alone knew how—but the scar it had left was soul-deep and hurtful. But she was sure there was more to the story than Jack had related. Perhaps more than he knew.

Jamison folded his hands in his lap. "Won't you sit down?"

It was an order. The first obedience lesson. She had graver matters at stake than pride. She sat.

He smiled with great pleasure. "Let's see now. What would make a man like Seward cleave to a man like me? Have you never wondered what happened that made him so finely tuned to pain, so delectable an object of torment?"

She stared at him in horror. "You *are* a monster."

"Oh, dear me, no," he said in genuine dismay. "I am a genius. A genius of human nature. You see, dear young woman, we all seek pain. We pursue it from the moment we open our mouths to draw breath. You yourself, have you not been pursuing death for many months now?"

She flinched in pain and surprise. His blank cold stare seemed to draw the warmth from the room, the secrets from her soul.

"I see I am correct," he mused, and then shrugged. "Matthew Wilder was apparently a genius in his own right. Look what he did to you."

She would not give him the satisfaction of a response.

"But we were speaking of *my* talent. I have spent a lifetime learning exactly what tender places in the soul and psyche to bruise, which pain to"—he paused, held up his hands as he sought his words—"administer and which pain to allow a man to inflict upon himself. It is a science, my dear. And I am its progenitor."

"What did you do to him?" she demanded, clutching the arms of the chair and leaning forward.

"You underestimate your husband, child. He wounded himself far better than I or anyone else ever could, except perhaps you." Once more his gaze grew speculative.

"Tell me."

"Delighted," he said with a bow of his head. "You see, I have a flaw." His smile told her he knew how monstrous such a coy admission seemed, and it amused him. "In my thirtieth year I was rendered infertile by a disease. The same disease that rendered me sterile also killed my heir and its mother."

Its? she wondered in horror.

If Jamison read the revulsion in her expression he gave no indication. "Some years earlier a former maid had named me the father of her unborn babe. Since I deflowered her, I had little reason to doubt her claim."

"Jack," she said.

"You get ahead of yourself," he chided. "I'd received a letter from her posted from Edinburgh. She informed me that she'd birthed a son and named him after me, Henry, and that she was ailing and most unlikely to live."

He picked up his cane and began running his long, bony fingers over the carved silver head. "I suppose she thought that naming him Henry would be inducement enough for me to come after the brat. It wasn't. So that was that."

Anne closed her eyes. "Monster" was too fine a term for him.

"Until"—he waggled his finger playfully—"until I found myself barren and without an heir. I remembered the name of the Edinburgh workhouse where she'd gone to breed and went there. The man running the place could scarce recall his own name let alone those of his countless denizens. But I was not to be thwarted. I'd come for a son and I'd leave with one. I had the man bring in all the lads of a certain age and line them up for my inspection.

"There were perhaps a dozen. I noted Seward immediately. There was violence in his carriage, antipathy in his stare, and desperation—a wonderful soul-corroding desperation—about him."

For the first time his voice carried a tinge of real emotion. Anne stared, riveted, her hands clutched tightly in her lap.

"All the lads looked up to him." He spoke with something like pride. "They deferred to him though he was neither the eldest nor the largest. He was thin and filthy and his nose had been broken, but still he had a comeliness about him."

The bile rose in her throat.

"I asked the boys one question: 'Which of you is Henry?' Of course, no one answered. They were suspicious of what would happen to 'Henry.' Exportation. Perhaps a brothel. You didn't know about boy children and male brothels? Young people today are too sheltered."

She choked back her sob. He would have enjoyed it too much.

"So I said, 'I will adopt the one named Henry and raise him as my son. He will be fed every day. He will sleep on a feather mattress and he will learn to read and write and when I die he shall have all that is mine.'

"Immediately a sickly little toad with a hunched back called out, 'I be 'enry!'" Jamison's face contorted with disgust. "And from the full minute that passed before the other refuted his claim, I knew he was indeed called Henry."

There was nothing more he could say to shock her. She gazed at him, made callous by his cruelty. "What next?"

"Every one of those boys shouted that he was Henry . . . except Seward. I will not forget the look on his face. He was near starved to death and no favorite of the workhouse gang leader. I knew he would not last much longer in that place, and he knew it as well. But neither would 'enry. I did not want 'enry. I *did* want Seward."

The ugliest of associations formed in her mind, sickening her. Jamison saw it and it amused him.

"Oh, dear, no. I am no catamite. Listen a bit longer."

"I can't."

"This is your husband. Any fool can see you are mad with love for him."

Anne stared at the man. How could he know what she'd only just begun to suspect herself?

He stared back at her and then began to chuckle. "You didn't know? How droll! I commend you, my dear. You have made me laugh! But where was I? Ah, yes."

Yes, I love him, she thought fiercely, denying his mocking evil from the very depths of her heart. *Yes and yes and yes.* She loved Jack. And she would fight for his life and his soul.

"I cuffed the runt away and pointed at Seward. 'You have the looks of a Jamison about you,' I said. 'What is your name?'

"'John Seward,' he replied. But I saw the effort the admission cost him. I could see him looking about that room at the pails of excrement overrunning in their corners, the piles of straw on low pallets, the animal fervor of his cellmates."

Dear God. She swallowed. *Dear Lord, please.*

Jamison continued. The head of the silver cane bounced lightly in his palm. "'Now lad,' I said, 'think again. When you were a babe someone surely called you Henry?'

"Seward still didn't reply and now all the others fell silent. Even they were able to appreciate the act of creation they were witnessing."

"Creation?" she murmured through dry lips.

"The creation of Seward," Jamison answered in a gentle instructive voice. "The act upon which all of his subsequent acts ultimately refer." Once more his eyes narrowed in remembrance. "For a moment, his soul hung in balance. He realized what he was about, what I was about. He knew that if he said yes, he sentenced 'enry to certain death and if he said no, his own death would be almost as sure. *Almost.* On such short words hang a soul's damnation. 'Well, what is your name?' I asked.

"'John Seward,' he replied, and his voice broke and I knew I was this close." Jamison held his thumb and index finger a fraction apart.

"'And, John Seward,' I said, 'if I say you are wrong, that I *know* you are Henry, do you know what you would owe me?'

"'Aye,' he whispered.

"'I call you Henry. Do you say I am wrong?'" Jamison leaned forward in his seat, the cane's silver head clutched in his fist.

"'I call myself John.' He stood like a young willow being whipped by a gale. I picked up his chin and forced him to look me in the eye.

"'But if *I* call you Henry, will you answer?' I said.

"Tears started in his eyes. Tears of fury. I would not release his chin.

"'I will answer,' he said." Abruptly Jamison slumped back in his seat. The silver head began bobbing once more in his palm. "Quite a weighty decision for a boy of, what? seven? eight? to make, wouldn't you say? Ah, you are overcome. Here, use my handkerchief."

She batted his hand and handkerchief away and dashed the tears from her cheeks with a hand shaking with fury and sorrow.

"He did not look either way as he walked out of that squalid room," Jamison went on softly. "He did not look at 'enry. He did not have to. He took 'enry with him as he left. He has carried the weight of that betrayal, that decision, for twenty-five years. He carries it still."

"Mephistopheles. "

"Why, yes, dear daughter." He sounded delighted. "I've thought that myself. How enchanting that you should be so well read."

"Evil man."

"Evil? But think. I have offered Seward the only true redress for his sin, another sin. Do you know he once killed a man with just one word from me? Is that not power?"

"Let him go."

"Let him go? I have invested nearly a quarter of a century in his creation. The earnest entreaty of a dark little hobgoblin of a woman is hardly enough to make me abandon my creation."

"He's not what you think." She heard the pleading note in her voice and she hated herself for revealing any weakness to this man. He would use it.

Something evil and quick slithered across the surface of Jamison's noble face. "You may be right. Perhaps his marriage to you has rendered him vulnerable. A weak weapon can injure its owner. Perhaps I *would* let him go, if I were to, say, acquire another weapon, one as potent and useful as he has been."

She saw now. She raised her head and met his eye. For the first time she was glad of her marriage. She saw in Jamison a familiar soul-devouring hunger. She'd seen it—God help her—in Matthew's eyes. She knew demons. Darkness was no stranger to her. If it had been, she would have run rather than face this man's monumental evil. She would never have had the strength to stay here and fight for Jack. She loved him with every fiber of her being, whatever that amounted to. "What do you want?" she asked.

"Ah." He *tched* gently. "And here Seward has always been such a stickler for fine manners. To find such a lack of refinement in his wife . . ." He shook his head in mild reproach.

"What do you want?" she repeated.

"That letter." The playful note was gone.

Her hope collapsed. She flung out her hand in supplication. "I don't have it! As God is my witness, I do not have this letter! I never did have—"

"I know."

She froze.

"Forgive me any unpleasantness I may have caused."

He called attempted murder an "unpleasantness."

"I only lately discovered you didn't have it. But I know who does. I want that letter, *daughter,* and you, as I have said before, have some unique talents. Get that letter and I will release Seward."

A surge of hope raced through her but she needed to get away from Jamison. She needed time to think. There was something in his expression, an eagerness, an intensity that unsettled her. She didn't trust him. Still . . .

Someone else had taken the letter. Jamison had no reason to kill her anymore. And if she recovered it, Jack could free himself from—

She stood up.

"Sit down," he commanded her.

She shouldn't trust him, but she could see no reason for him to come here and tell her these things and ask for her aid. But then, who could say what machinations he might place in motion? She couldn't think straight.

"The letter could be moved at any minute," Jamison said calmly. "I suggest you don whatever it is you don to do this sort of thing and hie yourself off to retrieve it. That is, if you accept my offer."

"Who has it?"

Jamison lifted a brow. "Lord Vedder, the impertinent pup. It won't take long for Vedder to find a most unsuitable home for it. For a most substantial fee."

"Where does he keep it?"

"However should I know?" Jamison waved away the question. "That's your job, m'dear. In his library, I should imagine."

"But *where*?" she asked, rising. "How am I to know it from any other letter?" She paced before him, her hands working fretfully. "I'll never find it. There won't be time to open all his correspondence, to read through all his papers," she said hopelessly.

Jamison's face took on a thunderous aspect. "You stupid girl. It came from the king. It will carry his wax seal on it!"

"You're certain?" she asked anxiously.

"Yes! Yes!" he snapped. "A single folded sheet of vellum with a red wax seal. You will have no trouble identifying it." He rose and pointed his walking stick at her. "Will you accept my offer? Will you do it?"

He needn't have asked. If he knew about her love for Jack, then he certainly knew that for even a chance to save Seward from his influence, she would have made a deal with the devil himself.

And so she did.

Chapter Thirty

Jamison allowed his driver to help him into the carriage and cover his lap with a rug. He glanced down the street at Seward's rented town house, secure in the knowledge that he had slipped out of it while the staff fussed over Seward.

He rapped on the carriage roof and called out his directions, settling back as the hansom lurched forward. He wondered if Tribble's girl had already donned her black mask. She'd certainly been impatient to be gone. He gave a slight smile. She'd be gone soon enough.

Regardless of the histrionics he'd adopted to press home his points, Jamison felt no particular satisfaction at his success. It was simply another success.

He'd played the role of heinous villain to the hilt. As with all of the most convincing artifices, there'd been more truth than lie in his performance. He *had* found Seward in much the circumstances he'd described, and he'd related that first conversation between Seward and himself nearly verbatim. The only embellishments had involved the degree and depth of Seward's loyalty and the matter of Seward's killing at one word from him. If only he was really so sure he owned Seward.

Jamison scowled and peered outside. A few fat snowflakes had begun drifting down from a heavy, turgid sky. He wanted Seward's allegiance again. He would do nearly anything to secure it.

And the first step toward that was ridding himself of this woman. Yes, Seward would suspect him when she turned up dead. Jamison's task was to make certain Seward's suspicions remained a matter of conjecture. If he could do that, he might eventually convince Seward that he hadn't been involved. He must arrange her death so that nothing led back to Jamison or indicated his connection to it.

If he did not handle this delicately, Seward could turn from an asset into Jamison's enemy.

And such an enemy. Could that be actual fear he felt? he wondered curiously.

This plan would go more smoothly than the debacle Vedder had arranged. Talking that pathetic drunk Frost into breaking into Seward's own home. The fool had nearly killed Seward. Jamison's jaw quivered with anger and self-disgust. He should never have trusted Vedder to come up with a plan. He was getting lazy.

Well, things had been set into motion properly this time. Vedder was waiting in his library right now. Soon that troublesome woman would break in and Vedder would kill her. Seward would assume that in her overwrought condition she'd given in to her compulsion to steal. It was, after all, mad behavior. What else could Vedder do when surprising Wrexhall's Wraith in his own home but shoot her? The mystery of where she put that letter would remain unsolved. Until Jamison decided otherwise. It's reappearance at some future time could be attributed to any one of a number of circumstances.

Then, upon discovering that he'd killed Jack Seward's bride, Vedder would turn the gun upon himself. At least, that's the way it would appear. Society might dislike the cowardly act, but knowing Seward's reputation, they would certainly understand it.

Of course, Vedder didn't know about that part of the plan. He knew only that his every debt had been paid off and that an equal sum was promised when Anne Wilder—Anne *Seward*—was dead.

No, Jamison thought, closing his eyes and letting the rock of the carriage lull him to sleep, there were only two people who could connect him to Vedder—Anne and Vedder himself. And both of them would soon be dead.

Pain drummed dully in Jack's temple and his mouth felt thick and dry. He squinted. His vision swam as he focused his eyes on the lantern. He was still in the study. Lying on the sofa. How long had he been—

"Anne!" He jerked upright. "Anne!" His shout turned into a groan. He grabbed his head, doubling over at the waist. The room toppled over itself and he clamped his eyes shut against the nauseating motion. He panted, counted ten, and then struggled to his feet. Spinning rooms be damned. Where was Anne?

"Anne!" he bellowed, his legs shaking with the effort of keeping himself upright. His stomach rebelled, roiling as he stumbled toward the door. "Anne!"

Hurried footsteps approached from down the hallway. He blinked blearily as the door swung open and Griffin rushed in. "Good God, Cap, what are you thinking—"

The floor pitched up to meet him just as Grif caught him under the arms. "You best stay down," he said.

"No. Where's Anne? Is she hurt? Did he—"

"Easy there, she's fine." Griffin lowered him to the sofa. "Right as rain. Probably upstairs practicing scaling chimneys again."

Such sweet relief rushed through Jack that he did not take umbrage with Griffin's sarcastic tone.

"Frost was going to shoot her," Jack said. "I have to make certain he doesn't get the opportunity. Ever."

"Fine," Griffin said. He picked a brown bottle up and measured some of its clear liquid into a glass. "But not right now. That's a nasty-looking furrow that ball plowed through your scalp." He filled a glass with water and handed it to Jack. "Drink up."

"What is it?" he said, eyeing the glass.

"Laudanum."

Jack handed it back to him. "No wonder I feel so weak," he said. "How much of that poison have you been draining down me?"

"Enough to keep you quiet and rested."

"How long?"

Griffin shrugged. "You were shot this morning. It's getting on eight o'clock."

A tentative rap sounded on the door. The maid peeped in. "There's a gentleman what says he must see you," she said. "A Lord Strand."

"Show him—" He didn't get a chance to finish his order. Strand pushed his way past the maid, his expression taut with worry.

Strand stared at Jack a second before sweeping his hat from his head and blowing a deep breath of relief.

"I didn't believe him," Strand said. "Thought the man had poisoned himself with drink and gone mad."

"You're talking about Frost, I presume," Jack said. Jack looked like hell. Blood stained the collar and shoulder of his shirt, and his hair stuck up in a golden thatch above the linen binding his head.

"Yes," Strand said, studying his friend. Odd, that it should have taken the news of his death to make Strand acknowledge what he'd known for years. Jack was, indeed, his friend. One of his only friends.

"Frost staggered into Watier's Club about half an hour ago, four sheets to the wind," Strand said. "He proceeded to announce that he'd shot you dead."

"A highly exaggerated notion of his own skills," Jack murmured.

Strand smiled. "Griffin, if you'd go and ask Mrs. Seward to join us at her convenience?"

Taking his time, Griffin collected the tray and departed. Jack got up and wobbled over to the hearth. He drained his glass onto the hot coals.

"Why did you come, Strand?" Jack didn't look up from the sizzling embers.

"I hastened to see—"

"To see what?" Jack asked. "If my widow could use some comfort?"

Strand flushed. Well, of course Jack would know. Being enamored himself, it would be easy enough to read the signs of captivation in another man, especially when those signs were directed at your wife. But that wasn't why he'd come, and it hurt a bit to hear his motives so clearly suspected.

"No," Strand said soberly, "I came to see if you lived. And to tell you that Lord Vedder dragged Frost out of the club. I think that he goaded Frost's actions."

"Vedder?" Jack frowned, stirring the fire, staring at it as if it held the answers to his questions. "It makes sense. Jamison and Vedder." He looked up, his expression grave. "Forgive me, Strand," he said finally. "I appear to have committed a horrendous gaffe. I misjudged you. Worse, I attributed my own low tendencies to you."

Strand relaxed. "Thank you," he said, striving to lighten the tone. "But I have low tendencies aplenty without acquiring yours. I actually came to see if you'd pegged it because rumor has it I'm heir to that disastrous pair of boots you're wearing and I wanted them buried before your executor could name me their owner."

Jack looked down at the offending boots. "Sorry, Strand. You'll have to live on your prospects awhile longer yet, I still have need of these."

They shared a companionable smile and Jack offered him a seat, taking one himself.

"About Frost," he said, sobering. "I knew he was angry with you, but to actually shoot you? Most unexpected."

"Yes," Jack said slowly. "But he hadn't meant to shoot me. He'd meant to shoot Anne. I got in the way."

"Anne?" Strand exclaimed incredulously. "But why? Is she all right?"

"They assure me she's fine." Jack's gaze grew contemplative. "Why Anne? I suspect Jamison as having put him up to it."

"But why would Jamison want Anne dead?" Strand asked in bewilderment.

"Because Anne is Wrexhall's Wraith, Giles," Jack said evenly, "and Jamison wants anyone who may have read that letter dead."

Strand slumped back in his seat, his mouth ajar. "Anne Wilder, Wrexhall's Wraith," he muttered incredulously. His gaze sharpened. "But why does he want people who've seen the thing dead? Seems rather an extreme measure."

Jack laced his hands together, his gaze distant and speculative. "That's what I've been thinking. He says it's for security reasons. I accepted that explanation at first. You know what Jamison is: paranoia incarnate. But now I don't quite believe him."

The door to the study suddenly opened. Griffin walked in. "She's gone," he said without preamble. "No one knows where."

"What?" Jack shouted, rising. "What the hell do you mean, no one knows where?" His voice was diamond hard. "That's why you're all here. To watch after one woman."

Griffin turned an uncomfortable shade of red, his eyes darting away from meeting Jack's. "I know, Cap. She went upstairs. The maid says she heard her talking to a man in her room about an hour ago. She thought it was me so she didn't pay it any attention."

"What else?" Jack demanded.

"The kitchen boy's missing his hat and coat."

Jack turned around. "Strand, you'll help me search?"

"Of course. But where?"

Jack was already in the hallway shrugging into his coat. His expression was grim. "Frost didn't come here by way of his own inspiration. He's been seen everywhere with Vedder. And Vedder has been involved in this investigation from the first. He's just the sort of malleable fool Jamison would use."

"My carriage is outside."

"Cap, you're hurt," Griffin said, barring his exit. "You don't have any idea where she might be."

An arctic landscape had more warmth than Jack's face. "Will you help me find her?"

Griffin's jaw thrust out stubbornly. "No. She's a thief and a liar and she'll get you killed. If she's fallen and broken her neck I say bloody well done. I don't care—"

His last word was cut off. Jack had seized Griffin's collar and jerked him close to his face. A snarl lifted Jack's lips. Pain caroused wildly in his pale eyes.

"*I* care," he ground out between clenched teeth. "*I* bloody care, Grif. She's not dead. And I'll not have you say it." He shook the older man like a pit dog shaking a rat. "Rip out my heart, Griffin! Cut it still beating from my chest before you tell me she's dead."

He flung the man away from him and stalked out into the night.

Jack slumped against the corner of the building, desolation washing through him. He'd been searching for four hours and he'd not found a single trace of her.

Strand and he had traveled at breakneck speed to Vedder's mansion. At first the butler had refused them entry, stating that his

master was not receiving, but after a short and violent conversation he'd divulged that Vedder had decamped at first light.

The frightened—and slightly bruised—man had sworn he'd
never seen his master so frantic to be gone or so adamant that his
departure be secret.

Jack's relief at discovering Vedder wasn't stalking Anne was
short-lived. He and Strand divided their search; Strand had gone
looking among the ton and Jack had gone to the Norths' town
house. Not only was she not there, neither were the Norths.
They'd left for a house party late in the afternoon and no, Anne
had most definitely not been with them.

He'd returned to his address and scoured the streets, asking the
vendors and shopkeepers, the street sweepers and the watchman,
if they'd seen a slight youngster in a torn coat and hat.

None had. But then their eyes were earthbound, and she,
she flew.

Each corner he took was preceded by a moment of dread as he
wondered if he would find Anne, broken like an arrow-struck
dove, lying crumpled on the wet stone. Each corner he took
brought relief and a renewal of his determination to find her. But
hour after hour of fruitless searching ground him down with the
certainty that she'd fled from him.

His head throbbed and his vision grew bleary and still he kept
looking. Looking until he had to admit that Griffin had been
right. He'd no direction to follow, no leads to trace. And so he'd
come back here.

He mounted the steps, failure and fear his unfamiliar companions, and let himself in. Spawling shuffled forward and took
his coat.

"Thank you. Where's Griffin and Lord Strand?" he asked wearily, expecting no good news. Without vanity he knew himself to
be the best tracker and most intuitive hunter in England. If he
could not find her, no one could.

"Both come and gone out again twice now, sir. There's a fire in the study. I'll have Cook make you something to eat," she said, bobbing a curtsey and hurrying away.

He walked into the study. A blaze crackled merrily in the hearth mocking his anguish. He stared down into its flames. Light and shadow licked his face.

Dear God, let her be safe. The prayer rose from the center of his soul, where his heart had always remained constant to itself. *Please God. Please.*

He heard the front door open. Griffin or Strand, he thought incuriously. A soft footfall came down the hall and paused.

"Jack."

He swung around. Anne stood in the open door, staring at him with huge, fervent eyes and—blessed Lord. A tear. "Jack, you're all right?" she whispered.

"Yes." His voice was hoarser than usual. *Now I am.*

She broke and pitched herself into his arms. He clamped her to him with a sense of relief so intense he would have fallen if he hadn't been holding her.

"Oh, dear God," she said with an odd hitch in her voice, her eyes traveling greedily over his face. "I was so worried. I thought you—Oh!" She rained little kisses over his cheeks and eyes and mouth. He closed his eyes.

He'd never experienced anything like it in his life, the pure joy she gave him. He lifted her high in his arms, uncertain whether he could ever let her go when suddenly she began to wiggle.

"Wait!" she said breathlessly. "I forgot for a minute. Wait!" She fought her hand into her pocket and pulled a thick, folded sheet of paper free. A broken red wax seal was still on it.

"Look what I've found," she said.

Chapter Thirty-One

Slowly Jack let Anne slide down his body, but he wouldn't let her go too far. He looked at the sheet of paper in her hand and then at her. "Is that what I think it is?"

She nodded eagerly.

"Where did you get it?"

"In Jamison's house. In his study."

His expression turned incredulous.

"He came here while you were . . ." The desolation that had wrapped around her when she'd seen Jack so still once more closed her throat. She tried again. "I thought you might not live."

Something of her anguish must have been reflected in her eyes for he stroked her cheeks with the back of his fingers.

"I'm sorry." He was always apologizing for his pain. "Tell me about Jamison."

And so she told him about how Jamison had come and what he had said and as she related her story, and therefore necessarily his, Jack studied her face intently, as if to penetrate her heart. Which, she thought bemusedly, he'd already done.

"Jamison told me Vedder was in possession of the letter," Anne finished. "He offered me a deal if I would steal it for him. I agreed. As soon as he left I nabbed some of the kitchen boy's clothes and climbed up the drainpipe leading to the roof."

Her words pricked a flash of amusement from him. "And . . . ?"

"I knew where Vedder lived and I headed for his house. But as I went something nagged at me."

A few strands of unruly hair fell across her brow. Jack brushed it from her face, tucking it behind her ear. "Yes?" he prompted.

"I was actually on Vedder's roof before I realized what it was," she said. "When Jamison sent me to Vedder's to steal the letter, I'd protested that I wouldn't be able to find it among all the correspondence bound to be in his study. Jamison grew impatient and described for me a single folded vellum sheet with a wax seal. But you'd told me that *no one had ever seen the letter*."

"Wise, wonderfully clever little thief."

"So I knew Jamison had seen it and assumed that having seen it, he would never let it out of his possession. And"—her voice dropped modestly—"since he expected me to be robbing Lord Vedder, he wouldn't be expecting me to rob him. So I did."

Admiration filled Jack's smile. "Where were you when I needed someone at Versailles?" he asked, shaking his head—and then the smile died. A grave expression replaced it.

"What?" she asked. "What is wrong?"

He looked down at her. "You might have been killed. You were *supposed* to have been killed. That's why Jamison sent you there. I suspect Vedder was to have done it. Happily, while a great ass, Vedder is not a murderer. Which would surprise Jamison," Jack said with a touch of bitter humor. "He has never understood people's odd reticence about killing their fellow man."

"But why would he want me dead if he knew I didn't have it and never did have it?" she asked in confusion.

He placed his hands on her shoulders. "Because he's mad, Anne," he said seriously. "I think he killed Atwood to keep his possession of that letter secret. You were the only one who knew that the letter wasn't in the jewelry chest you stole. Only you knew Jamison was lying and, too, Jamison wanted the letter to be thought irrecoverable. That's why as soon as I came close to catching you, Jamison began pressuring me to kill you. He didn't want anyone questioning you."

She stared up into his eyes. Killer's eyes, she originally thought them. Yet she could not find it in her to be afraid.

Gently Jack tipped her chin up with his finger. "I wasn't going to, Anne. I was never going to kill you. I'm not an assassin, no matter what he told you." He gazed deeply into her eyes, his expression growing more and more intent.

"What deal did Jamison offer you, Anne?"

She tried to look away, but he was having none of it. He held her chin still. "Anne?"

"Jamison promised that if I stole the letter, he would release his hold on you," she said gruffly.

"And you believed him?" Amazement lifted Jack's brows. "But then," he went on, "you do not know him as I do. He will never willingly relinquish the hold he assumes he has on me."

"He has to," she said, frightened. They were so close. Something wondrous and rare and fine seemed just within grasp. She wouldn't let Jamison destroy it.

"No, he doesn't." Jack shook his head. "He doesn't have to release or hold me. He doesn't *have* me. I'm not his creature, Anne. I repaid any debt I owed him long ago. But I realized it and he never did. I can walk away at any time."

"Is that true?" she whispered, wanting desperately to believe him.

"Yes," he said somberly. "I'm so sorry you put yourself in danger because of Jamison's delusions. But, God help me, to know that you—" He stopped. Slowly he withdrew his hands from her face, forcing them to his sides.

She cared for him. She risked her life to save him. Once he'd thought he wanted to act as her knight in shining armor. He'd never expected her to take that part, to dare the dragon, in the guise of Jamison, on his behalf.

The world seemed suddenly unfamiliar and alien and far too fragile and far too precious. He'd never wanted to live quite so much as he wanted to at that moment.

Because he wanted every moment, every second heaven would allow him in order to spend them with her.

He looked into her face, so dear and so perplexed. She didn't even know what she'd given him. She might not even know what she'd admitted.

He needed to be careful, to be patient.

"All for this letter," he said, hoping to distract himself from the desire to haul her into his arms. He must not frighten her. "I think we deserve to see what's in it, don't you?"

"Yes." She moved to the table that acted as his desk. "It's too dark in here."

He picked up the lantern on the sideboard and lifted it high, spreading a circle of illumination over the tabletop. Carefully she unfolded the letter, spreading open the luxurious ivory vellum.

The salutation and few dark lines were penned in an elegant, firm hand. Atwood, Jack suspected, had acted as His Majesty's scribe. But the thin, scrawled initial on the bottom was uniquely and familiarly the king's own, even if it was just the one initial.

Together they read the few written lines. Anne looked up first.

"Can this be what Lord Atwood died for? What Jamison would have killed me for to keep secret?" she asked in a shocked and confused voice. But then, Anne knew nothing of secret agencies and political intrigue, the power of innuendo and insinuation. "My God. Whatever shall we do with it?"

"We will see that it's delivered."

It was nearly dawn before Jack finished making arrangements and sending messages. Anne had curled up on the couch and fallen asleep. The sound of her deep, even breathing had kept him company through the loneliest hours of the night.

Griffin crept in once, just after midnight, bringing a pitcher of water and a towel. He left silently, perhaps understanding that his misplaced loyalty had very nearly cost Jack the one thing in his life he'd ever truly valued.

Wearily Jack rubbed the back of his neck and rose from his chair. His eyes ached and his mouth was cottony and he smelled rank, he thought with a sniff.

He shed his shirt and tossed it to a chair before filling the basin and dipping his hands into the cool water. Quietly he sluiced his face and upper body with water, scrubbed away dried flakes of blood and dirt, and toweled himself off. His skin pebbled with gooseflesh in the cold, dark room.

He walked stiffly to the window and pulled open the heavy drapes. Sunlight exploded into the small room like visual poetry. It poured through the glass panes, drenching everything in golden light, sweeping away the shadows and brushing each object it touched with color and warmth. The air itself sparkled and danced as tiny dust motes careened crazily in the sun shafts.

Jack lifted his face, relishing the soft radiance cloaking his skin and heating his chilled flesh. He sighed with deep, ineffable pleasure and inhaled deeply. The toasted air smelled clean. He'd spent too much of his life in darkness and in shadows. He craved the light.

He was standing thus, luxuriating in the soporific warmth, when she touched him. His eyelids parted slowly, as if he were afraid her touch was a dream and opening his eyes would dispel it. He remained motionless as her fingertips explored the span of his shoulders, followed the contour of a muscle, and dropped to describe the shallow valley of his spine.

"Anne." He turned and when he saw her, he couldn't speak. She took his breath away.

He had, he realized with a sense of wonder, never seen her in full daylight. Always their encounters had occurred during the fringes of the night: in twilight, just before dawn, or in the darkest hour of midnight. But now she stood in sunlight and she was beautiful.

Her hair was not black but sable with rich, plummy strands gleaming against the foil of the white shirt she still wore. Her face, far from being milky white, was suffused with the most delicate flush of pink, like the heart of a seashell. Only her eyes remained the same in darkness or in light, being a deep, rich indigo.

"Anne," he finally managed to repeat.

"Yes?" Her voice sounded far off, quizzical.

"Touch me, Anne." He hadn't meant to say that but it must have been the right thing because her luscious, tender mouth, a mouth he'd always thought misplaced in that stern and handsome face, broke into a brilliant smile.

"Yes." She lifted both hands and slowly skimmed her palms down over his chest. He sighed with pleasure. She stroked him in one long, luxurious sweep, coming to rest low on his belly, the heels of her hands on the waistband of his trousers.

"Jack?" She sounded tentative, a bit breathless.

"Yes."

"Make love to me." She said the words with delicious enjoyment, rolling them across her tongue with sybaritic pleasure. *"Make love to me."*

"Yes." His arms enfolded her, pulling her into his embrace, his mouth covering hers. His head spun with the richness of her response, the sweet abandon with which she opened her lips. He kissed her as if he would siphon her soul from between her lips.

He did not ask why she wanted this. He did not want to know why. She might leave him tomorrow or within an hour of seeing their plan come to fruition. She might be slaking the undeniable desire she felt for him, hoping to purge it so she *could* leave him. She might try to disclaim her feelings for him. Whatever her reason, he didn't want to know it.

It might destroy him.

He lifted his head and cupped her delicately shaped skull in his hand, holding it to his chest. She whispered little kisses along his collarbone and rubbed her satiny cheek against his throat. Her hair, warmed with the sun's blandishments, slipped beneath his chin and tangled in his incipient beard.

She tugged at his neck and he looked down. Her face was tilting up toward his, wanting more kisses. He wanted more, too.

Her mouth was carnal bribery. She chewed delicately on his lower lip, touched the tip of her tongue into the corner of his mouth, and when he groaned in response, she lapped into the hot interior. It was all he could do to stand. His whole body quaked with his efforts at self-control. But he'd never known much self-control where she was concerned and he didn't know much now.

He looped his arm around her waist and pulled her hips against his. She arched back, accentuating the pressure. He bit down in pain-spiked pleasure as his member went rock hard. Instinctively she rubbed her hips across his erection.

He caught her upper arms, staring into her eyes. "I want you," he said. "I want to be inside you. I want to be so deeply inside you I can feel your pulse, feel every breath you take."

She answered without words, twisting her arms free and slowly undoing each of the fastenings holding her shirt together. When she'd finished, she looked up shyly. The open shirtfront revealed the deep cleft between her breasts but her nipples were still covered.

He wanted her naked. He flipped back the edges of the shirt, exposing her small round breasts. He rubbed his thumb over one nipple. It was velvety, the skin there a little thicker, a little tougher, made to be suckled.

She caught the hand on her breast and held it still, staring up at him, her expression suddenly uncomfortable.

Did she want him to stop? he wondered. He wouldn't do anything she didn't want . . . He drew his hand away and pulled her to him. She'd liked kisses. Well, he would kiss her until they both fainted for lack of breath.

She responded eagerly. Her tongue tangled with his in hot intimacy, fierce and demanding. But something was still not right. There was a subtle desperation in her response, her kisses felt like pleas. He lifted his head.

"What do you want?" he asked, staring into her pretty, unfathomable blue eyes. "How can I please you?"

She blushed. Damned if she didn't blush, a furious rose color that began on the top of her breast and spread with riveting swiftness to her throat and cheeks.

She glanced away, obviously distressed. Tenderness and fierce protectiveness washed through him.

"Your mouth," she mumbled. She raised a hand and her fingers pattered lightly over his lips. "You kissed me."

"Yes," he breathed.

Her gaze was still averted from his, but her hand had drifted down between them. Delicately it brushed across her nipple. "Here."

Lord. He heard a sound of arousal rise from deep in his throat.

"Oh, Jack," she muttered miserably, "it was so much easier as the thief. When I had a mask. She could be bold. She took what she . . . I could—"

Jesus. Along with the white-hot desire her words set afire, a vague, unsettling suspicion rose.

"Anne," he said quietly, studying her intently, "didn't Matthew ever ask what pleased you?"

She shook her head. He frowned. He knew the upper classes adhered to odd and seemingly masochistic rituals where matrimonial sex was concerned, but to what extent had Matthew carried it?

"Did he"—Jack forced the words to come calmly—"did he make demands on you that you were uncomfortable with?"

"No."

He contained his relief.

"Did you ever tell him what you liked, what pleased you?" He hesitated. "Did he try to please you?"

"God, yes." He could barely hear her. "But—"

He didn't understand. "But what, Anne?" He smoothed the rippling hair from her temple. "What?"

"We didn't do what you and I . . . Sometimes he couldn't . . ." She let each hint die miserably. She tried again. "He was so gentle and . . . I was afraid that I would offend . . . I didn't know what he . . . And the one time I tried to please him, he was horrified." She struggled on. "That wasn't what he wanted from me. That wasn't love. It was lust, he said. So I didn't do anything again." Her eyes pleaded with him to understand.

He did. He understood too well. No wonder she'd responded so hungrily to his touch. She'd been starved of physical love. Though experienced in the sexual act, she'd never celebrated the pure sensual joy of it.

"I'm not a saint, Anne," he said. "I'd devour you if I could. I'd like to feast on your body and I'd have you feast on mine. I want to hear you panting in my ear and calling my name. I want you to use my body for your pleasure because that will make my pleasure greater. I'll take whatever you'll allow, Anne, and then I'll probably take more. That's what I want, Anne. Now what do you want?"

She did not hesitate. "You."

He scooped her and carried her to the couch. "Sometime," he said tightly, "we will have to make love in a bed."

The couch's back was to the window; the light was too far away. He kicked the end, spinning it around on the hardwood floor, and then shoved it out into the light.

"I want to see you, to feel you, all of you on all of me," he said roughly. He deposited her in the center of the thick, lumpy cushions and, as she watched, undid his trousers. He lifted his foot and dragged his boot off and repeated the procedure with the other. Then he stripped himself of his trousers and finally came round before her.

The muscles beneath the fine-grained skin flowed and tensed with fluent suppleness. His shoulders were broad and his hips were narrow. He was altogether lovely and powerful and masculine. *He is as fine as a blooded stallion*, Anne thought. *Straight as a lance and tempered like steel.*

His body was scarred, he knew. There were bones that had been broken and never knit properly. His skin was too leathery and he wasn't a young man any longer. But he wanted her. He loved her. He lifted his hands, palms out. "Such as I am, I'm yours."

"I want you to make love to me," she said. That is what she wanted. That thing they'd done before, that merging of physical desire and heart's pleasure. "Let me make love to you."

He bracketed her face in both his hands, tilted her chin up with his thumbs, and gave her another of those long, heated kisses. She clasped his shoulders and pulled him until he toppled beside her, breaking their kiss.

Slowly he undressed her, peeling the shirt from her shoulders and pushing the baggy breeches from her hips. His hands were everywhere: gliding, skimming, and burnishing. He touched her in a thousand places and with a thousand degrees of sensuality. And when his hands were done, his mouth took over.

He grazed over every inch of exposed flesh, whispering across her belly, polishing the pulse in her inner thigh with his lips, and nibbling on the taut skin beneath her breast. When he finally took her nipple into his mouth and suckled, her body jerked, arching up from the couch.

"Yes," he whispered as in answer to some request she'd made.

He rolled over, carrying her above him, and set her thighs on either side of his dense, muscled body, spreading her wide. His eyes held hers as he reached between them and positioned the head of his member at her feminine opening. "Take me inside of you. Whatever you want of me," he commanded in a strained voice.

His words released within her a sense of unimaginable potency. She sank onto his shaft, hissing a little as she adjusted to his breadth and size.

"I want you," she said. She wiggled, trying to take more of him. His hands clamped on her hips. He trembled beneath her, filling her, thick and strong and hers.

"There's more," he said. "Much more." He began to move, lifting his hips and letting them fall, each little movement sliding her teasingly along his shaft.

"More," she demanded, surprising herself. He smiled with lazy triumph and complied. His thrusts grew stronger, deeper, harder. She rode the rhythm, bracing her palms against his flat, rippling belly. The tension built inside her. The feeling of being near completion, of incredible pleasure just out of her reach, became almost unbearable.

"God, I can't . . ." he whispered.

She looked down at him. Sweat cloaked his body. His eyes were closed. His expression was strained, fierce and determined.

"More," she said.

Jack laughed and his laugh turned into a groan. She looked so adorably insistent, impaled on his cock, her face tensing with each of his thrusts. But she was driving him beyond madness.

So, she wanted more, did she? He rolled over again, capturing her body beneath his. Lacing his fingers with hers, he stretched her arms high over her head and held them there. She panted a little. Her pupils were like onyx stars.

"You want more?" he asked, his voice ragged.

"Yes," she whispered.

"Yes," he echoed, and thrust. Hard.

She gave a little gasp. He thrust again. Her gasp turned into a low sound of feline satisfaction.

"Please. I need it," she muttered, her hips meeting his thrust, her body straining. "Now. Please. It's too much."

"No."

He kept it up a long time, moving over her, pumping in and out of her body, and each time he felt her about to come, he backed off until the moment passed. And then he would start all over again.

Not once but three times he brought her to the edge until finally, the last time, as he held her squirming body beneath his big one, her eyes snapped open. Her feverish, accusing gaze riveted on his face.

"Now." She sounded defiant as she jerked her hands free of his. She twined her arms around his neck and lifted her body, crushing her soft breasts against his chest. Her thighs wrapped high on his flanks, and deep within her, he felt her muscles contract like a hot, wet silk fist around him.

"Yes."

"Yes," she echoed almost angrily, hitching her hips.

Only another thrust, she thought frantically. Just another thrust. Just a few more seconds. His head arched back and his lips curled, revealing his teeth clamped tightly together.

He looked so strong and beautiful straining above her, his chest dense with hard flat muscle, his pectorals snaked with veins, and his throat ruddy and suffused with blood. She sobbed, her hips rising aggressively, seeking an end to the interminable wanting.

"Jack!" Some desperate note in her voice recalled him from the interior place he'd gone.

His eyes flew open. "Yes," he rasped. "Anne. My own."

He lifted her, twining his long arms around her and rocking back on his heels, thrusting deep within her one last time. His body shuddered with his release and it became her own, catapulting her into a dizzying, blinding whirlpool of pure sensual pleasure.

He cradled her in his arms and traced the contour of her temple with his fingertip. Her breathing was shallow and one of her breasts was scratched from his beard. She'd live. He wished he could say the same about himself. He could not ever remember anything to compare with what they'd just shared.

Her eyes drifted open. Her gaze was lambent and sated.

"I love you." He didn't even realize he'd spoken aloud until he saw the words register in her eyes. A shadow clouded their brilliancy and then pain and finally they grew brilliant again, this time with tears. He cursed himself for being so obtuse, so precipitate.

He smiled sadly. "It's not worth tears, Anne," he said ruefully. "I've not all that much of a heart to love with. It's a barren bit of landscape, my heart. Post-harvest chaff mostly."

His dull attempt at wit did not raise even a trace of a smile. If anything her tears flowed faster, hurting him more than anything had hurt him in a long, long while.

"Don't cry, Anne. Our marriage is lawful but I wouldn't ever try to keep you with me against your will. You're free to go wherever and whenever you'd like. I'll not raise a hand to stop you or raise my voice to call you back. Don't worry, Anne, I'm not asking you to love me."

She lifted her hand and made a weak fist, drumming his chest. He stared at her in surprise.

"You idiot," she said with a sob, "I'm not crying because I don't love you, I'm crying because I do. I do. And because I didn't think I *could* love."

Chapter Thirty-Two

Nothing had ever felt so important or so fragile. He must be careful, as wary and wise as he'd ever been before.

"Why would you think that?" he asked. Without the heat of his body to warm her, gooseflesh had risen on Anne's naked skin. He picked up his shirt and draped it over her shoulders.

"Why would you think you were not capable of love?" he repeated softly.

She dashed some tears from her cheeks with her fingers and sniffed. "Because I married a saint and I didn't love him."

He waited, remaining carefully silent.

"And I fell in love with the man who hunted me. The man sent to kill me. It's wrong."

Seemingly casual, he guided her arm into a shirtsleeve. His heart beat thickly in his chest. "Why do you say that?"

"It is," she said, looking at him as if he were being purposefully obtuse. "I married Matthew because he was handsome and rich and so very, very far above my touch."

"And because you loved him," Jack said evenly.

"I thought I loved him," she said, her eyes mirroring her confusion.

"But he did not believe you." He pulled her remaining bare arm through the other sleeve and began fastening her shirt. He looked up. She was staring at him as if transfixed.

"How did you know?"

"I've listened. I'd developed a rather personal interest in the matter," he said with a crooked smile, "and I tried to mesh what I knew of Anne Wilder, what I'd heard of Anne Tribble, and what I recognized in the thief. You were running from something. I grew to suspect it was from the paragon whom you'd married. Or his corpse."

She tried to pull away from him but he wouldn't let her go. "You obviously hold yourself accountable for your husband's death. Or should we call it what he meant you to call it—suicide?"

Her lids fluttered shut, the pain on her face was excruciating to witness. Silently Jack cursed Matthew Wilder.

"At first it was like a fairy tale," Anne said, her eyes still closed. The words came out slowly, as if they might choke her. "He did everything for me. Everything. And all he asked was that I love him. I thought I did." Her brow was lined with consternation. "But he saw something, he somehow knew that it wasn't *true* love, that what I felt wasn't real, because he doubted it almost from the first."

"Yes?" Jack said.

"He would ask me if I loved him. All the time, he would ask me if I loved him." Her voice held an echo of exhausted harassment. "But if I answered yes, he'd be hurt and miserable."

"Why?" Jack asked.

"He said that if I *really* loved him, he wouldn't have had to ask me. Yet when I told him I loved him, he would probe, he would be suspicious, he'd keep asking me if I were sure. And then . . ."

"And then you were not sure," Jack said. And he'd thought Jamison was a monster. "And how did he react? By withdrawing from you?"

Anne shook her head in violent negation. "No! No. He wooed me." A look of utter exhaustion filled her face. "He courted me all over again. He gave me gifts, took me traveling, and plied me with attention. He did everything in his power to make me love him."

Her voice grew flat, lifeless. "And then he decided that I was not capable of love. That I wasn't ever going to be able to harbor for him even a degree of the love he felt for me. Because I'm not really gentry, you know. And my sort aren't capable of experiencing the same level of emotion that bluebloods can."

"Did he hate you?" Jack asked. His chest felt tight and he waited for the pain to wash over him and be gone. But it stayed, building in his chest.

"No." Once more she shook her head, wrapping her arms tightly around herself. She stared off into some distant past, and when she began to speak her voice had gained an edge of vehemence. "He still loved me. My deficiency didn't affect his . . ." She fumbled for the proper word.

"'Superiority'?" Jack supplied softly.

"Yes," she said, nodding, "yes, I suppose so, though he never put it that way. It was his curse, he said. To love better than he was loved. But it was a curse he would live with. We would just go on that way forever."

She looked at him with a blasted, cornered expression.

"But *I* couldn't go on that way!" she exclaimed. "One day, after one of our scenes, I told him I wouldn't hurt him with my presence any longer and that we'd both suffered enough. I told him I was going back to live with my father. He begged me not to. He swore he couldn't live without me. But, Jack, I could *not* stay there any longer. It was killing me! And I told him so."

"So you left," Jack said.

"I didn't have a chance. He'd spent a few years in the navy as a youngster and he had some sort of connections at the Admiralty and . . . I don't know." She pushed her hair out of her face. "Within the week he'd somehow finagled a captaincy. Jack, he wasn't fit to command. He led his crew to disaster and himself to death."

Narcissistic fool. So bent on punishing Anne that he dragged innocent men to their deaths to do it. Well, he'd done a fine job of punishing her. Might he find that comforting in whatever corner of hell he occupied.

"He wrote a letter, of course." Jack's jaw was tight with fury. He'd seen much evil in his life. He'd shaken hands with many devils and spoken with Satan in a hundred different guises. He thought he'd known its every aspect, but he'd yet to see this one.

"Yes." Anne nodded.

She didn't even have to tell him what it said. There would have been the thinly veiled accusation, the suggestion that if she'd been different, tried harder, he wouldn't have been thrown into despair, and then there would be a long, impassioned declaration of undying love and prayers for her happy future. Jack felt physically ill.

"And he called what he felt for you love?" he asked incredulously.

Anne looked up, staring at him in amazement, reading his fury. "Yes."

"Matthew didn't love you, Anne. He wanted to own your soul, and when he couldn't, he wanted to destroy it. And damn him to hell, he very nearly did."

"No, Jack," she said sadly, shaking her head. "He wasn't evil. He just wanted something from me that I couldn't give."

He wouldn't convince her of Matthew's malevolence. He could only hurt her by trying. So he told her what she needed to hear, the simple truth. "No one could have given him what he wanted, Anne."

She stared at him, releasing a long, shaking breath. Her back tensed, her shoulders went back as if she were preparing to accept a verdict.

"I never told anyone. I never said a word, not even to myself, but, Jack"—she turned her head slowly, her eyes stark—"I *hated* living with him. I hated the presents and the parties and the trips and the gowns." With each word, her voice gained strength and passion. "I hated his accusing glances and his suffering silences. I hated his sobbed pleas and vicious tantrums. I *hated* his adoration. It smothered me, it crushed me, and it choked the very soul of me. I tried not to." Her fingers dug deeply into her flesh and she began rocking back and forth in her seat. "God help me, I tried not to hate him!"

Tears began racing down her face. She made no attempt to wipe them away. She let them fall, hot, salty rivulets running from her eyes.

"It's all right, Anne."

"I swear, I swear to God, I didn't want him dead! Everyone told me how lucky I was to be so adored. And they envied us. You could see it, Jack. They envied me and I would have traded places with any one of them!"

"I know," he murmured. She buried her face in her hands and sobbed. He reached out and gently drew her into his embrace. She clung to him, crying softly now, the poisonous guilt and remorse finally spending itself in tears. And after a while she lifted her head and searched his face.

"Jack," she said, her gaze questing and somber. "I love you."

He weighed carefully the responses he might give her: vows of love, a promise for the future, pledges of fidelity, guarantees that her hurt would fade. But he couldn't promise any of those things but the first, and that she already knew. So finally he gave the one response he could and it proved the most healing one of all.

"I know," he said, gazing steadily into her eyes. "I know." And Anne smiled.

Anne's hand rested lightly on Jack's forearm as he escorted her down one of Windsor Palace's long, silent hallways. A sepulchral hush permeated the old palace though scores of servants and attendants hurried among the rooms and chambers, all assiduously at work on the monumental day-to-day tasks required in running a palace.

They came to a closed door. The liveried footman standing beside it bowed and preceded them in. "Colonel and Mrs. Henry John Seward," he announced loudly.

Inside a small, lavishly appointed chamber a gloriously handsome young footman stood behind the chair of a stout, balding man. Farther in stood Jamison, leaning heavily on his silver-headed walking cane. And at the far end of the room, her wizened and hunched body huddled beneath mismatched clothes, quaked Mrs. Mary Cashman.

She spied Anne and pitched herself forward. "That bald gent comes to me down t'Home, Mrs. Wilder. I thought he was from the Admiralty and that they finally be givin' me my Johnny's back pay but they drug me here. And I don't mind tellin' ye, I'm scared."

"It's all right, Mrs. Cashman," Anne said soothingly. "Let's find you a seat until all of this comes clear." She escorted the frightened woman to a small upholstered chair and bid her sit while she found her something to drink.

She returned to Jack's side. "Jack, do you think that footman could possibly find Mrs. Cashman—"

"Bastard."

Anne spun around. Jamison moved toward them across the floor, his progress painfully slow.

"Ungrateful, thankless bastard," he repeated coldly.

In alarm, Anne looked at Jack. Not a flicker of emotion passed over his lean countenance, not regret or injury.

"Yes, sir," he said.

"Do you know what you've done?" Jamison did not spare her so much as a glance. To him, she was supremely inconsequential. All that mattered was Jack and the letter.

For the first time, Anne realized that in his own, corrupt fashion Jamison cared for Jack as one cares for a possession of great and irreplaceable value.

"Do you?" Jamison demanded again.

"Indeed I do, sir," Jack replied calmly. "I am seeing that some personal correspondence completes its journey."

"The owner of that letter could bring down the government," Jamison said.

"I doubt that, sir," Jack said.

"Didn't you read it?" he asked incredulously. His voice was low; no one farther away than Anne was would be able to hear his words. "Do you know what that letter suggests? It suggests that the government, in complicity with the royal family, knowingly hanged an innocent man."

"Which they did."

"That's not the point," Jamison said angrily, stamping the end of the cane against the floor. The sudden sharp sound echoed in the big, quiet room. "We needed to make an example to these revolutionaries. John Cashman was not framed. He *was* in that gunsmith's shop."

"John Cashman was drunk, angry, and not in full possession of his faculties at the time of his 'crime.' I saw him hanged, you know." And now Anne heard a thread of anger, intense and white-hot, enter Jack's rasping voice. "I could not believe you were actually going to allow his death, so I went and instead witnessed your depravity."

"Bah!" Jamison swung away, but when Jack did not recall him, he stopped and turned again. "This letter could ruin us all. I could have used it to good advantage. I could have secured a position of power from which I could achieve great things."

"As I said, I think you far overestimate its importance."

"Are you mad?" Jamison asked.

Jack simply returned his gaze with his own cool, disinterested one.

This is how he survived, thought Anne. He'd buried himself; he hid his humanity from that evil man.

"Well, you've done it now, Jack." Jamison shook his head. "You and your bride have done it now."

Something in the way he glanced at her made Anne shiver. It struck Jack, too, because he moved closer. Jamison saw his protective attitude. He smiled.

"I hope this noble gesture is worth it, Seward. I hope you—"

"His Majesty, the king."

The announcement brought every head swinging toward a small door in the back of the room. A footman entered followed by a huge, fresh-faced young man carrying a small, elderly man draped in silk bedrobes.

The king, Anne thought breathlessly. He was pink and wrinkled and wizened-looking. Long wisps of white hair fell to his shoulders. His eyes were sunken and filmed over with a milky glaze. Completely blind, Jack had said.

Anne swept into a low, formal curtsey and Mrs. Cashman, seeing her action, stumbled from her chair and did her best to emulate it. The man who had preceded the king's entrance saw them and smiled.

"Your Majesty." The portly balding man who'd been sitting quietly watching Jamison, Jack, and Anne struggled to his feet. He bowed, followed by Jack and the blond footman and finally Jamison.

"What is this all about? Who is here?" The imperial voice had not lost its timbre or its accent.

"Visitors to see Your Majesty. Sir Knowles, Sir Jamison, Colonel and Mrs. Seward, Mr. Adam Burke, and Mrs. Mary Cashman."

The names obviously meant nothing to the frail old man. "We were talking to the queen and We did not like being interrupted."

Anne glanced worriedly at Jack. The queen had died some months before.

"Forgive us, Your Majesty." The portly old man sitting down lumbered upright. He had a voice as gentle as his mien.

"Who is that?" the king asked sharply.

"Knowles, Your Majesty."

"Knowles. Podgy fellow with more pockets than I've coin? And which pocket are you emptying today, Knowles?"

Anne glanced at Jack in dismay. But he was smiling slightly, and Knowles seemed in no way disconcerted by the odd turn of the conversation.

"I have a letter in one, sire. You'd dictated it and sent it off but it was lost."

"Did I? To whom did I write this missing letter?"

"A Mrs. Mary Cashman, sire."

The royal visage crumpled in concentration. The king's brow knit into a thunderous, bewildered aspect. Beside her she could sense Jack holding his breath, and then, like a minor miracle, the disoriented expression faded. Peace filled the old, seamed face.

"The sailor's mother."

"Yes, sire," Knowles said with alacrity. "We have recovered the letter, Your Majesty."

"Good," the king said. He sighed and tapped his finger sharply against the chest of the bruising young hulk cradling him as easily as a mother does her child. "The colonies must be brought to heel. See that Pitt comes to us tonight. We will not lose them, do you hear? We would be laughed at in all the courts of Europe. We will not—"

"Mrs. Cashman cannot read, sire!" Knowles shouted.

The king's mouth grew flat. "Cannot read? Well, then read the letter out loud to her, man!"

"Yes, sir." From his pocket, Knowles withdrew the sheet of vellum Anne had stolen. He opened it and approached the figure of Mary Cashman still trembling near a curtsey at the far wall.

"Mrs. Cashman?"

"Aye?" Her answer was nearly inaudible.

"Good," Knowles said, and offered her a small, encouraging smile. "His Majesty, George the Third, King of England writes:

Madam,

We, too, have lost beloved children. We regret Our Son and Heir did not do His sovereign duty on Our behalf and halt so grave a miscarriage of justice. Accept our condolences, madam, and know that Your King appreciates your sacrifice on His behalf.

G

"That is the sum total of this letter, madam. It is yours. You may take it if you like."

"You can't possibly—" Jamison stepped forward; Jack stayed him with a hand on his upper arm.

"You would be most wise to remain quiet," he whispered. "Most wise."

Jamison shook his arm free, staring at Jack with open enmity. But he remained silent.

"Well, Mrs. Cashman," Knowles prodded, "what of it?"

A single tear slipped from the corner of Mrs. Cashman's eyes. She straightened slightly, not much, but enough that one could see the innate dignity His Majesty's words had given back to this, the poorest of his subjects. And in that moment, Anne loved her blind, mad, ancient monarch. She would have put down her life for him.

"I gots no call to take that letter, sir, thankin' ye very kindly," Mary Cashman said quietly. "No one would believe this 'appened anyways and that letter would only be jeered at as a fake. I won't have no one jeerin' at this day and this moment. I'll keep it here"— she placed a gnarled hand over her heart—"and I'll carry it to me grave. God bless Your Majesty." Knowles stared at the woman, a complex and unreadable series of expressions passing with lightning rapidity over his soft, doughy face. Then he turned and called out, "Your Majesty, Mrs. Cashman bids God's blessings on you."

The royal head nodded, accepting the blessing as his due. He tugged at the shirt of his bearer. "The queen does not like being kept waiting, Bob."

"Yes, Your Majesty." The huge youngster turned and, gingerly bearing his fragile king in his arms, departed through the back door. The other attendant followed close behind.

"Mrs. Cashman, Burke here"—Knowles nodded to the glorious-looking youth by his side—"will see you home. I believe there is a matter of monetary compensation to be addressed. Burke shall address it."

The young man named Burke snapped into a bow over Mrs. Cashman's astonished face and offered his arm. "Right you are, Mrs. Cashman." He grinned and Mrs. Cashman blinked, smitten with his godlike good looks. "We'll 'ave—*have* you home in a dash."

Mrs. Cashman, Anne felt sure, would have gone to Spain had he suggested it. She certainly left the room quickly enough. Jamison waited a few seconds before walking stiffly past them through the door. Knowles sighed, pausing on his way out.

"A pleasure to meet you, Mrs. Seward," he said. She did not know his station or his rank but he'd aided Jack and that was more important to her than either of the other two so she curtseyed. He smiled at that. "She has as good manners as you, Jack. Just think of what your children will be."

His smile stayed on his face and his tone didn't change. "Jamison will assume you'll seek his . . . elimination. He'll anticipate it."

"I'm sure he will," Jack said levelly. "But I won't, sir. Not unless he—" For a fraction of an instant, Jack's eyes flickered toward her.

"Yes, I see." Knowles nodded. "Didn't think you would, him being your father and all. Still, wouldn't have been too great of a surprise."

He wouldn't have been surprised if Jack sought to kill the man as close to being a father as Jack knew? Anne wondered in horror. *Did no one know Jack?*

Knowles paused, his hand on the door. He looked out into the hallway and then, satisfied no one was there, turned his head. "To avert any further unpleasantness, I would consider relocation, Jack. I really would."

And he, too, left.

Epilogue

The fog rose early that evening, and it rose fast. It flowed over the ground and prowled up the sides of buildings, enveloping everything in its path with thick, soft plush. Anne and Jack stood on the balcony of Strand's mansion and watched the world being devoured by a cloud. Strand was not with them. Saying he preferred his club, he'd given them the use of the house.

Jack's arms enfolded Anne, pressing her against him. Trapped mist sparkled in her loose hair and dusted her cheeks with dew. The moon had risen and its chance light found depths in her eyes he wanted to spend a lifetime exploring.

"What about the Home?" she asked a little anxiously. "You're certain Julia Knapp will be allowed to supervise it?"

"Yes," he answered, brushing his lips over her temple. "Those papers you signed earlier gave her control of its administration."

Anne nodded. The fog had made its way to the balcony now. It wound around their ankles like little white phantom cats.

"Can you really do it?" she whispered, reaching her hand up to rest it on his chest. Tenderly he covered it with his own, lowering his head and brushing a kiss across her fingertips. "Can you really make people just disappear?"

He smiled. "Anne, I'm a master spy. This is what I *do*." He sobered. "And I do it well. But when we disappear, we will disappear for good. We leave everything behind: possessions, friends, family, and rank."

"The cat? Can we bring the gray cat?" she asked in a troubled voice.

"And that's all," he answered gravely. "It's the only way this will work."

"I know." Her breath came out in a long, shaky sigh mingling with the misty shroud that had swirled up around her shoulders, caressing her throat and tangling in her hair.

He tilted her chin up to see her face. Beautiful Anne. His thief. His wife.

His arms tightened around her. "Take one last look then, Anne. Say good-bye to all you hold dear."

But she looked instead at him, because in him she saw all and everything she held dear. She gazed at him long and faithfully. Filled with the singing sweetness of loving as well as being loved, she did not notice the fog finally enveloping them.

And when a chance breeze blew it away, they were gone.

Author's Note

John Cashman was a real person. He was tried, found guilty, and executed for treason in much the circumstances I have set forth in this story. New evidence suggests that King George III suffered from a disease called porphyria, some of the symptoms of which are hallucinations and psychosis. These symptoms, while recurring, would not necessarily be unremitting. History has well documented the antipathy between King George and his son, the prince regent. In having an enfeebled, powerless, mad monarch indulge in one moment of lucid charity, I have played the age-old author's game of what-if. I hope the results have proved entertaining.

About the Author

HEIDI EHALT, 2010

New York Times and USA Today best-selling author Connie Brockway has received starred reviews from both *Publishers Weekly* and the *Library Journal,* which named *My Seduction* as one of 2004's top ten romances.

An eight-time finalist for Romance Writers of America's prestigious RITA award, Brockway has twice been its recipient, for *My Dearest Enemy* and *The Bridal Season.* In 2006 Connie wrote her first women's contemporary, *Hot Dish,* which won critical raves. Connie's historical romance *The Other Guy's Bride* was the launch book for Montlake Romance.

Today Brockway lives in Minnesota with her husband—a family physician—and two spoiled mutts.

Sign up for more from Connie Brockway!

www.conniebrockway.com/mailing_list.php
www.twitter.com/ConnieBrockway
www.facebook.com/ConnieBrockwayFans